HEAVY
METAL
LOVER

HEAVY METAL LOVER

ISA AGAJANIAN

ISBN: 979-8-9873213-5-5

Front cover illustration by Noreamea

Book design by Isa Agajanian

PART ONE

1

From underneath two layers of sleeves, Liv Shankly scraped her silver prosthetic fingertips together, the way one might have done to measure humidity in the air by the friction of their skin or roll the flame off the blackened tip of a match. The clamor of the Eight Saints bar masked the faint whisper of curved metal against curved metal with the clinks and sluices of glassware.

Although no one else heard it, the metal was inescapably reverberant within her body; Liv heard it like she heard her own heartbeat, a constant, unshakable reminder of life. She buried whatever was noticeable of the hand into her pocket. With less evidence tying her back to the Eight Saints bar before the night's Drone Run, she had been able to preserve the secrecy of her favorite informant. If there was no sight of metal, there could be no sight of the mythically wounded rider, Liv Shankly.

Liv might have gathered the courage to get back on her bike after her last Run left her partially limbless and scarred, but her suspicions hadn't ceded. Something had interfered with the race. Something she couldn't stop. Something that she had spent months trying to convince her father was not her fault.

Whatever it was, she wouldn't let it happen again.

The hood of Liv's threadbare sweatshirt covered her hair, though it did nothing to mask the road scars splitting the side of her face, brow to chin. Upon turning to see the hooded patron at the bar, Liv's favorite informant—and, quite possibly, her only friend—grimaced before she could help it.

"Sorry. I still haven't gotten used to them," Lotte said, meeting her gaze briefly.

"Good, because I'm not here tonight."

Smiling to herself, Lotte poured the contents of the shaker in her hands into a stout glass and garnished it with a dried orange slice nearly the same shade as her hair. The bartender's ginger curls were cropped asymmetrically at her chin and shoulder, then pinned behind her ears for food service with the bronze, mainstay pins that Liv recognized from almost a decade of on-and-off companionship.

"You're never here, Shanks. When was the last time you graced Eight Saints?"

Liv's chest rose with a short-lived relief, then deflated, pushing out a soiled, sheepish embarrassment for the near year of absence in which she had avoided anything that had to do with the Run, which at that point had included Eight Saints, like she was the last shank of lamb and they were a den of starving wolves. She was going to have to atone for them someday: all the unanswered text messages she had sworn to answer once she was adjusted to the new limb and all the calls she had slept through during her first months of recovery.

Liv said, "Hey, I'm reaching out now, aren't I?"

In misplaced faith, she had assumed her first attempt at contacting Lotte again would be smoothed over by the understanding that losing her right arm—her dominant arm—in the last Run had plucked her out from every facet of life she'd been embedded in.

But she had been operating at a level that was probably as close as she would ever get to normal for almost five months now. Lotte was not forgiving enough to forget that Liv's recent silence was entirely her own, instead of her grief or her responsibilities.

The bartender answered Liv's raised brows and sad attempt at nonchalance with an unamused sucking of her gums, bracing herself on the counter. She cocked an eyebrow of her own as if to say that two could play Liv's game, or rather that she was good enough to play with only one (eyebrow, that was.)

"Okay, okay. I should have called."

"Mhmm."

"In fairness, never in my life have I sent you a message with only my left hand."

"But you'd think that after months of a life-altering injury and total silence, you'd want to, I don't know, call me to check in?"

That was a fair point. Liv's head cowed, and she slipped her fingers around the back of her neck to toy with the shorn fuzz at her nape. "Sorry."

A man standing to Liv's left waved for Lotte's attention, which the bartender ignored and passed along to someone else behind the counter. That familiar indifference made Liv's guarded expression thaw.

"So," Lotte said to her hooded patron, "what do you want?"

"Can I get a glass of water?"

The bartender sighed, wanting something else to fill her time while the other man leered for her attention. Her movements were exaggeratedly considerate to buy herself a longer moment with Liv. She grabbed a glass off a shelf behind her and studied the surface for residue, and that evidence included the swirling pathways of her fingerprints, which she wiped, then re-wiped for good measure. "Please. You don't come to Eight Saints for water unless you're doing the Run after."

After filling the glass with water from the tap, all that was left for her to do was watch Liv down it or listen to whatever the patron would say next.

Liv said nothing. She took the glass, measuring the grooved shapes around the rim with her fingers, buying time with the only thing Lotte hated more than her shit-talking: silence.

Lotte didn't know how right she was, and the suggestion alone was too impossible to consider. As Liv sipped, avoiding Lotte's honey brown stare with both elbows perched on the counter to hide her culpability, Lotte's congenial expression dropped.

"No," she whispered, scandalized.

"Yep."

"You can't seriously be considering it, Liv."

The girl in question looked down the length of the bar to her left, then her right. Everyone was so properly engrossed in their raucous conversations that they didn't hear either girl begin to share the illicit details of the Lower Cities' most dangerous—and possibly, the most profitable—after-hours venture.

Liv leaned forward, her fingers curled around the edge of the counter. "I need the money, Lotte. I heard the winnings are supposed to be big tonight."

"Who told you that?"

"So it's true?" Liv downed the water in her glass until most of the space was taken up by a large ice cube that she could swirl around with a flick of her wrist. "Do you know who's behind it?"

Another patron, far less leery but drunker than the first, leaned over Liv's body to fetch a fistful of napkins from the dented canister between them. His unsteady weight pressed into her back, and then the smell of alcohol on his damp breath. He slurred an apology and lugged himself away.

"I've gotta get out of here," Liv said. "What's the liquor equivalent of a contact high?"

Lotte swiped at her with a rag towel hanging from her belt.

"Shut up."

"I know, I know. I don't have much time to chat anyway."

"Look," said the beleaguered bartender. "As your friend, I implore you not to do the Run tonight if you care about your safety in the slightest."

Liv stared long and hard at her, clenching her jaw until her molars started to ache. "What about as my informant?"

"Liv."

"What about it, Lotte?" It came out less like a question and more like a demand. Like expensive wares, Liv laid her dilemma across the countertop for Lotte to look at plainly. "Maura has another treatment tomorrow in the Upper City, and Corey is underwater with insurance payments. If we don't pay off those debts by the end of the month, we're going to get a visit from collections. And you know how Corey is."

At least, Lotte used to know what Corey was like. Liv couldn't remember the last time she'd seen her adoptive father and her best friend in the same room together. If she thought about it enough, had she ever seen them in a room together? Her most recent memories were wind-streaked and shadowy from the lowlights of Run courses in the Lower City.

Back then, Corey was still her benefactor, willing to brave a later night out after work to watch his daughter bring home another cut of the Run's prize money. Back then, the danger had still seemed distant. Nothing had scared him yet, so he could keep his roles as a guardian and a benefactor separate.

The accident changed everything, so much that Lotte couldn't see or know, kept at such a far distance by Liv's lack of contact in the recent months. Corey had become a different man. The fractures in their relationship had widened, but the depths of their desperation remained just as deep. Holding each other together was harder than ever these days.

Lotte would have known this if Liv Shankly were a better

friend and kept in touch.

Only after half a minute of silence did the patron, still shrugging her round, muscular shoulders up into her hood as if she could make herself smaller, realize the entire point of her old friend's aversion. When had Lotte ever withheld information about a Run from her before? Hadn't they always known the dangers, even before the brunt of them cost Liv an arm and a smooth right cheek?

They both knew what she was getting herself into; the least Lotte could do was conspire with her toward her survival.

That was what a good friend did. Shit.

Liv's lip nearly split from how hard her teeth were digging into it. "Please, Lotte. You've got to know something about it. About the donor, at least?"

Tracing a shape in the condensation of the counter, Lotte said, "You can't race without a benefactor anyway. Someone has to clean up the mess, and who's it going to be if it isn't Corey?" Liv looked up at the bartender innocently, to which Lotte opened her arms pointedly to the breadth of the bar and added, "I'm here until closing, dipshit. Fielding the likes of you."

Liv was fucked. Even worse, Lotte was right; no rider could participate in the Drone Run without a benefactor. Liv had never been without one before, which was a shame considering she had never been in such dire financial straits either.

Corey had always kept her safe from the worst of it. Despite her grumbling, Liv knew he had removed himself as her benefactor because of what he thought he could save her from: another life-altering accident on the course.

But she was an adult, too. She had been racing for years, since before it was legal to ride. She knew the stakes more intimately than most riders did, and she knew now, just as much as Corey did, what else they might lose if she didn't get the money.

It might have taken two to enter the Run, but it only took one to win. If the money was as good as she suspected it to be, she could come home a proven-right hero, saving him from the burden of their unbearable medical debts and assuring them that this—she—was the big break they'd been creating together.

Lotte's eyes fixed on her, nearly black and spotted with yellow from the pulsating bulbs behind Liv. Liv also found, behind Lotte's untempered fondness for her, one final warning: Don't go.

Slowly, Lotte admitted, "It's a government official from the Upper City. Someone with a lot of money and a lot of protection to lose it."

Liv balked at her. "Racing?"

"Of course not. No one in the Upper City's got the skin to race the way we do, let alone a government official. They wouldn't make it halfway through the course without getting clocked by a drone. But they're betting, and there's a lot of money laced in the pride of an Upper City better. They won't be inclined to place money on a rider who doesn't even have a benefactor. Doesn't matter how good you are when they're betting large; whoever they bet on will have the means to win, however bloody those means are."

Liv gave herself a headache trying to do the math in her head. From what she knew of other riders and their benefactors, which was admittedly narrow, given that riders rarely spoke outside the course and had little opportunity for friendly banter on the course, riders gave their benefactors a cut between 15% and 35% of the prize money. The ones with higher benefactor fees were typically contract riders, racers raised by and indentured to wealthy families.

Liv had encountered only a few contract riders in all her

years doing the Run. The last contract riders Liv had seen wore fitted black uniforms stitched with noble house colors like honorable knights and helmets emblazoned with the names of their benefactors. The only riders who could afford to ride for such a low cut came from the Upper City, where there were countless other ways to make a living that didn't risk leaving one's skin on the road or one's blood on the metal of their bike.

She couldn't imagine how much a heavy bet from someone in the Upper City might influence their decision to enter. What would a contract rider wearing the name of their noble family do for a taste of more? For the whole bite?

Liv's problem persisted annoyingly at the forefront of her mind like the sharp beak of a woodpecker. She didn't have a benefactor. In fact, Corey had no idea that she was entering the Run tonight. He would be working late again, taking a house call in Grollingcross, the Lower City furthest from where they lived; then, he would return home in his company-supplied vehicle, kiss Liv's adoptive mother Maura on the forehead, and crash on the couch, having eaten only half of his frozen dinner. If Liv was lucky, Corey would forget to push Liv's bedroom door open and check to see if she was sleeping.

She nodded at Lotte after it had all sunk in, tapped her fist against the counter, and said, "It's going to be me then. And when I come back, I'll order something I actually have to pay for."

"What do you mean? We charge for water here—"

Liv pulled something from her pocket and slid it across the counter: a folded note with a large, sad face and the word SORRY drawn on the forehead that Lotte only realized wasn't a bundle of bills after Liv had cleared the Eight Saints' front doors.

The Drone Runs had been around for less than a decade when Liv started riding at the age of seventeen. By that point, there was a small but steady group of riders coming every other week to the courses shared with them by the pair of gamemakers.

From there, the weak were culled, the fast kept winning, and those with the need—or the desire—for more got vicious. Thus, the rules were established before Liv began:

First: Riders were not allowed weapons, but they were allowed shields. Almost any shield that a rider had fashioned could only protect them from other riders, not from the drones, so it was left to each rider's discretion whether the weight of an added shield (or comparable shield technology) was worth the fraction of extra protection. Most riders didn't bother with shields.

Second: Riders couldn't attack the drones. Control over the four drones lay solely with the wrangler, the nameless entity at the coursemaster's side who first managed to hijack the drones. He was a small, wickedly smart man in his late thirties who couldn't, or perhaps refused to, speak, though he signed often and too quickly for anyone except the coursemaster to understand. Without him, the Run couldn't have existed. They kept him safe and, in return, the drones didn't kill them.

Third: Every rider was required to have a benefactor. Benefactors were, in most cases, only ever business partnerships, except for when it was a precaution. Creating and facilitating the Drone Runs defied several different laws, including those for street racing and reckless driving, tampering with official government equipment, and unauthorized organizing in public spaces. If a rider ended up painting the asphalt with their body parts, they needed someone to clean up the mess before the night was over and the cops found them.

Liv appeared at the start of the evening's course without a

mask beneath her helmet. She knew some riders wore them to further protect their anonymity before the race, but she had never done it, and it seemed pointless to her to start now.

Her modest effort at anonymity was a sharp bastardization of her adoptive family's surname: Shanks. She didn't know if wearing it made a difference; names didn't last long on the course. But she'd liked it as a teenager and didn't hate it enough to change it as an adult.

It occurred to her after she had already arrived that the presence of a government official from the Upper City should have made her think twice about the lack of a mask. She didn't know why they were here and, based on the crowd's collective chatter, no one else seemed capable of telling her.

Whoever this mystery guest was, Liv couldn't see them. As she maneuvered her motorcycle to the start of the course, eyes darted to her, lighting her up as if she were in the crosshairs of a hundred laser sights. The sensation of being remembered so clearly after a year of absence unnerved her. It was probably the hair, she reasoned. She had kept it dyed black from its natural middling brown shade and close-cropped since she was a teenager. Then again, it might have been the tracks of scars that ran down her face.

With her hood off, it could have been anything.

Liv, on the other hand, didn't remember any of them except for the gamemakers. The racers were mostly unfamiliar, though their starting lines were stocked with an alarming number of contract riders. Compared to the nine Lower City riders, their meager three's-a-crowd should have looked like nothing to Liv, but they were typically the only ones who mattered to her, who could jeopardize her success.

Their black helmets boasted chromatic house names, none of which Liv recognized. She offered a friendly nod to the rider closest to her, who seemed particularly interested in staring at her (or rather, their eyes were fixed on the silver peering out of their right sleeve). They made no indication of cordiality; "Weird", Liv thought, before she noticed that the wrangler was beside her, tapping her right arm to get her attention. "Oh, hey." She decided that it was a ripe moment to remove her layers, place them in her backpack, and leave them beside the gamemakers' truck.

She shed the layer of leather to remove the sweatshirt beneath it while the wrangler tucked his wide, illuminated drone controller beneath his arm to sign something to her: "Benefactor?"

Liv shook her head, then got to work unclasping the buttons Maura had installed around the right shoulder seam of her leather jacket. "I was going to, uh, figure it out when I got here."

"What about C-O-R-E-Y?"

Liv's head shook in reply, and the walls of her throat tightened. "No. Not anymore."

The wrangler gave her a slight, affirmative smile and signed something that Liv only vaguely recognised as "Happy you're alive," then, "Wait here."

She had picked up a handful of signs during her years on the course. These, she had far less familiarity with.

Her right sleeve peeled apart from the rest of the jacket with the last unfastened button. She used it to tie the wad of her sweatshirt fabric into a compact shape and stuff the entire bundle in her backpack, tucking it near the gamemakers' truck before scrambling to replace the leather jacket over her arms. The wind hissed off her metal and stung straight to her bones. She zipped the jacket up to her throat and returned to her motorcycle to strategize a plan for swindling a benefactor.

When she returned, the coursemaster was waiting for her alongside his partner. He was large with muscle and soft in the stomach, with an impressively thick and well-groomed black beard. His eyes were soft with the same weakly paternal sentiment the wrangler had looked at her with when he said, "You're going to have a hard time getting a benefactor tonight, Shanks. This isn't the race you want to make your glorious comeback with."

The wrangler's mazing expression corroborated his partner's hesitance. Their warnings were not the same remorseful warnings her father had given her about returning. Liv felt an added pressure not to prove them wrong but to prove them right for all their faith in her. She stood tall against it, straightening her shoulders. "If anyone has seen me race before, they'll know I'm reliable. I've got to try."

The coursemaster didn't know what her circumstances were; neither did the wrangler, although Liv suspected there was more to what they knew than she thought. But entering the Drone Run required a certain amount of recklessness and, in her case, desperation. Given a better chance for money, most riders wouldn't even consider doing the Run. Had she not grown up with it, Liv might have discovered that she was one of them.

Being good at the Run didn't mean she wanted to live this way forever.

The wrangler signed something to the coursemaster that Liv couldn't understand. A blessing, perhaps. Or an endorsement. It swayed the coursemaster into a decision in the rider's favor, which was more than what she could have asked for. "We'll take offers for benefactors, if you'd like," said the coursemaster. "We'll make an announcement before the Run, but it'll be your decision to accept the offer."

"Thank y—"

"The rule still stands, Shanks: no benefactor, no race. Got it?"

She nodded, gratitude escaping her. It was clear the game-makers didn't consider it a favor to her but a death wish. The unknowable potential of the night's Run sent a dart of ice through her spine.

The crowd collectively rippled with gasps and other obscene utterances as the Run's Upper City intruder appeared. One appreciatively tailored trouser leg and leather boot extended from the backseat of an unblemished silver car.

Liv swore she had seen him before, but the connection evaded her. With slicked hair the color of chestnuts and the standard pinstripe design of the High Mayor's house, he stuck out among the usual crowd of race watchers like a lone salmon in a dry dirt ditch.

Her mouth curled into a grimace, a continuous motion instigated by the part of the crowd closest to him. However, some, to Liv's surprise, gaped and crooned at the man like he was a newly risen messiah.

She realized it then, all the parts clicking together like an aligned bite. It was the High Mayor's son, Caldwell Keaton. Not a politician per se, but nonetheless, a prevalent public figure with too much power. She'd seen his face illuminated on the tabloid broadcasts on the looming screens of the Upper City that taunted them from across the bridges.

On the other side of the car, stepping out from the passenger seat, was a less inspiring figure. A woman of comparable age to him, topped with the same chestnut-colored hair, which fell in pin-straight tresses down to the small of her back and gleamed with the lights of bikes and cars. It was inhumanly dazzling hair, Liv thought, noticeable mostly because it was longer than Caldwell's. The girl must have been his sister, though, for all Liv knew, they might have been partners. She didn't know what kind of incestual family politics went on in the noble houses of the Upper City. They were governed by pomp and privilege.

The crowd circled them like piranhas, keeping their distance, prepared to bite at the first wrong move.

The coursemaster's voice thundered through the noise with a sputter of feedback from the amplifier attached to him by a chest harness. "Weird night, isn't it?" he remarked in a gruff attempt to quell the crowd, except he was as visibly displeased as she was by the presence of the Mayoral figures due to the clarity in his T's. "We're joined by new faces. And some old faces that have..."

He cast a look at Liv, then at the wrangler who stood just beside her.

"Special circumstances. Bet wisely. Tonight, we're going to race like we always do."

Murmurs of proposed bets sifted through the crowd and rose like a tempest when Caldwell Keaton, having known what he was there for, gestured non-discreetly to one of the contract riders on Liv Shankly's left. The house name on their helmet read Margossi in a thick, angular font. The woman beside Caldwell eyed the rider with thin lips, betraying neither displeasure nor approval. If anything, she looked affronted.

Liv wouldn't have bothered with bets either, had she been the one surrounded by a sea of hungry, snapping teeth.

The black mirror of the Margossi rider's helmet visor squared at her. Even though Liv couldn't see the rider's eyes, she could feel them raking down the shape of her and through the machinery of her bike, appraising her acutely. She pressed her helmet between her hands. Paint chipped off the surface where her metal fingers scraped nervously. The sound, like silverware on a naked plate, made her body tense, but she couldn't resist the urge. Every time she stopped, she was left with the sound of the crowd's wide agreement to place bets on that rider.

What reason could Caldwell Keaton have had to bet on

them tonight?

The coursemaster continued, "Are there any prospective benefactors here tonight in search of a rider?"

"For Margossi?" The crowd erupted into nervous laughter like a hundred crossed fingers on the same needful hand.

Liv made herself as tall as she could, which was only about five feet seven with her boots on, raising her helmet like a flag in her unsleeved, metal arm. "For her," said the coursemaster.

She couldn't tell whether the following silence was piteous or insulting. A voice close to her mused, "Back from the dead, eh?"

"Just from Corcoran," Liv responded in jest, doing herself no favors on the anonymity front. It got a laugh and some short-lived interest from other Lower City watchers, likely the only ones who couldn't be swayed to support the Upper City officials with a bit of shiny hair product and neat pinstripes.

It surprised Liv how quickly the others were willing to abandon their loyalty to their local riders, their friends, and their collective disdain for the Keatons. Life in Corcoran, the most eastern of the five Lower Cities surrounding Morgallis, had ingrained an unwavering loyalty into her. They had to stick together to protect themselves.

However, no one offered themselves up to be her benefactor. Even those who shared her loyalty could not risk losing money on a rider they hadn't seen since she was in an accident that left her an amputee.

To the coursemaster, Liv asked, "Twenty percent," and hoped it might entice someone who would have otherwise elected to be her benefactor for fifteen. The coursemaster repeated it into his amplifier.

"Fifty," someone shouted.

There was no telling how much money Caldwell Keaton put toward the Run. Unfortunately, it made perfect sense to

Liv why no one would gamble on her, but that didn't diminish her need for it, nor did she know how much she could afford to share the winnings.

"Twenty-five," she raised.

"Forty-five!"

That cut was significantly larger than anything she would have ever agreed to. She couldn't expect them to budge much further. She offered, cautiously, "Thirty... Two?" which only made whoever was haggling laugh at her. Then, the offers ceased.

She was about to accept the forty-five percent reduction from her potential winnings, even if it was more than half of what most uncontracted riders gave their benefactors. A little money was better than nothing, she knew; though Corey himself, whom she had given almost all her winnings to unprompted, only ever asked her for fifteen.

She could feel the Margossi rider watching her through their visor and caught the smallest shake of their head, probably mocking her, before they turned to the rider beside them, their arms perched loosely over the handles of their motorcycle.

"I'll give her the eighty-five percent!"

Liv heard the voice but saw nothing from the seat of her bike where she was expecting to be axed from the Run. Someone jeered at them for accepting an offer that had already been negotiated down, a feat that made sense to no one less than Liv.

The Keaton boy stroked the sides of his chin like he was petting an invisible beard, caught in the questioning stares of countless members of the crowd who waited for an indication of what to do. Of course, he hadn't made the offer. His gaze returned magnetically to the Margossi rider's back. Thus, bets were placed, and seemingly none in Liv Shankly's favor.

"You don't have to do this, Shanks." The coursemaster had

turned off his amplifier and stepped down from the bed of his truck to exchange private words with her.

"What? I thought I heard—"

Again, that disembodied voice shouted, "I said I'll give her the eighty-five percent!"

From the sea of Lower City bystanders, Liv's benefactor appeared, revealing more than slick, chestnut colored hair and a stern line of lips. She had deep, black eyes, a faint smattering of freckles across her cheeks, and shoes tapered into a sharper point than Liv's pocket knife. She wore the same pinstripes of the Mayoral house on her vest over a white, balloon-sleeved blouse. She was neat, coquettish, and possibly even more out of place in the crowd than Caldwell Keaton was.

She stared at Liv with an equivalent unfettered curiosity, then cast her eyes downward when they met with the rider's. She addressed the gamemakers, as if the thought of their mismatched gazes fumbling over one another again would overwhelm her, and said, "I'll give ninety, if it helps. I just need her to win."

2

The coursemaster left the decision to Liv as he'd promised; and what could she say except yes? Liv was wary of appearing too eager for her help, her demeanor supported by the indecorous revelation that any representative from the Upper City would want so eagerly to help her.

The house of the High Mayor had kept her family in a grueling cycle of poverty her entire life. Racing for them, even if it meant earning the money she needed, made her stomach twist with unease.

"Why?"

The question rendered the girl momentarily dumbstruck, and Liv braced herself for the possibility that the girl might rescind her offer out of offense. Liv hadn't yet bitten the hand that could feed her, but she was circling it suspiciously, unwilling to eat from it.

The girl asked, "Well, can you win?"

"Of course I can," Liv said with a short huff. "That wasn't the question."

Lowering her voice, her generous benefactor replied, "My brother is placing a lot of money on the Margossi house rider. He..." She leaned closer, guarding her answer from curious onlookers. Even the coursemasters, who had granted the pair privacy, were glancing after them in their periphery, unsettled by the need-to-know. "He doesn't bet with a light hand. There's no question that his rider can reach the end of the course, but that won't be enough for him. The fewer competitors who are left standing by the end of it, the more money Caldwell gets back. At the very least, stay on the bike for me."

That was child's play to Liv; some faith from her benefactor might have helped her grapple with the decision to accept the offer. "Hang on. Why would you want him to lose it?" Liv didn't pretend to understand Upper City politics, let alone the family politics of the elite, but she couldn't imagine why the Keaton daughter would risk betting on a rider she didn't know just to potentially cheat her brother out of earnings.

"I want him to fail," the Keaton daughter said simply. "You'd understand if he was *your* brother."

"I dislike him enough when he's just some guy," said Liv.

"Commendable. So, do we have a deal?"

The helmets of all three contract riders pivoted toward them, compelled by the utterance of a threat. Liv had expected a certain amount of chatter from showing up here without a benefactor, but not to this extent. Had she known this would be the risk waiting for her, would she have heeded Lotte's warning?

Probably not.

Liv wished she could remember the Keaton sister's name. She had seen the faces of the Keaton patriarch and his playboy son too much, considering how vehemently she avoided them, but the girl... Vaguely, Liv recalled a tabloid mention of the High Mayor's *twin* children, but the memory of the girl's face and name evaded her.

Thwarting Caldwell was a common objective that Liv could set aside her aversions for. She extended her metal hand, which, despite the lack of feeling, was still the one she insisted on making deals with. "You know, if I lose, it's your job to clean me off the course."

The Keaton daughter gripped her new rider's hand. The

force reverberated through the connection point at Liv's shoulder. "Okay. Don't. Good luck."

Liv returned to her bike, grinning to herself as her benefactor confirmed her participation with the gamemakers. Sabotage as a motivator for the rich was so comically predictable that the rider could ignore how much she hated being used as a pawn.

She tugged her helmet over her head. The contract riders dipped their heads to her in what might have been a sign of respect or a challenge, and it dawned on her how royally, absurdly fucked she was if she didn't succeed.

She was a person of interest now, a viable threat to Upper City contract riders. Fighting the rising tension in her chest, she swung her leg over the seat of her bike and gave a thumbs-up to the wrangler.

The riders arranged their bikes four rows deep across the width of the road. The course changed with every Run to keep local law enforcement from pinpointing the illicit operation. Did anyone know what it meant for government representatives to come as spectators? Did any of the riders know what it would mean to *win* while they were being watched?

Everything changed once the countdown began. Liv didn't think about Caldwell Keaton's government money or the controller in the wrangler's hands, waking the drones. Her vision narrowed on the road ahead, the patterns of light distorting the asphalt, and the horizon line of dilapidated buildings where everything terminated.

Ten. Nine. Eight.

Other riders had said the beginning mattered most, that the most important moves you could make happened within one and ten seconds of the airhorn, but there were typically over fifteen miles of road between the beginning and the end of any course. The best riders were not the ones who rode fast and straight. No, the best riders rarely concerned themselves with outrunning each other at all.

Once the glowing eyes of a drone had fixed on a rider, the most important thing they could do was make themselves disappear.

It took an expert navigator to handle the unfixed roads in the Lower Cities. Liv had encountered gashes in the road that were deadlier to meet at a high speed than a bullet.

She tapped a button on the side of her helmet above her ear meant to register voice commands and held it until the outside roar dulled to a whisper and the whir of the drones' thin propeller blades had gone totally silent from within the wrangler's locked truck trailer.

In five seconds, the door would shutter open and release four hijacked police drones programmed to survey and secure the perimeter of the course, and the coursemaster would sound the air horn for the Run to commence.

At that point, the eyes would find them all.

Liv's fingers curled around the clutch. *Five. Four.*

"Riders!"

Three. Two.

The coursemaster floored his finger on the trigger. The drones poured out into the skies above them, lit at the crux of their propellers by glowing, absinthe eyes. They crept upward like spiders—that was, if each spidery leg had been fitted with knife-sharp propeller blades and the spider's head could spit darts.

Liv had never been hit by one before, but now wasn't the time to get comfortable around them.

Her tires bled out against the asphalt several paces behind the more zealous riders, but equal to two of the three contract riders—the ones who weren't from the Margossi house. She didn't have time to read the names on the sides of their helmets before one of them swerved in front of her and turned sharply down an alley on her opposite side.

The move did something worse than simply give her pause; it made her wonder how familiar these riders were with her streets. She had assumed, perhaps naively, that all contract riders came from the Upper City, but it had also never mattered to her if they won as long as she won too.

She couldn't think that way anymore.

The rider who remained at her side matched her next turn, following her past two potholes on the main road. They clung to her back tire, so close their tracks could kiss, and one slight shift could send her tumbling. She was at a disadvantage in the front. Her bike wasn't fast enough to drive straight out of the point of tension with a bike like theirs, but it was durable enough to withstand a blow.

Liv pivoted sharply to the left and braked, clipping him with her back tire. Her bike spun and tilted, which she accounted for and rectified with the careful placement of a protruding curb. The other rider launched forward, unable to steady their bike or their body.

The collision was not fast enough for the friction to burn through their uniform, but it was disruptive enough for a drone to spot them from overhead, cast its darted net over the rider's head, and then fix its glowing eye on Liv.

She was already gone when another dart struck the contract rider's leg, pacifying them instantly.

The road was almost peaceful once she'd sufficiently scrubbed the image of the rider's tangled body from her mind. Anyone who wanted to hurt her would have to catch her first, and she'd shaken off her most immediate threat. She passed two riders from the Lower Cities who had moved to the side street she was on and decided to reroute to the main road again to recover some distance between them, lest a well-positioned drone cast a net over all three of them at once.

She saw no sign of the other contract riders. Above her, the sky was deceptively clear. No glowing drone eyes. No stars. To her right, through the gaps between buildings and across the tall bridges dividing the Lower Cities from the Upper City, High Mayor Keaton's perfectly preserved pink face grinned at her, only the size of her pinky nail, via a digital broadcast hanging on a holographic screen over the skyline.

Again, Liv wondered why she had never seen the High Mayor's daughter until tonight.

There wasn't much opportunity for deep contemplation on a Run, but Liv managed to steal moments here and there. High Mayor Gaines Keaton's presence, like his son's, was such an invasion that it made her sick sometimes. It was impossible to ignore. The effects of his reign had seeped into every facet of her life, from her family's pilgrimage to the Lower Cities to their subsequent fight to survive there. It inspired a particularly strident disgust that Liv hadn't reserved for a living person before.

The peace she found on the course lasted only minutes. In its place was an oath. She had to win. Not for the Keaton daughter and her sibling feud, but for her family.

The second contract rider split between two buildings on Liv's left—*airborne.* The culprit: an unmarked tear in the road. A drone spotted them, casting its net and dart.

Its eye then locked onto something ahead of her.

She'd reached the Margossi rider. They had a small enough lead that Liv could see them, but only as a speck against a sea of flickering light bulbs.

The contract rider took a sharp right and disappeared down a side street. Liv was tempted to follow them, put some faith into Caldwell Keaton's massive bet, and see what lay down the unlit corridor. She seized the rare chance to look back. No one was following, save for the faraway drone slowly creeping toward her.

She could make it to the end with speed alone. She wasn't far from the end of the course; as long as nothing else touched either rider, they could both reach the termination point and earn a cut of the winnings.

It wasn't a bad deal, especially if Caldwell had invested a hefty sum into the evening's Run. Even with all the bets for the Margossi rider, there was still at least one for her.

Since losing her arm, she had made significant modifications to her bike. Pressing a trigger on her left handlebar moved all her controls to that hand, freeing her prosthetic. It limited sensitive changes to her current ride settings, but it allowed her to do certain, trivial tasks. She could press down on the comms button beside her ear and answer a call or fidget with the high neck of her leather jacket.

Tonight, it gave her permission to be ruthless, to do more than share the winnings, the way she had always done under Corey's safekeeping.

She had never ridden this way before, with a point to prove and a hardened offense. No Run since her first had thrilled her so much, either, and she was practically burning within her protective layers to go even further now that she knew what was possible.

The Margossi rider would require more than a tap of her tire. She needed to fight dirty. Angry.

Prayer went against everything she lived through before her family migrated to Corcoran, so she sent a directionless wish into the night that her decision to change her ways wouldn't end up fucking her over.

Then, once she had gained on the Margossi rider, Liv hit her metal arm against the hard shell of her protective knee brace in such a way that caused the cylinders making up her fingers to twist, collapse, and narrow to spikes.

The rider effortlessly swerved to avoid her bike. Liv could hear their subdued shouting through the muting of her helmet's current setting. She reasoned it would be easier this way, hearing nothing and caring little, but she was still left with Corey's voice in her mind, quietly disappointed.

She had always ridden for the adrenaline rush and the sting of air that slipped between the bottom of her helmet and the collar of her jacket. Most Lower City riders risked everything for a sliver of the winnings, and whatever they couldn't win in money, they could win in these stolen moments of wildness and freedom.

She didn't pretend to know what the Upper City rider's reasons for entering the Run were, but she'd bet anything she needed the money more than they did.

In one fluid motion, Liv jabbed the metal spikes into the back of their tire and tore them clean before the rapid deflation dragged their back into hers.

It slowed her momentarily, causing her handles to wiggle and her bike to swerve unsteadily. She heard a string of curses loud enough to break both helmets' soundguards and corrected her position hurriedly.

The rider more hurriedly reached for something in a hidden pocket at their hip. Their palm curled around black metal, and the shape gleamed with the yellow of the streetlamps as they extended it squarely from their chest.

"Shit," mouthed Liv.

A bullet clipped the seat of her bike, narrowly missing her side. The rider fired three more, but none hit her or her bike after the first. She took a hard left back to the main road before the rider could fire another. Only once she had covered another two miles did she finally take another breath.

Liv felt the inside of her helmet decompress, as if her head had been ballooning with hot air. Warmth rushed to her ears, but she was shivering all over.

There was a drone not far behind her, but with only one more mile to go before the termination point, she let her shoulders slump in relief.

I've done it, she thought, and in less than a minute, the statement became true.

She slowed her pace. Every muscle in her body unclenched, and she barked out a laugh that no one else could hear.

She relaxed into her seat and threw back her shoulders, feeling all the ridges of her spine shift back into a reasonable position. Behind her, the shapes of two other Lower City riders reached the end of the course, small as flies. They, too, would get something from the race pool, even if it wasn't as much as her cut. She wondered if anyone placed bets on them—friends, family, benefactors...

Outside the boundaries of the course, though, and past the termination point was a drone. Its eye flashed at her like it was blinking in suspicion, and Liv blinked back, undetectable through her tinted visor.

She mumbled, unfastening the buckle beneath her chin. "Where d'you think you're going?"

Then, it shot, hitting her metal arm at the elbow.

The force of the dart tugged sharply at the connection point on her shoulder. Her vision went white with pain. Liv grabbed for the handlebars with the helmet halfway off her head and struck the kickstand with her heel.

She couldn't have miscalculated the course perimeter. Liv was at least a quarter of a mile past the designated boundary. The shot shook the other riders with surprise, though neither of them faced the same wrath.

She couldn't concern herself with questions about why the drone was shooting at her. She had no time to reconnect the buckle at her chin once gravity had helped the helmet back onto her head. She fled from the boundary and the other riders, only to find that the drone was hastening.

Out here, she had no one to call for help. The only person she could think of was Corey, and he was also the only person she couldn't tell. Her fingers had instinctively raised to the button on her helmet to call him, but she put them back on the handlebar.

She would have to tell the wrangler himself. Her tires screeched against the pavement, heading in the direction of the course again. If Corey couldn't tell the gamemakers that something was wrong, it had to be her. With all four drones scouring the area, the course would be a hotter danger zone, but she couldn't think of anything else to do.

If the drones were following her out here, it wasn't worth the added time of rounding the perimeter.

She didn't concern herself with racing strategically; she had won the Run and beat the contract riders. All that mattered now was survival, and she could manage that with speed alone.

She passed the downed second contract rider, who was sealed to the ground by a barbed net. Their helmet was off, revealing bright blue hair and dark brown skin. Their sedative-drugged gaze shifted from Liv's bike to the drone above her, and they tried in vain to tuck their arms over their head to brace for another dart.

The drone's eye didn't waver from Liv's bike.

It levied another shot, hitting the asphalt behind her.

"Stop!" she shouted.

The drones couldn't hear her, but the wrangler should have been able to see her through its eye. Couldn't he terminate it manually?

She shouted again as the beginning of the course came into view. Even if no one could hear her, they could see her clearly. The crowd began to disperse, leaving few remnants at the starting line.

The wrangler was shaking the controller, slamming his fist against its digital surface, while the coursemaster wrapped his arms around the smaller man's shoulders and pulled him to the ground for cover beneath the truck bed. The Keatons were being ushered by a personal driver into the silver car.

The drone behind her faltered in the air as the wrangler's slipping grasp caused the controller to tumble against the ground, but it corrected its course instantly. The wrangler reached for it, but the coursemaster held him back, keeping him under the cover.

"No," Liv pleaded uselessly. Under the wrangler's control, the drones shouldn't have been able to kill anyone, but Liv had seen what they could do without his measures in place. Outside the course, darts were coated in a tranquiliser strong enough to kill, and their nets were wired to electrocute. It was easier to assume that people in the Lower Cities wouldn't have the strength to withstand the violence of a police drone than to fight its clutches. What would happen if the wrangler's measures couldn't keep her safe?

Another dart hit her bike.

She took herself down a smaller street, buying time for the wrangler to grab his controller. If Liv continued forward, she would pull the target toward the remaining bystanders.

Her speed was too substantial, the ground too uneven. Worse, she had miscalculated the road she turned down, and she would run out of space quickly unless she could turn again in smaller confines.

Her tire snagged on a cardboard box flattened on the asphalt. Her handlebars twisted despite her corrections. She turned toward the main road again, facing the drone head-on before she could pass it again, and the millisecond of eye contact between her eye and the drone's eye nearly made her wet herself.

It fired again, but she was already moving. Her bike screeched with an unidentified puncture, slowing incrementally.

She made it to the main road before it could fire again, hitting the right side of her helmet.

Liv's vision blanked from the whiplash. Her hands were jolted from her handlebars, stealing the rest of her control.

The bike teetered with her toppling weight, throwing her body sideways. Everything in Liv's body felt like it'd been lit on fire.

Someone on the road shouted her name, but something was covering her eyes. Her helmet, maybe. She couldn't take it off, immobilized by something hard against her side.

She'd stopped moving and started burning. Was she bleeding? She couldn't tell.

Over several harrowing seconds, Liv became cognizant enough of the situation to realize that half her body had been crushed by the weight of her bike, and she could do nothing to change it except wait for whoever had shouted to reach her. Her call for help was a mere wheeze, only tight puffs of air between two barely-there consonants.

Eventually, her savior pulled the helmet the rest of the way over her head and laid her skull against the hard ground. Their hands were cold and stiff, as was the road, and Liv couldn't tell where one ended and the other began.

"Did I win?" she croaked.

"What?"

Liv blinked, but the figure never manifested more than a smear of contrast in the blur of her vision. She tried to swallow, then asked again, "Did I..."

But there was nothing else after that.

3

Not even one year from her first accident, Liv Shankly woke up in a hospital again to blinding lights above her head and a dry mouth from insufficient water. This light was brighter than the first, accounting for a smattering of blue holo screens behind her bed that housed her vitals, and her mouth was considerably less dry, as if she'd been taken somewhere new for care, somewhere other than her regional hospital in the Lower City.

The fact that she didn't know where she was made her stir awake out of her placid state. There was a wire in her arm, funneling a drip IV stream straight into her veins, and a body folded over in the seat beside her that she didn't recognize. Her left leg was bandaged from the middle of her thigh to the bottom of her heel and strung aloft in a slightly crooked position with an array of lifts and supports.

Did Maura and Corey know she was there? Would anyone have told them? She was wearing only a hospital gown, which meant someone, probably a doctor, had removed her clothes and taken her things.

Liv then remembered that she hadn't been carrying her comms device during the Run and that she had, in fact, been thrown off her bike to achieve the injuries she was currently bedridden with; and since that was the case, it was better that Corey and Maura didn't know the full truth of her circumstances.

Slipping into clarity, Liv realized the person asleep in the nearby chair was her one-time benefactor and High Mayor's daughter. "Hey," Liv said, rousing her awake. "Where am I?"

The Keaton daughter rubbed her eyes and gave a soft hum, fighting the pull toward waking. Liv repeated, "*Hey*. You there."

Upon realizing her rider had become conscious, the Keaton girl snapped to attention, lowering her bent legs from the seat of the chair and dragging herself closer to the bed. "I knew you'd wake up the second I stopped looking. How are you feeling?"

"Fucking brilliant."

"Really?"

"No. What's going on? What hospital am I in? Where's my shit?"

Her benefactor stood from her chair quickly, albeit unsteadily, to fetch Liv's backpack from the foot of a nearby countertop. "You're at the Hillfetter Memorial Hospital in West Morg. It's been about fourteen hours since you first arrived and fifteen since you fell off your bike. The worst of the damage was a crushed patella and a mild concussion, but the doctors deemed you stable a little while ago."

The girl lifted the backpack off the ground with some difficulty, reticent to place the weight onto Liv's bed.

"You put something in there?"

"Had to put your winnings somewhere," the girl replied. "Dr. Tewer told me when you'd crossed the boundary. I almost couldn't believe it."

Liv's mouth had begun to shape the name questioningly when the sight within the open backpack caused her to shout. "Holy *shit,* is that—?"

"It's yours now."

Liv's body lurched forward with arms outstretched—

No. Her prosthetic was missing from the connection point

at her shoulder. She possessed only one arm and a great sense of imbalance in her body.

This fact dampened her enthusiasm first, followed shortly by the ever-present reminder that the money was meant to pay off her family's existing medical debt; then, most dreadfully, Liv sobered to the realization that no matter how much she had won, it would likely be insufficient to cover this accident, too.

Her head rolled back onto the pillow, defeated instantly. "Is my comms in there?"

"This thing?" Pulling the compact, folded device out of her pinstriped coat pocket, the girl laid it on Liv's stomach. "I tried to look for your emergency contacts: parents, siblings, and the like. Couldn't find any contacts under the usual roles. Then, I figured that you might just have them listed by their names rather than mother, father, et cetera; so I went about my search using official avenues."

"Official avenues?"

"Records," said the Keaton daughter, culminating in a grievous pause. Liv swallowed. She considered offering the simple explanation that Corey and Maura were not called such parental terms in her phone, but then she would have to explain why. Or that her true surname wasn't even Shankly, but something else about her that had been adopted through unofficial, murky means. "I couldn't find anything on you. The Total City has no official records of your existence, rider, let alone the identities of your parents or other family members."

What had been, just moments ago, a triumphant discovery slowly devolved into Liv's worst nightmare. She wondered if she could close her eyes and fake sudden somnolence to get out of the conversation. Maybe she could come up with a clever ploy during the time it took for the Keaton girl to call for a doctor.

"Well, I definitely exist," Liv begrudged, "much as the world keeps trying to kill me."

"I did try, though," offered the girl, as if Liv's irritation stemmed from her lack of success rather than her fickle status within the Total City's records.

It would be easier to avoid the topic altogether. "Do you know what they did with my arm?"

The girl said nothing but reeked of apprehension. She turned and paced toward the foot of the bed with agonizing slowness, avoiding her rider's gaze while she spoke. "It was confiscated."

Fuck, thought Liv. *Fuck fuck fuck.*

"You're not in any trouble."

"Oh, so you donated my limb to science, then?"

"The modifications on it were unsanctioned," the girl hissed. "I'm not saying it wasn't wrong of them to take it. I'm not saying I didn't try to get it back. What I *am* saying is that you should be lucky you weren't arrested for it. Modifications to that extent—and to what end, I can't even begin to fathom—would be considered totally illegal if anyone had had the foresight to anticipate them."

"But they're not illegal yet," Liv mumbled, the last of her enthusiasm quashed. If the police, or whatever other investigative branches wanted her arm, decided to punish her for the countless modifications she'd made to her prosthetic (which were, admittedly, not limited to fingers that sharpened to spikes and included a sliding panel in the palm that could release certain fixtures like wrenches for her job and a baton for bad bar fights), her family would have a worse fate to reckon with than medical debts alone. And the debt was bad enough. So bad that she had put herself back on her bike for the Run and kissed the asphalt for it.

"No. Not at *all.*" The girl's fingers curled around the bars at the foot of Liv's hospital bed. "You're equally lucky that I was here to vouch for you. I couldn't get them to release it, but I could disprove your possession of it. The mods you made to it rendered its registration information unreadable, where it wasn't totally scraped off. It'll have to go through forensics for them to figure out who it could have possibly come from. And with your insufficient records, there's a high probability that they'll have nothing to show for it."

Liv thought that was all impressive and convenient, except for one major piece that the girl had missed. "You don't think a hospital patient with a missing arm and a matching connector point won't tip them off?"

The High Mayor's daughter looked at her with what Liv recognized as pity, and it almost pleased Liv that her face had shown no traces of it until this point. "You must not be familiar with Morgallis's history of cosmetic amputation. A limb like yours..." Her speech slowed. The girl spoke as if she had to fit every sentence into the span of a single breath, with tight syllables and a high-pitched, musical intonation. But she'd become grave, suddenly. Hesitant. "It'd be quite the fashion. There could be hundreds in the area who were missing an arm like yours, and plenty who would like to get their hands on machinery like your prosthetic. Whether or not it's attributed to you is secondary to the willingness of someone else to claim it."

Liv's chest squeezed. The loss of her arm had been traumatic, no matter how capable she was to carry on without it. How anyone could choose to get rid of it... How anyone could afford to...

She wished Corey were there. She wished she could go home and talk to her parents. When all they could manage against their circumstances was camaraderie and a listening ear, sometimes, that was all Liv needed; and she doubted she would find that in the High Mayor's daughter. She wished more than anything that she had not placed herself in such a tenuous position where she would be afraid to call them.

The guilt would hurt Liv much more than their anger would. She had wanted to believe she was doing the right thing, fighting against the possibility that this could happen, too. Would he and Maura even be angry? Maybe after the fact. They would be terrified, first. Not by her actions or her negligence, but by the prospect of nearly losing her again.

"Well," she murmured, feeling sicker with every second the conversation veered into misery, "I bet none of them are as ripped as me. They'll figure it out soon enough."

A nurse entered the room to check her vitals. She flurried around the bed, typing notes into a tablet periodically, obscuring the Keaton daughter from Liv's view. The girl idled by the counter across from Liv's bed with a forefinger loosely crooked against her lips.

The rider still didn't know her name. At this point, she felt like it was too late to ask, and she watched her silently, considering every news broadcast and article she could remember about the Keaton family, conjuring up the names of only Mayor Gaines Keaton and his son.

"Can you feel anything in your leg right now?" asked the nurse. Liv wiggled her toes at the end of the cast. "Miss Keaton has already squared away the insurance details, so we're going to keep you another hour or so for some final monitoring and recovery planning, and then, you're free to leave."

"What do you mean?"

The nurse tucked the tablet under her arm to fidget with a wedding ring on her finger. "The recovery plan or the insurance?"

"We'll discuss that in a moment." Such gently spoken words from the High Mayor's daughter could halt the nurse's next words like a scythe.

"Yes, Miss Keaton. There's someone here to see you, also."

"Who?" asked the girl.

"A couple of visitors. For her."

Liv pushed herself upright, expecting to see her father and Maura. With her bad luck, the hospital would have managed to find them in spite of the non-existent documentation tying them together.

Instead, the broad-shouldered shape of the coursemaster filled the doorway, and then, his slight, mute counterpart, the wrangler, both wearing more elegant clothing than she had ever seen them in before.

The clothing in question was a button-up shirt, which the wrangler had fastened to the neck while the coursemaster had left two buttons open to reveal the white hem of an undershirt; a pair of neatly brushed black corduroy pants and one pair of rust-brown linen trousers; and some kind of jacket, unzipped over both their torsos.

By principle of the Runs, they were not supposed to exist to her off the course. It felt like a cosmic breach of the universe that they were standing in front of her, wearing identifying wristbands.

They looked at her like she was a gift. The coursemaster approached her first, arching down to lift her upper body from the raised bed and embrace her. "This is the second time you've scared us to death, you know. What's the matter with you?"

Liv waited for the nurse to remove the IV rooted in her left arm to return his hug. "What are you doing here?"

The wrangler embraced her next, more gently and for a longer time. Never would she have expected to see them like this, worrying over her like her parents did. She could feel the wrangler's chest catching with breath. He was trying to say something, but couldn't find the energy, or the words, to voice it.

It was enough. He pulled away, gripping her by the shoulders. The bare inches of his wrists that she could see beneath the hems of his coat were embroidered with fresh scars.

Liv's line of sight betrayed her curiosity. The wrangler took his hands off her to sign, "The controller is destroyed."

Once the nurse had left the room, the coursemaster, whose wristband identified him as Michael Golovsky, said, "We came to visit just after you were admitted, but Miss Keaton said you were being prepped for surgery at the time."

"What happened to the controller?" Liv asked. "And the drones?"

The gamemakers looked at each other, which gave Liv a chance to read the name on the wrangler's wristband: Stanislaus Tewer.

"We don't know what happened to the drones," said Michael. "Three of them were still under our control, but one of them was rejecting our commands. We test them religiously. We've never had an outburst like that."

Interpreting Stanislaus's signs, Michael said, "It won't happen again. It can't happen again. That drone was still using the signal from the controller. Stanis had to break it to sever the connection."

"Not quickly enough," remarked the Keaton daughter. "It went on long enough to injure my rider significantly."

"It's in the nature of the Run for things to happen, Miss Keaton," said the coursemaster, too patiently to reveal true upset. "The drone shouldn't have been chasing her at the time, but the injuries she sustained were well within the scope of normal Drone Run possibilities."

Liv added, "He's right, pinstripes. I got myself into this mess."

The High Mayor's daughter leaned against the counter, her fingers tapping restlessly.

To the coursemaster, Liv muttered. "You didn't tell Corey, did you?" Both gamemakers shook their heads. "He's going to be so disappointed in me."

Michael placed his hand on the top of her head and ruffled her short black hair like dog fur. "He'll get over it. It's not your fault, Shanks. You raced well. This shouldn't have happened."

"Have you had her emergency contact information this whole time?" the Keaton daughter asked.

"With all due respect, a lot of folks in the Lower Cities have circumstances that require shut mouths. It wasn't my place to tell her father. That decision lies with her and whoever her benefactor is. Trust me, I did consider it. She was stable. We had our eyes on her if anything were to change."

Liv's lip warbled. She didn't know when the urge to cry had struck or where it came from. Equal parts hopelessness, relief, and gratitude mingled in her chest, all of it taking up the space she needed to breathe. Stanislaus laid his hand over her wrist and squeezed.

"We can tell him now, if that's what you want," the coursemaster offered.

Liv mulled it over. She owed it to her parents to tell them she was safe. Still, she didn't know if she could reckon with the full weight of everything that had happened in the past twenty-four hours so quickly.

"Can you tell him not to come?" she asked the gamemakers. "Tell him I'll be home soon."

The pair answered with a simultaneous nod. Stanislaus stood up from the side of the hospital bed, and they both left the room together. The Keaton girl watched them from the doorway until they had gone a sufficient distance for her to take a full breath.

She dropped her head and folded her arms across her chest. "Did I just make a fool of myself?"

"In front of the gamemakers?" Liv asked.

"I don't think Dr. Tewer remembers me. He used to be a guest instructor for my youth robotics league. He was a bit of a legend for us as kids. I'd hate to think I looked like a self-righteous idiot in front of him just now."

"So? What else are you supposed to be?"

"I don't know," the girl said. "Composed. Sophisticated. Capable."

"Sure, if you're a brochure for high-end security enlistment. I doubt they care, pinstripes. You're probably never going to see them again anyway."

Chewing the inside of her cheek, the High Mayor's daughter stared at Liv for a long time as if the rider was a puzzle she couldn't solve. She took a seat beside Liv's bed again, sliding the chair closer. "I'm out of my depths here. I wasn't supposed to be there last night, let alone place any bets."

"I don't know why you would, considering the house Margossi rider was carrying a pistol."

"What?"

With the events of the evening behind her, Liv had the courage to scoff. "Do you expect me to believe you two waltzed out there ready to bet your dirty money on a rider without any insurance that you'd win?"

The other girl's shoulders set proudly, her chin sharp and tense. "In case you've forgotten due to your concussion, my money was on *you*. Why would I do that if I thought you'd end up with a bullet hole in you?"

"I don't know. Sadism?"

"I wouldn't. If I'd known he had an illegal weapon on him, I'd have kept my mouth shut and let Caldwell do with his money as he pleased."

"Ah. What a relief." Liv surveyed all the blinking machines in the room. Even the noise in this hospital was different. It gave her thoughts room to fester, which she detested. "So, you placed a bet on me, too?"

"I did place a small bet on you, yes. But most of the money in the bag is Caldwell's." The girl laid her head on her forearms on the side of the hospital bed. She looked as if she hadn't slept at all aside from the brief refrain before Liv woke from her sedatives. Her eyes closed. Her straightened back collapsed into a slouch, as if the gamemakers' departure robbed her of a spine.

"What is it between you two that makes you so keen on him losing?"

With barely-restrained exasperation and a downward, avoidant gaze, the High Mayor's daughter said, "Sibling rivalry. Resentment. I don't know. It's not really your concern, is it?"

"Maybe I'm just having a hard time understanding how someone can afford to put so much on the line over 'sibling rivalry.' You paid for the surgery, didn't you?"

Her eyes remained shut. Perhaps, Liv was being too vicious in her interrogation. The girl couldn't comfortably admit anything when all Liv had done was stick pins in her motives like a dead moth. They didn't know each other. Liv didn't even know her name. As soon as Liv got discharged, they would go their separate ways, and nothing they said to one another would amount to anything.

"Last night," the girl muttered, "when you asked me about why I wanted my brother to fail so badly, I didn't know how to answer. It wasn't a lie, what I told you. But how do I condense twenty-six years of our history into something palatable for a stranger? It's impossible. And maybe my omission was dishonest enough. He lives for games—Caldwell. He has built his entire life around competition. But he and I couldn't be more different. The kinds of games he plays, I have no desire or wherewithal to win. It makes me look weak, and at present, that isn't something I can afford to be."

The girl didn't seem to notice when Liv went quiet, too lost in thought about her brother or the question or, perhaps, a dream she'd been woken up from by Liv's sudden consciousness.

"Well. Thank you," the rider said. It was so earnest that she felt flayed open on the asphalt again in front of the Keaton daughter, even though she had long since left it. She supposed she should be grateful that someone had taken a chance on her winning, however misguided and lofty it was, when they'd had no reason to.

The girl couldn't have known how rare and awful the humiliation of an apology was for Liv. She must have been expecting something much more volatile. Liv watched all the hard lines of her face soften incrementally.

"It's nothing, really."

"I won't say it again, pinstripes. Just take the thanks."

"My name is Vaughn," the Keaton daughter corrected her. Her eyes flared toward Liv, wide and unguarded. "I took a gamble on you, rider. It was, in hindsight, a very stupid decision to place money on someone Caldwell hadn't vetted, given that I know little about this game. What you won... It wasn't about the money for me. What you did was more valuable to me than a little lost money, and I'm very grateful you're still alive for me to admit that."

"You don't know my name either, do you?"

"Haven't the faintest clue. Thought you might have preferred it that way."

Liv adjusted her cheek against the pillow, not remembering when she put it there in the first place, when she realized that she had been staring, drowning in the dark, starry galaxy of Vaughn Keaton's eyes. "It's Liv," she said. "Olivia Shankly. Sometimes, it's just Shanks, depending on who you ask."

Vaughn's mouth quirked up at the corners. "Hello."

Liv parroted back to her, having no goddamn clue what to say next, "Hello."

The next person who entered her hospital room was one of the attending doctors, an older man with sea-green scrubs beneath his white coat, the name Hathaway stitched above his breast, and a thick pair of rectangular glasses on his round nose. "Your vitals look even. We're going to finish casting your leg in a second, and then I'll hand you off to Dr. Ochoa to discuss a temporary prosthetic until you have the means for a custom. In the meantime, my scribe has some options for cast tape you can choose from. You'll be free to discharge after that. In your own words, how are you feeling?"

The quiet scribe beside the door readied herself to record Liv Shankly's response on a tablet.

"Like I could run a marathon. Or fight a mad bull."

Blankly, the man replied, "There are no bulls in West Morg."

Vaughn's eyes crinkled at the corners. "What color are you thinking of for your cast?"

"Fuck if I know. Choose for me."

"It's not my knee."

"Well, it's not my money paying for the surgery. Pick something good, though." Liv stretched her arm above my head. All her vertebrae realigned with loud clicks. "Something that makes me look rugged for when I return home a hero."

Dr. Hathaway spread his scribe's selection of fiberglass casting tape out on a robotically assisted desk beside Liv's bed like a child showing off his favorite toys. Vaughn looked them over, considering each one with an unnecessary closeness, the burden of the decision weighing heavily on her shoulders.

"This one?" Vaughn plucked a roll of burgundy. "Brings out the color of your biceps."

"Fantastic."

"I'm going to talk with Dr. Ochoa about the temporary prosthetic. I put my information into your comms device earlier, in case you need to reach me." Vaughn stood from her chair, brushing past Dr. Hathaway. "Try not to, though. I have some calls to make."

4 ———————————————————————

When they removed the connection point from her old prosthetic, Dr. Ochoa had quipped lightheartedly about how old her model must have been. "They must have had an overstock of this or something. We haven't used shell models that fuse directly to the skin in decades. You'll find this connector much easier, I think."

Its other half, the arm itself, was somewhere in police custody, and Liv wanted to defend its dignity, even though everything about it that was good came from mods she made. The model was shit, but it was all she'd been given at the time. The disparity in what she could afford with her lacking Warner Med insurance policy and what the doctors in West Morgallis could offer her under Vaughn's protection was astounding.

At that point, a nurse helped the doctor wrap bandages around freshly sanitized puncture points where the connection point had been speared into Liv's skin with dozens of prongs. Her nerves were numb by the end of what felt like an eternal, internal flaying. She'd been watching the nurses work but couldn't stomach it anymore. She rescinded her typical sarcastic jabs.

The connection point fit like a sleeve over the bandaged stump of her arm, sewn to a high-necked, button-fastened bodice made up of a slanted bandeau and a collar. Vaughn had returned to the room, and she averted her gaze as her rider slipped the hospital gown off her shoulders and wriggled the odd garment over her naked shoulders. The nurses handed Liv a bag with all her clothes, and she put them on, her new arm hiccupping to life.

The mechanics of it were hidden by shiny, white panels. The motions were fluid, and when Liv expected to hear the gentle scrape of metal, she was sorely disappointed to hear nothing at all. With her former prosthetic, it had been obnoxious at the worst of times but a small comfort at the best, being able to slide her fingertips together and hear the hiss of steel. Her new fingers clicked together gently, which made her think of exposed bone.

The hand was a comparable size to her left. The width of her new arm was scrawny, which made Liv wonder if the optimal starting point for the average Upper City prosthetic accounted for a widespread lack of muscle mass.

A nurse slid her old connector into the bag her clothes were in and handed it to Vaughn Keaton for safekeeping.

Once the last of the medical personnel left her room, Liv asked, "Can I go yet?"

The High Mayor's daughter nodded. Her eyes were less red than before, as if she'd taken a moment somewhere between their last conversation and the extraction of the old connector's prongs to squeeze a few eyedrops into them and rinse her face in the bathroom.

Vaughn approached the side of the hospital bed where Liv's legs hung aloft, holding a set of crutches in her right hand. She offered the left to Liv. "I have a car outside. Tewer and Golovsky should have delivered your bike to your place by now."

Liv's parents would have discovered what had happened to her and where she had been the previous night. By the time Liv acclimated to the crutches underneath her arms and waddled outside, it was night again. The sky was cloudy, catching the changing lights of the towering digital billboards in the Central Morgallis Square.

Most of the billboards had been built into the mirrored windows of skyscrapers when the city first remodeled to weather the storms, their screens waking when the sun set. Morgallis's remodel happened first, and the Lower Cities should have happened shortly after, but their efforts to weatherproof had long since been abandoned. When Liv rode at night, the screens boasted a city that was whole and complete from beneath the layer of gray that hung heavily over Corcoran. Above those screens hung the proud face of Gaines Keaton, stamped in holo blue on a display of his own.

The car waiting for her was different from the one that had brought the Keatons to the course. It was deep black, like an oil slick swallowing a starless sky, and there was no Caldwell to step out of the backseat. A man in his late twenties leaned against the driver's side door, murmuring something into his cell phone when Liv and Vaughn appeared. Hastily, he finished his voice note and pulled the door open for them.

Non-discreetly, Vaughn's hand splayed delicately over the center of Liv's back, ushering her into the car. "Thank you, Clav," Vaughn said to the man.

"Yes, Miss Keaton."

Vaughn shimmied in afterward, leaving the passenger seat empty. Liv stored the crutches at her feet with the tops balanced on her shoe and the bottoms angled toward Vaughn's neat loafers.

Liv closed her eyes. She breathed in and held it for a long time, waiting for Vaughn or the driver to say something, before releasing it. Her temple tilted onto the window beside her. The connector of her new prosthetic gave a grating squeal as it compressed between her layers and the wall of the car. Vaughn dictated an address—*Liv's* address—to which the driver, Clav, replied, "In Corcoran?"

"Yes, Clav. Is that a problem?"

In the oblong sliver of the rearview mirror, Liv saw the driver's heavy-lidded, dark eyes crinkle. "Of course not. Just a surprise, is all."

They spoke little after that, which Liv would have hated if there wasn't so much happening outside the car for her to look at. The hospital was in West Morgallis, and Corcoran was the most eastern of the Lower Cities that arched around the capital, bordered only in the east by the ruins of a collapsed flooded city, and then the sea itself. They would have to drive through the Upper City's heart to get to the Corcoran bridge, while the luxury of nightlife curled its seductive fingers, beckoning them to indulge until they had escaped.

The Upper City was altitudinous compared to the Lower Cities. This hadn't been the fact that gave the Upper City its moniker; no one called Morgallis the Upper City until long after the storms, when all the disparities came floating to the top of those floodwaters. It had only been Morgallis, a frivolous, tech-obsessed, neon corner of the region that the fringe towns lived with rather than the bright beast of progress they cowered under now. Liv could see it shining from the outskirts of the Lower Cities with all its glowing bridges leading to it like veins toward the beating organ.

Their car slowed as they passed through a dense cluster of high-rise buildings underneath a web of walking bridges. Liv didn't have any reason to venture this deeply into the Upper City; the city center consisted primarily of novelty shops and corporate offices with apartments stacked over them.

When night fell, the city seemed to boast new vices. Signs, closer to Liv's level than the billboards, illuminated exclusive clubs, live music, new acronymized substances to dissolve into drinks, and flesh.

Flesh. Liv squinted at the sign, wondering if she had read it correctly, and puzzled over the missing context once she concluded she had. In Corcoran, brothels might have referred to such services as "bodies," though even that was more impersonal than most clientele preferred. Their brothels were full of people who yearned for connection, for a touch they were missing, or high praise they didn't get for doing lackluster, degrading work.

Of course, Corcoran was nothing like Morgallis. The Upper City was an overwhelming, overpopulated anthill where unfulfilled desires came to be sated as long as one had money to burn.

The sheer radiance of its lights entranced her. She first marvelled at the coats. This time of year, the muggy, porous weather gave way to dry days and crisp breezes. The divide between springs and summers had once been more than a closed- and open-mouthed breath; now, the most effective passage of time in their flooded region was a periodic refrain from the feeling of living in an armpit. Liv knew this refrain was close whenever Maura asked her to dig her coats out of a storage bin and hang them in the closet for her to get rid of the wrinkles.

The coats in the city center were colorful like the plumes of exotic birds. Some were puffed with fur that glowed like shards of uranium glass, while others were deceptively transparent, glowing only where rare droplets of rain made contact with their surface.

Decorated pedestrians covered the sidewalks, snaking through the city center. Pointed ears, upturned noses, and faces adorned with silver bolts and bars glanced briefly at the string of cars pulsing through. Vaughn turned her face away from her window, opting to fix her gaze on the unimpressive middle seat between them.

Liv locked eyes with a trio of women huddled around the hood of a parked car, who were wearing little else underneath their transparent coats. The cruxes of their toned, tanned legs were covered by elaborate lacework of leather. Liv wrapped her fingers around her cheeks and kneaded her jaw to hide her deep flush. Seeing her through the dark glass, the trio postured proudly. One offered a demure wave that probably would have worked on Liv a year ago. It took more than the promise of a good time to seduce Liv Shankly.

She noticed the marbled turquoise of the girl's hand, and the realization that she had only been paying attention to the vulgar things made her realize 1) that she had completely overlooked the trio's color-varied prosthetics, and 2) that it might not have been as difficult to seduce Liv Shankly as she'd thought. The sensations reckoned violently inside of her, warring until she felt sick again, although that might have also been the car.

She removed her temple from the window and dropped her head back against the headrest, breathing slowly until her newfound nausea subsided.

"They're not real," Vaughn noted.

With no recourse for her leering, Liv asked, "What do you mean?"

"Those girls outside aren't real. You won't find any living, breathing sex workers outdoors in Morgallis."

"So the prosthetic—"

"It's not a prosthetic," said her benefactor. "Our droids are convincing. Soft where they need to be, but durable enough to withstand even the worst inclinations. If you looked closely, you'd see that those hands are registered to the Kilgarre Corporation."

This was said as unimportantly as a cereal brand, but Liv couldn't place the name.

Once Vaughn deemed the silence unbearable, she added, "They're most notably a weapons manufacturer, but in the past decade, they've branched out with consumer-direct products like the droids."

"So, sex and violence."

"I believe their official motto is 'Making love, war, and everything in between.' But yes. It's significantly cheaper here to buy artificial company, and the brothels tend to cater to more affluent types who can afford human companionship. But for every person looking for a cheap, quick release, which is the majority of the clientele, Kilgarre gets a little richer. Those hands are the mark of a Kilgarre Corp droid. Between us, it's where their trackers are hidden."

"How much did you have to undress to figure that out?"

Vaughn's pink face flushed a deep brick shade. "I'm fairly well-informed about the droids navigating this city."

Clav's eyes shifted into view in the mirror again to study the pair. Interrupting his glance, Liv asked, "Are *you* a droid?"

"Not since the last time I checked."

"Clavernus Lim is my private driver," Vaughn explained.

"Another pinstripe then."

The High Mayor's daughter shifted uncomfortably in her seat, her spine as stiff as a knife. "He doesn't work for my family. It's easier that way."

For what, Liv Shankly didn't need to ask, though she was certainly keen to know. The less they knew about one another, the better off they would be in the future.

When it became clear to Vaughn Keaton that her rider had no interest in furthering the conversation, she leaned forward, curling her fingertips over the top of the driver's seat, and whispered something to Clav. It sounded like a question, but Liv heard neither the query nor Clavernus's answer. The Keaton girl's eyebrows furrowed. She sat back, folded her legs, and said nothing about the interaction.

It took a few turns after passing through the city center to reach the bridge to Corcoran. It was one of several bridges connecting the Upper City to its minor siblings, each bridge a decorated finger on a rich, heavy hand. Liv's temple knocked against the window as she turned to rest her head, and she left it there uselessly, gazing toward the miles-long bridge suspended over the rising water.

Before the Lower Cities had become what they were today, sealed off from the fineries of the Morgallis and the faith-mongering of the Holy Commune, they'd been the bridge itself. The divides between their cities had been little more than lines in the sand swept over by high tides. Floodwaters from a barrage of hurricanes had forced them all up to higher altitudes. People packed their belongings and went where they could afford to weather the storms.

Storms hadn't been unusual in the area, but they'd never been so strong nor as frequent; and for those who could not afford those properties high above sea level, rebuilding had never been so difficult or so *expensive*.

It only got worse once the Upper City restricted provisions. Scarcity, Liv had learned from her school teachers, prevented Morgallis from sharing their means of production. It was a rich lie, backed by cheap lobbyists and other politicians hell-bent on keeping their pockets deep and full with exploits. People in the Upper City boasted of excess in every facet of their lives. The displays were a backhand and a betrayal.

Liv looked across the vast expanse of water, counting the scars on its surface from discarded debris. Something bobbed above the murky ripples of green. She was too far up to discern whether it was an animal or a shredded car bumper. Her vision blurred from the slow-pulsing colors of light that framed the sides of the bridge.

Crossing into (or, in this case, crossing out of) Morgallis was like stepping into a separate world or a dream. It seemed beautiful and extravagant so long as she didn't think of what was behind her or how it came to be. Its history had rejected her. Morgallis wasn't a place she belonged, and underneath each invitation was a reminder of the place she would always return to.

This excursion was a one-time thing.

"Where did your family think you were last night?" Vaughn asked suddenly.

"Nowhere," said Liv. "Home."

"They wouldn't have known you were gone?"

"One of them works late. The other's probably too tired to realize I never came home. She doesn't leave the apartment much."

"And that's everyone."

Liv couldn't tell if that was a question or a conclusion. "Yep," she said, popping the 'p.'

Then, after a pause, the High Mayor's daughter asked carefully, "Is she old?"

"She's sick."

"How sick?"

What was Liv Shankly supposed to say? "She's not contagious, if that's what you want to know."

"No," Vaughn answered. "But I'm assuming it's a personal topic."

"Mhmm."

"Is there anything I should know before we get there?"

"Like what?" Liv looked at her for the first time in minutes, her brow lowered quizzically. "You don't have to act interested, pinstripes. It'd be easier for both of us if you dropped me off and forgot about what happened at the Run. Scrub it from your mind. Spend your cut of the earnings on something cool until there's nothing left of last night. Get the Lower City out of your system while you can. There's no reason for you to be here longer than you have to."

"You have my cut."

"Couldn't be my fault," Liv noted. "I was unconscious."

With mild disconcertment, Vaughn said, "It's no one's *fault*. It's there on purpose."

Clavernus, who likely had no idea what kind of money they were discussing, glanced back at both of them through his mirror like their heads had been replaced by chickens. Liv was just as perplexed as he was, though the other girl was watching her intensely, tracking every involuntary twitch in her face. "Oh. Fuck, you're being serious right now."

"Obviously."

"Why?"

Vaughn's head tilted to the side considerately. "I told you. I wasn't there to bet."

"But you said—"

"Yes, and if I'd said I'd give you *all* the winnings, I'm sure that would have attracted some unsavory attention from folks who assumed I had money to throw away." Liv's demeanor broke in a flash of amusement, and Vaughn, who clearly had that kind of money, added, "That's not the point. The point is, I'm no worse off than how I started the night. You rode well. And the doctor told me you handled surgery like a champion."

"Again. Unconscious."

"As if I was going to ask what he meant by that. My god, you don't know how to take a compliment, do you? I tell you you're a magnificent racer, and you look at me like I just shattered your knee myself with a toy hammer." Vaughn slumped petulantly in her seat with her arms wrapped around her body. "How far are we, Clav?"

"Twenty minutes."

"Hm."

Liv wondered if this was the point where she was supposed to thank Vaughn Keaton. She had thanked her once at the hospital, and that seemed like plenty considering how little she wanted Vaughn to be her benefactor. Of course, she was grateful. No one else would have handled her impromptu surgery with such willingness or capability. It was a miracle she had fallen into such gracious hands.

Liv felt a twinge of guilt that quickly gave way to clarity. Vaughn was, first and foremost, a Keaton. Her hands were only capable because they'd been building castles on the backs of impoverished cities like hers. Liv then wondered if Vaughn had ever built anything in her life and peered at the girl's hands for some evidence of labor.

There was... *something*. Blemishes around her knuckles and in the flesh web between her thumb and forefinger interrupted her otherwise pristine exterior. *Whatever,* Liv thought. It was probably from the previous night, from the shards of metal like shrapnel that had broken off the drones and her bike.

Then, there was the matter of her bike. Liv felt like throwing her arms around the beast when she got home and murmuring, "You poor, poor thing," as if love alone would fix it. It was broken because of the Keatons and their inexplicable interference. What did it matter that Vaughn wasn't directly at fault? She was one of them, complicit in the sabotage, just like she was probably complicit in everything else.

Surely, Liv could attribute her supposed lack of gratitude to the delightful concoction of painkillers she was currently on. Despite her misgivings, her mind kept turning over a word the High Mayor's daughter had said. "Magnificent, huh?"

Vaughn sighed with exasperation. "Slip of the tongue."

The rider's remaining fondness for her benefactor dissipated. "If you say so."

Her apartment building sat on the innermost edge of Corcoran, bordering another Lower City called Matrevillea. It was surrounded most closely by other dense apartment buildings, then by an outer circle of factories. The products originating in Corcoran varied: clothes, processed foods, and most household devices one could dream up. If it existed within the Lower Cities, it had likely passed through several Corcoran workers' hands at some stage.

Liv had grown up feeling great pride in how good with their hands they were—people from her city were resourceful, sturdy, steel-forged, and a bit raucous on account of always shouting at each other over loud noises. She was easily placeable here, always a little dirty from oil or rust from hours at her long-term mechanic job at Bronlow's family garage.

Her biggest blemish was Corey Shankly.

She could see him from the end of the road, standing at the entrance of the building with the gamemakers. Liv's bike sat beside them, tilted on its kickstand, looking battered and worse for wear, though all the essential parts seemed to be present at first glance. The car was an obvious transplant in Corcoran, new and sleek; Corey's eyes fixed on it immediately, even if he didn't know she was behind the glass.

Like a pair of stark white shoes, Liv had half a mind to tell Vaughn and her driver not to let it sit still for very long, or else some kid might try to vandalize it. There was little to do as a child in Corcoran. The black roads had become gray with countless layers of driven-over chalk drawings and poorly cleaned spray paint.

Liv nudged the door open before the car came to a full stop. Corey rounded to her side, twitching against the urge to pull her out as if the car had been wrecked and lit aflame and she might otherwise burn up with it. But she was eager, too. Eager to be home, to hug her parents, to talk to someone other than the High Mayor's daughter who, despite her immeasurable efforts, wouldn't understand what sort of mental gymnastics Liv was doing to justify the events of the day.

Corey looked as if he had just woken up, his full head of silver-streaked hair falling limply around his ears and an unshaven shadow on his jaw, but his entire body woke into motion at the sight of her. He eased her crutches beneath her arms before he could register her condition. Though her jacket hid the length of the new prosthetic, her unfamiliar, ivory fingers were stark against the black leather. He wrapped his arms around her, lifting her an inch off her crutches. "Jesus, Liv. What the hell were you thinking? I asked you not to go back there."

Liv grumbled against his shoulder but said nothing of value. Over his shoulder, Liv could see Maura wavering gently on her feet. The coursemaster was standing beside her, his arm poised against the door frame to catch her if she fell. Vaughn had shut the car door and was conversing with her driver, saying something that made his shoulder sag comfortably. He pulled a carton of cigarettes out of his suit jacket pocket, offered one to her (which she primly declined), and then stalked off to light it.

Corey pressed his hands to the sides of Liv's face and turned it upward. His eyes were ringed with red from crying or sleeplessness or perhaps both. "What am I going to have to do to get you to protect yourself, kid?" He planted a kiss on her forehead. "Come on. Let's get you inside."

From the other side of the car, Vaughn said, "Olivia."

Once again fully supported by her crutches, Liv pivoted to the other girl, feeling vindicated in the presence of others.

"You've forgotten something."

They all shared a single held breath as Vaughn Keaton

hoisted the backpack out of the car. Liv had forgotten to ask how much was in the bag. It was cash, and it was plentiful, and she had only gotten as far as to wonder if bringing such a stuffed bag to the bank would look suspicious. Vaughn delivered it to the coursemaster, being both the strongest, broadest person there and the closest to the front door of the building.

He was also, Liv realized, close enough to Maura that she could deduce its contents easily. Liv's adoptive mother inquired to him softly, and by then, the High Mayor's daughter had left to speak with Liv alone. "Inside," the coursemaster seemed to be saying, though Liv could only read his lips. "You'll want to count it inside."

With Vaughn in front of her, Liv lifted herself as proudly as she could, narrowly missing the other girl's height by an inch. "So, you'll be on your way, then."

The natural, plump curve of Vaughn's mouth thinned to a straight, hard line.

Corey piped up, "Thank you. You've been extraordinarily generous, but... We can't— I don't know how to pay you back."

"Don't," Vaughn said. "It's hers. She has earned it tenfold."

"But the surgery— I mean, I work in healthcare across the Lower Cities, and I know how much a patella reconstruction can be."

Vaughn was nibbling on the inside of her cheek again, fussing with her long hair, which had fallen in pieces out from a loose elastic at the nape of her neck. "Consider it a favor. For the, um." With her gaze snagged on the bottom of Liv's red facial scars, she added, "The magnificence."

Before Vaughn could recollect her driver, Liv shook off her father and said, "Hold on. This isn't adding up, pinstripes."

"Hmm?"

"I've still got a debt to you, then. I thought we were on common ground."

"I would certainly like to be, but you seem insistent on not letting that happen."

Liv hissed through her teeth, "You said we were even."

"I never said that. It might have been implied, but—"

"What do you want from me, Vaughn Keaton?" Liv leaned unsteadily toward her. "Sparing me from my financial debts just to drag me into a personal debt? What's your game here?"

"My *game*."

"Yeah, pinstripes. Your game. Paying for my surgery, vouching for me with the police, giving me your cut." Liv, who had lowered her voice to dissuade the curiosity of her parents and the gamemakers, lowered it even more until she was whispering beneath the residual clatter of night-shift factory work. "You don't know me. And whatever feud you have with your brother can't possibly be worth what you've already done for me. I couldn't even race for you again if I wanted to. So, what's your game?"

"My answer isn't going to satisfy you."

"Try me."

"Alright. There is no game. That's the honest truth."

"No—"

"See? Unsatisfied. I know enough about games to tell you truthfully that I'm not here to play games. I'm not here to hold you hostage or make you repay debts."

Vaughn took a small step backward, at which point Liv realized how close she was to teetering into the girl's private sphere.

"Still," said the Keaton girl. Every word she spoke had sharp points. "I expect this isn't the last time you'll be seeing me. Favor or not, we have things to discuss."

Liv looked at Corey over her shoulder, who had rejoined Maura and the gamemakers. His fingers were absentmindedly petting through Maura's hair as she spoke, one of his favorite small affections. Liv was tired of having conversations on the outside of them, saying things as if they were dark secrets.

"Okay."

"Okay?" Vaughn's face brightened at the first sign of armistice.

"But I owe you nothing," Liv said.

"Obviously."

"And you're not turning me into the police for the arm."

Vaughn nodded. "A given."

It seemed too simple to be true. "You're not going to report it? Make them scrap it for parts?"

"Betrayal isn't something I consider beneficial or remotely helpful, and I offered to help you. It's not my business what you've done with the prosthetic, nor is it my place to speculate what you use it for. I don't know what it's like in the Lower City other than that you entered that race out of desperation. I'm sure you have your reasons."

Liv's face warmed with shame. Or, perhaps, an unease from being met exactly where she needed to be met by a person who had to defy her embarrassingly low expectations to do so. Liv had expected her to call the arm contraband or use it as a bargaining chip. She had never trusted Upper City politicians. What regard did they have for her? It was their legislation that made the kind of struggles her neighbors were living with. People like Vaughn Keaton were virulent like weeds and inescapable like smog.

"I don't like accepting help from Upper City folk," Liv admitted. "I don't take it lightly, what you did for me. I just can't figure out what would make it worthwhile for you except that you would want something from me in return." The confession opened her up like a scalpel, laying her out for the Keaton daughter's scrutiny. She might have been less honest or more stringent in her conviction against the Upper City if she hadn't been so medicated.

But what good would that do? The winnings were never meant for Liv but to claw her entire family out of the deep, dirt grave they'd been slowly digging themselves into. Her pride would only hurt Corey and Maura, whom she cared for more than a hit to her ego.

Vaughn spotted her driver returning from his smoke break and took a long, shaky breath. "In a few days," she began, "I'm going to give you a call, and I need to know you're going to answer. Can you do that for me?"

Liv blinked, stupefied. "Is that it?"

"It'll be important. You'll want to hear it."

"And you don't want to, I don't know, tell me what this is about? Give me any clues?"

"I shouldn't make you any promises. But don't think too hard about it. Get some rest. And if you decide to take anything I say to heart, keep your head down and your mouth shut about the money." Vaughn placed her fingers on her rider's right shoulder, squeezing gently, not enough to disturb the tender pierce-wounds of the old connector but enough to feel the thin ridges of the bandages. "I'll see you soon. Enjoy your winnings."

Liv didn't move from where she was standing until after Vaughn and her driver had hauled themselves into the front seats and the car was halfway down her street. It was Corey who moved her, placing his hand on her shoulder in an echo of the way Vaughn had touched her. "Let's sit down, Chopped Liver."

Of all the things she shared with Corey and Maura about that night, she said nothing about seeing Vaughn Keaton again.

5

Corey spent the evening fussing over Liv the way he fussed primarily over Maura, fully aware that he would be called into work early the next morning, losing valuable time for sleep over reprimand. Maura joined in on the fussing to the best of her abilities until her fatigue sent her back to bed. Liv surmised that this was probably the best case scenario, given how much grief she'd given them over the past year.

It would be a shut case by morning, and no one would want to dredge up the issue any longer, so they would all assuredly move on to more important things. Corey would return to fretting over his busy schedule, while Maura would stay home and craft until her fingers were punctured and sore with sewing needles. Liv would have to return to work soon, offer the owner of the garage a half-baked explanation for her leg, and be relegated to tasks that required minimal bending and rising; meanwhile, she would steal an extra hour or two every night, like she had done before, trying to alter the peculiar machination of her new prosthetic.

Liv noticed, while Corey was oscillating between disappointment over her actions and relief for the fact that she lived and breathed, that Maura was in her pajamas. She wouldn't have deduced anything strange from this normally—Maura stayed inside most of the time, and her wardrobe consisted mostly of pajamas—except for the fact that, by now, she would have just been getting home from her scheduled doctor's appointment.

She must have cancelled it.

Briefly, Liv felt a choleric pang of guilt. Then, while Corey was insisting, albeit rather sweetly, that Liv risking needless injuries would hurt them too, she remembered she was an adult and had been for some time. She didn't have to take this shit, especially when the shit in question had affected no one more than herself, and she was the only one with a full picture of last night's events.

His lecture came from the attached kitchen over the sound of running water. Liv sat on the couch, fielding the worst of it. Maura listened less keenly from the bedroom, twisting open the cap of an extra-strength ibuprofen. "Have you even looked at the winnings?" Liv asked.

"It shouldn't matter, Olivia," said Corey, scrubbing at a piece of oven-baked, frozen lasagna stuck to the bottom of a baking sheet. "I should have been better at seeing that before, I know, but we've talked about this. What's it going to take to keep you from entering the Run again? I thought it would be the end when you lost your arm. I thought that it would be enough to persuade you to step back—"

She wished he were happier about the money. He was a good doctor and a dedicated man. Everyone here knew it, and they loved him sufficiently to remind him why he shouldn't leave.

But the Lower Cities didn't have enough doctors to give Corey time to rest. The lack of money and the excess of broken bones throughout the industrial regions, particularly in Corcoran, kept him miserably consumed with work. Any doctor in the Lower Cities who was less committed, or perhaps even more desperate, would go to the Upper City for better pay or to pursue a specialized cosmetic field. Few were willing to stick around during the worst of things.

On principle, it was impossible for Liv to hate him, even in a juvenile way.

"I don't know," he added softly. His fingers loosened around the sponge, and he shut off the faucet. "Maybe this is what I get for raising a little brute. A lifetime of bruised knuckles and broken bones. I thought you would grow out of it, you know."

He had been inconsolable beside Liv's hospital bed the first time, unable to treat her on his own and too invested in her recovery to return to work. He blamed himself for the accident, for allowing her to do the Run to supplement our mounting monthly expenses, and Liv could tell he blamed himself for what happened last night, too, even if he hadn't been there to see it.

"If it helps, none of this happened until after I won," she said.

"How could you get so hurt from a winning race?" He sighed from deep within his stomach, which had gotten softer with age. "Clearly, I can't stop you. I thought you might have some difficulty finding another benefactor if I stopped going, but..."

Liv leaned back against the couch, wondering if she was treading ground the gamemakers had already covered with him. "I don't think it'll happen again either."

Maura steadied herself in Liv's periphery, approaching the couch where she sat. "Oh yeah? Why's that, honey?"

"They smashed the drone controller last night."

"Smashed it?" asked Corey. "On purpose?"

"They obviously wouldn't have wanted to, but it had stopped working. I had already crossed the boundary when it started shooting at me. I've never seen that happen before. It just kept *chasing*."

Liv shuffled aside to make space for Maura on the couch. The older woman laid her head against Liv's shoulder and threaded her fingers into hers, musing quietly as she noticed the unfamiliar white fingers, "Oh. This is new."

Corey asked, "Was anyone else hurt?"

"Fuck if I know."

He leveled her with his sudden weariness. He looked as if several days of sleeplessness had been preying on him and had only just decided to charge.

She knew she ought to be more considerate with how she spoke to him. Her patience had been wearing thin for some time, wrought largely by the Keaton daughter's presumptuous line of questioning.

But she was the one with the bag full of money and, despite his best efforts to draw attention to her recklessness, he was the one hungriest for it.

"It's the Run," Liv posited. "Of course, people got hurt. I couldn't really stop to administer first aid or make a thorough assessment of injuries, though, could I? Given there was no doctor on sight..."

Corey murmured something to himself that sounded awfully close to a prayer. This temporarily rattled her, for if there was anyone who thought of praying less than she did, it was Corey. He had grown up among the Holy Commune long enough that leaving them was a choice.

When Corey and Maura had stolen away to Corcoran with her at the age of seven, Liv had only two prayers memorized because they'd been sung like lullabies by her birth mother. Faith, at most, was a foggy, half-remembered facsimile of early childhood.

Often, when she was younger and still grappling with the uprooting of her life thus far, Corey would tell her about how things used to be, before faith overcame the Holy Commune and his courtship with modern medicine became taboo. Not everyone had held such a staunch disbelief in medicine and science, but there were enough people there—a great majority, in fact—who were threatened by it to keep the rest from taking their chances.

And what was Liv doing with her tenuous health and safety now? Perhaps Corey thought she was throwing it away or that she was ungrateful. Maybe he hadn't looked in the bag yet and seen just how hard, and for how much, she fought to keep this life they had made in Corcoran.

So she sat there quietly. It seemed like no matter how many times Liv made subtle inclinations of her head toward the bag for him to look, Corey was determined to feel his Big Feelings at her.

Normally, she didn't mind it. Of all the inexperienced, unsuspecting teenagers her birth mother could have handed her off to, Corey and Maura had become the most willing to handle those feelings in a healthy way. They straddled a crooked line of friendship, brotherhood, and parenthood, bent thrice over but never totally connecting again to make a closed shape. Something was missing. They couldn't ground her. She was an adult now. And for a brief moment, Corey and Maura had been kids at the same time Liv herself was a kid. They couldn't very well kick her out like an unwelcome roommate.

They all sat there quietly, shifting their cluelessness from person to person until Liv finally asked Maura, "How was your appointment?"

Maura didn't look at her again and returned her attention to the white fingers poking out of her sleeve. "Didn't happen today," she murmured. "It's been a bad pain day. I thought it might be better if I rescheduled."

Corey placed his hand across his brow and started to knead ruthlessly. "There's no point lying about it. Shit's already weird."

Maura made no effort to amend her statement but offered him a drawn-out sigh and a suggestive, irritable prodding of her cheek with her tongue. Unlike Liv's spirited attempts to diffuse the tension, this was enough to make Corey drop his chin like a scorned pet and remove himself from the situation. He began to pace in a route so familiar that a trail had been worn out of the sticky linoleum in a slight dip.

"You should have gone," Liv whispered.

"I *was* having a bad pain day," Maura replied.

"Haven't you wanted them to see you while you're having a flare-up?"

Maura's eyes were a freckled blue so light and striking they reminded Liv of robin eggs. People in the Upper City paid to have eyes as bright as hers. The older woman finally laid her line of sight on Liv, and the blatancy of being addressed so closely made the last brazen bits of pride in the girl's chest sink into the pit of her stomach.

"You want to make me some tea, baby?" This was Maura's cue for Corey to leave, which he weathered like a soft slap and promptly obeyed. To Liv, she said, "I shouldn't have to say it. You know why I didn't go. I'm not trying to guilt you; all I want is to be there for you when you need me, but you know I can't do that. You can't expect me to get on with my life while I'm wondering what's happened to you."

"How much did the gamemakers tell you?"

"Not much... But our assumptions were already at the worst-case scenario. They came to bring us the news and spent most of the time reassuring us that you were, in fact, alright. You can't blame us for worrying."

"I don't blame you," said Liv, "I just—"

"You just did the Run anyway and got yourself hurt in the process." Maura looked at Corey as if she had spoken too loudly and let spill an irrevocable, dark secret. Her voice was generally quiet on account of the others always giving her their undivided attention. Liv's methods of deducing when Maura was angry were different from anyone else's. Maura would shut her mouth, shift her jaw to the left and right to prod the insides of her teeth with her tongue, and take a much longer time to inhale a breath than she did to spit it back out.

"I didn't mean to scare you," Liv said.

"No. And you're not a child, so I doubt it does us any good to play the blame game."

Liv's fists had turned to tight little knots on top of her stomach, the flesh harder than the plastic. Maura placed her hand over them and eased them open. "It wouldn't hurt to have said something. Sent us a message, gave us a call..."

Liv's weight sagged into the back of the couch. She turned her face in the opposite direction, where there were no windows to gaze out of or birds to study, just an array of wires from all the lamps currently attached to the wall outlet to give the room some semblance of natural lighting. She thought it senseless to argue about how un-childlike she was and note to her mother that she'd been out late before, getting drunk, having sex, and doing remarkably stupid things; no matter how old she was or how much money she put toward their family debts, Liv was still Maura's kid. The person she was now coexisted in Maura's mind with the little girl who had sat on her lap on the bus, having her short hair braided into two tiny stumps.

"What kind of tea do you want, baby?" Corey asked from the kitchen.

"The cherry blossom one."

He nodded and rummaged loudly through the cluttered cabinets for a mug. Before the gentle clanging of clay ceased, Liv whispered, "I'm sorry. I took care of it, though. Everything is okay."

"You got lucky," Maura replied. The woman pushed herself off the couch, giving her daughter's bandages a gentle tap. "But I thank God you did."

Then, she retired to her room for the evening without

saying goodnight.

Liv's crutches were propped up against the couch on her right side, and just on the other side of them was her backpack, zipper open only a quarter of its teeth on the top. As Corey tensely lowered the cherry blossom tea bag up and down into the mug, Liv grabbed one of the crutches and strung it through the fraying loop at the top of the bag, coaxing it closer.

"So." Liv's throat felt tighter, warmer. "Do you want to know how much is in here, or should we just pretend I did all that just because I felt like it?"

Corey's fingers halted around the mug. His shoulders were hunched, and he looked... small.

Liv wasn't a child anymore, and even if she knew perfectly well that they would always see her as their kid, they had never fully become her parents, which made the patronization feel a little off every time. They were a little bit of everything: mother, father, friend, sibling, benefactor.

She hoped that this eternal degree of separation would come back to Corey and allow him to show some interest in the contents of the backpack. He couldn't stand there and sulk forever. At the end of the day, their debts loomed over them. If he could just look at the money for himself—

Corey gave the teabag one last dip, tossed it, and left to deliver it to Maura. When he returned, he shut the bedroom door behind him, less for Maura's comfort and more to hide his distasteful curiosity.

Liv would never call it distasteful. Money troubles made desperate people. This was the reason she had gone to the Run in the first place. She only wished Corey would stop trying to pretend he wasn't interested.

He took the spot where Maura had been sitting. Liv hauled the bag onto the couch between them.

"Hold on." His hand clamped around the open gap in the

zipper. "This changes nothing, you know."

"It should," said Liv. "I don't want you to be angry at me."

"What?"

Before Liv could say her piece about why he should be at least a little grateful for her willingness to put herself on the line, her father reached over the bag and wrapped his arms around her, pulling her head against his shoulder at an unsavory angle. Her left shoulder was pinched between them, and her head tilted beneath his chin to keep from knocking his teeth in with her forehead. "What would you have me say, instead? You scared the shit out of me. Let me be mad for a minute."

"You're crushing me."

"Well. Big Feelings," Corey said, shutting his eyes tight. It was grossly sincere for a phrase he used to tell her when she was ten years old and speedrunning toward pre-teen nihilism: 'Feel your big feelings. I know you've got them.' Like a flipswitch, the phrase would make her sob and wail until she was tired; and Maura would tell her she'd been so brave while Corey rubbed his hand in little circles on her back.

Liv sighed and weasled herself into a slightly more comfortable position, fitting her arms around his stomach. "Okay."

"No amount of money in the world can bring you back."

"*Okay*. I get it."

"No, you don't. I don't even get it. Nothing prepares you for how it feels to be faced with that reality. I can't imagine a world without you in it, and you've asked me to do it for you twice now." Corey kissed the top of her head, an affection he saved for only the most mammoth feelings, the ones with enough weight to shake the ground. Liv squirmed free and kneaded the top of her spine until it felt adequately realigned.

The bag shifted onto his lap with a little pull. Several seconds passed between them with total stillness. "No amount of money," he repeated as a full phrase. "Whatever is in here, remember that."

She nodded.

"And you're done with the Run."

This, she did not respond to at all. Corey raised his thick eyebrows at her to prompt her willful acceptance of the terms. "There is no Run," Liv said.

Deep down, she knew the gamemakers would think of something. Hundreds across the Lower Cities relied on the Run for a little extra money. They would resurrect it somehow.

And after they had miraculously necromanced it back to life, no one could predict what other punches Liv's life would throw at her. Even the most permanent bonds in her life had the capacity to break. It took only one sordid argument with their insurance company to drain them down to nothing again.

Sure, she didn't want to rely on the Run forever, and it was probably a good thing for the adrenaline junkies in the Lower Cities to find less gruesome vices in the meantime. She would, however, be lying if she said she wanted it to end entirely.

"Holy shit."

Corey had unzipped the bag. Liv shuffled closer now that the bag was no longer between them. The cash was piled to the top, not just with ones and fives like it usually was when there were no lofty donors. Corey made a second, incoherent noise.

"How much do you think is in there?" Liv goaded.

Stacks of hundreds looped at the center with paper sleeves peered through the upper curtain of small dollars. Corey thrust his hand into it, searching for the place where it ended, but it went all the way down to the bag's seams.

His eyes grew wide and glassy, and his breaths unsteady. Liv smiled at him and lifted her eyebrows as if to ask, "No hard feelings?"

Caught midway between a frenzy of exultation and panic, Corey only stared back. "Olivia. Whose money is this?"

The root of his panic wouldn't settle in until much later; all Liv felt was triumph. "It's ours now."

6

Ten days had passed since the Run, and it was the first instance of rain in two months. Winters were typically drier than the summer and mercifully cooler. The shaders programmed into the outer walls of Vaughn's glass house were shut off to give her a clear view of the gnarl of greenery that stretched around her on the hillside; thus, she could see the shape of her twin brother lounging on her couch with a magazine from outside.

It didn't surprise Vaughn to see Caldwell in her house. This was unfortunate because he had not been invited and never came with an announcement. She keyed into the property, the soggy knot of hair on the back of her head adding what felt like ten pounds to her neck. She would have twice the headache for the rest of the long day if Caldwell said something stupid (and he usually did).

Sighing, she untucked and unfurled the wet knot of her hair to wring it out. She considered ignoring him completely, like a recent addition to the furniture. Caldwell swung his legs off the short side of her L-shaped sofa and beamed devilishly. "My darling sister, out for the night?"

"No," she said.

"No? Where'd you come from then?"

It was nine in the morning, too early for him to be there and even earlier for her to have been returning home if not from a night out—except, Vaughn didn't have nights out. Caldwell, who rarely had nights *in,* knew this better than anyone and couldn't mask the facetious implications in his question.

"Coffee," she answered simply.

"That's pretty big for a coffee." His eyes flickered to the duffel bag hanging from her shoulder.

As large and unignorable a conversation topic as it was, Vaughn didn't want to talk about it. She replied with a dismissive grumble and hoisted it further up her shoulder. "It's a lovely morning, Caldwell. You should spend it outside and not in my house."

He gestured nonspecifically to the glass walls and followed her from the living room toward the sprawling workshop at the back of the property.

Vaughn lifted her feet as she stepped to clear the short rise of the training mat in the front half of the room. It was often too wet to run her fencing drills outside, and she had ruined one of her foils by leaving it propped against the wall before a flash storm hit. Since then, the front half of her workshop had been cleared to make room for a training mat and a well-worn piste, and the odd conglomeration of workshop machinery had been moved into the back half, where it shielded her workbench like a short wall.

On the other side of the room's clear walls was a short stretch of uncut grass, bordered by a thick cluster of moss-dressed trees. A lone shooting target stared back at her, punctured with a few more bullet holes than the last time she had looked at it. It was Caldwell's; Vaughn never liked guns. Because she had refused to touch it since Caldwell first put it in her yard, even to move it, she last looked at it yesterday.

She set the bag on her workbench gently, careful to hide the scraping and sifting of metal inside from her brother's rapt attention. He came behind her chair as she took a seat. "Can't I visit my beloved sister for unselfish reasons?"

"When was the last time you knocked?"

"What good is my key if you make me knock?" Her brother stripped off his pinstripe suit jacket and hung it over the back of her chair, prompting Vaughn to fix her ammonite posture like a caning from their old governess. "You've gotten too used to it. If I change my habits now, you'll think there's an intruder outside."

Rounding in front of her, Caldwell reached for the bag, trailing his fingers along the zipper like a query for permission. Vaughn sharply pulled it closer to her, despite the lack of open room on the bench, which meant two small circuit boards and a bottle of adhesive fell into her lap.

"I do have cameras."

"How often do you check them?"

"*Often,*" said Vaughn, only proving a point that Caldwell had been trying to make with her ever since she moved: isolation has planted a seed of paranoia inside her. It was obvious to everyone, no matter how vehemently she tried to suppress it for her own sake. "What do you want?"

"What's in the bag?"

"You didn't come to ask me that."

"No," he said, "but I'm curious now. New project?"

"It's none of your business."

Her brother folded his arms across his chest in a methodical gesture of feigned ambivalence; the tricks he deployed for others never worked for her. She'd seen her twin cry over playground disputes and watched him vomit up an entire bag of spicy chocolate candies. The corrupted image of Caldwell's new adulthood existed beside the image of his harmless, pudgy youth.

A line of bruises peeked over the undone collar of his linen shirt—*fingers,* she realized, from whatever debauchery he had fallen into the night before. His mouth turned up at the corners, his eyes crinkling with a deceptive good humor.

Sometimes, it was hard to look at him.

"What'd you do with the money?"

"Nothing."

"Nothing?" he asked. "You're not, I don't know, financing a new project with it? Buying yourself a rare bottle of wine and doom-drinking up here?"

With a heavy sigh, Vaughn answered, "No, I'm not."

"So where is it?"

"I don't have it."

"What do you mean you don't have it?" His voice possessed the basest hints of irritation, the only betrayal to an otherwise unwavering demeanor.

Vaughn didn't have the energy to argue with him (although, when did she ever? More often did they argue than she ever wished to, and it was typically about pointless drivel like her lack of social life and his abundant audacity.) "Exactly what I just said. I don't have it."

Her twin brother's head dipped into his hand, and he groaned, pulling it down his face until his features stretched like loose threads. "Come on, Vaughn."

"You ought to be more careful with it next time. A gamble's a gamble for a reason."

"Yeah, well. I shouldn't have lost. It should have been a foolproof way to get the money to the Margossis without any interference."

"Since when do you need to give the Margossi family any money? Don't tell me you're in trouble."

He closed his mouth, looking at the metalworking pieces strewn about the workbench, screwing them together in his mind into shapes that didn't make sense. Vaughn stood abruptly and wandered toward her kitchen before he could take notice of her open notebook, where there was clear evidence that she'd been drafting something new.

"I *shouldn't* have lost," he repeated, as if Vaughn was meant to derive further meaning from it.

If only he hadn't. Everyone felt his losses. Caldwell was a bitter loser, incapable of owning up to his mistakes. Vaughn had some sympathy for him, the poor thing, having to learn how bad the consequences of his actions could be. It must have been difficult for him to get what was coming to him from his ill-advised exploits.

Vaughn opened her fridge and searched it with a tapping heel. "So you say."

"So I know. There was no way the Margossis' rider wouldn't have won unless some sort of foul play occurred *or*—" he drew this out while placing himself on the other side of the open fridge door. "Your rider had some kind of tip."

"And what exactly would I need to tip them off about?"

He wasn't clueless enough to disclose the Margossi rider's gun, but Vaughn was marginally impressed that he had the foresight to know about it in the first place. He could be methodical when he needed to be; only she didn't know why that would have to be the Run or what kind of money he had tied up in the Margossi family. They had new money, but they weren't frivolous spenders. Their progress in communication implants was only growing more profitable and expansive. The Kilgarre Corporation had been trying to license their technology for years, and their offers had been rejected every time.

No one who wasn't fully financially secure from their own business prospects would reject a deal from the Kilgarres.

Caldwell's decision to bet at the Run had seemed random and uncharacteristic at the time. It was, in Vaughn's view, the least predictable of his ventures, which included high-roller tables at the casino in Morgallis and mech boxing. The games he played rarely involved a victim or a vessel in which to sink his repercussions. His bets hardly concerned humans at all. There was only him and Lady Luck.

To discover that there was any form of his gambling that Vaughn preferred landed a peculiar blow to her psyche. She closed the fridge door, having grabbed nothing, but her brother was no longer there.

"Caldwell?"

The blade of her epee sliced through the doorway to the workshop before she could enter it. "An idea," he proposed, guarding a second epee that she only used for pageantry behind his back in his other hand. "For every bout I win, you answer a question for me."

"You can't just ask me like a normal person?"

"That's getting us nowhere."

His knuckles were near-white around the handle of her epee, notably too tight. He had never excelled at fencing the way she did. He held the sword like a hammer, while she held hers with the deftness of a rosined bow.

Still, it didn't matter how one held a blade if it was close enough to their opponent's neck. The flat of it pressed against Vaughn's skin.

"I'm telling you the truth," she said.

"Okay," he said, extending a sword to her. "Tell me more then."

Vaughn took it and turned the handle in her grip, feeling the difference in its weight when there was no opponent on the other end. "I don't want to spar with you."

"Too many secrets then, eh?"

"You won't win. I'll puncture you like a tire. And then, I'll have to answer to Papa."

"That does sound dreadful."

He swung the blade down in a wide arc. Vaughn's epee chipped against his, parrying the illegal move with little more than her bell guard. "Watch it!"

"Did you go to the Run with me to bet against me?"

They circled each other like predators, their regard for a piste nonexistent. Caldwell wouldn't play by her rules if he intended to win, and as long as he was wielding a blade, she couldn't relinquish hers.

Still, he hadn't won anything yet. "No," she said. "You know why I went."

Caldwell laughed, and Vaughn leveraged a controlled attack toward his shoulder, which her brother blocked with a formal parry, rendering her low expectations of his fencing technique untrustworthy.

"Vaughn," he said. "V. *Vinny*. Don't tell me that's your rider's arm over there."

Damn it, she thought. He had seen the mockups in her notebook. "So?"

"*So?*" he echoed, goading her to attack. "If you're going to buy anyone's friendship, make it someone who matters. Not some amateur Lower City racer."

She met his next attack with a counter, and his blade struck the bell guard with a hiss. "You don't know what you're talking about."

"Except I do. You don't hide it well; everybody knows. Nothing on the internet dies. 'The Keaton girl is a recluse. A has-been. A child prodigy who became a sub-par adult. A failed tech experiment.' You'd do anything for a little attention, wouldn't you? Even from the people who want nothing to do with you."

Vaughn attacked with a wide, illegal slash of her sword, then parried his counterattack with a repressed grunt. "She needed the money, and I'm not a monster."

Caldwell shook his head to toss a strand of loose hair away from his forehead. "No, you're not. You're pure of heart and virtue, and yet no one seems to care. Why is that, Vaughn? Is it because you aren't interesting? You're such a good person—a better person than I am, in fact. No one cares about good people. Not unless you've got something else they want."

Vaughn glowered, wishing she could skewer him like a tender piece of meat and feed him to the possums.

"You don't have to do all this." Caldwell's next move was playful, void of malice. It was the closest thing to true sparring he had done so far, which made Vaughn loosen her grip and her guard. "It isn't worth the effort. You should come out with me sometime. You'll make plenty of friends in the city, friends who are *fun*. And the best part is you don't have to give a shit about any of them, because none of them give a shit about you; and that's okay!"

Vaughn lunged forward with an irrevocable attack. Caldwell twisted sharply. The edge of the blade nicked his shoulder, but his hand fastened around her wrist.

The epee clattered out of her grasp. She stumbled, then collapsed as his weight dragged her down. Caldwell's knee pressed down on hers. He took his sword and stuck it into the training mat beneath her.

"'S not fair," Vaughn huffed, short of breath.

Caldwell wiggled his finger in her face, then pressed it against her forehead to hold it down on the mat. "What does it matter if it's fair? You're a fucking Keaton. You should start acting like it." He tapped the center of her forehead. "No one can afford to deny the Keatons. No friend is going to stand you up or curse you when your back is turned, not if they know what's good for them. You don't have to live like this, you know? You can have your little workshop and your trinkets, and then you can get shitfaced with your new friends in the city and come back home before the sun is up. You can have it *all*. You've just got to take it, Vaughn. Come on."

Vaughn's head rolled to the side as Caldwell rose to his feet with a small, "Oomph." She trained her vision on the stretch of trees outside her workshop window.

She most loathed Caldwell when he was right. No one denied the Keatons, and it overshadowed every agreeable interaction she had ever experienced. Since moving to the glass house in the heights of Morgallis, she had traded one paranoia for another, and she would be a fool if she didn't consider fickle friendships more manageable than the former. Every kind word was a double-edged sword, at once deceptively kind and cruel.

He gathered their swords into his right hand and offered her his left. "Now. Where's the money, Vaughn?"

She let him pull her halfway to her feet, then slipped her hand out of his grasp and knuckled him in the groin. "Told you. I don't have it."

"What the hell!"

"Go away, Caldwell."

She pried the swords out of his feeble grip and slid them both back into their cases while he doubled over in pain. "But the money—"

"You shouldn't have given it away in the first place."

"Does she have it all? That rider?"

Vaughn's blood seared. The noise between her ears was swelling calamitously with her change in altitude. Her heartbeat manifested everywhere, from the tips of her fingers to the pit of her stomach. Whirling on him, she brandished a screwdriver from her workbench. "If you so much as touch her, Caldwell, I'll—"

"Whoa *whoa*." He stumbled toward her chair and stole his jacket back in a pointless attempt to cover his punched crotch. "You're jumping to conclusions."

"Because I know you."

"Have some faith in me, then. The truth is, no one gives

a shit about us except us. We've got to stick together, you and me. You can't—" he took a step back, grimacing. "You can't punch me in the dick whenever you feel like it."

"Get out of my house."

"You don't want to do something today? Come for a drive with me?"

"No," Vaughn insisted, returning to her chair. "I don't. You can leave my key on the counter when you leave, too."

Caldwell scoffed. "Suit yourself. I lose years off my life whenever I come here, you know."

"Yeah."

"It's *depressing*."

And then he left, sparing her no formal goodbyes or even a wave from the front door. He took his key with him; she sensed the absence like the closed space where a wisdom tooth once lived.

When the door shut, Vaughn spread her fingers across the surface of the workbench, and she pictured all her loathing flooding out through her tensed, bony fingers. She took a minute to breathe, although her perspective on meditation was too militant for her deep breaths to bring her closer to comfort.

"Bullshit," she said aloud; for unlike her fruitless attempts at meditation, talking *did* accomplish something. Sometimes, it helped her plan out all the eloquent things she would never have the courage to say to her father's face. Other times, she would talk herself through engineering puzzles until her hands turned unsteady or her vision went blurry.

Most of the time, she used her self-talk to pick imaginary fights with Caldwell and work herself into enough of a rage that she would find the pressure point that brought her to tears. She didn't cry often. Crying felt performative, and there was no one here except for herself to perform for, but when she was alone and running on empty, it would make her so tired that she fell dreamlessly, lovingly into sleep.

Murmuring to herself, Vaughn unzipped the duffel bag and inspected the untethered metal parts that had been organized into plastic bags. One of the bags was simply labeled *Prongs* with a large question mark at the end. This was an apt description for the slender wands of varying shades of metal. "Are you... whittled? No. Course not. God, how do you even... And they didn't even bother to note how any of it was assembled. Could you be any less helpful, Detective... No— Scratch that."

She laid the pieces of her rider's arm in front of her like the keys of a church organ. There was something musical, mechanical, and elaborate in the way the mixed metals harmonized across the bench. Her prototype ideation had been so different from the rider's execution of the same thing. She could deduce several things from the pieces and, upon first glance, think of refining no less than fifteen.

She straightened her back and returned to the piste, wearing footprints into the track with five minutes' worth of pacing, trying to shake off the last traces of adrenaline in her system. "It's not depressing," she mumbled. "It's picturesque. It's idyllic."

It was not usually this silent, though. She would have already turned the music on if Caldwell hadn't been waiting for her. She logged into the central command system with a voice command: "Lunokhod."

A transatlantic accent greeted her from all around her. "Good morning."

"Did you hear my brother this morning, Lunokhod?"

"Does Vaughn want Lunokhod to hear her brother?

"Yes, I do."

"Lunokhod heard Vaughn's brother this morning."

"He was acting like a moron, wasn't he?" she mused.

"Nothing to report."

"What? Nothing?"

"Lunokhod was not active at the time Vaughn saw her brother and, therefore, has nothing to report. Would Vaughn like to report an error?"

She halted her pacing. "No. You're doing wonderfully, Lunokhod. Vaughn just... needs friends."

"Searching the internet for friends near Vaughn. Results are inconclusive. Many users report vibrant nightlife nine miles away, but some users are dissatisfied with the traffic in the area. No results within five miles—"

"Goodnight, Lunokhod."

At the sound of her shutdown command, the voice answered, "Goodnight."

She wished the AI could have lied to her, just in that moment. The problem with having the city under any of the Keatons' thumbs was that no one was willing to speak ill of them to their faces. She would kill for someone to tell her that Caldwell was as loathsome as she often thought. Someone who meant it. Someone she didn't pay or *program*.

She picked up her cell phone and dialed her rider.

7

Bronlow's Garage had no work for Liv while she was recovering. Had it not been for the winnings weighing down her backpack, this would have been world-shattering, but it was mostly annoying because it meant she couldn't come in anytime soon to run diagnostics on her bike.

That would have to wait anyway. She moved around solely with crutches, and the strange, plastic prosthetic they had given her made the fit of the crutch beneath her right armpit significantly more uncomfortable. She usually woke up early, went to work by the time the sun came out to fiddle with something on her bike before opening, stopped at the gym after closing, and then rode home in time for Maura to ask what they should do for dinner.

With her leg cast into an immovable line, she couldn't even climb into her loft bed, which meant she had been sleeping on the couch for the past ten days, while Corey, who usually slept on the couch, had to sleep in her bed for the time being. Her nights were so restless from the deflated cushions and hard arms of the couch that she slept in late, trying to chase good sleep and woke to Corey shuffling around before he left for work. Then, Liv would spend an hour molded into the shallow dip of the cushion with her headphones on, her fingers tapping against her stomach unrhythmically (the plastic ones couldn't keep the beat), thinking of ways she would spend her money if she wasn't so terrified of losing it all again.

"We should deposit it on separate trips," Corey had said. "You take some, and I take some."

"How much are we taking per trip?"

At that point, they had sorted all the loose bills and split the total into several different hiding places. Corey walked around with his head down and his anxiety high, thinking an Upper City official would knock on their door at any moment to collect the money that they shouldn't have had. "Four thousand?" he had proposed.

"That's going to take forever," said Liv.

"It'll be twice a month for each of us. Eight thousand total, to align with our paychecks."

Maura, who had been sitting on the couch with Liv's cast in her lap and a permanent marker in her hand, noted to both of them, "You can't attribute it to the paycheck schedule without claiming you got different jobs. When has anyone ever paid you in cash?"

Liv had sighed while Maura continued diligently tracing the sketch of tropical birds on the cast. "When has anyone at the bank ever asked what you did for work, anyway? At that rate, we won't have enough to cover our outstanding debts by the end of the month—"

"But we can stall collections," Corey had said, which was enough for Maura to discard all her arguments. They shouldn't have needed to wait to pay off the debts if they already had the money.

It took a lot more for Liv to hold her tongue, and she countered, "Five thousand dollars, twice a month, and all three of us make deposits."

Corey had mulled it over for a long time, running the numbers through his mind with flitting vision. With Liv's casted leg and creaky, unchecked motorcycle, he would have to be the one to take Maura to the bank; could he fit it into his schedule?

But Corey had agreed, and they had each taken five thousand dollars to the bank. The tellers had said nothing, and no one got caught. Liv boarded the bus home and felt, in spite of her remaining debts, like the richest person in the world.

However, she was extraordinarily bored with the required amount of rest for her recovery. Not even two weeks had passed since the night of the Drone Run, and she and Maura had caught up with the last three seasons of Matchmakers and Heartbreakers, Morgallis's most aggravating reality TV show about the love lives and strategic partnerships of the Upper City's elite families. Liv had eaten more popcorn in those six days than in the past two years combined, and by the time the call from her one-time benefactor came, Maura had covered her burgundy cast in an array of herons, pelicans, skimmers, and flamingos, birds from a bygone era when the Total City region was still called Florida.

Maura was in the bathroom when Liv got the call, but the rider shut herself in her empty bedroom for privacy anyway. Vaughn Q. Keaton, entered as such into the comms device by the girl in question, flared across the screen. Liv swallowed hard, remembering the assurances the Keaton girl had made: Liv owed her nothing. Liv wasn't getting turned in to the cops.

Yet, something stirred restlessly in her stomach. "Hello?"

"Good morning."

Good morning? "Yeah. What's up?"

"How are you feeling?"

"I'm fine," Liv drew out. "Is this really why you're calling me?"

"Why? Are you busy?"

"What do you think? It's nine thirty in the morning and I'm out of work. I just thought with all your foreboding from the other day, you might have more to say than 'how are you.'"

"Ah." Vaughn sighed audibly, and something on her end of the call creaked. "Not one for formalities, I suppose. I have something for you. Can you be ready in half an hour?"

"For what?"

"I'm sending Clav to drive you up to Morgallis for a chat."

Maura's knuckles tapped on the door gently, and Vaughn nearly leapt out of her skin like she had been caught with a dirty magazine. "Just a second!"

"You okay, Chopped Liver?"

"Just on the phone—with Lotte!"

"Lotte?" asked Vaughn.

"Don't worry about it. Thirty minutes? I can do that."

"Excellent. Same address, yes?"

"Can you have him park down the street? Maybe on the corner of 116th and Clover."

"Whatever you prefer. I'll see you soon, Olivia."

Hearing Vaughn call her by her full name and with such ease made Liv's skin warm profusely. "It's just Liv," she said softly, as if the omission of those three letters would make it less personal.

"Okay. Goodbye, Liv."

Clav stubbed out his just-lit cigarette when Liv approached him. His clothes were less refined than when she had first seen him, less like a uniform and more like something someone in the Lower Cities might wear for a funeral: a black polo shirt and neat wool trousers for warmth. His nose wrinkled, trying to hold up the sunglasses that were slipping off his nose while he fiddled with the carton and his lighter.

"You can smoke it," Liv said. "I can wait."

"It's probably better if I don't. Do you need any help?"

Liv reached for the passenger seat, which made the driver

flinch. "Nope. Thanks, though."

To her knowledge, Clav had no implant or earpiece to tell him where to turn, and his dashboard held no hidden navigation instructions. His familiarity with the tight streets of Corcoran seemed bone deep, so Liv asked, "You come down here often?"

He looked at her over the right leg of his sunglasses like she was an unconvincing sleight-of-hand magic trick. "Not anymore, no."

Whatever that meant. Liv made herself as comfortable as she could, adjusting the seat backward for her outstretched right leg. Her crutches knocked around in the backseat with gentle *clicks*, and her scarred cheek was perched in the cool, plastic palm of her right hand. "So. If you're not a pinstripe, how'd you end up driving for the Keatons?"

"I don't," he said. "Just Vaughn. We grew up together."

"So this is a personal favor for a friend?"

Clav's tongue poked around in his mouth. "She pays well. And she's very nice. I wouldn't say we're friends, though. My mom worked for the family for a long time and would take me to the house with her on occasion. We saw a lot of each other as kids."

"What'd she do there?"

Again, the driver put up a wall between himself and Liv's line of questioning.

"I fix cars for a living," she offered, "and deal with loads of other shit on the side. Nothing fazes me."

"Doesn't really matter what she did. She worked herself to death up there anyhow."

An embarrassingly long silence had passed until it dawned on Liv how literally he meant it. "Oh. Sorry to hear that."

Clav shrugged. "It's been a few years. We used to live in Corcoran, though. She'd been saving up to move into the

Upper City all her life. Ironically, the only thing that got me there was her life insurance policy payout." Then he snorted, sharp and bitter. "She's not a bad person—Vaughn. But I can't say the same about the others. That city breeds greed, and it comes from the top."

He was beginning to sound like someone from the Holy Commune. Her memory of faith may have been cloudy, but the principles instilled by the people there were unshakable: Morgallis was a godless place, and therefore, sin was abundant. Greed would fell that shining city of progress one day. Most of the people living in the Commune thought it was long overdue.

Liv didn't attribute much importance to their piety. They were also the kind of people who believed God could cure them of their diseases if they were repentant enough, and that the floods were His rapture. It was as hostile a place as Morgallis for anyone who didn't fit their mold.

Liv asked after they had crossed the bridge, "Do you know what she wants to talk about?"

"No idea."

"Brilliant."

"I'm not being avoidant on principle. She just hasn't told me."

Despite the fact that Liv was just as far away from her answer as before, she felt the tension in her body slip out from every pore. At least she wasn't the only one privy to the Keaton daughter's cryptic tendencies.

Clav added many seconds later, "She never sends me back to the Lower Cities, though. I was surprised to hear that she wanted to see you again."

Liv's head tipped back against the headrest, giving in to total comfort while it lasted. Seeing the High Mayor's daughter again would cause her to tighten like a spring. "Yeah. Me too."

As the car climbed steadily up the cliffy peak hidden behind Morgallis' city center, the tangle of tropical foliage grew denser and darker. Liv rolled her passenger window down to bear witness to a chorus of birdsongs above her head in the trees. Heavy mist in the air crowded her lungs. Liv always liked the weather this time of year, but she seemed to have forgotten it after living in Corcoran so long; even the coolest months were stuffy with smog from the nearby factories.

Her face grew pleasantly damp as she poked her head outside the window.

"We're not far," said Clav. "Then again, there's not much farther for us to go. We'll hit the peak soon, if we keep driving."

"Do you ever go to the top?" asked Liv.

"I don't need to." Then, with a smile, "You can't top a view like that. If you enjoy nothing else about Miss Keaton, you can't deny how nice the quiet of her house can be sometimes. There's a big difference between Corcoran noise and Morgallis noise. It almost makes you forget that total silence is achievable."

Neither of them spoke again until they reached Vaughn Keaton's house. Liv's stomach twisted into tighter knots. The car slowed, the driver's turns smoothed, and they soon reached a tall white gate buried in a thicket of dry vines.

The sound of screeching metal gates heralded their arrival. Liv didn't know why it surprised her, the sound. Metal was familiar to her the same way flesh and bone were. She lived in a city of industry, woke to the sounds of clashing machinery, and slept serenaded by its late-night, powering-down whistles.

The screech of white iron was the only thing she could hear in the hills. When the gate opened fully, silence suffocated her once more.

The house appeared to be a single, sprawling level from

the outside, with labyrinthine walls that looked as if they were meant to be fitted together with a missing half, like a puzzle. Through the clear walls, Liv could see a kitchen, a sparsely furnished living room, and a white-walled hallway, the visible frame of which resembled a greenhouse or a birdcage.

Vaughn stood outside with one hand curled around a salmon-colored mug and the other squeezing a navy blue cardigan shut around her body. She took her hand off the ribbed band of the sweater to wave at Clav. The man gave a nonchalant lift of his fingers in response, betrayed only by the amiable smile that lifted the lenses of his sunglasses.

"Thanks for the lift," Liv said.

"You don't need any help getting out?"

"Well." Liv considered her crutches in the back seat and the soft dirt of the driveway leading up to Vaughn's house. "It probably wouldn't hurt."

Clav loaded her out of the backseat like a sack of coffee beans against his side, which made her reunion with the High Mayor's daughter less mysterious and unbothered than she had initially expected. Liv hadn't been small or light enough to be lifted by anyone close to her since she hit her teenage growth spurt. Her face was bright with a juvenile, mischievous sort of glee when Clav eventually dropped her on the stone steps of Vaughn Keaton's front porch. She shook her short hair out, feeling winded. "Fantastic service here."

Vaughn blinked in quick succession. "Yes, he's quite good company to keep. Speaking of which," she said to her driver, "I've made a little extra coffee for you if you want some."

Clav returned from the car with Liv's crutches and now-empty backpack. "Maybe some other time, Miss Keaton."

"Are you sure?" There's plenty in here if you—"

"I might take a walk around the property. I'm sure the fresh air'll shock me back to life."

"Ah." Vaughn trained her disappointment into a poorly practiced mask of indifference. "I'll be sure to leave the door open for you then."

Unperturbed by tobacco smoke filling up his fresh air, Clav slipped the pack of cigarettes out of his pocket again and placed one in his mouth.

Vaughn asked, "This stays between us, yes?"

Clav lit the end and stuffed a heavy, silver lighter in his pocket. "Always does, Miss Keaton."

She gave him a thin smile. Her long, bony fingers curled around Liv's elbow, almost possessively. An odd thought, if Liv considered it for more than two seconds. There was nothing about her to be possessed or even coveted by someone like Vaughn, except maybe the unspecific promise of company. Clav's avoidance left Vaughn Keaton with a deficit of it, which would have made Liv feel some pity for the girl if she didn't feel so much secondhand embarrassment.

"How are you?" asked the Keaton daughter. The sincerity in her voice and the tenderness in her grasp as she led Liv through the front door made her lightheaded. "How was the drive? Not too bumpy, I hope."

"Bright," Liv proposed, unsure of how else to describe a journey she was only half-paying attention to.

"Did you talk much?"

"Enough." When Vaughn didn't respond, Liv added, "He's a prickly one—your driver."

Vaughn sighed. "That sounds like Clav. What about you, then? Do you want coffee?"

The first thing Liv registered as she stepped into the house was the quiet, steady stream of high, staccato notes on a piano and intermittent bursts of strings playing all around her. She searched the clear walls and corners of the house for speakers but was met with a startling blankness. "Uh. Sure."

"Is the music bothering you at all?"

Liv shook her head. "Expected some techno."

Incredulously, Vaughn asked, "Really?"

"No. You look exactly like someone who listens to this."

If anything perplexed Liv Shankly, it was the utility belt fastened around Vaughn's waist, peering out from beneath the hem of her sweater. The heads of several tools—like delicate wrenches, pliers, screwdrivers, and other handheld tools Liv might have carried on her at the workshop—hung half-hidden beneath the navy mohair, while the handles sat perched atop a pair of matching navy blue trousers. Picturing her in more appropriate clothing for a day of metalshop tinkering led Liv down a dark path of fondness for the High Mayor's daughter.

The edges of the tools clinked against the edge of the kitchen island as she poured some coffee into a second mug. Liv wiggled herself onto one of the barstools across from her.

"Do you want milk or sugar? It's non-dairy, unfortunately. Well, not unfortunately for me, but maybe for you, if that's what you—"

"Surely, you didn't have a driver pick me up from Corcoran just to talk coffee prep. So? What'll it be?"

The girl was a flurry of motion, always itching something with her fingers or scouring the room for something new to look at. She ran her fingertips along the inch of her neck beneath her ear. Her hair hid a patch of raised, red skin. "Well, I have... good news and bad news. What would you like first?"

"Good news now. Bad news when the coffee's in my hands."

"Milk and sugar then?"

Liv's mouth lifted at the corners. "Fuck yeah."

While Vaughn spooned the sugar in, she began, "The good news is I was able to collect your arm from the station."

Liv's pulse quickened. She had already grown irritable with this prosthetic. All the ways it failed to match her body and her needs grated on her more and more each day. "And? Did they give you any trouble?"

Vaughn shook her head. She poured the milk next. "But that answer errs into the realm of bad news. The good news is, everything is in my workshop. You've done something really incredible with it, Liv. It's astonishing how you pulled off so much with so many mismatched parts. I was able to identify at least four different extensions tucked within the body of the arm alone. And toward what purpose?" She slid the coffee across the island carefully. "Work? Violence? Mayhem?"

How Vaughn could only find four extensions within the casing of the arm should have raised her alarms. Had the police confiscated the others she had hidden in there? It wouldn't make sense for them to take some and leave the rest...

Liv could only speculate about which extensions Vaughn had seen. Whether she'd come across something like her tools, which had plenty of purpose, or the baton, which had no purpose at all, except to prove to herself that she could have it.

"Just for shits and giggles, I guess. I only use some of them." After a brief pause, Vaughn's implications struck her. "Hang on. Did you disassemble it?"

Vaughn swirled her coffee around in front of her. "It had been disassembled when I picked it up. I was actually able to piece it back together, although you'll have to tell me if I got it all wrong in a minute. The thing is... The *bad* thing is that it's totally non-functioning. I thought I might be able to repair it and return it to you in one piece, but it's completely bent out of shape."

Liv had come prepared to face disappointment of some kind. It had the benefit of being only one of the many harsh blows she had been dealt lately, so she felt mildly desensitized to it. The alternative to getting her arm back broken was not getting it back at all. She supposed she should be grateful that its modifications didn't get her into deeper trouble with law enforcement after the Run, but she couldn't quite muster that either.

"That's not to say I can't fix it at all," said Vaughn. "I know I could, at the very least, recreate what you had already built. Although I'm not sure you would want me to."

"I don't know why *you* would want anything to do with it in the first place."

A crease formed between the other girl's eyebrows.

"My arm isn't your problem," Liv explained.

"Sure," Vaughn said. "I suppose it doesn't have to be. But I took some of the dented panels off to examine the switch mechanism underneath them. There's so much weight in there. How you manage to carry all of that around every day is just..."

"What?"

Liv may as well have asked the question in another language. Vaughn stared at her blankly, then, as if remembering the coffee clutched in her pointed grip, she replaced it on the counter and took a deep breath. "Well, the mechanisms are quite *crude* and unnecessary."

That bleeding stripe of fondness for the Keaton daughter turned to a dark smear. "'Crude?'" Liv's jaw hung open, her ego thoroughly shot through. "What the hell do you mean 'crude'?"

"It works!" Vaughn rushed to amend. "It's certainly an innovative design. It's also a miracle you managed to fit so many mechanical parts in that small space, but it could use a significant refinement—or even a digitization! The unmarked button switches are a *total* hazard, Liv. There are no sufficient guardrails to activate those tools. It should take more than a little pressure to get the extensions out. How have you not skewered yourself already?"

This left Liv fumbling for words. Her thoughts were plentiful, but she couldn't seem to grasp any of them. "But..."

"Come with me," Vaughn said. "Bring your coffee if you want. Everything's stained in the workshop anyhow."

Liv slid down from the stool, pushing herself lethargically through a central hallway toward the back end of Vaughn's home.

Crude. That word echoed through her head with every thump of her crutches. It twisted inside her, soiling the good humor that Vaughn had been unknowingly laying a foundation for with her offers of coffee and too-earnest concern. *She doesn't know jack shit.*

The workshop door at the end of the hallway was wide open, and light from the clear wall at the other end sifted through the holographic outlines of what looked like rabbits leaping a path around the perimeter. The stubby ends of her crutches sank into the first inches of a soft floor mat meant for training. To her left, tucked into a corner, was a piled assortment of hole-poked targets falling over each other and a discoloration of shoe marks that reached from that corner to the opposite side of the room.

Those oddities were reserved for the front half of the workshop. The back half bore a deeper resemblance to the garages and workshops that Liv had worked in. An array of metal structures and unfinished contraptions obstructed a clear path to the back corners of the room and split the center like thick stalagmites around the open mouth of a cave. Liv's gaze flitted between all of them but didn't stick. Nothing looked familiar to her. The machines were as sleek as machines could possibly be, like final evolutionary forms of all the basic tools she had ever touched in her life. It was as if someone had shown her one of the High Mayor's holographic service announcements, but she had never seen color TV before.

Past the room's contents, the exterior glass wall gave them an uncensored view of the lush canopy of jungle descending from Vaughn's place on the hillside. Sunlight dappled the roof of the trees, sinking through the gaps and freckling the tangle of grass ahead. Clav's figure slinked by behind the first layer of trees, his footfalls heavy against the wet mulch and his cigarette dangling precariously out of his mouth.

Liv had meant to ask about the machines, but her mind was split between ten different things at once. Vaughn was saying something introductory to Liv about the space, but Liv was watching Clav through the glowing rabbits with amusement as he paused and pivoted to take in the tree shade above him before puffing out his chest with an overdue sigh.

She was continuously aware of the other girl's placement in the workshop, following closely until they were both positioned in front of a long workbench against the back wall, and Liv's crutches were tilted forward, with nowhere left to go. Liv swallowed, and her throat thickened with something insatiable and immune to the comfort of a drink. Jealousy, maybe. The view had far surpassed the expectations that Clav's earlier comment had begun building in her head.

After a long string of ignored ramblings, Vaughn asked, "So, what do you think?"

Liv blinked until the other girl came into focus again. Vaughn was leaning her weight against the workbench by a bony hip, having unclipped from her utility belt at some point and laid it on a swivelling chair that sat between them.

"Oh... Um."

Vaughn's arms twisted around her chest. Her fingers itched gaps into the fine knit of her cardigan. "I was just saying... Well, I wasn't saying it to persuade you into staying longer. If you'd like to go home with the pieces of your original arm today, I can at least help you flatten some of the dented metal to a more suitable degree." She nodded vaguely to the chair, which Liv cleared and promptly accepted. Vaughn hopped onto a clear sliver of the bench with ankles crossed primly. Liv's line of sight travelled to the dainty indigo slippers, so subtly mismatched in hue from her sweater that Liv wondered whether she truly knew which color was which. "But," Vaughn continued, "as they are now, all the parts have been so deformed from the drone dart that they can't function properly. And since you've used so many different metals—by the way, where *did* you get all these metals from?"

Liv's flush swelled stormlike. "I work in a garage."

"Like a *car* garage?"

"We come across a lot of scrap metal. Some of it seemed salvageable."

"Well, the fact that there are so many different kinds means that some of it's more formidable than others. Most of the pieces won't withstand me bending them back into shape, and the pieces that could were all attached to pieces that won't. Some of the thinnest levers have already snapped; I fear the ones that haven't will snap the second I try."

The inner workings of Liv's beloved, dismembered prosthetic lay arranged across the workbench beside Vaughn in neat rows like the dits and dahs of Morse code. Like this, with all the variation in browns, grays, and silvers, it looked just as crude as Vaughn made it out to be, like illegible scribbles of ink before they were puzzled together to compose decipherable letters and words.

Her arm shouldn't have looked like this. With her elbows perched on the edge of the bench, Liv laid her cheeks against her palms and mourned the dissected beast of metal. Vaughn wouldn't have thought it was crude if she had seen it before the dart. Her initial amazement—the innovation she had first pointed out to Liv—would not have been contradicted if it still worked as it was meant to. Its true form had been dismantled. Demystified.

It looked awfully like bones to Liv, though they were not like any bones she could think of except, maybe, those in the fingers and toes. Rather, they looked like fish bones, the metal panels of the arm's outer shell like iridescent scales catching in the light. All Vaughn could make of its bones were rudimentary post-mortem estimations of life.

Wedged inside that tiny vessel, it probably looked overly complicated to the High Mayor's daughter. Then again, so might clockwork, and Liv, who had grown up fascinated with intricate clocks, could think of few things that were simpler.

"Okay," Liv said, and drew out a long, elegiac breath. "Okay. What's the alternative?"

"To what?"

"To getting my arm back as-is." She leaned back in the chair, her hand resting on the top edge of her cast. "Let's say I'm okay with letting you make your refinements, or whatever else you want to do with it. What does that look like?"

Vaughn's dark eyes widened. "Do you want me to?"

"This is hypothetical."

"Well, I would have to try things out... Truthfully, I've never worked on such an advanced prosthetic before."

"I thought you said it was crude."

"The mechanics are crude, but the arm itself is advanced beyond any prosthetic—or admittedly prosthetic-adjacent thing—I've ever worked on. It's going to take some trial and error, but more trial than error, I can assure you. Digitization alone should take me less than a week since I'm already plenty familiar with working on pieces this fine. But seeing as this is totally off-record and I'd have to model it myself, it might take me a bit longer—"

"What is it you do, exactly?"

As if the answer couldn't have been less obvious from the machines packed around them, Vaughn's head swivelled from point to point. "I'm an inventor. Otherwise, I wouldn't be furnishing my house with big gadgets."

Pointedly, Liv added, "Or targets."

"Ah. Those." The Keaton girl dropped to the floor again with a gentle *thunk.* "The shooting targets aren't mine. I'm not keen on guns myself; I'm a fencer, you see. I like something with a little more finesse. Caldwell, on the other hand, likes anything that makes him feel like a big, strong man, which *naturally* meant that he couldn't tell a parry from a Passata Sotto. One day, I came home and found him standing on the other side of that window with these targets lined up along the treeline. He'd been shooting for half an hour since there aren't any properties in that direction of the hillside—loading and shooting and reloading until my eardrums felt like they were going to split."

Vaughn reached through the standing, holey target's legs and plucked a slender case for a sword that was propped against the wall. From it, she removed a silver epee and let its fabric jacket slip onto the ground.

"I brought the targets in, thinking he might find somewhere else to galavant, but I should have known: he's an unending nightmare, Caldwell is. He lives to torment me, and Papa requires us to have keys for each other's homes, so he does it often."

"That's *crazy.*"

Unperturbed, Vaughn said, "That's family." She flourished the epee decoratively for Liv's consideration, then assumed a side-step stance with the whining blade pointing toward the targets, parrying an imaginary opponent's swing.

With a swift lunge, the epee strikes the target, the blade bowing slightly under her heavy pressure.

"At least, that's *my* family."

Vaughn unstuck the epee from the target, the blade

balanced horizontally in front of her straight torso like a cross.

"He took them all out about a week later and lined them up in the same spot. Except this time, he wanted me to shoot. At the time, I thought, 'Why not?'" With the tip of the blade, she prodded at the case on the ground. "I wasn't hurting anyone. It's only the woods out there. As long as I aimed straight and kept my grip steady, the worst thing I could do was miss and hit a tree. He lined me up and told me where to aim. Then I shot. And Caldwell smiled."

A cold shifted throughout Liv's body slowly, sinking from her shoulders to her stomach, eventually settling in the tips of her fingers and toes. Hints of it meandered around her body aimlessly and wouldn't clear with any of the deep, meditative breaths she forced upon herself. Why did it unnerve her so much?

"I should have known it was a strange request. Have you ever seen Caldwell Keaton's smile? He has our father's smile, which is always a little off. And by that I mean—" Vaughn cut herself off and pressed her curled knuckles against her lips, pensive. "I know what it looks like when Caldwell is happy. He looks like a boy again. He was feeling righteous about something, about having *proved* something to me by having me shoot the gun and hit a target; and then, he asked me to help him move them inside to get them out of the oncoming rain, and I saw he had taped a photograph to the other side of the one I'd shot."

"Of you?"

She shook her head. "Of our father. It'd be less strange to have a photo of me there, I think. Then, I could have pretended he'd done it to play games with my head or intimidate me into something. Like I said, I'm used to his games. It wouldn't have shaken me. But Papa... That, I can't understand. They're closer to each other than I've ever been with either of our parents, and that closeness happened sometime in adulthood. Love is a deliberate choice at our age. Papa was mostly absent, raising us. I think he realized, at some point, that there was someone in the wings now grown enough to be primed in his image. So, Caldwell got weird."

"That's a grisly understatement, pinstripes."

Vaughn's right hand came down on the back of the chair. Her left gingerly traced the gutted infrastructure of Liv's metal arm. "I'm not like him, you know. I wasn't at the Run to gamble, and I didn't ask you here so I could toy with you."

"Why did you come then? Anyone with working eyes could see that you were completely out of your depths there."

"Can I lie?"

Liv snorted. "Why would you ask me that?"

"Because my reasons are paltry, and you'll laugh at me if I'm honest with you."

The rider laughed anyway, because the defense was comically juvenile for someone who held herself so righteously. "I don't think you should give a shit about what I think."

"Why wouldn't I?"

"That's just how things are. When has anything I've done mattered to your family, except for when it gets in the way of your gambling ventures? And when have the Keatons done anything that mattered to me, except for when Gaines passes another stupid law that kicks us down harder?"

Perhaps Liv should have exercised some restraint when she talked to her and subdued the fire behind her disdain for Upper City types.

Vaughn wanted an answer, and all the bones of Liv's metal arm were lying on her workbench. Liv had to give her something. "It doesn't make a difference what I think—not in the Upper City. Never has and never will. Pretending like it does only makes it personal. Right now, the Keatons are a disembodied malevolent force that haunts Corcoran."

The inscrutable expression on Vaughn Keaton's face betrayed a warm-blooded shame. Beneath Liv's harsh words, her face was just as hot, stuffy, and traitorous. All her stubbornness had grown with her, a thin strand from childhood that had calcified and hardened in her hands as she slipped unnoticeably into adulthood, but so had her fear of authority.

Corcoran, unlike the Holy Commune where Liv was born, lived half-smashed under a fat, ruling thumb. Her family had learned to live life looking over their shoulders, making little noise, drawing the least amount of attention to themselves as possible. It was hard enough to survive, let alone to revolt.

Perhaps, this would be the extent of it. Liv's only attestation of how she'd lived and her principles. It was all she could muster when she was still entertaining such a large, personal favor from the High Mayor's daughter.

"You don't have to get cozy with me," she added. "All this you're doing... It's nice, but it's unnecessary. I wouldn't have batted an eye if you sent me home and wanted nothing else to do with me."

Vaughn studied the metal parts to avoid meeting Liv Shankly's gaze. "So you don't think... that could change?"

"What kind of substantial change comes from helping me fix my arm? It takes a lot of complacency for a problem to get so bad."

Vaughn nodded solemnly, lifting a particularly dented metal prong that Liv recognized as belonging to the lever of the wrench extension. She bent it back into shape with some force and bit down on her lip, focused. She laid it back on the workbench, fixing the uneven separations between the adjacent pieces. "I went with Caldwell to the Run because, in spite of everything, my brother is the closest thing I have to a friend. And I was lonely. That's it."

Liv didn't laugh. Out of all the reasons Vaughn might have offered up, that one filled Liv with pity.

It was a short-lived pity, and Liv quickly came to her senses. What kind of person sympathized with the Keatons? Vaughn's words possessed a sincerity that Liv had heard in her last confession, too—'I'm not like him'—that would make Liv inhuman to ignore.

She stared at the other girl for a long time, alternating between a misplaced apology and a complete loss for words.

"Look, Vaughn—"

"Maybe you're right." Vaughn pinched her fingers in front of her stomach as if they were caught in a paper trap. "I can't really fix anything. I'm not a politician, and I'm hardly a politician's daughter so long as he's got a son who serves him better. But I'm not a monster, either. I want to help. I... If I can fix anything, it's *this*. Will you let me do that?"

Liv was silent for a long time. Pinpricks of heat drilled into her face where Vaughn's relentlessly observant gaze searched for her train of thought.

Liv looked at the bones of the arm laid out beside her instead of looking forward. The piece that Vaughn had just tried to bend back into shape had an irreversible dip in the metal. Some damage could never be totally undone. Those bends would always leave behind evidence, unless she could somehow melt the metal down and forge it anew. Liv didn't have the time or resources for that. Not to mention the willpower.

"I spent months figuring out how to make a prosthetic that worked for me." Liv offered a small, apologetic smile to her. "Even if it was crude. Even if it wasn't as good as it could have been. It took me a lot of work that I won't get back. If you really think you can fix this... Vaughn, if you think you can do it, I'll do whatever it takes to make that happen."

"You would?" Vaughn's eyebrows were tense and straight,

and dark eyes searched Liv's for the punchline of a joke.

"You and I both know you have no obligation to help me fix this, but truth be told, I need the help. I've already done this once without an arm, and it sucked. I was spending hours after work trying to rig the pieces together in there with borrowed shop tools, just so I could eventually make things a little easier for myself. To have done all that work and taken all that time to get my body acclimated to the arm, only to lose it again doing the thing that made me need it in the first place? I can't let that be for nothing. What'll it cost me to come back and help after all that? You're doing me a big favor. I'd be an idiot to turn you down."

Vaughn studied her closely, chewing on the inside of her cheek. "Very well. We can... do that."

"Yeah?"

With renewed spirit, Vaughn's pointed chin lifted, and she repeated with a fair stutter, "Yeah. That sounds nice. I'll just, um. I should tell Clav—"

"Tell me what?"

Vaughn's driver was only halfway through the hall when he interjected. He had something pinched between his left hand that clinked with the familiar timbre of metal. In his right were his sunglasses, his cigarette long since disposed of. He strode in blithely, none the wiser to the emotional unrest building up between the two women. "Found a couple more of these outside by the way."

He held out his hand. Vaughn did the same. In her palm, he placed four silver bullet casings streaked over with damp mud and freckled with rust. With a shamed, sharp intake of breath, Vaughn closed her fingers around the metal and placed it delicately on a corner of the workbench where it could not mix with the metal of Liv's tarnished arm.

"It's been a while since you've worked on one of those, honey."

Maura's interjection shocked the soldering iron out of Liv's hand and onto the table. She snatched it up before it could score grooves into the coffee table. "Jesus. How long have you been awake?"

Liv let the iron cool and took her hands off the broken pieces of the old clock to fumble around the couch for the remote. She muted the warehouse pillaging TV show that had begun playing half an hour ago, wedged unpleasantly between two frivolous reality shows she actually cared about. Three men on the screen were negotiating the price of a 2000 Bugatti Veyron, and they were drawing up short straws since some of the original parts had been swapped out at some point.

It served as ceaseless background noise in lieu of the Bronlow's Garage clatter that she usually tinkered to; she had modified most of her arm to her coworker Luis's classic mariachi, interlaced with the occasional crank of a car lift. But it played quietly so as not to wake Maura before she was ready. Liv pressed a button and checked the time. It was nearly noon.

"You didn't hear me walking around earlier?" asked Maura. Liv shook her head. "So, is this a new one or an old one?"

As Maura sat beside her on the couch and beheld the hand tools and cogs splayed out on the table, Liv cleared her throat, failing to recall how many years ago this particular clock had found its way into her possession. She had worked on so many over the years, but the fascination—or rather, her time—had dwindled since she had started working in the garage. The sudden vacancy in her schedule had left her itching for something to work on.

This was all she could do to take her mind off her rendezvous with Vaughn. It was something she could actually talk about.

She lifted up a rag. "The dust didn't give it away?"

"Oh goodness."

"I know."

Maura's lips tugged upwards. "I'm glad I didn't miss you this morning."

Liv threw her hunched shoulders back and kneaded the nape of her neck. "Oh yeah? You want to do something today?"

"If you have time for me. Funny, I thought you were meant to be *resting*. Not having such mysterious trysts away from home."

Indignantly, Liv said, "I rest! I rest plenty. Too much, even. I'm tired of resting."

"Where do you go, then? Because I know Bronlow's isn't budging on their leave."

"Says you."

"Says me? Says you!" Maura gave Liv's arm a gentle shove. "Fine. Don't tell me. You're being safe, though, aren't you? Not getting into any trouble?"

If there was any trouble afoot, Liv felt it most when she was at home. Ever since she had come into that bag of money, she had brushed her teeth, eaten her cereal, and watched her shows with a shadow of dread cast on the wall behind her. She was constantly squinting through the peephole of their apartment door and listening closely to the thumps beneath the couch for signs of wrongness. Of someone different and dangerous on the other side of her walls. Someone whose money she had stolen. Someone who desperately wanted it back.

She had staved off the fear for only a little more than a week before Corey's paranoia finally reached her. She could decry Corey's foreboding as nothing more than a side effect of his exhaustion and hunger for the money; years spent driven by survival could do that to a person.

It was Vaughn who had finally broken her, and she hadn't even been trying. All the close concern that couldn't possibly be meant for someone like Liv—it came from a place she could only assume was a premonition. What did Vaughn know? What did she think would happen to Liv when Clav took her home from that faraway house?

Naturally, she shared none of this with Corey or Maura. Not the dread or about the bullets in Vaughn's backyard.

"You have such little faith in me," she replied, trying to seem lighthearted. "I can behave."

"When you're keeping secrets from me, my mind doesn't resort to good things. What do you think I'm going to do to you if you're in trouble? With all five feet, one inch, and two bad lungs of me? I just want to know you're keeping yourself safe." Maura palmed the top of Liv's head and dragged her closer to kiss her hair. "Give me some credit. We've kept you alive this long. You can't expect me to give up that effort now."

"Yes, yes, I'm okay."

Maura's hand tightened around Liv's hair, and she swiveled it around like an eight ball before releasing it. "I'm going to get some orange juice. You want some?"

"Sure."

On the screen, two of the men were sitting in a van, driving over the Grollingcross bridge to Morgallis, having unsuccessfully acquired anything from the Lower City warehouses they were rummaging through. The Grollingcross bridge was a little nicer than the one from Corcoran, and the floodwaters below were noticeably less murky. Liv suspected it was an editing trick. They couldn't possibly fool anyone with that shade of blue, except for the richest of the rich, who didn't make journeys to the Lower Cities anyway.

Maura was in the kitchen, squeezing frozen orange juice concentrate into a pitcher, when Liv's comms device began to vibrate on the sofa cushions. She answered quickly and quietly. "Yeah?"

"Hello! How are you?"

"Uh—" Liv pushed herself up to her feet, shelved the phone between her cheek and shoulder, and hopped unceremoniously toward her empty bedroom, which was taken up by a smattering of Corey's belongings since they'd been sleeping in each other's usual spots. Unquestionably suspicious, Maura's eyes followed her, though she stayed put, stirring her frozen concentrate until it had melted and dissolved.

Liv shut the door behind her. "What's wrong? Did something happen?"

"I had an idea," Vaughn said simply. "I know we had planned to see each other tomorrow, but I just thought I could run it by you and, depending on what you thought, potentially start working on it today so I had something to show for it when you—"

"Okay. What is it?"

"Is everything okay, Liv? You sound a bit—"

"Yeah, totally," she rushed. "I'm a little preoccupied right now, if you could just, um..." In her moment of silence, Liv pressed her ear to the closed door and listened for her mother's footsteps, but heard nothing. With a skittering breath, Liv dropped her side against the wall and continued. "Sorry. Go ahead."

Vaughn's end was quiet for a long time. "Clav told me he

still picks you up down the road."

"Did he?" Liv shut her eyes and mentally cursed the driver.

"You're ashamed of working with me, aren't you?"

Liv said nothing and, therefore, could not say anything that wasn't untrue. In a tone gentler and more collected than what she'd greeted Vaughn with, she asked, "What was your idea, pinstripes?"

She would deal with a frigid confrontation with Vaughn tomorrow. Whatever that looked like.

"Well. I was thinking about all the extensions you had in your last arm. They couldn't have all been sturdy, considering both the stems and the tools at the ends would have to fit alongside each other in that limited space."

"Mhmm?"

"How would you feel about reducing it to three stems?"

"*Three?*" Liv's old arm, as heavy as it was, had fit at least ten, ignoring the fact that some tools, like the pocketknife and the corkscrew, were thinner and more brittle than tools like the baton or the Phillips head screwdriver, whose heavy metal made up for their thinness.

"But we thread the ends! Make them versatile. You could switch the tools out as needed, and the whole thing would be worlds lighter."

"Yeah, but..." Liv wanted to throw her comms device onto the dresser and pace, but could do neither with her injured leg. "The entire point of having them all there was to eliminate the need for forethought. I could get *any* of the extensions at a moment's notice, whether I needed them or not."

"Did you get much use out of that baton, Liv?"

Liv paused, sensing a trap in the hints of irony Vaughn had let slip. "You're funny. Ask me about anything else."

The High Mayor's daughter responded with an amused huff. "Very well. I'm going to see if I can put together a prototype for you before you get here. See if I can change your mind."

"You can try. It took a lot of time and intention to make the arm I made. I wouldn't have made those decisions without a reason."

"Luckily, neither would I. Goodbye, Liv. Tell your family I said hello."

She heard a creak in the living room—Maura nearing. "Sure, sure. Gotta go."

The older woman was still stirring her orange juice concentrate when Liv left the room, reeking so pungently of shame that she pressed her back to the bedroom door and didn't move closer.

"Going somewhere?"

"No. Not right now."

"No trouble, I hope?"

Liv waved the question away. "I wish. You have such exciting expectations about what I get up to in my free time."

"Obviously," Maura said, smiling to herself. "I think the Runs are pretty glamorous."

"Do you?"

"I mean, don't tell Corey I said that. And *don't* let that get to your head. As far as he knows, I'm a staunch objector to your involvement in the Run." She trailed off, watching the last of the concentrate dissolve into the swirling water. "It must be very thrilling in the moment, though. Riding fast, adrenaline racing... Corey was always so proud of you."

That look of pride was branded into Liv's mind. It haunted her and spurred her forward concurrently when she got back on her bike to look for a benefactor who wasn't him. They didn't do much together anymore. Not since she had gotten injured. He had little time for anything that wasn't his work. He didn't have time for the Run either. But the Run was already a place he shouldn't have been for reasons other than time, so the issue of time itself seemed arbitrary.

The Runs were the only time Liv ever saw Corey hopeful, and it was one of the only places he hugged her anymore. He would cheer, exuberant, as if no record of success would ever prepare him for the relief and the thrill of watching Liv win. He would grab her helmet with both hands and tip his sweaty, stress-creased forehead onto it, laughing triumphantly. Liv would laugh back. They would express more in those laughs than they did over the breakfast table.

The older she had grown, the less she needed that sort of thing, at least in the fundamental way that children did. It might not have bothered her so much if their circumstances didn't always seem so dire. The absence of warmth and the lack of hope made her wonder frequently if the joy of her, of the child she'd been, had worn thin to the burden of her, and if she was living in their apartment on borrowed time. Was he still proud of her? Was there anything to be proud of when she wasn't racing?

Liv sat back down on the couch and stared at the clockwork on the table. She picked up a thin cog and rolled the teeth along the pad of her thumb, leaving indentations in it like pavement markings. Maura placed a glass of orange juice in front of her. "Thanks, Maura."

"Of course, honey."

"Do you want to watch something?"

Maura shrugged. "Nothing new to watch. I've seen *everything*."

"You can't just sit there in silence and watch me."

"I'll do what I want. And who says that's what I wanted to do? I've seen you plenty, too."

Maura lifted her feet onto the couch, shifting herself downward until her head rested upon the arm, and her toes were wiggling through the worn fabric of her socks against

Liv's thigh. "I'm just going to take a little nap, okay."

"But you just woke up." Liv laid the backs of her fingers across Maura's forehead, then her cheek. "You feeling okay?"

Maura replied with a sharp hiss through her teeth and a small grin. "Maybe. Maybe not. You have your secrets, and I have mine." Her eyes closed. The muscles in her cheeks smoothed, and her crows' feet unfolded. In her sleep, beneath her prematurely silvering hair, Maura looked her age. Neither of Liv's adoptive parents had ever seemed much older than her.

Once Maura's steady breaths turned to the occasional snort, Liv unmuted the television but kept the volume low. Maura, too, missed all the usual sounds and signs of life.

Clav had begun working through his cigarette before Liv got to the end of the street, which meant there was only a little stub left, and the scent of tobacco had already seeped into his clothes. He was dressed even more casually than the time before, in a long-sleeved sweater and faded jeans. In the car, he pushed his sunglasses snug over the wide bridge of his nose, then reached up into the compartment above their heads and handed her a spare set. "I'm not averse to conversation, you know."

Liv was twisted halfway over the console when he said this, hoisting her bag into the backseat after kicking it around too much. "Did Vaughn tell you I said that?"

"Not in such concise words."

"Is that why *you* told her about picking me up out here?"

The sunglasses dipped as his brows tightened. "No. I didn't think that'd be an issue. Certainly isn't an issue with me."

Liv slid the sunglasses onto her face and examined her reflection in the overhead mirror. Car mirrors always brought out the worst in it. There was a slight discoloration where her roots were growing in; her natural hair, though dark brown and thick, was still lighter than the perma-black hanging onto the ends. She didn't feel like dyeing it yet. She shut the sliding panel over the mirror and settled in for the long drive. "It's not an issue with me either, but Vaughn seems to think so."

Liv stared out at the slowly shifting cityscape, tongue poking around in her mouth. "I didn't think she would get mad at you about what I said. I didn't mean anything by it. You're not obligated to make small talk with me anyhow."

All of Clav's teeth appeared, and he barked out a laugh. "Oh, that's— That's not really how she works. She just mentioned it to me."

"But it bothered you?"

The driver shrugged. "I'm just messing with you. One Corcoranite to another. Besides, she doesn't get mad at me about stuff like that. I think she just wants something to talk about, and right now, that's you. You want to listen to something?"

Liv didn't know what to say except, "Sure." She knew some part of people's minds was occupied by the memory of her; otherwise, she wouldn't have risked her chances at the last Run trying to find a benefactor, armed only with a proven track record of success. Still, she expected any public perception of her to be conditional upon a race. To think that anyone was talking about her when she wasn't around made her feel feverish and strange. There was a soreness in her face and a shallowness in her chest.

"She seemed bothered by it," Liv eventually said. "By you picking me up down the road."

Clav said nothing for a long time, drumming his fingers against the wheel, but Liv could see a thought turning over in his mind like a sticky cog. "I don't know what your reasoning is. It's not my business or hers unless you want it to be. My job is to pick you up, take you there, and drive you home."

"But?"

With a sigh, "She's... embarrassed. Maybe you've already noticed it, but Vaughn— I mean, Miss Keaton has a lot of anxiety."

"About me?"

"About everything. She's worried about her work, her family, her image... Ever since she moved up to the Morg hill, she's been worried about her house and living on her own. The truth is, we stopped talking for a long time after we got older, before she officially hired me. Nowadays, she asks me for things all the time, things she doesn't really need me or anyone else to do. I can tell she gets nervous on her own. It's serene up there, alright. But I can't imagine what all that quiet all the time would do to someone."

You're ashamed of working with me, aren't you?

"Don't take it personally," Clav said. "Like I said, it's not my business. You're in the car. I'm getting you there in one piece. Technically, that's the extent of my job."

Liv, however, had no job and no obligation to spend time with Vaughn or let her driver pick her up, and so she was going to that glass house out of her own volition. She supposed that, since Maura already suspected the worst of her, she *also* had no reason to make it harder for herself by making herself walk to the end of the road on her crutches. So what if Maura knew? Wasn't Maura also yearning for something new to talk about?

Liv couldn't shake her misgivings. If she made the concession and let either of them come any closer, it would have only been for Maura's sake, because the idea gave her no comfort. Those concessions punctured holes in her pride. She didn't *need* Vaughn Keaton or her driver getting any closer, not to pick her up or become her friend. Even if it made things easier.

Instead, she skulked around her apartment carrying a little secret on her back as if it were a freight load. Maura might forgive her for working with a Keaton, but Liv couldn't forgive herself.

Vaughn's eagerness didn't make it easier. She watched them pull up to the house, smiling with all her teeth. They were bright and straight, save for the two front and center, which were more prominent. Her lips were blushed with the kind of fruit punch, pomegranate juice stain that lipstick couldn't fully accomplish. Her long hair had been fastened loosely into a braid and gathered into a knot. She took a hand off her coffee mug to wave at them from the doorway. "Good morning! Are you hungry? Or thirsty?"

Drawing herself through the front room, Liv could see that the coffee pot was still halfway full, with enough for her and Clav to pour themselves one large cup each if they parsed it out correctly. Vaughn looked at her with large, expectant eyes; Liv's eyes dropped to the floor, guilty. "Sure. Famished."

Clav stayed longer than the last time, idling on one of the barstools next to Liv until he had finished at least one cup. The more they drank, the more Vaughn's tension seemed to dissipate. The cloud of anxiety hovering over Vaughn's head was impossible to ignore now that Clav had mentioned it, and so he had downed his coffee almost in service.

He left afterward, neither of the others asking him where. Vaughn's fingers tapped restlessly against the porcelain. Her nails were short, having been bitten and chewed rather than filed or cut, but they were polished with something transparent. "So," she said, "how are you?"

"Better."

"Really?"

It proved difficult pretending to be unfazed and unsympathetic to her earnestness. Liv took a sip from her coffee and replied honestly, "Well, yeah. I've been thinking a lot about this—I mean, about the possibilities of a new arm."

Vaughn leaned over the counter, hastily moving the long, untethered pieces of hair at her temple behind her ears. Her fingers knitted together on the countertop, inches away from where Liv's were. "And? What do you think?"

"None of it was productive, if that's what you're asking."

"It wasn't," said Vaughn. "Otherwise, I would have asked you a very different question."

Once Liv realized the only thing that would stop Vaughn from continuing to level her wide-eyed, relentless curiosity was an answer, she gave her coffee another long swallow and pushed herself to elaborate. "The arm was the last thing I worked on. Up until then, I'd been tinkering with much older contraptions. Clocks, automata, that kind of stuff. But the arm was the last thing I worked on that wasn't a car. Most of my time has been devoted to physical therapy and recovery, and then it was financial recovery. I signed myself up for more hours at work to make up for all the wages I'd lost. I'm not going to say working on the arm *wasn't* enjoyable, but I didn't do it for fun. So, I had forgotten how much I loved the feeling of working on such a small scale. It's more stimulating than a car."

The other girl nodded, scrupulous in her stare.

The attention made Liv's temperature rise. "That's it. Seriously."

"Your mechanics make more sense now. You don't like working with electricity. That's why the only evidence I could find of wiring was from the original electrode setup."

"I never said I didn't like it. I just..." *Just what?* Liv had no strong opinions on electricity as a whole, other than that it was around her all the time, flickering overhead, forgettable, essential, and unfathomable to her. "I'm more familiar with automata. The wiring I work with at the garage is a whole different beast."

"You're powering the arm with two different sources, though. You must have felt some disconnect between normal movements and the extensions."

"Yep. Hence the *crudeness.*"

All of Vaughn's curiosity and eagerness curled back into her like a touch-me-not, and all the ease with which Liv had expressed her last thought calcified. "I shouldn't have said that," Vaughn said. "That was rude of me. I'm sorry."

"Look—"

Vaughn did look, which worsened Liv's efforts to come up with the next thing to say. It was clear to Liv that she had thought about it a lot, whereas after that day, Liv had barely thought about it at all, except as an inward joke made toward the rich girl's expense. "I got a little defensive, okay? You weren't wrong. It's not as good as it could be, but—"

"It's brilliant," said Vaughn. "And it was brilliant before I knew why you didn't power it electrically, but I was so caught up in how I thought it should have worked and how I could have made it differently that I said something uncouth about it to you."

"Brilliant?" *Magnificent.* Liv studied the other girl until a crack formed in her rigid sense of formality, and she realized how phlegmatic she was about an issue that meant little to Liv in hindsight. Vaughn closed her eyes and hid a laugh in her hand.

That festering, virulent fondness had come back to bite Liv behind the neck like a mothering cat.

"I am regrettably prone to choosing the wrong words at the wrong time," said Vaughn.

"No, no, keep going. It's not every day someone tells me I've done something brilliantly."

Vaughn's lips lifted at the corners. She curled her fingers

around her mug and slid it like an offering across the counter-top to Liv. "That makes two of us. Cheers?"

Liv's cup met hers willingly, already emptied and dry.

Two chairs sat beside the workbench this time, and some of the smaller, unrecognizable machines that had been scattered around the room were now hiding somewhere else. "I tried to clean as much as I could." Vaughn was actively tidying as she said this, but the only things left to move were small handheld tools and spare parts that had no better place than the bench, so she placed them inches away from their original positions and fiddled with them until they were all made parallel or perpendicular to her liking.

Liv laid her crutches against the far end and placed herself heavily into a chair. On the workbench, along with the old pieces of her arm, sat an assortment of sketches in various sizes. First scribbled hastily into a black notebook, which lay face-open against the glass wall, Vaughn had then moved more intricate numbers and neatly drafted diagrams onto lightly gridded, single pages. Those neat drafts illuminated the glass wall with a sudden verbal prompt to her AI.

Liv wondered how much time Vaughn had already dedicated to this. Her work had not been even half as involved as Vaughn's initial thoughts for the arm. She, of course, had much less to work with and lacked an arm. Despite all the exceptions and justifications she could make for herself, Liv's chest was struck with a hollow, hive-like feeling of housing a hundred angry bees; she was completely out of her depth next to Keaton girl.

"You've... put a lot of thought into this."

"I know, I know. It went a little overboard. Half of that's unusable."

Liv poked around her teeth with her tongue, the bees even more disturbed than before.

So much for brilliance, she thought. Sometimes, all it took to get a job done was some well-timed willpower. Up against knowledge and practice, what good was willpower, which only worked if the rest of the pieces in play lined up perfectly?

"Have you spoken to Dr. Tewer lately?"

"The wrangler? Why would I?"

Vaughn settled into the second chair. "You all seemed awfully close at the hospital. I assumed they would have checked up on you. I'm sorry, I can't remember the other man's name."

Michael. Their names were generally treated as forbidden knowledge to riders. "We're not supposed to know them."

"Why not?"

"To protect them. To protect ourselves. The less we know about the Drone Runs, the better. It keeps us from spilling information to the wrong people. For some of us, these races are the only way to make a living."

The unspoken fact that Liv was the reason it no longer existed passed between them. Liv brushed her fingers across the open page of Vaughn's notebook where she had scribbled over a line of notes so viciously that the paper had nearly torn.

Slowly, as if cajoling a frightened animal, Vaughn said, "People know about it, Liv. The kind of people you probably don't want attention from."

"How do you know that?"

The other girl shrugged, kicking her crossed ankles forward to strike one of the wheels on Liv's chair. "It's rather common information in the Morgallis government. In fact, they're probably the only ones up here who know about it. It's bothersome to them, but not so much that they'll do anything to stop it. The residents, on the other hand, don't typically concern themselves with things in the Lower Cities. They try not to be so *civilian* about where they spend their free time. Bit ironic, isn't it?"

Liv slouched back and pushed her chair into a lethargic spin. "Really fucking rich."

"I wondered if that was why your wrangler used old drones."

Everything in Liv's body seemed to prickle with awareness. "What do you mean by 'old drones'?"

Vaughn looked to one corner of her room, then another, for something she didn't find. "I *mean* that the drones he's using are an outdated model. That model has been decommissioned for a few years now. It was needlessly forceful. Haven't you seen the current police drones that are employed around the city?"

Of course, she had. But their very nature was reprehensible to Liv. She refused to meet their glowing eyes or stay too long in their scopes. Too much presence in a surveillance state wouldn't have amounted to anything good or safe. They were looming, threatening shapes that Liv had always responded to with feigned indifference; she had no idea what they could pick up on, whether they could sense her fear like a wary dog.

Liv itched her scalp with the hard fingers on her prosthetic. "It's typically better for me to have them at my back than in my sights."

This irked Vaughn for some unplaceable reason. "I suppose it makes sense to me now, especially if they still believe the Runs are something covert. It'd be more difficult to hack one of the current models for use in the Drone Runs, and if they did, there'd be a higher risk of punitive action from the police if one of their active drones went missing. But there's a reason the design was changed."

Already intimately familiar with what the hijacked drones were capable of, Liv let some of the tension roll off of her. The worst had already affected her. Certainly, they couldn't hurt her anymore. "What's a Run without the danger? The only reason anyone cares about the Runs—the reason there's any money behind it at all—is for the thrill behind the threat. Besides, the other night was an anomaly. What happened to me... That has never happened before. The gamemakers keep us safe."

"I know," said Vaughn. "Which is why I'm so surprised they still use that design. All the drones that are currently in service in the Upper City have been updated to be *completely* non-lethal; no darts, no tranquilizers, and no nets capable of strangulation. But they're still usable. Police use them all the time and with less risk of physical injury to the people they're in pursuit of."

"Why are you mentioning this?"

Vaughn leaned across the workbench and swiped her notebook out from underneath Liv's wandering fingers. She flipped to the beginning, searching. "Because it was *my* design that neutralized the drones. Despite the, um..."

She turned the notebook back toward Liv, thumb pressed hard against the spine to keep the pages down. "Despite the *crudeness* of the drones you were using for the Run, they seemed to have, at least, been more tractable than the ones we have now. Mine can be monitored from multiple points within the police department. Whatever Dr. Tewer had done to commandeer the old ones with his controller is more advanced than what the police are doing to operate theirs, now and before the model update. It's a strange choice to use them at all. Even stranger, though, that something should go wrong with the controls."

Vaughn trailed off, gazing at the evidence of her engineering prowess. The first scratches of a design were faded and smudged with fingerprints on the page before them. She looked at it with equal parts reverence and regret.

With Vaughn's eyes trained on the once-familiar arcs of

graphite, Liv scrutinized all the signs of worry in her face. They were all subtle enough to go unseen if not viewed from up close. A slight depression between her eyebrows. A firmness in the muscles beside the corners of her lips. Even within the small scope of the pages, her eyes were restless.

Liv closed the notebook. "You seem to know more than what you let on the other night, pinstripes."

Vaughn tucked a stubborn, wayward strand of hair behind her ear again, the dip undisturbed on her forehead. "I didn't say I didn't know anything. Just that I might not have gone without a little incentive. And it's good I did, in the end. Otherwise, we wouldn't have met. And I couldn't have taken care of your leg."

"My leg wouldn't *need* taking care of if you and your brother hadn't been there."

For a moment, Liv worried that she had pushed her again, the same way she had pushed her the last time they had seen each other.

Vaughn moved the swivelling seat closer and lowered her voice as if they were sharing a secret. "Do you really think it happened because we were there?"

"It's just—"

"Be honest with me, Liv. I'm being honest with you. I went for my own self-pitying reasons, but Caldwell went for something else. I don't know what it is or why he chose the Run to gamble on that night. It beats me even more than it satisfies me to have won." She seized Liv's wrist gently. Her thumb slid over the protruding bone, setting all the hairs along Liv's arm upright.

"I don't know. I've been doing the Run for years, and nothing like that has ever happened. No amount of contract racers or betting money has ever resulted in a drone malfunction. Not until you came."

"But the Margossi house rider has been there before, yes?

What about the other house riders?"

Liv shook her head. "Contract riders are Upper City, but they aren't outsiders. They know the rules. They know not to spill any details about the Run. Their stakes are different. To us, illicit money is just money. To them, it's only ever illicit, which means they make themselves scarce at the Runs, and they keep their mouths shut. They wouldn't tamper with the drones if they knew what was good for them."

"But you think Caldwell would?" Her grip unfurled with deliberate slowness, as if Liv might not have noticed they were still on her wrist, and she thought she could release it without her rider noticing.

"I think..." What did Liv Shankly think? The only metric she had to measure Caldwell Keaton by was the distant, glowing screens showing tabloid news—and his sister's word. Liv must have trusted her enough to let her fix the arm, which was, considerably, a lot; but could she trust the bias Vaughn held against her brother enough to defend all other options? "He's probably the only one the consequences can't reach. The gamemakers couldn't penalize him for interfering, not without him bringing the law down on all our heads."

Vaughn bit her lip and turned her head to think in another direction. "What would your organizers have done if I'd told them about the weapon the Margossi rider had on him?"

With a useless shrug, Liv admitted, "I don't know. No one risks violating the rules of the Run. A lot of people need that money."

"As do you, I take it?"

"Whoa whoa, we aren't talking about me right now." Liv didn't want to get into her family's insurmountable medical debt, even if all her comment did was pique the other girl's suspicion. "I didn't do anything to the drones. I just... I don't want to get into debt right now."

The High Mayor's daughter acquiesced. "Sorry. I wasn't thinking."

"It's fine."

"You're here for the arm." Vaughn seemed to use this as a reminder for herself, less than she did for Liv. She collected her notebook again and opened it to one of the last pages she had written in. Only a few pages remained until she reached the end. Liv longed to know what other kinds of things Vaughn kept in there. It would probably make her feel small and unimportant. Still, it might also revive something dormant inside of her, a lost desire to build and repair and make perfect. The motivation was worth a little ego bruise.

Vaughn started to write something down in an unmarked corner of the page. Numbers. She wrote fast, like they had been pent up for a while and could only now shake loose.

"Vaughn?" Liv asked.

The girl paused her script mid-sentence.

"What does your brother want with the Margossis?"

The pencil shifted in her grasp, needling back and forth. "I... I don't know. He was paying them for something. He won't tell me what. I don't think it was good."

Liv waited for something else. For an idea or a hunch. Caldwell Keaton couldn't pay the Margossi family for anything with money he didn't have. Neither Vaughn nor Liv dared to mention that part, as if having this money within reach was an unspeakable sin.

Vaughn scribbled the rest of her note down before closing the book around the writing utensil again. "Keep that money close, okay? Don't let anyone take it from you."

9

No one came for the money. The Shanklys deposited more of it into their bank accounts, made at least one frivolous purchase with the overwhelming sum of it, and chipped away at their debts.

It had seemed insurmountable and inescapable. Without the crushing weight of it above her, Liv felt like a different person. Little had changed at home. Maura teased her often about the secret, devious things she must have been up to while simultaneously caring even less. The threat of danger subsided. The debt slowly disappeared. Liv and Vaughn made strides with the construction of her new prosthetic.

And Liv's leg only had a couple more weeks in the cast.

Somehow, despite the gravitas, Liv's dread began to fall away in pieces. Vaughn cut Liv out of it like a diligent gardener clipping her from a thicket of thorns.

She didn't know how she managed to square away so many of her problems with only a broken knee to show for it. She would soon have to contend with physical therapy to rehabilitate her leg, which would certainly hurt like hell.

But for everything else she had gained? No win from the Drone Runs had ever felt so sweet.

The only one who didn't seem to agree was Corey.

The money had not affected his work schedule. His hours remained full and plentiful, half due to the demand and half due to his own request. Even with Liv's regular outings to the

Upper City, Maura saw more of her than before, but Liv wasn't Corey. Liv wasn't her *partner*. It was one of the few roles Liv simply couldn't fill, one that kept them all from fully indulging in their newfound stability. Maura was mostly there when Liv was home; a small, fractured part of her was stuck to Corey, so it was always gone.

Liv knew she shouldn't have taken it personally, but that hadn't stopped her before. That was the thing about having parents who never expected to have her. She couldn't shake the feeling that she was an interloper, a constant guest. This life was never supposed to be hers. She had become ingrained in every part of it—their successes, their failures, and their endeavors. They undeniably needed her. But would they have chosen her, given the chance?

The weather was shifting in Corcoran. The dull, bright consistency of the sky reverted back to its temperamental, impulsive mannerisms, sunny and clear one moment, then weeping and thundering the next.

It took its time getting there. More than a month had passed since the night of the Run. Winter, like all of Liv's other misgivings, peeled away to something fresh.

It was time to make another deposit.

For as long as Liv's leg was still in the cast, Corey insisted on her taking his work-provided car, even if that meant a longer commute.

She woke up earlier, sparing no time to lie on the couch with her headphones like she usually did. While she aligned her prosthetic with the stump of her shoulder in the bathroom, Corey shuffled through the living room, discordantly chugging his way through half a cup of orange juice on a peppermint-fresh mouth. Two wheat slices popped up from the toaster, hurried as he was. The flat of his knife and the hard, unmelted butter cracked through the toast. He cursed softly. "Hey. You ready to go?"

The arm gave a sudden, contained jerk as the electrodes aligned. "Almost."

"They called me into the Matrevillea location today. Last minute. Their Urgent Care unit is short-staffed."

Liv nodded, speeding through her final morning tasks. "Does that mean Corcoran Regional is going to be understaffed?"

"I don't know." Corey wiped his hand down the front of his face, pausing to knead his temples. "I only had two appointments today, which I'll have to reschedule. Let's just hope we don't have an overflow of immediate care requests. If the city could just hold itself together for a day, Corc Regional will be fine. Did you say you were ready?"

"Just a second," Liv said, just sharply enough that they both angled toward Maura's door to see if she had woken up. Liv tied her tennis shoe, grabbed her crutches, and pushed herself up.

She sat in the passenger seat, backpack and crutches tossed in the backseat upon a pile of unaddressed, empty coffee cups and crumpled paperwork. Corey quietly mumbled an apology to her while buckling himself in; he hadn't gotten to it yet, but he would. He had staved off Liv's helping hand too many times for her to offer to help. She would have had time today to clean it out for him after she went to the bank, but she knew he wouldn't accept it. She couldn't strip that simple responsibility, which made him feel more like a functional adult than his public servant job did, from him.

But the smell of old, dried coffee had begun to sour, and her lack of work meant that she, too, had no method of proving her functionality. Maybe a compromise could be made. She could feel useful, and he could have a clean car. A win-win.

He kept two drinks in the center console between them: a large, metal bottle filled with water and a disposable cup of coffee to prompt his body into alertness before his all-day shift.

The backseat was a graveyard of attempts made and finished.

"Maura says you've been busy lately."

"Bronlow's won't let me come in until I'm done with the cast *and* the brace. I'm so tired of recovery."

"Are you taking it easy? You know you'll prolong your recovery period if you're putting undue strain on your leg."

"I know."

"She says you've been going somewhere."

To this, Liv shrivelled against her seat like a just-poked worm.

"It's okay, you know?" The car rolled to a stop behind a long line of morning traffic. No amount of coffee cleared the plump, weary shapes around his eyes. "She says you've been safe."

"Mhmm."

"And *happy*."

That seemed like a stretch, but Liv thought better than to dispute it. She needed to make a point, maintain their expectations of her safety. She'd be a moron to tell them she didn't really care.

It was, admittedly, untrue. Who wouldn't feel lighter or more hopeful when their efforts were amounting to something good? Her reckless decision to enter the Run again was curing their family's biggest ailment, and her contributions to Vaughn's invention were amassing into the shape of a new, functioning prosthetic. The High Mayor's daughter didn't need to threaten or coerce her into providing input; in fact, she was sickeningly, uncommonly considerate, which often left Liv nonplussed where she had previously been so firm in her convictions.

"I feel," Corey articulated, "some degree of parental insufficiency in that I've never asked you what you want for the future."

"Of course you have."

"Maybe, when you were little," he said. "But back then,

I didn't really know how to talk to you. And things were so different..."

He meant new, hopeful. Back when Liv had first been sent to Corcoran with them. At the time, it was the greatest step any of them could have taken toward a better future. Anything seemed possible. For a child whose reality was bowing under the loss of her mother, all Corey and Maura could do to soothe her was tell her to look toward the future.

That had become exceptionally harder to do in recent years.

"I don't know," Liv said. "I haven't really thought about it."

"You don't ever—I don't know—think of moving out? Think of leaving Corcoran?"

"Where else am I supposed to go? Back to the Holy Commune? No, thank you."

"Anywhere," Corey refuted. "Anywhere in the world. Where do you see yourself?"

Liv's future looked just like the present. It looked like working at Bronlow's Garage until she was old, possibly aging into a leadership role. It looked like dinners with Maura in front of the TV and taking her to appointments when Corey had work. Breakfast, gym, farmer's market, and the Eight Saints bar on the weekend.

Few possibilities existed for someone like her, who didn't have a college education, official documentation of her existence, or any generational wealth to fall back on. This was it. She had to be content like this.

Defensively, she asked, "Do you want me to move out?"

"Oh no! Nothing like that. You know you can stay as long as you want. I just thought I should ask, because—"

"Because I'm twenty-five years old and have no other prospects except getting out of this cast?"

Corey's sigh melted into a defeated laugh. It eased Liv's

nerves to shake off some of the sullenness, even if she didn't know what to make of it.

"I haven't thought about the future in a long time," Corey said. "The present feels so goddamn demanding, sometimes. Like, why should I think ahead if I can barely keep up with what's going on now? Everything is so insular. I forget that there's more out there, over the water. There are three-quarters of the country that haven't been touched by the floods. I don't want you to forget that, not when you still have so much ahead of you."

The density of factory buildings at Corcoran's western border split open. Between this city and Matrevillea, and beneath the border's plain, weather-worn bridge, lay a sprawl of farmland that sloped downward into the old, rushing floodwaters. A cluster of cows gathered around a wood-and-wire fence as if to watch the water below race by. It smelled musty and rotten from the dirty water and manure, even with all the windows shut. Liv wondered what the cows were looking at in the water and what could possibly entice them besides fallen debris from the bridge. She couldn't see it. Instead, over the horizon, the faint intrusion of the Upper City skyline speared through the gaps in the smog.

During the daytime, it looked as unglamorous as any other place. No billboards, no hovering, smug face of Gaines Keaton turning in the sky. Liv could look forward and see Matrevillea just as clearly, cut into a similar silhouette.

"You know, Liv, we would never ask you to leave."

"You could," said Liv, less like a jeer and more like an offering.

"But we wouldn't."

That feeling, which typically only manifested as a persistent, unreachable itch, came back in full swing to make everything ache. She was never supposed to come with them.

Even if they would never send her away, even if they loved her now, she wondered if she stood in the way of the future Corey and Maura once dreamed of sharing.

Liv dropped her weight onto Vaughn's couch with a grunt.

"Sorry!" Vaughn sang from the bathroom. The door was open, and Liv could hear the contents of the cabinet mirror shuffling around. "I'll be right out there."

A full fifteen hours before they were supposed to meet, Liv had been sitting with her big feelings in the bedroom that she was no longer sleeping in, rifling through a box of her old knick-knacks when, at the very bottom, she unearthed the letter that her birth mother had tucked into the pocket of her little backpack before sending her away from the Holy Commune forever. On any other day, this reminder might have afflicted her with a temporal twinge of longing for what might have been, but today, it was a wall erecting, closing her in. Maura had been sitting on the couch, knitting needles clacking furiously through the front panel of a fair isle sweater. Liv couldn't bring herself to break the precarious silence.

However, closed within that wall was her comms device and an unread message from Vaughn Keaton. Liv read it, deemed it important enough to justify a call, and asked if the other girl would be willing to accommodate her this evening. ("What for?" "Just some company.")

Clav's car was parked down the street within what seemed like minutes, two buildings closer to her apartment than usual. "You're not slick," she'd told him, to which he'd laughed and answered, "Get in the car, Shankly. You're wanted at the glass house promptly."

Liv contented herself with simply stretching back against a couch that wasn't her own, one that could fit the entire, extended length of her without relying on the arms, and falling asleep to different noises. However, Vaughn had decided that the situation called for urgency. Liv smiled to herself, listening to Vaughn curse beneath her breath at whatever beast she was currently fighting in her bathroom cabinet.

The Keaton girl came padding out into the living room seconds later, nimbly braiding through the lower half of her hair. She sped through her usual salutations. "Okay. Hello. Good afternoon. How are you feeling?"

"Were you okay in there?"

"What?" Her fingers moved like spiders' legs. She tied the thinning end of the plait and held it like a comfort toy. "Oh. Yes, of course. I was still in my pajamas when you called. I hadn't expected company."

"You got out of your pajamas for this?"

Vaughn frowned, unenthused by the scrutiny imposed on her by her houseguest. "You said you needed to talk. Is everything okay?"

Liv laced her fingers over her stomach. All her big feelings suddenly felt frivolous. Certainly not worth getting out of one's pajamas and into nicer clothes when it was already the end of the day. But if Vaughn had worried over her, she ought to confess. "Sometimes, I think... Sometimes, I think that this is the best I'm ever going to get. That this is the most I'll ever have."

Sitting on the other leg of the L-shaped couch, Vaughn's weight caused Liv's head to loll to the side. Vaughn had changed into jeans, of all things, and Liv could tell only from the seams and the folds around the knee that it was *nice* denim. The stiff kind that lasted forever. Liv's confession must, at least, be worth changing into stiff jeans.

"There has never been a time since moving to Corcoran that Corey and Maura and I weren't struggling with bills. I started racing before it was legal, just to help with the basics."

"Like rent?"

"Mhmm." Liv's eyes traveled up the dark seams of Vaughn's jeans to the belt cinched tight around her waist, and thought her confession must also be worth a stiff belt. "You'd think, on a doctor's salary and a small apartment, we wouldn't need that. But he's drowning in med school debt from his compounded degree, and Maura's got a condition that needs constant medical attention. All his money goes to that. Rent is the least I can do."

"Have the winnings helped?" Vaughn asked. Her face was almost upside down from the way Liv was oriented.

"Yeah. I mean, they don't fix everything. We're paying off debts to our insurer now, but eventually, that money is going to get used up and run out. It's only a matter of time before we red-line again. Corey isn't letting himself take days off. And I'm obviously not bringing in any wages right now. The winnings gave us some hope, but it's impossible to enjoy it when you remember you're going to be stuck in this position forever. And then, what would have been the point of any of this? Ugh."

Liv rolled herself over so as not to be faced with the rest of Vaughn Keaton, for whom she was flaying herself open to try to keep up with. The redness in Vaughn's face from a recent, steaming face wash had begun to subside. The hem of her mohair sweater was only half-tucked. These imperfections, this evidence of incompletion, allowed Liv to bury her face into a pillow and muffle a groan.

Vaughn warily rested her hand on Liv's shoulder. "Would it help if I—"

"You don't need to help. Just..." The problem was institutional. Bigger than her family, than her wages. An infection among the people with the most power, so ingrained in them that the Lower Cities had little hope for reform anymore.

But wasn't Vaughn one of those people? Who could be more equipped to help than someone from whom help would cost nothing? Someone who didn't consider help as a debt to be repaid.

Liv pushed herself up. "I don't know. I'm just spiraling. Happens sometimes. It'll pass, and I'll get better, and things will go on. I just needed to talk about it. Don't worry about it, pinstripes."

This didn't appease the High Mayor's daughter, whose fingers had returned to worrying the end of her braid until half of the strands had broken loose of the elastic. "For what it's worth, I'm happy you came."

"I'm not. I feel guilty that you put on jeans for me."

"If you hadn't called, I would have probably stayed in bed all day. Today hasn't been particularly easy to get through. Papa called earlier."

Vaughn lifted herself from the couch and went to the kitchen, the thought left incomplete.

"Did he say something?" Liv didn't give a shit about Gaines Keaton. She already warred with her sympathy for Vaughn. It kept her awake at night, anguishing over her commitment to animosity toward all the Keatons and the fact that her time with Vaughn was the only thing she looked forward to these days. Liv suffered with subtlety, and she found it impossible to toe a line that made any sense.

Vaughn poured them each a glass of water. "Lunokhod," she said to her intelligent house. "Play the last minute of my call with Papa, please."

The AI, awaking from its slumber, replied, "Playing minute nineteen of call with Papa, March third, twenty eighty-eight."

The commanding voice of Gaines Keaton surrounded them. "Do you really think that'll hold you forever? You've got to do something new, sweetheart."

"I don't *have* anything new." Vaughn's voice spat back. "I've already told you that. Why don't you ask Caldwell what he's doing? Hold *him* to a standard for once."

"You shouldn't be jealous of your brother. It's not good for you two to be fighting."

"I'm not jealous."

A bitter chuckle. "I know you are. But he's the only one who cooperates anymore. Look, let's get dinner next Wednesday, just the two of us. I'll tell Mirata to clear my schedule so we can have a chat about your next projects. How does that sound?"

"I'm busy."

Liv's eyes met Vaughn's as she pushed herself up to a more dignified position. Vaughn typically reserved Wednesdays for Liv, but the rider was always back in Corcoran by dinner time. Liv didn't mind being a scapegoat if it meant Vaughn had less contact with her father. Her conscience was certainly clearer for it.

"Too busy for your old man?" Gaines paused, and a deep breath filled the phone line. "I taught you better than that. Family's all we've got. I never expected Caldwell to be the only one to remember that. Get dinner on the docket with Mirata as soon as you can. I'll be expecting a date shortly."

"Okay."

"I love you."

"I know, Papa. I—"

"Maybe you should reconsider the chip."

The background noise ceased. "Call ended," said Lunokhod.

Vaughn returned to her spot on the couch, and Liv took the glass from her. "When I redesigned the standard police drone, it was postured as a testament to his continued competence in office. He'd been so proud of me. Once the patent was sold to the Kilgarre Corporation, and I could afford a place of my own—*without* help from Papa—he helped me design the workshop and visited me constantly to make sure I was making good use of it. But nothing else came to mind. No new inventions. Nothing that made a difference to him. At first, he would provide me with these ideas for what he considered revolutionary new technology. Stuff that the Kilgarres would want. It was mostly war machines. I couldn't make one of those. Not just because it was morally antithetical to everything I believed in, but because I didn't know how. You can't design widely destructive weapons irresponsibly; they're all meticulously drafted and planned and methodical in how they destroy, which is what makes them so awful. I've never once given myself the chance to think that way or *build* that way.

"He hated that. By the time he realized I wasn't going to make him something he could sell to his favorite weapons manufacturer, I had been falling out of his favor for some years. And Caldwell, who had never given him what I'd given him or done much of anything except garner tabloid attention for his debaucherous behavior, suddenly stopped looking like a fallen angel to him and started looking more like a promising mound of clay with which he could mold a Gaines-shaped mask." Vaughn set her elbows on her knees, looking beyond the glass walls. "He had become impatient for a new toy, it seems."

"Has he always been like this?"

"He used to tell me that people in power must always demand more. So, yes."

"What did he mean about the chip?"

Vaughn lifted the slack hair above her braid over her ear and caressed the red mark. "About two years ago, when Caldwell started endearing himself to our father, Warner Medical asked for volunteers to participate in a trial run of implanted mood stabilizers. I've... cycled through a few different mood disorders with therapists. Different ones tell me different things. I've been medicated for all of them at some point, but no one really knows what's wrong with me. The chip, in its current state, is supposed to affect your mood by responding to triggers you provide via an app. It's on the market now and probably works just fine."

She let her hair fall over her ear again. "That's not the version I had during the trial, though. I was hopeful. I have faith in medical science, and I wanted to believe in the good intentions of doctors. A few weeks in, I noticed the chip wasn't responding to my controls. I swear, it was like someone had decided my commands for it were insufficient or that I didn't know what was best for myself. No one believed me. The chip would do things I never asked it for, and it made me paranoid. My mental fortitude collapsed in a very public and embarrassing way. They found out that something *had* gone wrong with the chip, but by then, I had already been dismissed as a hysterical little girl. Papa was upset I had it removed. I think that's when my trust in him disappeared."

Liv didn't know what to say. Some of the pressure lifted from her chest, and her lungs had filled with this precious, reciprocal confession. She had been bestowed something personal—one of Vaughn's very own Big Feelings. It was an awful thing, but being allowed to harbor it for her prompted a swell of affection she didn't know what to do with.

They each took a large swallow of water and drifted into silence.

"I used to live in the Holy Commune," Liv eventually said, now that her own confessions felt less expensive.

"With the zealots?"

Liv smiled. "Sure." The Holy Commune was a charitable albeit supercilious moniker for the region. Having left it, Liv knew how twisted and hateful it could be, but she never referred to it with such strong terms either. Calling it zealotry aloud was a step further than she usually went. Not everyone who lived there stayed by choice.

Surely, her birth mother didn't either.

"Is that why I couldn't find any information on you at the hospital?"

"Don't read too much into that," Liv said. "Seeing my records wouldn't have made a difference."

Vaughn's lips pursed. She set her glass on the table, leaned back against the couch, and slowly lifted her socked feet onto the edge of the table. "Do you ever miss it?"

A million-dollar question. The Holy Commune would hate her if they'd seen what she had become: strong, butch, non-virginal, and a little uncouth. She did not fit the mold they wanted to stuff her into. The cities, for all their problems, did not run on hate the way that the Holy Commune did, but rather on apathy and a general lack of regard for her life. She was better off in Corcoran, and yet, still in need of so much.

"I don't know. I've been to the Commune plenty of times since leaving; that place is never going to love me. But I miss not knowing what the rest of the world was like. I miss the time when everything seemed so simple, and I was so sheltered. I miss when the cities' problems weren't *my* problems too. Maybe it's just because no one was telling me about all the things that were wrong. I assume they ignore everything that goes on with us." Liv's head dropped down. Exhaustion ripped through her like a shock of cold. "I swear I don't usually get this existential unless I've had something to drink."

"I could get you something to drink if it makes things easier," Vaughn offered.

"I shouldn't. I don't want to know what I'll say if I'm already talking like this now."

A grin baited across the other girl's mouth. She pulled her

knees inward, curling into a knot atop a single, wide couch cushion like a cat. "You should keep going."

"I really shouldn't."

"Why not? I've never been to the Holy Commune. I've always wondered what it was like. If it's as lawless as everyone in the Morg government likes to say it is." She laughed softly, in spite of her best efforts, then covered her mouth with the back of her hand. If Liv didn't know better, she would have thought Vaughn had drunk something alcoholic before her glass of water. Her pupils were hugely dilated, her gaze impossible to pin down. Her head rolled heavily against the perch of her hand. She had stopped fidgeting with her braid, and it trailed half-plucked down to her stomach.

Liv's inhibitions had fled, too, which she noticed only after her gaze had reached the tip of Vaughn's braid. The untethered ends resembled the hard-bristle paint brushes she used to repaint old clocks. She blinked. Cleared the thought. "You want me to take you?"

"Really?"

Liv shrugged. "You won't like it, but I'll do it if you're curious. Just—" she gestured to her cast, "give me a chance to get this off first. Then, we can take the bike."

"The bike," Vaughn echoed, enchanted.

"I get the cast off in a couple of weeks," Liv told her. It was probably the only thing she'd said tonight that was actually worth mentioning. "I'll have a brace for a little while and some PT, but then, we can—"

"Do you need me to be there?"

Need. No, Liv didn't need Vaughn to be there, but she'd reminded her as more than a courtesy. Liv would be getting the cast removed at Corcoran Regional Hospital, where Corey usually worked; having Vaughn there would, in fact, be detrimental to her efforts at concealment.

But it would be nice to have her there. Liv might feel less like a liar and a burden to her parents if she didn't treat Vaughn like a dirty secret around them when all Vaughn had shown her was kindness—unearned, wholehearted kindness. That Liv truly *wanted* Vaughn to be there was an inexplicable, alien phenomenon.

"You think you'll be busy on March 15th?"

"Only with you," Vaughn said, before quickly making an amendment to the too-sincere sentiment. "It's a Wednesday, Liv."

"Right." Liv's fingers tightened around the glass in her hand. She cleared the last of her water in one painful swing, but the heat was still blooming on her face when she replaced it on the table. "Of course it is."

Several days of working on the prosthetic would pass between that evening and the removal of her cast. Vaughn's notebook grew fat with creased, used pages and an assortment of pasted-in notecards. Liv made concessions, won over by the other girl's enthusiastic, overzealous proofs of concept for interchangeable tool attachments and digital control panel designs. Vaughn awaited those concessions and spun results from them like gold. She sent blueprints to her metal fabricators and pictures of her progress to Liv when she wasn't there.

Mid-March came quickly, and Liv had not yet told Corey to anticipate Vaughn's company at the hospital. She joined him for his drive to the hospital and idled alone in the patient waiting room for her appointment time. Patients were called and discharged. Hours passed. Liv had brought only a notebook of her own to pass the time and did not expect to spend so many hours alone, waiting for Vaughn. She filled pages with wobbly, left-handed ink sketches by the time a nurse called her name.

Her left leg looked deflated. She expected it to expand into its original, muscled shape the way a new, plastic-wrapped comforter became pillowy enough to sink into. It needed a thorough wash and a hard scrub, but she was grateful to see it again, even the scar along her kneecap.

Then, Corey came. He sat in the chair beside the hospital bed and handed her doctor the brace on cue. After nearly two months in the cast, Liv was relieved to be one step closer to a functioning left leg.

Soiling this, however, was Vaughn's absence. Liv had scripted several things to say to Corey when she arrived: defenses, endorsements, explanations, and whatever else the situation called for.

"I know you've been sitting here all day," Corey said, "but I can drive you home with me if you want to wait until the end of my shift."

Liv checked her comms device, where a rare text message had been left unanswered and unseen by Vaughn. She turned the device over again, tested the bend in her knee with a pained hiss, and shook her head. "It's okay. I'll meet you back at the apartment."

"How are you getting home?" he asked.

She shrugged. "I'll call a friend."

"If you change your mind, come back inside and tell whoever's working reception that you're waiting on me, okay? I've got to get back to the other wing."

Corey stood and pulled Liv's head close by the overgrown back of her hair. He placed a kiss on her scalp. "See you at home, kiddo."

That small act of closeness brought a well to the corners of her eyes. How stupid she felt waiting on a Keaton, of all people.

She nodded, remaining on the edge of the hospital bed to test more and more weight on her braced knee before she finally stood. Her heart was racing, furious, spurned, and inconsolable. She signed her discharge papers under the waiting room television screen, where the news was on a forever loop, all the changes in broadcasts demarcated by ads for workplace injury lawyers and a frozen meal brand. She sent another text to Vaughn, too pissed to dial her outright: *going home now. see u some other time.*

"Do you need any assistance to the driveway?" The receptionist's question had a pointedness to it, as if intended to break Liv from hypnosis.

"I should be fine. Is there a 33 bus stop nearby?"

"You're Doctor Shankly's kid, right? He told me that I should not, under any circumstances, let you take the bus home."

"You're kidding me."

"It's just a precaution so you don't put too much weight on your leg so soon after the cast comes off. It's quite a walk to the 33," she said, killing Liv's original question with avoidance. "Sorry. We do have resources for cabs if you're interested."

Liv shook her head and resigned herself to the hard waiting room chairs again. Her mind was fuzzy and unsettled, and her ears felt as if they'd been plugged with cotton.

So, she paid little attention to the screen above her head, spiralling deeper into her silent discontent, until a patient in his seventies sitting to the right of her shouted, "Holy shit. Someone got him."

Everyone in the room looked first. Some stood, blocking Liv's view of the screen altogether. With her newly exposed, tender left leg at risk of a sudden trampling, Liv nudged the arm of a woman in front of her and asked, "Hey, what's going on up there?"

She started to cry, her first word to Liv stifled by a violent hiccup. She covered her mouth, and the other side of her hand hid a wide, triumphant smile. "I'm so sorry, hon. I know I shouldn't be smiling, but— Oh my goodness, someone's actually killed Gaines Keaton."

PART TWO

10 —————————————————

Seeing him like this—with eyes shut, forever pensive, and motionless—was not unusual. In recent years, Vaughn's father had become quieter and less present in their conversations, often turned away, kneading his jaw like a tough mound of clay. She knew what his eyes looked like. They were the blueprint for hers and Caldwell's, and since she saw them every day in the mirror, she assumed nothing unusual about them.

The fact that Gaines Keaton's dead body did not look unlike the man Vaughn had spoken to a week ago made her uneasier than the body itself did. The coroner stood with his shoulders against the slick, metal wall, shifting against the handle of a drawer as if he had an itch deep within his spine.

More likely, the coroner had never been faced with such silence from a living person. Vaughn said nothing, and her breaths were equally soundless. The coroner pushed his wire-framed eyeglasses up the bridge of his nose with his knuckle and cleared his throat.

Vaughn's attention lifted from Gaines's covered body on the table. "He looks good." The High Mayor had been dressed in a casual linen shirt, unbuttoned at the collar to expose a pale, almost translucent throat.

"Thank you," the coroner said sheepishly. "I mean, the team has already embalmed the body, so his decomposition process is delayed. The funeral director will give the skin on his face a little..."

"What?"

"I was going to say liveliness, but I don't mean to be insensitive."

Vaughn's nose began to run, and only then did the heat pressing behind her eyes turn equally porous. She hated her father. Hated his carelessness, his indifference. Still, she didn't want him dead. Did she?

Bubbling up inside her was an anger she couldn't place. She'd lost something, surely—not a father per se, because that would imply he had ever been a strong presence in her life, and her relationship with him was as fleeting as the dry season. But his absence meant that he had taken whatever it was with him.

She pushed through a tight breath. "You've done a great job."

"Well," said the coroner. His Adam's apple bobbed above his tight, white shirt collar. For once, Vaughn's anxiety had quieted beneath the larger sensation of emptiness, but she could sense something similar in the coroner, as if he didn't know whether he was allowed to be proud of his job when his job was handling her dad's dead body. Again, he said, "Thank you, Miss Keaton. I'll be sure to relay your gratitude to the team."

He lifted the sheet over the High Mayor's solemn face.

A dreadful thought struck Vaughn. She would have to see him again tomorrow, publicly. Would the broadcast be unkind to her if she didn't weep over him when they televised the funeral?

Outside the viewing area, Caldwell paced back and forth down the hallway, waiting for her to emerge. His back straightened. Then, his arms opened. It was difficult to figure out the protocol for an event that one was not typically supposed to attend often. Vaughn let him hug her, but nothing about the embrace was comfortable. His shoulders were bony, jutting into her arms and her cheek. Hugs were foreign. She half-expected him to pinch her once she was folded into his arms.

"Weird, isn't it?" he said.

The tension of having to perform the right kind of misery drifted away. "I don't want to think about it."

"Good." Caldwell untangled, grasped his sister by the shoulders, and gave her one firm shake. "We're needed at High Hall."

"Right now?"

Caldwell shook out his twisted, unbuttoned suit sleeve and checked his wristwatch. "In thirty minutes, give or take. It's probably best if we don't look entirely wrought with anguish."

Vaughn didn't ask for whom. She could think of no one, except maybe Clavernus Lim, who wouldn't be critical of her reaction. Still, she expected people to take issue with her supposed indifference more than the anguish.

She wouldn't be able to please everyone; this she knew more than anything, which was why she had self-exiled and excused herself from trying to please *anyone*. So, who was Caldwell performing for at High Hall? The officials there—and she assumed they were officials, for only mayoral cabinet members and their invitees had the security access to enter—would not be swayed by the kind of performance that Caldwell put on for his circle of glamorous socialites.

He wore their navy house pinstripe design, a trouser and suit jacket set over a white collared shirt buttoned closer to his throat than Vaughn was used to. His fingers curved like claws around her shoulder. He eyed the coroner over her head as he exited the viewing room, a glint of paranoia hidden underneath his furrowed brows. Under his nose, caught in the dry crust of tissue irritation, was a dusting of white from the previous night's (or possibly, the morning's) exploits.

"Come on," he whispered, corralling her alongside him.

"Let's get the fuck out of here."

She walked half a pace behind him, trying to juggle short conversation with him while she typed Clav a quick message: *he's taking me to High Hall. can you follow?*

"I dismissed Mirata from the house for the next week," Caldwell was saying. "Don't worry. She's been compensated well."

"Isn't she the executor of the will?"

"In due time. She's particularly distraught about Papa's passing." In his tetchy, hastened state, Caldwell let slip an embittered edge into his words. Vaughn was appreciative of Mirata for the distance the woman put between her father and herself. She placed a degree of separation between them that made up the difference between a hot-blooded quarrel with her father and a business-formal email signed, "With regards, the office of High Mayor Gaines Keaton." She was the stone that dulled her father's sharp words before they could reach her.

Caldwell didn't need that sort of sugarcoating. Not when their father's words were proud and glowing.

Vaughn followed him to his car, where a stripe-clad driver ushered them both into an open backseat door. After he shut it, she asked her brother, "What about you?"

"Am I distraught? Are you?"

Vaughn pressed her lips together, patient for his response.

"For all intents and purposes, yes. What else do you want me to say? He was a public figure, V. He had strong opposition and questionable allies. Besides, they're still investigating the murder. We shouldn't be saying anything that draws attention to ourselves."

"They say it was poison."

Caldwell faced away and wiped his nose, and the white powder residue was gone. "And you believe that? Papa was on a diabolical concoction of medications, maybe a third of it prescribed through legal means. We should be skeptical. We should be demanding answers."

It sounded like an instruction. Like a stage director's note for a paltry player. That skepticism was not for the benefit of their father or their peace but for an audience that was always watching.

God, she hated being back in the city.

"You should have warned me about going to High Hall," she said. "I would have—"

"Dressed to match?" Caldwell craned toward the passenger seat and retrieved a matching pinstripe coat. "You had one at the house."

And he had brought it. He'd come prepared. Vaughn's gaze traveled along the stripes. Her cell phone buzzed against her hip, and she slipped it out of her pocket while Caldwell stared out of his window. *I don't have clearance for High Hall,* Clav said. *I'll follow up to the gates. I can't go further than that.*

At one point, she could have weathered anything with Caldwell at her side. She couldn't have anticipated how lonely she would feel having him there now.

Like castle walls, the buzzing, electromagnetic ward wrapped around the High Hall government building with only a heavily guarded iron mouth to allow passage through. Caldwell rolled his window down and flashed his identification at one of the armed Central Morgallis officers, who made an indiscriminate waving gesture to someone in a watchtower before the iron gates parted for the car like hungry teeth.

High Hall was a mystery to most. Anyone who was not a government worker was lucky not to know the building, for the only reason an outsider had to visit the Hall was to face judgment for a high-caliber crime. Having known it for most of her life, Vaughn could not say she had ever gotten used to it. Its white walls were kept clear of storm weathering through several tireless groundskeepers, and its impeccable, stark cleanliness gave it an uncanniness, as if it were a judicial dollhouse fresh from its box.

They stepped out of the car and ascended the long flight of stairs, flanked by a row of guards. "You should put that on," Caldwell said quietly, referring to the striped coat hanging over Vaughn's arm. "We're a united front, you and me. It's just the two of us now."

She took a deep breath and swung the garment over her shoulders. Through the open doors, red dripped from the atrium's staircases and unfurled into patterned rug tongues. The lights were warm, piercing the dark sky like a bullet wound. The mayors of Wagner's Bay and Grollingcross stood at the bottom of the left staircase. At the sound of twin footsteps, they turned, greeting the siblings with a cordial extension of their hands.

It was safe to assume the remaining mayors were hidden behind some closed door. Who else would Vaughn have to make nice with today? The mayor of Grollingcross, a large white man with thinning corn-colored hair, shook Vaughn's hand first. "It's good to see you. I'm so sorry to hear about your father's passing."

Vaughn would have only believed that statement coming out of his mouth. Mayor Levine of the northernmost Lower City lacked a spine, a widely acknowledged fact among his own municipality. Had the Total City been a democracy, he would have been voted out years ago. His time in his local office was second only to Gaines Keaton's.

But the Total City hadn't been a democracy in a long time. So, Levine kept his role by the unspoken decree of Gaines himself. Vaughn wondered what the man mourned most.

A shorter man with oil-black hair and unnaturally red cheeks, Mayor Breunerman, shook her hand next without comment. At Caldwell's behest, the four carried their collective condolences to one of the meeting rooms.

Then, there were seven.

Spread out around the wide, round table, all the mayors of the Lower City stood behind their seats, their stares pointed and unflinching, with all this distance between them. Exactly seven chairs for seven attendees. Whatever Vaughn had just walked into, she couldn't confess to her painful obliviousness. They were expecting her. Probably at her brother's request.

The door to the meeting room shut.

Around the table, the mayors sat the way their cities did around Morgallis: Jeanette Hokada of Corcoran on Vaughn's left; then, Everett Walberger of Matrevillea; beside him sat Iman Jimenez of Leuwe; then, the feverish face of Andras Breunerman; and finally, Edgar Levine of Grollingcross on Caldwell's right. Walberger's fingers tapped impatiently against the smooth, marble tabletop, occupying the silence. Jimenez's eyes slid to Breunerman, distrust ricocheting off the cufflinks of his jacket.

"It'll be an evening funeral," Caldwell said.

"No reception?" asked Levine.

"I didn't want to put that on Mirata. Or myself, for that matter. You'll understand if it's a little soon to be entertaining a big crowd like that."

An unintentional chorus of relieved sighs filled the room, which they all proceeded to ignore.

"What of the vacancy?" Jimenez asked. "I mean, that's what we're here for, isn't it? We can't just make small talk around the situation. A week of inaction this early in the year is going to have a disastrous ripple effect on us."

"Two minutes of small-talk isn't going to bury you, Jimenez," Breunerman scolded. "Let the boy grieve his father. Gaines was still a man behind his title."

"We rely on that title," Jimenez said, thrusting her forefinger hard against the marble. "All of us. I've exchanged my condolences in private. What happens here must be for the benefit of the people. Unless you disagree."

Breunerman put his hands up defensively, leaning back in his chair with an ease and nonchalance that indicated he didn't really care about the grief either. Vaughn suspected they all had that in common.

"She did offer condolences," Caldwell said. "My sister and I appreciate it. We've all needed some time to recalibrate. I wanted to approach this as soundly as possible, and unfortunately, that's meant pausing several of my father's ongoing transactions."

"Transactions?" Jeanette Hokada's voice was strikingly smooth and low. She did not move an inch but wrested the others into her command. "With whom?"

"There was a five-million-dollar supplemental payment to Morgallis PD for uniform updates. Some money for the Warners, the Kilgarres, the Margossis. All the usual suspects," Caldwell said dismissively. Then, in a more serious tone, "I know that all your municipalities are anticipating substantial payouts. Until someone accepts the role of High Mayor, those payments are on indefinite pause."

"Pause?" Walberger's posture stiffened. "Are you saying he didn't authorize the payment? Matrevillea *needs* that money. He's weeks behind on it already."

"We can't wait much longer," said Jimenez. "This *will* bury us."

"My father's second in command won't take the position. We have to find another way to fill his role, even if it's just during the interim of an election."

"It should have always been an election," said Hokada. "As far as I know, Gaines's purported second in command was not elected by the people. Why should we have let them fill that role even for the interim?"

"But that will take months, Miss Hokada," Levine said. "If your cities' budgets need replenishment now, you can't wait to elect."

Jimenez argued pointedly, "What about *your* city, Mister Levine?"

Vaughn cast a sidelong glance at Caldwell, whose jaw tensed and shifted nervously. Under the table, she took out her phone and sent him a message: *How much of this did Papa tell you himself?*

While she refocused on the escalating conversation, she kept him in the corner of her sight. He put his hand into his pocket, then left his phone there, having silenced it.

"Of course, I'm unhappy with the delay," Levine was saying. "You think Grollingcross doesn't rely on Morgallis' money, too?"

Walberger shifted closer to Jimenez's side. "You seem to be implying that this affects us more than it does you, and you know damn well why that is. The eastern municipalities have some of the largest labor industries in the Total City, and yet, we somehow need twice as much in supplemental payouts from Morgallis for basic funding."

"He's right," Hokada said. "If I were you, Levine, I would be terrified for the near future of my city. When was the last time you were rightfully elected?"

"What are you getting at?"

"Gaines keeps that mayoral chair warm just for you," said the Corcoran mayor, "but he's not here anymore. What are you going to do when due process comes back around for you? What do you think the Grollingcross people are going to do with you when the money runs out and it comes time to shake your seat loose? Maybe that's why you're so afraid of an election."

Breunerman, still leaning back in his chair, defended Levine with a primitive sneer. "You sound so sure of yourself, Hokada. Are you going to put yourself up for the position, then?"

The hall went silent. Across the table, glares shot like silver pinballs. Mayor Hokada didn't speak up but stared unflinchingly at the Wagner's Bay mayor, pushing against his ambivalent wall.

Then, with an almost juvenile optimism, Caldwell said, "I have a suggestion."

Vaughn turned to watch him play at politics, and for a moment, she saw him as a child—like they were both children again—playing make-believe with heroic, ambitious visions of the future. When they were young, he had seemed so courageous and had such large dreams. It was the kind of foolish, charming courage that she could laugh at in retrospect, but in the moment, it felt monumental.

"I'm open to hearing it," Breunerman said. Caldwell, like the diplomat their father had begun raising later in life, waited for the others' permission. How lovely and amiable he could be when he wasn't losing himself to the thrill of gambling tables and high-speed races. For the first time in what felt like years, Vaughn admired her brother.

If only she could trust him.

"My father has served as High Mayor for almost twenty years now. Regardless of his designation, few people could rival his experience running Morgallis, if there are any at all. Having grown up in this family, I know that Mayor Hokada is right. This city deserves an election. It deserves a fresh start. I think we all want to give it that, as long as we don't collapse in the meantime.

"None of your cities can afford that time. Not Grolling-cross, not Wagner's Bay. None of them. Morgallis taxpayers have been subsidizing the Lower Cities for longer than my father was in office, and we can't just change that since he's no longer here to authorize the payments. We need immediate attention. Immediate authorization. And right now, my city is in a tenuous state where no one is looking after it. With whatever authority I have, even if it's just my conviction, I would trust any one of you to fill that spot for the time being. Yes, we need an election, and yes, I believe in the letter of the law. But we can't leave your cities without funding. This relationship is symbiotic. Your pillars are as important to the structure of the house as Morgallis is."

Mayor Hokada spoke first, after a long, permeating silence. "This is a delicate, transitional period for all of us. I cannot... reasonably offer myself up for the task without abandoning Corcoran. And regardless of who sits in Gaines Keaton's seat tomorrow, Corcoran will need me to support them."

Vaughn let out a tight, shaky breath as one of the only officials she trusted to take her father's place turned it down.

Then, went the second.

"Matrevillea is an agricultural hub," said Mayor Walberger. "I'm enormously proud of it. They're resilient and strong, and I know they can withstand anything. But I have to agree with Mayor Hokada as well. They shouldn't have to withstand anything more than what we already have. They need me more than Morgallis does."

Then, the third. "There must be someone in his cabinet who is, at least, capable of keeping Morgallis from crumbling during the interim. None of us can be expected to leave our municipalities at the drop of a hat."

Vaughn bit down on the inside of her cheek while the

last two deliberated. "If the other mayors think my position as mayor of Grollingcross to be undeserved," Levine began, "it should be stated that I keep this position because I love my city. It's where I chose to raise my family. My kids. Gaines knew what that was like—to choose family."

Beneath the edge of the table, Caldwell's hand flexed open from a tight fist, unseen by all but Vaughn.

Breunerman, after half a minute of silence, simply laid his hand flat on the table and shook his head, declining the responsibility for himself.

"My father," Caldwell spoke through gritted teeth, which might look to anyone else like repressed anguish. Vaughn could not help growing wary, awakening to a new kind of anxiety. "Our father was not a typical guardian. But goddamnit if he didn't make us. We've spent years watching him run Morgallis. Instead of playing house, we were playing Total City government. I may not have much to my name but his legacy, but my sister has made something wonderful for herself. Papa was always so proud of her contributions to his cabinet."

He smiled, and his smile, like the tension between his teeth, looked like something else to people who weren't Vaughn. It looked trustworthy, dashing. Only she knew—

It's never quite right.

She could hear it in her rider's specific tone, as clear as if she'd been right beside her. Of course, Liv Shankly could see it, too. Liv, whom she had let down, who would feel the effects of Gaines Keaton's death in an entirely different way. Vaughn had a mountain of things to apologize for. Things that Liv wouldn't even know about yet.

Vaughn sighed and gave her brother a half-hearted smile in return. It was earnest, if not a little sad. She had not made Papa proud in years. Why Caldwell had claimed otherwise, she didn't know, but it attuned her to the identity of that loss she'd felt earlier. She would not make anyone proud anymore.

And so, the former child prodigy would fade entirely into obscurity as the small mark she'd made on her father's legacy would soon be buried with him.

Caldwell stood up then, emboldened, and braced his hands on the marble. "That's why I'm proposing that Vaughn Keaton take his place until the next election."

11

The knife dropped in a steady, thumping rhythm through the halved corn tortillas. The basic prosthetic she'd been given was certainly a step up from the original model that Corcoran Regional Hospital's specialist had given her when she first lost her arm, but the finer movements in her fingers were less fluid, less exact. She adjusted her grip around the handle before using the blade to push the pile of tortilla shreds into the pan of hot oil in front of Maura.

Over the crackling of oil, the doorbell buzzed. Maura held up her hand before Liv could drop her knife. People waiting at the front door of the building buzzed the wrong apartments all the time. Maybe they had already realized their mistake and buzzed the right one. Liv stayed at her post, dutifully cutting more short piles of corn tortillas into smaller shapes.

The doorbell buzzed again.

"Are you sure you're not expecting someone?" Liv asked.

Maura looked at the blinking digits above the stove pointedly. Why would she have company at this hour? She shook her head. "It's probably just Corey with his hands full. Go check on him, honey."

Nodding, Liv pushed her chopping board away from the edge of the counter and went to check the front door display. A little, square screen beside the apartment door had lit with a CCTV view of the building's entrance, where whoever had buzzed their apartment number was twisting impatiently on the steps.

Vaughn. It was unreal how sleek her hair was, even through the screen. The girl had her long braid twisted into a knot at the back of her head, light catching each tiny ridge. She turned toward the curb and said something, probably to Clav.

Liv bit hard into her bottom lip and gently tapped her fist against the wall beside the display. She had no calls from the Keaton girl and no texts since before her cast was removed. But she had shown up anyway at an inopportune hour for conversation.

"What?" Liv's inaction had made Maura's spine stiffen. "Who's there? An auditor?"

Liv gave a nervous laugh. The sudden onset of panic manifesting in her stomach might not be too different if the person outside *were* an auditor. She wasn't prepared to face either possibility. "Everything's fine. I'll just, um, be right back."

Before Maura could inquire further, Liv shoved her feet into her permanently tied sneakers and slipped out the door, skittering toward the elevator like a clumsy fawn. Her mind was an unpleasant string of *shit, shit, fuck, why*, until her elevator reached the ground floor, and she eased her clenched fingers apart from each other, shaking them out with her final few curses.

How did one greet the person who had left them waiting at the hospital, with no notice or apology, because their tyrannical father's long-awaited death had publicly come to fruition? Surely, there was no framework for it. Liv's life had become rife with annoyingly singular experiences for which she had nowhere to look for guidance.

She gave herself no chances to dwell on it. Better to dive in now before she could realize just *how* out of her depths she was. She forged ahead bravely and stupidly, hoping something clever would come to mind that made the plight seem less hideous.

"Liv," said the other girl, with such incredulity that Liv wondered if Vaughn knew why she was even there.

She watched the door's latch click into place behind her. "Ah. You haven't forgotten about me just yet."

As Liv faced her one-time benefactor, she was confronted by a dense cluster of colorful flowers. Her mouth paused, suspended mid-*Oh*.

Vaughn extended them until the edges of petals grazed Liv's fidgeting hands. "They're for you."

As if Liv's stupor had stemmed from a lack of recipient specificity. "Oh, um."

"I know flowers are usually meant for hospital bedsides and special occasions, but... I suppose a normal apology is insufficient."

"An apology," Liv repeated, incredulously.

"I know how reluctant you are to let me anywhere near your personal life. You gave me a chance, and I let you down."

Liv took the bundle from Vaughn's hands and inhaled the fragrant blooms discreetly. How was it so difficult to be angry, or *stay* angry, at Vaughn Keaton? It should have been a straight-forward task. "You know, I would have been okay if you'd just given me a heads up, right?" Liv set the flowers on the concrete slab beside them.

"Don't say that." Pulled free from the braid and the knot were short, sparse strands at Vaughn's temple. She smoothed them against the side of her head with an open, flexed palm. "I should have been there. It was important to you. And to me—I swear—"

"Your dad just *died*."

Vaughn flinched as if Liv's words could strike her. She looked at the closing pavement between them, her chin warbling. Clay, who hadn't moved an inch from the surface of his car, lurched forward to console her by simply standing a little closer, quiet and untouching.

"It's a good thing, isn't it?" Vaughn looked at the tips of her shoes.

"For you?"

Vaughn sighed. Of course, the collective response in Corcoran had been elation. Gaines's death stoked a fire under a working class whose spark had long since been dimmed.

Liv kept this to herself.

"It's fine." Unconvincingly, forced through a tight breath, Vaughn said, "We... never got along, anyhow."

She maintained this supposed indifference for a total of three seconds.

Liv scooped the other girl into her arms. Clav was another arm's length away, and Liv held him there with a warning gesture behind Vaughn's back.

A dribble of tears stained Liv's hair and the shell of her ear. Vaughn shelved her arms atop Liv's shoulders and squeezed hard.

"Hey," Liv murmured, "you're shaking."

"This is a nightmare, Liv. He's left us with the most obscene mess, and I fear I've just made it all worse."

Just when Liv thought enough time had passed to release her, Vaughn's words devolved into hiccups. "I'm sure you haven't," she said.

"I just let Caldwell take over a *city*, Liv."

The hand that had been making small rhythmic circles down each of Vaughn's vertebrae ceased its movements. Liv's eyes connected with Clav but only briefly, as he tore them away, suddenly avoidant. *God*, Liv thought, *I've opened a can of worms even he won't touch.*

Slowly, Liv asked, "And how did you do that?"

"I should have known he was going to do something

ridiculous like this. No warning, no discussion. He proposed that *I* take over our father's role until Morgallis could have a proper election, and I panicked. Why the hell would I want to do that? In what world could I do that?"

"Slow down." Liv removed herself enough to look Vaughn squarely in the eyes. "Start from the beginning."

The girl was porous, leaking from her eyes and her nose, while half-intelligible fragments of explanations were still coming out of her mouth. She turned away from both of them abruptly and, in this self-exile, forced herself to take three deep breaths, leaning against the concrete slab on the other side of the steps. "Okay," she declared. "I'm sorry, I just... This isn't what I came here for. Flowers—yes, that's it. I came to give you those and say that I'm sorry, and we can talk about this another time."

"Vaughn."

"God, Liv, it's all so terrible. Papa left a gap in what is arguably the most powerful force in the Total City, and no one else stepped up to fill it. Caldwell knew I wouldn't be up to the task, even if it was only until the next election period, and it made his willingness look all the better for it. What a *saint* he was to step up," she complained. "Some nerve he has, telling me it was for us. I just... God, Liv. Everything's in shambles."

Liv absorbed it slowly. "You turned the role down?"

"What else would you have me do? I don't know how to keep the cities from falling apart. It's not enough to want to make things better if I don't know how to do it—not in a position like that. And Caldwell, much as he thinks he's learned enough from Papa, has nothing but his own interests to protect. Who's to say what those interests are? He hasn't even told me what he wants with the Margossi family or what the purpose of that transaction was. He tells me he's taking care of things, that I should have faith in him, but he's lost to me. I don't know who he is anymore. My parents are gone, and now my brother is too. Everything has begun to implode on me, Liv. Enormous, cataclysmic implosions." Her gaze levelled on Liv, then on her driver. In a much softer tone, she added, "It all feels so immediately pressing and huge to me that I forget that you two aren't feeling it too."

Just then, Clav's mask of concern split, baring a trace of amusement to Liv Shankly. A trace of mean-spirited satisfaction with the High Mayor's death. For all of Vaughn's stresses, she couldn't convincingly say that she'd liked Gaines Keaton either.

"To be fair," Liv said, "it's a bit hard to know what you're going through when you haven't talked to me in over a week."

Vaughn's initial prerogative returned to her: Flowers. Groveling. She covered her eyes and let out a frustrated groan.

Liv squeezed the other girl's shoulder, having exhausted her capacity for earnest and public gestures, like hugs. "It's okay, Vaughn. We're okay. I get it."

"No, you don't."

"Maybe not exactly. I rather like my parents. But, you know."

It was clear that neither Vaughn nor Clav knew, but when the topic of discussion was Gaines Keaton, no one could be bothered to dispute it.

"Look," said Liv, "I can imagine how heavy it must feel to have to deal with all of his shit so suddenly."

Wiping her nose with her wrist, Vaughn replied, "It really *is* shit." Her eyes were bright with the lingering sheen of tears, and they shone with the reflection of the true white bulbs above the doorway. She turned to Clav. An unspoken assurance passed between them. Technically, they had finished what they came to do. It felt final. Too final and too sudden for Liv's liking. At any moment, Vaughn could leave again and take both her confession and her fumbled apology with her.

Such a short-lived truce between them didn't justify all the worrying Liv had done over Vaughn. Her reappearance had ushered in new troubles to fixate on. She'd said so much and not enough. Liv needed to know more. Dread loomed over them, a morbid uncertainty of the future. When faced with the reality—Caldwell Keaton rising to his father's place—Liv couldn't tell whether what Vaughn had done was right. Liv trusted Vaughn more than either of them.

If Liv wasn't careful, Vaughn would push her answers somewhere she couldn't reach.

"You want to come inside?" Liv offered. "We're making dinner right now. I could take her home afterward, Clav."

The driver's eyebrows raised. "Not on your bike, surely."

Liv hadn't intended to take it, but the unfavorable mention of it made her nose wrinkle. "*No.* I'll have a car as soon as Corey gets home. What the hell have you got against my bike?"

"Nothing," Vaughn supplied, then, addressing him directly, "I'll be okay, Clav. I'm... sorry for all the trouble today."

Hesitant, the driver shifted his gaze away from Liv. "Text me when you get home, alright?"

"Of course. And you."

He left with a curt nod. Liv saw him reach instinctively for his packet of cigarettes, abandon it, and climb into the car.

She watched the car leave her block, pass her usual pick-up spot, then disappear into the dark horizon line, because beside her, Vaughn was studying her with an equal fervor that Liv did not know how to face.

"Right." Liv collected her flowers, holding them with the buds forward like the point of a sword. "Dinner. Upstairs."

"And your family."

Like everything else she did, Liv dove headfirst into the problem with shut eyes and unflinching immediacy. She ushered Vaughn into the building and toward the elevator. Maura had probably seen everything, spying through the little screen beside the apartment door. Liv's throat felt thick with anticipation.

"Corey should be getting home any minute," she said. "It's just me and Maura right now."

Vaughn nodded, running through an assortment of minute, gestural preparations to recollect herself before the elevator ascended to Liv's floor. "I'm not an imposition on your dinner tonight, am I?"

Liv hadn't thought that far ahead. She was refusing to think of it to quell the panic.

By the time she had mentally prepared herself for these two pieces of her world to collide at Corcoran Regional Hospital, Gaines Keaton had died unexpectedly, and Liv's glowing opinion of Vaughn had sunk to new depths. Since then, Liv's picture of this moment had gotten scribbled over with a return to (what should have been) normal: reality TV shows with Maura, physical therapy to retrain her knee to bend properly, and sporadic efforts to repair her damaged motorcycle.

What she hadn't been anticipating a return to was this effervescent enthusiasm from Vaughn Keaton to enmesh herself further into Liv's life. The thought terrified her more than any Run.

"No," she said. "No, you're not an imposition at all."

Ding.

Liv placed herself between Vaughn and the parting doors. "Just promise you'll be good to them. Like, really good to them."

"Of course. Why wouldn't I be?"

"I mean it. My family is important to me."

Vaughn inched toward the elevator doors, her head lowered as if Liv's words were reprimanding her for some *inadequacy*, or some lack of understanding. "Yes. I know."

The apartment was cleaner than usual. Maura's dinner efforts were a leftover of her relatively good pain day, the aftermath and reward for a day spent cleaning house, running to the bank, and being otherwise advantageous. Still, some of their furniture sat askew across the living room in a way that made the apartment look like a shaken dollhouse. Liv had pushed one edge of the couch toward the television, the coffee table toward the kitchen, and a chair to the newly open floor space to do her knee exercises.

Maura stood in the kitchen, sliding yet another portion of cut tortillas around in the oil, pretending not to have seen anything.

Liv kicked her shoes off again beside the door. "Maura. This is Vaughn."

Maura considered the girl and, upon recognizing her sans Liv's money-filled backpack, gave up performing her airs of nonchalance. "Oh. I've seen you before, haven't I?"

Vaughn flashed her a smile, unfathomably hopeful for someone who had seemed, just moments ago, like the world was ending. How much of it was true or tried on like a sweater, Liv didn't know. Vaughn's face was full of subtleties that few people knew how to read, but her large eyes and expressive brows were consuming enough to draw one's gaze there first. "Just once," said Vaughn.

Dwelling on it would stress her out.

Liv handed back the flowers and asked Vaughn to find a vase in the kitchen, sending her into the mouth of danger.

She shut herself in the bathroom, turned the sink handle as far as it would turn so the water would spit hard, and dropped her face into her wet hands with a groan.

I just let Caldwell take over a city.

Said like a doomsday prophecy and then buried like the

dead. Above the buzz of smaller panics—Vaughn meeting her parents, Vaughn in her apartment, Vaughn digging deeper into her skin like a thorn—that one sentiment prevailed, daunting. Dinner would be hard enough to handle without the imminent threat of society's downfall hanging over her head.

Downfall was obviously imminent. Otherwise, Vaughn would not seem so bereft. How stable was their government anyway, when the weight of money and the future already rested on Morgallis's shoulders, and the weight of industry was resting on everyone else? She could not imagine it getting worse.

Quiet through the door, Vaughn shoveled politenesses onto her unsuspecting host, and Maura assured her everything was okay; she loved the company. They were making extra chilaquiles anyway. Did she like them?

The fact that no part of Liv's home had fallen apart yet quelled some of the smaller worries. In its wake bloomed a secret relief. Vaughn was here, still in her life, and normalcy sustained.

Her expression was tense and urgent in the mirror. Hot from the strange amalgamation of shame and excitement. Her neck held evidence of the place where Vaughn's arms had wrapped around it, patchy from the warm contact.

I just let Caldwell take over a city.

She rubbed her eyes, dried her face, and returned to the kitchen.

"It's so good to finally meet you," Vaughn was saying. "Liv's told me so much about you."

"Has she?"

With one of Maura's vases on the counter before her, Vaughn carefully arranged the bouquet. "She talks about you guys all the time. All good things, I promise."

"Is that right, Chopped Liver?"

"Yep." Liv swung the displaced chair back toward the table where it belonged. She pushed the couch into place and smoothed out the folds in the rug.

"So," Maura pushed one final portion of tortilla shreds into her pan and spooned out the last of her store-bought sauce can. Vaughn's portion. "Do you see each other often, then?"

Liv laughed at Maura's sideways mention of her mysterious rendezvous. "It's okay, Maura. Acting coy is pointless now."

Maura lifted her spatula like a hand in defense. "I wasn't going to assume."

"Assume what?" asked Vaughn.

Crowding into the small kitchen with them, Liv reached up and over the counter that Vaughn's back was digging into, sliding a drinking glass out of a cupboard. Her upward stretch eased an amused sigh out of her. "Maura has suspected that my midday trysts are something illicit and dangerous. And judging by the look on her face right now, she's jumping to conclusions that are, frankly, worse."

The expression in question was a barely masked, self-satisfied grin. When Maura could not successfully suppress it in front of her unexpected guest, she turned her back to both of the others to re-rack her spices and loudly declared, "Am I so wrong for wanting one of my favorite people in the world to be happy and more widely beloved?"

"*No.*" Liv leaned back against the counter where Maura was cooking, and from here, she could take in both of the other women's contrasting expressions. "That's just not what's happening here. Sorry to burst your bubble."

"Oh!" Vaughn's face reddened with the realization of what Maura was eagerly insinuating, and her hands shot to her hair to twist and fuss with it, only to find purchase on the collar of her shirt when she remembered that she had tied it up. "We're just— Well, we—"

The resulting disappointment on her mother's face in the foreground of Vaughn's full-body alertness made Liv laugh. "Just friends," she said.

To this, Vaughn said nothing. Only folded her arms over herself and squeezed tightly.

"Well, friends are important too," Maura replied, luke-warm. "More so, in fact. But it's not like you've had any of those over in a while either, Livvy, not since Lotte came over to play games that one night. You can't blame me for jumping to conclusions here."

"Who said I was blaming you for anything?"

"I don't know. I was being optimistic. Take this." Shoving a bowl of chilaquiles sprinkled with cheese into Liv's hands, Maura sent her out of the kitchen.

Corey joined the three women after they had all filled their glasses and chosen seats around the table. A space was kept empty for him on Liv's right, while Vaughn sat to her left and Maura directly across from her. His recollection of the houseg-uest was immediate, but any further familiarity with her first name or her family eluded him.

Which was good. Easy. No one spoke about the Keatons, not as a family or the namesake of their dead High Mayor. Neither Liv nor Vaughn let slip her Keaton surname or that she was mourning a sudden, identifiable loss. Although Corey, seated across the table from Vaughn, puzzled over her periodi-cally throughout the evening, he cared less about clarifying any memories he might have had of her than he cared about the fact that Maura had made dinner and set the table for them, a feat she typically did not have the energy to execute.

Beneath the table, his hand clasped hers, and above the surface, a sleepy smile stretched over his face. Gratitude. Relief.

Liv turned to Vaughn, feeling effectively demoted to a third wheel by her parents, only to find that the other girl was an equally dismaying sight. Although the corners of her lips remained upturned from a joke Maura had made seconds earlier, it didn't reach her eyes. She eyed straight through her half-eaten plate, miles away. Her fork rotated slowly, thoughtlessly within her left hand.

If only the same comforts applied. Liv considered slipping her hand beneath the table around Vaughn's knee, leaning over to ask in a dulcet tone, "You still with us, pinstripes?"

But this didn't happen. Until the table was cleared, goodbyes had been said, and they were both shut inside Corey's car for the drive back to Morgallis, Liv wouldn't mention a word about the countless worries simmering beneath Vaughn Keaton's placid exterior. It would lead to a torrent. The second she gave Vaughn space to say more, everything would pour loose like water from a splitting dam.

There was nothing wrong with it. Nothing wrong with being the recipient of Vaughn's Big Feelings. In fact, Liv had a desire, to which she would never admit aloud, to hold all of Vaughn's secrets and quirks. But it would be much easier to do all of that while her parents weren't sitting across a table.

In the car, Liv adjusted the driver's seat and the rearview mirror. The *clicks* of their seat belt buckles reminded her of Clav's earlier comment about her bike, and she sobered to the fact that sitting in her passenger seat was a high-profile Morgallis elite. An ugly fact, Liv thought. She tried to dispel it from her mind, but she watched the road with more caution than usual.

"So." Liv's grip tightened around the wheel. The radio played low. Neither of them moved to turn it off, but neither was listening to it. "Do you want to talk about it?"

Vaughn's cheek lay in her hand. Her body was tilted away,

knees pointed towards her window, and her arm propped against the door. "About what?"

Your family, Liv thought. *Or my family.* Her world presently revolved around those two things, with Vaughn somewhere in the middle; she didn't truly belong to the Keatons, and her status in Liv's life was... unsettled.

"You tell me. I'm all ears."

Vaughn's head tilted imperceptibly in her driver's direction. "Are we really friends, Liv?"

Her tone was undecipherable. "It just seemed easier to say that than to explain our arrangement. I don't want Maura to think... I don't want her to think you're holding onto some bargaining chip against me."

"Ah."

"We don't have to be friends. I know that wasn't part of the arrangement. I'm sorry if Maura's comment about us earlier made you uncomfortable, but—"

"It's not that," Vaughn said simply. She shrugged against the door and held herself tight. "Have you ever noticed that Clav doesn't call me Vaughn?"

"Sure."

"He used to, though. When we were kids and his mother worked for the family, he called me Vaughn. Sometimes V. After she died—after I reconnected with him and offered him the job—he hasn't once called me anything other than Miss Keaton. Makes me feel old. Certainly doesn't make me feel like a friend."

Slowly, Liv reached for the volume control on the dash and shut the music off.

"In my life, there are only two people I confide in who aren't my family. Up until I met you, for a very long time, all I had was this person who I paid to spend time with me, who probably resents me because of my family, who doesn't even call me by my name anymore. I've learned to be okay with that because friendship is hard when you're a Keaton, and everyone has ulterior motives for getting close to you. But then, suddenly, this new person comes into my life, whose only reason for seeing me is to get her necessary mobility aid repaired, who is too afraid to let her parents meet me; but sometimes, she seems to be enjoying herself around me. Sometimes, she shares things with me like she trusts me, and the nickname she calls me has stopped sounding so much like a mean-spirited taunt. She calls me a *friend*. But only because it's easier than explaining the truth.

"I don't know what to call this," Vaughn continued, giving her hand a half-hearted flourish. "This arrangement, as you call it, is the closest thing I've had to true friendship in a long time, save for Clav. But is that what it is? If you can't even commit to calling me a friend after we've left your family?"

Liv's heart surged into her throat. Her skin burned with shame, and her palm went sticky with sweat against the peeling fabric of the wheel. "I didn't mean anything by it. Being the easy thing to say doesn't make it untrue."

"I don't blame you. I'm not angry. You've been upfront with your intentions from the beginning. But you'll understand why I have trouble measuring this kind of thing, won't you?"

In the back of her mind, Liv could hear Clav's voice. *'Miss Keaton has a lot of anxiety. About everything.'*

She nodded, only listening.

Vaughn's placid gaze fixed on Liv's profile, and Liv couldn't help the narrowed sensation of cold in all the points where it wandered, like an ice cube dripping over a scalding metal handrail. Slowly, Vaughn said, "There's something I need to tell you, but... I need to know that I can trust you. And more than that, I need you to trust me."

Sincerity did not suit Liv. Still, she conjured it up when it was needed. "Of course, I trust you."

They were crossing the bridge out of Corcoran, and the lack of cars on their side of the road left the view into the floodwaters below clear for both of them to see. Black stretched all the way down. The sky, starless, fell seamlessly into the abyss. Vaughn's eyes were just as dark, trained on the unyielding clench of Liv's hands.

"I know Caldwell killed our father. I have no one else to tell."

"H-how do you know? I mean, I thought the culprit was still undetermined."

"I doubt anyone else suspects it except me. It isn't like he told me outright, but it's obvious. I know him. I know what he's like and what he's capable of. I had assumed that he and Papa were on better terms now since they were spending so much time together—that I was just the odd one out—but Caldwell has always been preparing for this moment. He played a long game, endeared himself to Papa, and got all his ducks in a row before he could usurp his position.

"In a very backwards way, I suppose I should have had more faith in him. It was always Caldwell who kept me safe and defended me when we were younger. Caldwell, who put himself between us when Papa was in his violent rages. For a long time, we were inseparable. I mean, he has been by my side for my entire life. When he started getting closer to Papa, I felt us drifting apart. I would have never said it to his face, but he was the only friend I had, and it was as if he betrayed me. Chosen our closest enemy over me."

At the end of the bridge, Vaughn lowered her voice like the city itself would overhear her. "After the meeting today, I asked him what he was thinking, volunteering me to oversee the city when he knew I couldn't do it. He told me, 'Of course, you can. You can do anything, V. Because you have me. We have each other. And we can do greater things than Papa ever did, but we have to do them together. Otherwise, none of this would have been worth it.' Even if I think he's wrong and I suspect ulterior motives, his belief in me was real."

Liv didn't respond for a long time. They navigated through the urban sector to the canopied foot of the hill. Vaughn's knee bounced as she grew impatient. What could Liv say? What comfort could she offer? Sure, Caldwell's seizure of power would end up fucking everyone over, but Vaughn stood closest to the source.

She tallied up yet another dreaded, singular experience: *friend's brother seizes unchecked political power, compromising all*. Why could she not have manageable problems anymore?

At last, once her tongue no longer felt like a lead block in her mouth, she asked Vaughn, "Are you going to tell the investigators?

The other girl shrugged, hiding her face in her hands. "What's the point? No one with the power to hold him accountable *will* hold him accountable for it. And how do I prove it? Caldwell has covered his tracks masterfully. He has important people under his thumb, and all I have is a hunch. If I show him I've lost faith in him, I put a target on my back."

"Vaughn." Liv swallowed hard. "Do you think he would hurt you?"

"I don't know. I can't imagine..." She shook her head. "Even if he didn't hurt me, where does one go from there? I would lose my brother once and for all. That's bad enough."

Vaughn buzzed the car through the gate to her house, and Liv parked. A single light outside Vaughn's door turned on when she prompted something on her phone. She was otherwise still as stone in the passenger seat and silent as if she wasn't even breathing. Conversely, Liv could hear her heartbeat in her ears, smashing against her skull. Vaughn angled her head towards her driver but kept her eyes on the steering wheel, where Liv's hands were tightened mercilessly.

"I don't want you to worry," said Vaughn. "I know that's asking something impossible from you."

"That's... an understatement."

"He mentioned a pending deal with the Margossis earlier. He said that Papa had dealings with them in addition to some of his more frequent partners, like Kilgarre Corp and the Warner Company, but I don't think that's true. Even though we spent little time together in the recent months, Papa has told me about nearly all of his current affairs. None of them involved the Margossi family, except for when it had to do with something Caldwell was pursuing, and he seemed to think nothing of it. Like Caldwell's objectives would amount to nothing. He seemed to think they were childish.

"Now, nothing can stop my brother from making whatever deal he wants to make," Vaughn explained. "I don't know what it is. I don't know if it's enough to make him want to kill his own father. But the money he lost at your race can't matter to him any more than this new development does. Now, he has all the money in the city at his fingertips."

That gave Liv only a little comfort. It meant she wouldn't have to fear an auditor or a Keaton family representative showing up at her door to inquire about the money or its source.

But no one should have the kind of power that now rested in Caldwell's hands. He could do anything with it, especially to spite someone like Liv, who had ended up in possession of something she shouldn't have.

Liv said, "It was enough to get him to meddle in the Drone Run in the first place."

"The lack of regulation in your sport made it a perfect opportunity for sabotage," Vaughn said. "He has always been a gambler. Virtual betting tables in the Upper City are too heavily regulated, and in-person betting tables are too crowded with people who'd do anything for dirt on the High Mayor."

"He was playing with lives. Put aside the money for a minute, okay. Not only did he manage to rig the drones; he'd placed a middleman on the course as a contract rider and given him a loaded gun. Someone could have died anyway. *I might have died.*"

"I know. Yet, you're here, and we're in an entirely new mess that will affect more than your races. My point is, he's taking his eyes off you."

"Were they on me before?"

Vaughn's expression softened, and while it made her a blank slate, it wiped clean an expression of concentrated stress and replaced it with something that rivaled amusement. Endearment, at least. This only confused Liv, as the prospect of fielding Caldwell's attention had struck her with paranoia, and the only thing worse than an unfounded paranoia was one that proved accurate.

Vaughn's tone was mostly affable. "Do you think I'm good for nothing? That I have no power whatsoever in this situation? If he had done anything to you, I would have brought something much worse upon him than the law. I'm not the only one with sharp teeth in this family. I just have enough sense to hide it. *And—*" Vaughn pushed the passenger door open, "enough shame to know that I should use my words first. Most issues can be handled logically without murdering our family members. Are you coming?"

"I should probably go."

"It's getting pretty late," Vaughn said, unlocking her front door. "You're welcome to sleep here. I'd be a terrible friend if I sent you back in the dark after all that." Hovering beneath the light in the doorway, she turned and came face to face with a Liv that had followed her much too closely. Liv shifted awkwardly to mitigate the mismanagement of weight on her bad knee. Denying the offer, even if it was for a valid reason—that Corey needed the car to get to work early in the morning—felt like a retread of all the large steps they'd taken.

"I, um." Liv didn't know what to do with her hands. She tried shoving them into her pockets and faced the more uncomfortable dilemma of having forgotten she was wearing pocketless athletic shorts. "I have to get the car back to Corey, because—"

"Of course. Makes perfect sense."

"And to be honest, I think I just need to sit in the empty car for a while."

"Ah." Vaughn lowered her head and pressed her lips into a thin line. "Well, let me finish my earlier thought before you leave."

Liv didn't think she had more room for these thoughts. Not without a long night of sleep first. "Alright."

"You said that participants in the Drone Run don't have any further communication with the organizers, yes?"

"Nothing past what goes on at the Runs."

"So, you wouldn't know how to get in contact with them if you wanted to make an inquiry."

"What are you proposing?"

Vaughn folded her arms across her chest and rested her shoulder against the doorframe. "I suppose, as long as you have no moral objection to it, I could find them through offi-cial records. I want to ask them a few questions about the work they did to override their drones' official police systems. Figuring out how the drones were hacked the first time might provide some insight into their malfunction during the Run. Caldwell may not be a fool, but he isn't a tech genius either. If he hacked the drones, too, he would have hired help. To what end, I'd like to find out."

"I doubt the gamemakers would tell you," Liv said. "A Keaton poking around in Drone Run business is exactly the kind of thing their elusive behavior was supposed to prevent."

"Which is why I'd tell them it was for you. I could tell them you were in danger. Confidentially, of course; you obviously wouldn't have known I was coming to them for help because I wouldn't want to frighten you. They care about you, though. They would share that information if they thought it might keep you safe."

"I think you overestimate how willing they are."

"You underestimate how persuasive I can be. So. What do you think?"

Liv chuckled. "You don't need my blessing, pinstripes. Do whatever you want, and I'll pretend I didn't see it."

That was good enough for Vaughn Keaton. She nodded, stepping backward into the glass house, and it was colder in Liv's immediate sphere, as if all the warmth in the air had come only from her. "I'm sorry for being a stranger these past few days. I forgot to mention that the sculpted exterior hardware for your arm was delivered to me a couple of days ago. I haven't touched it yet. Been a tad preoccupied with other things."

Though Liv simply gave a reciprocal nod, her spirit sparked with hope.

"Do you want to come over on Wednesday to check it out?"

"Sure," said Liv, unable to suppress her relief. Everything around her had become so convoluted that she'd nearly lost sight of the entire point.

Her prosthetic, remade. Her body, just as she wished it could be again.

12

Vaughn's first mention of the wrangler's name was the first time Liv learned anything remotely personal about the game-makers. However, before that, Liv sought information about the Run from only one person, and she was on even thinner ice with them now than she had ever been before.

She walked into the Eight Saints bar with no plan except to find Lotte behind the bar counter and dig for some tidbit of information she didn't already know. Lotte seemed to know everyone or had heard *something* about everyone, which made Liv's continued participation in the Drone Runs possible.

Since that fateful night at the Run, Liv hadn't once reached out to Lotte again; a grisly personal failure, considering Lotte had spent half that conversation trying to remain ambivalent to her over their lack of contact just to prove a point. Liv shouldn't have been surprised to find the orange-haired bartender fuming when she sat down at a stool.

"If you want to know about the next Run, I'm not telling you shit. You have some fucking nerve," Lotte said.

"Hi, Lotte."

"Are you trying to kill yourself?" Lotte slammed her hands down on the countertop and pushed herself up and over. "I don't even know how you're still alive. Actually, scratch that. You survived miraculously and didn't think to call me or text me to let me know that you were still coherent? You are my least favorite person in this bar right now. I hope you know that."

Liv lifted her hands. "Okay, okay. Noted. I'll fuck off after this and leave you to your shift."

"There's no 'after' anything, because I'm not doing you any favors right now."

"Come on, nothing?"

Lotte's eyes narrowed. "Tread so carefully right now, or I'm going to throw a corkscrew at your head. What do you want?"

Liv was responsible when it came to drinking before getting back on her motorcycle. If she had somewhere to be, like another Drone Run, she would ask for a soda or a tall glass of water. But Lotte knew this wasn't Liv's typical order, which was a rum and Coke with cherry syrup. If Liv ordered anything else, Lotte might shut down and go quiet. And Liv *had* come to the Eight Saints bar for something important, something she refused to leave without. Something only Lotte would know, if anyone did.

She ordered her usual cherry rum and Coke and kissed her money goodbye, knowing she could not drink much if she expected to leave any time soon with total mental clarity. Beneath her stool sat a dense pile of her protective gear: her helmet, riding leathers, and some low-profile kneecaps that she typically only used when she raced.

Lotte made the drink with hunched shoulders and imprecise, uncaring movements, but the order—the reassurance— had settled her nerves slightly. Liv hadn't yet let her down. Maybe, she would even grovel again for her forgiveness. What a night that would be.

"You know," said Liv, "the Run's no more."

"Hmm."

"What? Have you heard otherwise?"

Lotte pushed the glass across the countertop gently. "No, you're right. There's no Run. No talk of the next best solution either. So many of the former racers have come in lately to ask. They're itching for money. Is that really why you're here, though? To ask about the Run?"

Liv shrugged, swirling her glass around. "Not the next one. I have about as much faith as anyone else that something like the Drone Runs will exist again, at least within the immediate future. But the last one—"

"You were there for," Lotte finished. "What do you need my help with?"

Liv only had a pair of black knee-length denim shorts and a faded, gray T-shirt. The seams beneath her shoulders were damp with sweat. The protective layers had warmed her up, as did the added adrenaline of being back on a heavy metal beast of a bike. Liv pressed her upper arms to her sides and propped her bare forearms on the cold, hard countertop to lean closer. "You knew about the presence of an Upper City official endorsing the Run that night. Do you know who it was?"

"Well." Lotte's eyes searched for curious listeners over Liv's head. "Not at the time, but I heard about it afterward."

"How?"

"What do you mean, '*how?*' Lots of our patrons go to the Drone Runs, and they all come back to talk about it. You think I wouldn't have heard about your sudden sponsorship from the Mayoral family?"

Liv shifted in her seat. Her friend and informant only had half the story if she thought the Keaton family was backing her. Being supported, even if only for the Run, by Vaughn Keaton was entirely different from being supported by her family. She couldn't expect anyone else to know that. Still, she wondered what else Lotte had heard about Vaughn. What did she think of Liv if she thought the rider was allied with the entire Keaton family?

"It's not what it sounds like. Caldwell Keaton had skin

in the race, a contract rider for another noble family. Do you know who it was?"

"Which family?"

Liv blinked at her expectantly.

In a matter-of-fact tone, Lotte said, "The Keatons wouldn't have a contract racer. It's odd enough that our new little boy Mayor was at the Run in the first place. To have a rider..."

"It wasn't *his* rider, per se. You said it yourself the other night; he was there to bet on someone."

A point of understanding sprouted between them. Their gazes met over the counter, eyes flashing with the bright synthesis of one family name: Margossi.

"What a snake," Lotte said. "And now he's sitting in the High Mayor's office, looking down at us. I hate it when rich boys don't get humbled."

"Cheers to that." Liv took her first drink. It was heavy on the rum and cherry, light on the Coke. She tried not to grimace as she swallowed. Maybe one drink was enough. "So, do you know anything about that contract racer?"

"Depends."

"Don't get precious on me now."

"There's nothing noteworthy about him," Lotte explained. "I mean, he seems kind of *sad*. He came in here before the race, you know. Maybe two nights before you did."

"He's local?"

"I guess. It's not like I've looked him up. He mentioned doing maintenance for an apartment complex and having his hours cut. He was drinking really heavily and had this doom and gloom demeanor that put me on edge. I've had people come in here for their last drinks, you know? I thought I ought to keep him company and see what was bothering him. I couldn't have been more wrong. He had come to the bar to get something really expensive to drink because he was certain that good fortune was about to come his way, and his money troubles were about to be eradicated. I think he meant the Run, but no one is ever so sure about winning. Maybe it was something else."

So much for good fortune, thought Liv. She had shown up at the Drone Run like a lightning strike of bad luck and taken all the money for herself. It wasn't as if she'd been the only one who walked away with any money. Two other racers had received a small cut of the winnings by simply reaching the end of the course.

The Margossi rider was not one of them. And if Lotte was correct, the rider was not some well-off, cushioned Morgallis citizen with minimal stake in the outcome, the way Liv had originally assumed. He could have been her neighbor.

"I need to talk to him," Liv said. "Do you know where I can find him?"

"Maybe. I know where he works, at least."

"Okay. Tell me."

The bartender's tongue poked around in her mouth, and she stared at Liv for a while, blinking as if it was a challenge.

"Please."

"Why should I? You got a problem with him?"

Through gritted teeth, Liv hissed, "Because... Please, don't make me explain it all."

"So, you want me to just give you some guy's residency info because you asked?"

"I thought you said you didn't know where he lived."

"I mean, what are the chances that he does maintenance for a different apartment complex than the one he lives in?"

If Liv had to guess, judging from the amount of time her own apartment building's maintenance team took to answer requests, the chances were not as high as Lotte assumed, but she had a point. That point and that possibility were promising, though. How much would she need to share for Lotte to trust her? As it stood, Liv's needs were still a question, only half-formed. It'd take returning to the night of the Run and the people behind the Drone malfunction to get any closer to an answer.

Eyeing her still-full glass, Liv answered, "Fair enough. He obviously expected to win that night, and he didn't. I want to know what was promised to him in exchange for a win. I suspect it was more than just the money."

"It's always about the money," Lotte said, with a bitter snort. "Whatever you think it's about, the heart of it is probably just money. Why do any of us do anything except to get by financially?"

"Love. Family. Loyalty," proposed Liv. "Money is as important to me as anyone, but I'd still pass up a good payout for you. The people you love should be priceless."

To her left, someone returned their empty glasses to the bar. Lotte left to remove them and wipe the moisture rings off the laminated countertop. "Is that why you're asking me, then? Are you doing this for someone else?"

So what if she was? Her reasons were plenty sufficient, and the problem affected her greatly, regardless of whether the scenario had come from Vaughn Keaton. The problem would affect all of them. They were inextricable from the machine of politics. With no one to catch Caldwell before he could move one, two, or three steps ahead, he could cause irreparable damage.

Before Liv could say anything (she hadn't decided whether she was doing it purely for herself or partly for Vaughn), the bartender murmured, "You *are*. Don't tell me you've started seeing someone who's involved with shady business."

"I'm not seeing anyone, Lotte. And this is hardly shady; trust me, I'm only trying to ask this guy some questions."

"All noble family business is shady. Otherwise, they'd tell us what they're doing, but here we are. You've said nothing that would assure me you're up to any goodwill. Hey, why aren't you drinking your rum and Coke?"

After an exasperated sigh, Liv lifted the glass to her lips and took a minuscule sip, disheartened to discover that the fingers of this prosthetic did not fit the grooves in the glass the way her old ones did. It was such a small expectation to have missed.

"*Please*," Liv said, trying as much as she could to imbue her words with importance. "I just need to talk to him. I'm not here to make trouble for you or anyone else. You have to believe me."

Giving no immediate answer, the bartender busied her hands with various tasks. She turned around and took a drink from her own glass of water, swished it around in her mouth, and pulled a tin of mints out of her pocket. Popping one in, she began to tidy small things across the countertops: glasses, lemon and orange rinds, used metal stirrers. When she returned to Liv's counter, she moved her hands to the cupboards hidden beneath the surface on her side, seemingly to continue her busywork.

Her hands rose to the countertop, one covering the other, which lay flat over a folded slip of paper. "I can't keep giving you free drinks, you know."

Liv didn't acknowledge the hand-off but took the paper and covered it up with her leather jacket as she searched for her wallet. "Now that you mention it..." She slid a one-hundred-dollar bill discreetly toward her friend. "I'm not closing my tab or anything. Just getting ahead on payments."

Thankfully, no one around them cared about their conversation. Otherwise, Liv's flagrant display of on-hand cash might have elicited leering, no-good gazes. Lotte placed the offering in a pocket on the apron around her waist. "You gonna finish that drink up?"

Liv's head tipped side to side in an exaggerated display of indecision. She got what she came for. "Honestly? It's a little sloppy."

The bartender narrowed her eyes and mouthed, *"Fuck you."*

There were few things one could say to come back from a slight like that. So, Liv gathered her belongings from around her stool and exited the Eight Saints, having paid most of her dues. She would have to thank Lotte for the note later.

Canary Marsh Apts, East Corc
his name is Bjorn

The edges of the note furred against her fingertips from the incessant fidgeting. She waited across the street from the complex, a series of three-story buildings spread across a minimally fenced-in block, leaning against her bike. She could have waited until morning, done some basic research on men named Bjorn in her area. But Liv had just taken a performative swig of her rum-heavy drink when she had gotten onto her bike. Whether she was at the apartment complex now out of an unclear mind or by her best judgment, she couldn't say. One thing prompting her to visit the facilities was the fact that tomorrow was Wednesday. If she found anything useful about him now, she could tell Vaughn in the morning.

For good measure, she took out her comms device and dialled Vaughn. At nearly midnight, she didn't anticipate the swiftness in Vaughn's answer. "Liv? Is everything okay?"

"Great," she said automatically, before shaking her hand and backtracking. "I mean, nothing's terrible. Not really great either. Anyway, are you busy?"

After a pause, Vaughn said, "Sort of." *Sort of?*

"Is someone there?" Then, itching the back of her hair, "I'm not interrupting some late-night company, am I?"

Vaughn's amusement was evident in her words. "Yes, actually. I have a hot date with your right arm. Do you hear that?" *Tap tap.* "That's your wrist. I'm assembling the outer shell right now."

Liv's face flared with abashment. It wasn't her business anyway. Still, the thought of existing in Vaughn's private thoughts in some capacity when she wasn't there sobered her up, if she hadn't already been sober. "I hear it. Do you think you could do me a favor?"

"Of course."

"You don't have to panic. Seriously, don't panic."

"Very comforting, Liv."

"I'll tell you all about what I'm doing tomorrow. Just make sure you hear from me in the next two hours. Otherwise... I don't know, get me a lawyer."

With more curiosity than serious concern, Vaughn asked, "Are you in immediate danger?"

Liv laughed and pushed herself off her bike. "No. Probably not. Just felt like I should let someone know to look out for me."

"Okay," Vaughn concluded. "Thank you."

"I— What?"

"Thank you for calling me. You can do that anytime, you know."

"Oh. Sure thing."

"Maybe, try not to put yourself into compromising situations so often, but—"

"This is a one-time thing," Liv assured her. "Honest to God. I'll talk to you soon."

"Okay. Behave," Vaughn said. The call ended, and Liv

tucked the device deep into her shorts pocket. A sudden sense of reservation bubbled up inside her. She had not cared much for her own safety until someone else was keeping tabs on it, which was, perhaps, the point of calling Vaughn in the first place. She turned her attention back toward the apartment complex. The task at hand.

The fence surrounding the complex was impractical for keeping real threats out and was easily scalable. Liv was studying the uneven gaps in the bars, trying to deduce whether she could slip through instead of crawl over. Her knee, still wrapped in its brace, was surprisingly durable, but she didn't want to test it. The main building, in which Liv could see a vacant office, sat near a closed car gate. Pedestrian gates (probably locked) flanked the sides, and thick vines draped over the faded brick pillars that sat on both sides of them.

Surely, the quickest way to get in would be to lug herself up and over and hope the landing didn't fracture her wired-shut knee again.

Her plan entailed no urgency, only a loose displeasure at having to stick her hands in a knot of dark vines that housed at least one family of spiders. Then, around the corner, a vandalized, creaky truck wheeled up to the gate, and the driver non-specifically waved a key fob out of his window at a sensor. Liv could trail in afterward, no climbing involved.

She just had to do it *now.*

The street was otherwise empty. A great convenience, considering she was incapable of looking nonchalant while simultaneously rushing to get across the road and through the gates before they closed. The truck sped through the complex, leaving Liv alone at the entrance. Completely alone. She checked for lights in nearby windows—nothing.

She pulled her hood tight around her face. In her left fist, tucked within her pocket, were some crudely sourced prongs meant to pick a traditional lock, provided the facility didn't have a digitized lock or something else she wasn't equipped to pick. She had come prepared to break and enter. Still, if she could avoid it, it'd save her from legal culpability and lessen her chances of getting caught.

She crept around the main building, sourcing a less visible entrance, and found a door in the back, nearly pressed against a dividing brick wall. She shimmied around it, leather jacket scraping the moss-padded wall. Dropping to her knees, she shoved the ends of her prongs into the opening. Metal scraped metal for a few minutes, punctuated only by Liv's utterances of "shit," every time her prosthetic hand lost its purchase on the tools. Then, with weight bearing on the doorknob, the lock twisted into the Open position. The door split from the frame.

Quickly, she returned the tools to her pocket and stepped into the building. She stood in a short hallway with a restroom and what appeared to be some storage closets or auxiliary rooms around her. At the other end was the office. She opened each of the doors, surveying. A file cabinet, cleaning supplies, a private snack stash, and, to no surprise, toilets. She stopped in front of the small closet and opened up every drawer of the file cabinet, looking for employee records.

She was met with a disorganized assortment of housing applications, transactions with utility companies, and receipts for various services. How they kept track of anything, Liv couldn't imagine. Finding Bjorn's information could take hours.

With two minutes to midnight, Liv began to rummage through the drawers to find some semblance of organization. When she found nothing that hinted at employee information, she deduced they must have kept it somewhere else or in their computer systems. She made for the front office and woke up the computers. She searched through the drawers and underneath the trinkets scattered across the desk for a hidden password or code to unlock the computers. Liv had little experience with computer systems, none whatsoever with hacking them. At last, on the edge of a crumpling notepad page, she found four digits scribbled on down. She typed them into the system. *Try again.* Higher up on the page was a series of 6 digits. Neither set was labelled because, of course, who would make it so easy for someone to log into a private computer system?

Again, failure. Liv shut the desk drawer and returned to the filing cabinet down the hall.

A key turned in the front door lock. Liv froze to see an equally shrouded figure behind the glass, swathed in a hooded sweatshirt and baggy pants. Fumbling over the lock, he didn't seem to see Liv. She threw herself into the closet and closed the door over her. The handles of the cabinet dug into her spine. The sudden force of her body caused the whole thing to teeter and shift against the linoleum with a screech. Liv kept it still behind her back and held her breath.

The man mumbled to himself. Nothing Liv could understand; she barely heard it over the heavy thumps of his boots. He laid something heavy on the floor and stalked into the hallway. Shadow passed over the gaps in the doorframe. Then, a bright light. The sound of a zipper. He was in the restroom directly across from her, pissing with the door open. Liv quietly released her breath when the feeling started to swell in her head. *Flush.*

The man left without washing his hands, flicking the light switch off again. His footsteps only made it into the hallway, pausing just as Liv expected them to grow quieter and leave.

The computer. Liv had assumed, at this late hour, that it would go back to sleep after a few minutes, and no one else would be coming to the office. From where he stood, the monitor's lit surface was clearly visible. His boots twisted against the floor, thumping toward the back door, which Liv had left ajar.

Blood rushed like a scream into Liv's ears. What was he doing here at midnight? This had seemed so simple in her mind. Even if she had set off any alarms, she could still *run*.

It was obvious to him now that someone else had been in the office. "Kiara?" the man called out. "Este?"

Liv bit down on her lip. Her eyes, unblinking, started to burn.

"This isn't funny. If someone's in here, I'm calling the police."

He scoured the front office, circling the twin desks and the front curtains. He typed something into the computer, logging himself in, and Liv cursed herself for the irony of her timing. There were probably cameras. She had expected them, but the most they could confirm with how little of her figure was visible was that *someone* had broken in, not who had done it.

Since she was still there, they could direct the man to her hiding spot. She debated making a run for it, slipping through the back door, and sneaking past the tight wall. That path led to the front of the building, where he could catch her anyway.

She had to face him or find a way out the front door and beeline to her bike. If she could get there, she could outrun him, and that was only if he decided to chase her.

The shadow of his footsteps stopped beneath her door. Liv shoved forward with as much force as she could muster. The wide punch of the door sent him backward, stunned. He had closed both the front and back doors again, but Liv could reach either. She twisted on her left leg and—

She cried out as pain darted up her knee, and her first, most consequential steps faltered. It was not enough to keep her from running, but it was enough to slow her down and keep her within the man's grasp.

His fingers hooked around the edge of her jacket. He

yanked backward hard. "Get back here!"

Coupled with this twinge in her knee, it brought her to a skittering halt.

"I didn't do anything!" She squirmed and pulled against him. "I swear, I didn't take anything! Let me go!"

"What do you want?"

Mercifully, the man released the tension. Liv's momentum sent her toppling onto her wrists. Her fingers scraped the linoleum with an ear-splitting whine. Amidst the larger issue, the noise was what made her flinch. "Nothing! I'm leaving! Don't have to tell me twice."

The man said nothing as she regained her footing with all the grace of a newborn doe. His eyes were fixed on the white fingers poking out of her right sleeve. "You," he said. "I know you."

With her pulse throbbing in her head, Liv reached for the front handle, then stalled. She looked at the man; he was unintimidating, unshaven, and barely taller than herself. The first thing she deduced was that she could take him in a fight, which seemed unlikely to begin, as he seemed committed to balking at the mere sight of Liv's prosthetic fingers.

Hesitantly, she released the handle. "You were at the Run— the Margossi contract rider. You're Bjorn."

"Who told you that?"

"No one." Then, realizing how stupid that sounded, Liv said, "It doesn't matter. I just..."

He raised his eyebrows, the anger and adrenaline still present in his expression.

"You don't usually race for the Margossis, do you? I've never seen you at the Run before."

"I've only done a few of these," Bjorn replied. "What about you? I've never seen you there, yet you somehow swayed the favor of the little boy mayor's sister."

"I wasn't planning on it. I would have rode for anyone else."

"So, what makes *you* special?" He removed his attention from Liv and gave a disparaging huff. "Forget it. What's done is done. Go home."

"Hold on. I have questions."

"You're lucky I'm not calling the cops on you. *Go*, before I change my mind."

Liv demanded anyway, "What was the money for?"

"It's none of your fucking business. You won."

If she had a better sense of self-preservation, Liv would have accepted his dismissal, turned on her motorcycle, and gone home, but she'd wanted this. To face Bjorn and ask her questions. She wiped her sweaty palm down the front of her thigh and proceeded, careful as if he might snap and undo all of his tenuous patience. "I didn't realize you were from Corcoran. I thought you were a contract rider."

"Just for the night," he grumbled.

"I don't know what they were paying you, but I thought, if you were with the Margossis, you would fare just fine without the winnings. I didn't realize you were one of us."

"I've lost races before. All those losses, I could shake off, but not this one."

"You must have known the rules of the Run. No weapons?"

As if he'd forgotten it, the dread of remembrance leeched the color from his face. "Look, I'm sorry. It wasn't my gun. I would have never accepted it if it wasn't absolutely necessary for the money to get where it needed to go."

"Who gave it to you? The Margossis?"

Bjorn shook his head and shut his eyes.

"Caldwell Keaton?"

"What, you're not in on his scheme?"

"No." She laced the word with an impressive amount of disgust. "I don't give a shit about Caldwell Keaton, except for the fact that he's a horrible motherfucker with too much power and bad intentions. I'm not here to help him or do him favors. He has made it my problem, though. He's going to make it everyone's problem unless I can figure out what he was using that money for."

A burden fell from Bjorn's shoulders. He turned his back to Liv and collapsed into one of the rolling desk chairs with a sigh. "Shit. I thought he'd sent you after me."

"For what? It's not like you have the money."

"Ouch. Pour salt in the wound." Bjorn ran a beaten hand down his face. "Obviously, he had a lot riding on that win. He made it clear that it wasn't my business to know what the money was for. All I had to do was win. The Margossis would take sixty-five percent, and I would take thirty-five. Then, we'd all go our separate ways, never to contact one another again."

He folded his fingers together and laid them on his stomach, eyeing Liv curiously, as if he expected her to have a strong reaction. She already knew this, and it only aggrieved her to have broken into a building and potentially re-injured her knee for more of what she already knew. "Wow," she said, carefully perching herself on the edge of the desk. "You would have shot me for thirty-five percent."

"That money was important. Not that you need to know my personal business, but I need insulin, and my insurance isn't covering it anymore. Fixing AC units and filling cracked plaster doesn't pay well. It's only a matter of time before my blood sugar levels go haywire, and the signs of DKA start to show up. Do you know what DKA is?"

"Ketoacidosis?" Liv recognized the acronym from her initial recovery, when her amputation was new and painful. A diabetic girl, only a few years older than her, had recently lost her left foot from incurable ulcers, but she had been further along in her recovery than Liv, and she'd left before they could really become friends.

"Bingo," said Bjorn. "I've got just under two hundred units of insulin left before I need to refill. But it's unsustainable in the long run. I can't manage it with my wages."

It was difficult to hold such violence against him, much as she wanted to maintain a brave, stubborn front. She'd spent most of her childhood in and out of hospitals, watching the healthcare system drain her family of all its hard-earned money and lay waste to their efforts within a single appointment or with one clerical error. Liv herself had taken extreme measures just for a chance to win the Run and undo some of the financial damage her family had long since been taking. After her accident, returning to the Drone Run was no easy feat. For Maura, however, nothing daunted her.

"I get it," she said. "I want to say 'no hard feelings,' but—"

"I *did* shoot at you."

"Right."

"I truly am sorry," Bjorn said gruffly. "Losing the race when there was so much on my shoulders... I wasn't thinking straight. I shouldn't have even accepted the offer for the job."

"You're not a bad rider," replied Liv. "I would have liked to win a fair race against you."

The man nodded, exhaustion clouding over his eyes. "We'll see."

Nothing else at the Canary Marsh complex interested Liv. She pushed herself up, testing her weight on her knee as she prepared herself to leave. "I should go. I'm sorry for breaking into your office."

"I just keep my shit here," Bjorn said, nodding to a toolkit he had deposited near the front door. Liv swallowed and stuffed her hands in her pockets, embarrassed to feel the pieces of her crude lockpick. "I do know one thing that might interest you."

With her hand already wrapped around the door handle,

Liv paused and lifted an eyebrow. Bjorn's expression was unreadable in the dark, from a distance. He leaned forward, bracing his elbows on his knees, touching the tips of his fingers together. "After the Run, I was supposed to hand the money off to someone named Greer. Only Greer. It didn't matter whether any of the other Margossi family members came to retrieve it. The money was meant only for Greer. I don't know if that helps you."

Neither did Liv. But it was something new, something that gave her direction. Greer. Even if Liv had never heard of them, Vaughn could find them.

"I'm sure it will," Liv assured him. "I'll see you soon. Seriously."

"For what?

Her smile split like a stormy sky. "All good things."

13

The gamemakers may not have been intentionally elusive, but Liv had never seen them outside the Drone Runs until she ended up in the hospital again. She had no conception of what kind of lives they lived apart from the Runs, whether they were traitors to the comfort of the Upper City or tradespeople, like most of the people in Liv's life.

She carried plenty of stresses throughout her days, but *people*—with them, she had the object permanence of a toddler. When they were not sitting in front of her, it was easy to forget them, and the people whose roles in her life were neither continuously offensive (e.g., Caldwell Keaton) nor ostensibly positive (e.g., her parents) simply ceased to be.

The gamemakers rested in this middle space, present but not enough to speculate on unless someone asked her to. She didn't expect to find them gathered in Vaughn's house, where the afternoon light was plentiful and exposing, with all the shaders in her walls lowered for anyone to see them.

They were, again, dressed casually and neatly, comfortable but not rich. Hard to place, now that the opportunity to place them was in front of her. They didn't seem to notice her until she was at the door.

Vaughn smiled and waved her through. She was dressed no differently than usual: dark-wash denim trousers and a delicate sweater hanging off her body with a fashionable lack of tension. Liv felt underdressed in her cutoff shorts and a white tank top that permanently bore oil stains from her mechanic job. Being the most underdressed person in a room of two was manageable. A room of four, however, riddled her with an annoyingly persistent insecurity.

The coursemaster (she didn't know if she should get used to knowing his real name, Michael) beamed at her, his hair freshly cut and beard full and wiry. He clapped a hand over her shoulder and pulled her closer. "Look at you. 'S good to see you upright and kicking again."

Both he and the wrangler embraced her briefly. The compression between them drew out of her a muffled, "Oof." The scent of soot and sawdust filled her nose. "Not quite kicking. I tweaked my knee yesterday."

"No," Vaughn drawled.

"Unfortunately, yes. What are you guys doing here?"

The other girl answered first. "We were just discussing the drones. Dr. Tewer was gracious enough to share his theories about how they were hijacked from his control."

The wrangler added, signing, "I'm getting to the bottom of this. This can't happen to anyone else."

"I'm sure it's not your fault," Liv assured him, but no one in the room agreed or chose to acknowledge it, as if they were all in on a contradictory truth, and no one wanted to break the news to her. "Okay. We'll just forget I said that."

"Later," Vaughn said, shelving the topic. Gently, she ushered Liv out of the gamemaker's personal space and to her own side. "Revelations can wait. You, however, have something waiting for you."

A smile nested in the corners of Vaughn's wide eyes. She searched Liv's face for a reply.

"My arm? It's done?"

"Well." Vaughn's head dipped to one side as she weighed her next words, causing the undone tresses of her hair to spill onto her shoulder. "It's only done if you deem it done. It's constructed. I was up all night finishing it so I could get a third-party opinion on it from Dr. Tewer this morning, and possibly— No. I'm getting ahead of myself. The most important thing right now is that it works for *you*. We won't know until you try it on."

The gamemakers watched her patiently. Dr. Tewer's eyebrows were pursed deep in concern, his thin mouth pulling taut across his bony face. Liv couldn't speak, didn't know what to say. She hadn't come emotionally prepared to face this possibility so suddenly. When Vaughn had mentioned working on it the previous night, she didn't think they'd reached the end. She assumed it was merely a continuation of the process.

To face it now, with all of them beside her, rendered her speechless and blank-faced.

"I... um."

Dr. Tewer, whose first name had been predictably lost by Liv's toddler-level permanence, signed once more, translated by Michael. "We'll leave you to try it. We don't want to overwhelm you; we're excited for you, though." Then, after he had stopped signing, Michael added, "You've remained in our thoughts, Shanks. We just want what's best for you, and this is objectively impressive work."

"Oh." Too many times this week, Liv had been caught short on the right words. More than once, she had been reminded of how much she lived in the minds of other people. *And in cutoff shorts, no less,* she thought.

"You don't have to be a stranger," Michael added. "Miss Keaton has our address. Write it down and keep in touch, okay?"

Vaughn's role as a mediator between the gamemakers' unexpectedly kind words and Liv's unguarded feelings was Liv's only defense against the overwhelm. Liv found herself reaching for the other girl like a crutch. "Yeah. I can do that."

Dr. Tewer motioned for Vaughn's hand and shook it cordially. Ever the formalist, Vaughn's handshake was firm and final. No one was holding onto Liv, which felt unfair for some reason. Vaughn thanked him before he and his companion exited the glass house.

"Lunokhod," Vaughn said, without taking her eyes off Liv's. "Lock up, please."

The house gave a cheery, two-tone acknowledgment.

"Do you want it to be a surprise? Like a 'close your eyes and hold out your hands' kind of surprise?" Vaughn moved slowly toward the workshop, stepping backward, with her eyes trained on Liv's face. Liv was paying attention to the slow toe-heel motion of Vaughn's Mary Janes to ensure the other girl didn't trip.

With everything else on her mind, she almost didn't register the question. "Yes. I mean— What?"

Vaughn gracefully cleared the raised edge of the floor mat in her workshops. In Liv's chest, her raised heart rate dipped to a less concerning speed. Vaughn grabbed her by the shoulders. "Wait here. I'm making an executive decision."

"Should I—" Liv closed her eyes, assuming this was also part of the instruction, "take the other one off?"

Metal lifted off the workbench with short, characteristic scrapes. Vaughn did not reply until she had returned to Liv's orbit. She spoke with the sort of reverence that was reserved for prayers. "Tell me if it looks alright first."

The rider opened her eyes. In Vaughn's extended hands was a silver arm sculpted with dozens of thin, polished cuffs. On the outside of the bicep, a sleek, open panel revealed a set of low-profile buttons, denoted only by Roman numerals. In the place where Liv's former right palm had a sliding panel from which all her tools and hand-helds emerged was a similar sliding panel; although its seam was barely visible, tightly closed, whereas the former was obvious and dented.

It was everything Liv's first prosthetic had been—just better. She wouldn't have dreamed this on her own. Her expectations were less ambitious, more grounded in the realm of her capabilities. But this— This had been a possibility all along. It had taken a twist of her willingness, a particular, inflexible series of events, and months of amassing trust to make it real.

"It's perfect," Liv said, strained. "Can I?"

"Please." Vaughn angled it toward her, then paused. "Should I get the connection point?"

Liv hadn't even realized that the arm was half-formed. Only one half of the connection point was attached to the arm, a ring with rivets along its outer face. Its other half, the one that would sit on Liv's skin, she hadn't yet seen.

Vaughn carefully rested the new prosthetic in Liv's hands and fetched a sleeve similar to the one she currently wore. A black tank, cropped higher than the breast, with a high neck and a hole for the left arm, was clamped between the rings of the connection point's other half. It was made of an unwieldy scuba knit. Vaughn stretched it demonstratively between her bony fingers, knuckles going white. "I can remake it if it doesn't work. I found an online forum where other amputees were discussing what kind of fasteners and closures were easiest, and this seemed to be the winner." The closures in question were lined up along the top of the shoulder and beneath the armpit, narrow buckles with pullable, concealable straps. "It should be secure enough to prevent any unnecessary movement. Put it on. Tell me what you think."

As swift as following an order, Liv took the prosthetic and the bust sleeve and closed herself in Vaughn Keaton's bathroom. She looked at herself in the mirror. Her hair was overgrown, and the difference between her dark brown roots and the rest of her dyed-black hair was stark against the white light of the mirror frame. She pulled the tank top over her head and debated on the sports bra. Not even her regular undergarments had these closures. The task of adding them had seemed trivial to Liv, worth saving for a less busy moment.

She left it on but unfastened the closure of her current prosthetic from her arm. She pulled the sleeve over her right shoulder. The silver ring was cold against her feverish skin, and the buckles were quick to fasten and pull tight once she figured them out.

Like her original prosthetic, this one fused together with two silver rings. While the first threaded together with a twist, this one was magnetic, assisted by snaps.

It was also heavier than Liv expected, given all of Vaughn's talk of reduction and refinement. The weight comforted her. The shape *matched* her. The asymmetry of her body no longer hinged on her shape but on her skin: silver and bronze.

She flexed the fingers. No delays. The articulation in her elbow hinge and sculpted knuckle joints was precise and smooth. She shook it out like a dog shaking moisture off its fur. It didn't budge, and she nearly cried. Could it be so simple? Could this feat, which had taken her almost half a year to make half-well on her own, truly have been conquered so fast and without error?

Liv opened the bathroom door, placing Vaughn in the mirror's reflection. She said nothing aloud, but her eyes said, *Come here.*

Vaughn wavered underneath the doorframe for support, bracing for criticism and hungry for approval. Her gaze was on Liv, but Liv was watching her through the mirror.

That hunger was... open-ended.

Liv, generally, did not care about how other people viewed her body. Her body kept her alive through a limb loss and could withstand most of the long hours of work and hard exercise she put on it; to hell with other people's opinions of it. Despite the brief interruption to her usual gym routine, ample evidence of muscle remained on her shoulders, her arm, and stomach, and Vaughn mapped it through a long stare. Curious, voracious, *hungry.*

Liv didn't think this was uncharted territory. Her tank tops did not leave much to the imagination. The sleeve, along with her sports bra, left only her stomach bare, so the difference was minimal. She didn't know how to respond to Vaughn's unabashed study of her. She cleared her throat, twisted her body left and right, and tore her eyes away from the glass.

"It's heavier than I expected. An ideal weight," Liv clarified, raising her fists up to her chin and throwing a few quick punches into the empty space. The thought of all this weighted metal striking someone in the jaw made her laugh nervously. "I love that you just let me be a public menace."

Vaughn smiled. "I do not admit to that. The weight's just a byproduct of the sheer amount of mechanisms stuffed into it. Let me show you how the controls work."

She reached permissively toward the prosthetic and angled Liv's forearm in front of them. She unflipped the panel, one hand on the metal and the other folded softly around Liv's shoulder. If Liv turned her head, the closeness might have alarmed her. Vaughn was close enough that Liv could see her freckles, the scar from her chip removal, and the flutter of her eyelashes in the mirror.

"This one here?" Vaughn's fingers ghosted over the top left button, but didn't press. "It's a general toolkit. The first press will trigger a compact set of tools for you to manually sift through."

Liv pressed it herself, repressing another laugh, when she identified the assortment of compact tools that sprouted from her hand. "You know, I was thinking, when you asked me about what modifications were in my last arm, about having created a Swiss Army Knife of an arm. A Swiss Army Arm, if you will."

"Is that why you asked me to put that in there?"

"It was a pleasant coincidence," Liv said, raising her hands defensively, with her right thumb hooked around her obvious spoof.

"You're ridiculous," Vaughn murmured.

"What can I say?" Liv said, before saying something very deliberate. "I cling to silver linings to get through a life full of bullshit. Sometimes, those silver linings are bad puns. What's next?"

Vaughn walked her through the recall command and the other extensions. She had preserved only the idea and used none of the mismatched, salvaged metal scraps belonging to Liv's first arm. Liv almost felt bad to use it, like she'd been gifted a shiny new toy rather than a mobility aid. She felt she ought to treat it preciously and regard it like a holy relic.

At the end of Vaughn's instruction, the Keaton girl watched her impatiently. "So? Verdict?"

"I think you're a genius," Liv said. "And I think we should celebrate."

"You like it?"

"Jesus, Vaughn, of course I like it. I don't know what I can say that'll convince you if you don't see it already. This is..."

Everything. It was everything to Liv.

"It's perfect," she said. "Thank you."

This restored the confidence to Vaughn's pulled-taut, focused expression. "Do you really—"

"I swear to God, if you ask me if I like it again, I'm going to shake you like a broken vending machine."

Before Vaughn could confirm or deny the prediction, Liv threw her arms around the other girl's stomach and lifted her onto her toes. "I'm taking you out tonight, pinstripes. My treat, as many drinks as you want, okay?"

"What do you mean 'out tonight'?"

"Out of this damn house!"

The rigidity in Vaughn's body vanished as she began to laugh. "Okay! Okay! Put me down before you hurt your knee."

Liv did as she was told. She pushed the stray strands of Vaughn's hair back behind her ears, returning it to its ultra-sleek resting state.

"Don't think I've forgotten your request from last night," Vaughn scolded, but it lacked any fire.

"I know, I know. Yell at me about it later." The small exertion of energy made the blood rush to Liv's face. She felt wild, recharged. "I need to tell Maura the news! I've got to call my friend!"

"Wait, what should I—"

Liv brushed past her, tank top in hand, and left to fetch her comms device. "Just get ready for a night out."

Liv made a fool of herself taking photos for about ten minutes outside of Vaughn's house, but she was a happy fool with no one around to laugh at her. She called Maura after sending some of her favorite photos. Maura struggled to maintain an air of enthusiasm for Liv's new prosthetic. "Honey," she said at last, "I know you're going to tell me all about it when you're home, and I can't wait, but I'm *so* tired right now."

It'd been so long since Liv had a Big Feeling that was so positive. She didn't know what to do with it. She texted Lotte, *BIG NEWS*. Before she could say anything else, Lotte replied, *are u in jail?*

Vaughn emerged nearly an hour later from her bedroom while Liv chugged a glass of water, remembering she ought to pause her excitement and hydrate if she intended to drink something alcoholic later.

This time, she *did* mean to take the bike, which meant the responsibility of safekeeping Vaughn Keaton, the crown jewel of Morgallis, fell onto her shoulders.

She hadn't planned to see a finished arm today and, therefore, hadn't packed her second helmet or additional protective gear. When Vaughn emerged, she stiffly modeled a pair of black, seamed stockings, short-heeled boots with knife-sharp toes, pleated shorts, and the shirt she was wearing earlier, though it had obviously been discarded and replaced at least once.

Liv handed her the leather jacket she usually wore while riding. "Put this on. I can't have the people's princess getting injured on my bike."

"No one is calling me that."

"I'm calling you that right now. The mayorship is a monarchy at this point. I've never met someone who fit the title so well." Liv then handed her the helmet, which Vaughn took after zipping the jacket up to her throat. "Normally, I'd give you different pants too, but we'll just have to make do with what we've got."

"What about you?"

Liv shrugged. She walked outside and ushered Vaughn onto the seat first.

The silver of her arm glowed under the dimming afternoon light. The sight, the familiar weight, made her giddy, like catching a glimpse of a crush somewhere she already knew they'd be. She was eyeing it, studying the sunbeams as they shifted across the sculpted metal, when Vaughn's hand slid around her waist from behind. "Is this okay?"

The words, already quiet in Vaughn's mouth, were further muffled by the helmet. "Yeah," Liv said. "Of course."

She struck the kickstand with her heel and started the bike.

Vaughn's grasp tightened. She leaned forward, flush against Liv's back. The rider's pulse spiked. Her cheeks were hot from the weather, the glee imparted by her new prosthetic, and now, a pretty girl on the back of her bike, holding onto her.

And Vaughn *was* pretty. It was harder to ignore when she was dressed up. She wanted to trace the seams on the back of her stockings like a river on a map. Her hair, possibly the sleekest hair in Morgallis, trailed out of the back of her borrowed helmet and down her borrowed leather jacket.

Liv's things. Liv couldn't divorce her from this unfounded, non-platonic context coming together in her mind. Every part of this position pointed to something deeper.

She kept her head straight, trying to mask the unease without the help of a helmet. Vaughn held herself close, rigid against her rider.

They descended the hill slowly; Liv regarded her own safety with enough importance to know that she wasn't above wrong turns or snags in the road, and a spill with no protection might be the thing that finally ended her.

It really was a miracle that she'd survived two bad crashes already.

The city had a scent she'd never noticed before, a melange of the nearby bakeries' sickly-sweet and the affected savory of dinner restaurants that loaded their entrees up with synthetic flavors. It was only slightly less unpleasant than the fermenting smell of flooded dumpsters across Corcoran that had been forgotten or ignored by the trash collectors. It was ugly because it was garish. She thought she might be the only person in the Upper City to notice it.

Once they'd reached the outskirts of the city, they rode straight across the bridge toward Corcoran. Through the helmet, Vaughn shouted something that sounded like, "Where are we going!"

Liv shouted back, fighting the wind, "Trust me!"

"What!"

She laughed and shook her head. Her hair swatted at her forehead, just short enough to miss her eyes. The sunlight assaulted her bare arms and scrunched-up face. Riding without a helmet was miserable and offensive to most of her senses, not something she did often. Their destination lay close to the end of the bridge, and the steady motion of Vaughn's thumb against her stomach drove her forward.

The speed limit lowered when they reached Corcoran. Again, Vaughn asked where they were going, and with little time left to preserve the surprise anyway, Liv said, "I'm taking you to meet a friend. Her name's Lotte."

"You've mentioned her before."

"I went to see her last night. She works at a bar in Corcoran. I'll have to take you there sometime, but we have other plans for now. All my information for the Drone Runs comes from her. She knows everything. God only knows how."

"Are you going to tell me about what happened last night, or are we going to pretend that didn't happen?"

"A very fruitless attempt at espionage," Liv said. "I found the Margossi rider. He's just a repairman from Corcoran. No Upper City ties or former affiliation with the Margossis. A small fraction of the money Caldwell was moving was meant to be paid to him when he secured a win, but that never happened."

"You're kidding."

"Why? Does that surprise you?" Liv pulled the bike into the parking lot of a nightclub just as the sun disappeared beneath the horizon. Downtown Corcoran had fewer impressive skyscrapers than Morgallis, but they loomed daunting nonetheless, blocking out the light long before the late sunset did. She parked the motorcycle in the back of the lot.

Vaughn unclipped the buckle from her chin and tugged the

helmet off her head. "A little. I expected some sort of allegiance for such high stakes."

"I don't know. You don't think someone in Corcoran could be desperate enough to throw out their morals for some Keaton kind of money? I'm not saying I would have done it, but I get it. I'm thinking of giving him a cut of my winnings. I can't manage to part with much, but he was obviously counting on it."

Vaughn laid her hand against Liv's back. "Don't. You should keep it."

"But—"

"Let me handle it. You *won*."

Liv had nothing to hide her overwhelming satisfaction at those two words. She felt like a winner.

They arrived too early for the club but could kill time and swap theories about the Run at the pizzeria across the street beforehand. Such romance, Liv thought, before quickly scrubbing the notion from her mind. Her emotions were already high. Vaughn's stockings were making her stupid. A slice of cheap, greasy pizza would surely cure her of this compulsion.

Liv took her helmet back and clipped it to a lock-shut latch on her bike. Vaughn's hands were buried in the pockets of the jacket with no intention of taking the garment off, so Liv let her keep it.

They ordered their pizza and took their slices to a corner booth. The noise from the kitchen and chatter around them sufficiently masked their hushed tones as they debriefed. Vaughn leaned over the table and said, "Well, I talked with the gamemakers about the same thing this morning."

"Was that the 'third-party opinion' you mentioned earlier?"

A hard swallow slid down Vaughn's throat. "No, actually. That was something else. I don't know why you thought they'd be unwilling to talk about the Drone Run, though. I only gave the briefest mention of you at first, and they were completely willing to talk."

"And you don't think they gave you any false tips to cover their tracks?"

The slim end of Vaughn's pizza slice dangled from her teeth, hot cheese melting off it. Liv watched amusedly as she tried to take the too-hot bite into her mouth and reply. She spoke through hurried little bites. "I thought so— but— they seemed just as confused— and there's no reason they— there's no reason they should want it to happen again. God, this is good."

"I guess you're right. What'd they say, then?"

"They think I'm placing too much of the blame on Caldwell alone. It had to have been a joint effort between him and the Margossis, and Michael suspects the Margossis were the ones who tampered with the drones, which speaks to my suspicions that Caldwell didn't do it himself. How familiar are you with what the Margossi family manufactures?"

Liv chewed and swallowed a bite of her own and said with a stuffed mouth, "Not at all."

"They make communication technology. The most notable product that's currently being coveted for use in other large-scale projects is a transmission chip—the kind of transmission chips you might find in phones. It's exactly the kind of refined, signal-reading technology that we might have used in the manufacturing of our police drones if we weren't already using Kilgarre Corp tech."

"Do you think it could have been used to override the drones used for the Run?"

"That's their best guess, but the drones would have already had one of those chips installed for the Margossis to establish communication with them, and they keep their drones under heavy security."

"What kind of security?"

"Honestly, I forgot to ask. I was focused on the possibility that the Margossis might have developed something newer that was capable of interfering with the drones *without* an existing connection through a chip. There's no reason why Caldwell would want to buy the transmission chip when we have an existing contract with Kilgarres, because it's only incrementally better. But if the Margossis had developed something that could override existing transmissions between weapons tech? That might be worth a ploy like this."

Vaughn took another bite of her pizza and made a low hum of enchantment. Advancements in high technology seemed to happen far away from Liv. If it reached her, it only did so in the form of widespread surveillance, like the new police drones, which she avoided at all costs. She couldn't comprehend the ramifications of that kind of thing. Not like Vaughn could.

Liv stared at her pizza, lost in a memory of the drones' black eyes locking on her. She said, "The rider gave me the name of the person he was supposed to hand the money off to. Someone named Greer."

The girl across from her perked up visibly. Softly, as if only speaking to herself, she asked, "Greer? What would Greer want to do with Caldwell?"

"You know him?"

"Her. The Margossi family consists of parents, Girard and Trulia, and three kids: Margitte, Greer, and Emmanuel. Greer, famously, had a falling out with her siblings, who hold a majority of the power over the family empire. A quick online search will tell you she doesn't partake in their business past leaving with her cut of their profits. It's a public point of contention. Why should she be making any deals on their behalf?"

"Maybe that's why your brother was passing money through the Run instead of legal means. Maybe it wasn't family business.”

“But what would she have that the rest of the family doesn't? She has, notably, the least amount of involvement in all their manufacturing and invention processes.” Vaughn lowered the half-eaten slice of pizza in her hand into the metal tray. “I suppose I could just ask her.”

“Are you friends?”

Vaughn gave a loathsome scoff. “No.”

Liv waited patiently for the rest to come out, with only the hum of the kitchen fan to serenade her. A lonely minute passed wherein Vaughn picked up and set down the crust of her slice repeatedly. “I don't have friends, Liv. You know this. I wasn't trying to be hyperbolic about it, but it's the people like Greer Margossi who pushed me to become this...“

“Guarded?”

“That's a generous word for it. I'm surprised you didn't know this. I figured, after our initial meeting, you might have looked me up. I don't know what's online about me anymore. I avoid it at all costs. It used to be filled with things about us.”

“Were you, like, an item?”

Vaughn smoothed her hair behind her ears. “I don't know. The last time I saw her in person, she was telling a friend of hers how she would do anything to secure a deal with Gaines’ administration for her family's latest tech, including fuck me when I was one of the dullest people she'd ever met. So, whatever we were before is a moot point.”

Liv had never heard Vaughn Keaton swear. A word as stubbornly commonplace in her own mouth as ‘bathroom’ or ‘pothole’ sounded like a proper curse when the other girl said it. It shook the hunch out of Liv's posture. She blinked, registering the sentiment slowly, as if the information was being delivered to her through a strainer; and in the weave of that strainer, through which all other, less important information passed through, was written: *Vaughn says 'fuck.'*

She then promptly apologized for it. "Sorry. You didn't need to know that."

No, that information could only make Liv's unwelcome, uncharacteristic fascination with Vaughn harder to shake. She did not need to think of anyone fucking Vaughn Keaton right now, especially when that person was assuredly wrong.

"Don't talk to her," Liv said. "We can get around her. Figure this out some other way."

"We ought to try first. I suspect if I sent her a message saying I wanted to make amends, she might open up about my brother—"

"Greer Margossi can kick fucking rocks. Don't do that to yourself, Vaughn. We'll think of something else."

Vaughn pressed her knees together and wiped her palms back and forth along the tops of her thighs. Her eyes lost focus somewhere past the table. Liv's questions had pushed her somewhere that Liv couldn't follow. She roused to attention when the cook shouted out an order number. She smiled at Liv, quick as lightning. "Yes, of course. Sorry, my hands are just a little sweaty."

"I didn't mean to dredge up buried history."

"It's not that. I mean, it's a little of that. I'm nervous to meet your friend. You said her name was Lotte?"

"Yeah, why?"

"I should be prepared. I haven't done something like this in a long time," Vaughn said. "Not with new people. Do you think she'll like me?"

Liv did not bother to train her expression and simply stared at the Keaton girl with the puzzlement of a newborn discovering his own toes. The earnestness of the question warranted an earnest prediction. Liv studied the version of Vaughn Keaton in front of her and momentarily let herself be swept away by it. Large, bright eyes. Full, pink lips with a rounded Cupid's bow. Vaughn's neck was long and slender, and the undone top buttons of her blouse accentuated an untouched plane of skin that Liv sought to press her cheek against.

And the sleekest hair in the world.

Lotte would probably overlook all of it after a minute in Vaughn Keaton's presence. That's what Liv had done. Pushed aside those huge, pleading eyes with a reminder of her surname, who she represented.

But Liv had been wrong about Vaughn.

"She's going to love you."

Vaughn rolled her eyes. "You're just saying that to make me feel better."

"So? Even if I was, it's because you have no reason to be nervous. Lotte's a bit neurotic, but she's a lover. She loves *me*, and I'm a non-responsive bitch who never tips her at work. There's nothing wrong with you, Vaughn. You're not *dull*. You are probably one of the most interesting people I know."

Vaughn propped her chin up on her palm and sighed, unconvinced. "Are you going to tell her who I am? That I'm a Keaton?"

Liv leaned forward, pushing both their trays of pizza aside. "What do you want me to do? I'll call you whatever you want me to. Whatever makes you comfortable."

After some consideration, she said, "Just call me V. Should be easy enough to remember."

V. They could be separate entities in Liv's mind, both brilliant, both enigmatic. If Liv bisected the idea of Vaughn into separate people, it meant she could also leave one of them right in this moment, perfectly preserved and willingly departed. This feeling she had—this unshakable, gruesome desire—to thread her fingers through Vaughn's hair and trail them up her stocking seams? That was V. And V didn't have to last longer than a night.

Liv took an obscenely large bite out of her side-swiped pizza and said with a full mouth, "I hope V knows how to tear up the fucking dance floor."

14

On the count of three, Liv and Lotte downed their vodka shots. Liv coughed a little, turning in her seat to hide the overwhelm in her face. Lotte wiped the moisture from the corners of her lips and squared Vaughn in her sights. "Are you *sure* we haven't met before?"

Vaughn's answer was a belated and long-drawn drink from her own shot glass. The off-duty bartender hadn't thought twice about Liv's companion upon their first introduction, except for a pause to place her in some forgotten context.

"She's not from Corcoran," Liv supplied.

"Most of the people I talk to aren't from Corcoran," said Lotte. "It's crazy how busy the Eight Saints gets sometimes. It's not some prolific establishment by any stretch of the imagination. I mean, we pass all of our health inspections, don't get me wrong. It's just that the stability of the place is kind of unfounded. Liv likes to bother me there all the time."

"All the time?" Liv laughed. "I thought you said I didn't come round enough."

"Two things can be true at once."

They sat huddled on the edge of a small table on the outskirts of a dance floor. Drinks here were meant to be consumed quickly and then discarded, unlike at the Eight Saints, which was expected to house steady drinkers for hours until they sobered up. The effects of the Vodka rapidly took root in Liv's body. To her left, Vaughn's body began to lose all its sharpness. In front of them, the frizziness in Lotte's orange hair looked more like a halo, catching the pulsing, neon lights.

"So," Lotte said, "let me see the arm."

Liv laid it on the little table, squirming through the tiny glasses and other tableware. She gave Vaughn a proud smile as Lotte admired its craftsmanship. "This is amazing. *You* did this?"

Vaughn nodded. "It wouldn't have been possible without Liv's previous design, though. It was all her ideas, her prototype."

"She's undercutting herself," Liv interjected. "She's a genius. Truly."

"Where did you learn this?" Lotte probed.

Vaughn's brow furrowed. "School?"

With a laugh, Lotte said, "I forgot that some of us actually went to college. Geesh. That's sobering to think about."

"Stop thinking about it then," Liv said. She trapped Lotte's wrist in a loose grasp and tugged her up to her feet. "I told V to expect dancing, and I aim to deliver."

It wasn't late enough for the crowd to fill the floor. The early birds sipped down their drinks, not yet drunk enough to justify looking stupid in front of others. Liv Shankly had no reservations when it came to looking stupid. She was generally hard to miss, more so with her silver limb, whose panels picked up the light like a disco ball. She had come to dance, to shake Vaughn out of her shell, and feel like a person again; personhood came with a slew of embarrassing Big Feelings like this.

Lotte feigned reluctance as she slid off her stool, but Liv couldn't have asked for a better dance partner. She motioned to Vaughn and mouthed, *Come on.* Vaughn danced with only half her body, with eyes still clear from the alcohol's influence. Liv wanted to take her by the shoulders and shake her until her composure shattered. There was no point in taking oneself seriously on the dance floor.

Liv took Lotte's hand and spun her, her orange hair fanning around her from the pinned-down points of her barrettes like a cocktail umbrella. Lotte spun herself deliberately into Vaughn's orbit just to pull her closer to them.

She leaned forward and whispered something in Vaughn's ear that Liv didn't catch. They laughed together, looking right at her.

"What?" Liv shouted over the music, but no one responded. Lotte added something else for Vaughn's ears alone. They laughed again until Vaughn's face turned as red as the strobe lights and Lotte doubled over mid-sidestep.

Whatever it was, it opened Vaughn up like a music box ballerina. Lotte took her in her arms and spun her too until her face held no remnants of reservation. It made Liv dizzy to look at it. The melange of affection and desire and joy dizzied her as much as the motion did.

She blamed the vodka. It could turn even the shittiest dance joints into heaven, a foggy warehouse made beautiful and rich with drapes of an ephemeral gauze.

The purpose came together like a symphony. Liv threw away any pride she might have been holding onto and gave herself over to the music. The song sucked. Terrible, terrible high-pitched vocals and a grating synth. She could dance to anything with good company. She had only the best beside her, around her, enjoying her.

For a moment, it was enough to absolve herself of all the usual aches of living. She took Vaughn's hand and dragged her closer. Close to her ear, still swaying to the shitty music, she said, "Told you."

"Told me what!" Vaughn shouted.

"To trust me. You look like you're having fun."

Vaughn's brows furrowed; she couldn't hear. "What!"

"I said—"

Vaughn laid her hand on the back of Liv's neck and drew her even closer, until Liv's mouth touched the shell of her ear. Liv grabbed the other girl's shirt for balance. Suddenly winded, she repeated, "I said you look like you're having fun!"

Vaughn looked at her, losing count of her steps and the rhythm, with her hand still on Liv's nape. "I'm having a really good time!"

Liv knew she was still moving, still dancing, but everything felt impossibly distant when Vaughn was right here, right in front of her. Touching her. Holding onto her. Faintly, she registered those long, knobby fingers in the back of her hair, with no other purpose than that they could be there.

"I need to get some air," Liv said.

"What!"

"I need to—" She looked at Lotte over Vaughn's shoulder. A challenge flared in Lotte's eyes. *What are you going to do, Liv?* "I'll be right back!"

Liv's fists unfurled from the fabric of Vaughn's shirt, and she fled. She passed the coat room, where her jacket hung forgotten, then the bouncer in the front. He stared at her, assessing her for signs of a struggle. No struggle. She just couldn't juggle the effects of a single shot of vodka and someone's hands in her hair. She gave the bouncer a nod. He ignored it.

She fell back against a thigh-high brick ledge jutting out of the wall and dropped her face into her hands, groaning.

"What's wrong with you?"

Liv did not look up to face her curious friend. "Go inside, Lotte."

"I should have known something weird was going on when you asked me to hang out outside of work. You brought me here to third-wheel."

"Please don't say that. I need this to be as platonic as

possible."

"Oh, Liv." Lotte smoothed her hand in comforting circles across Liv's upper back. "That's even worse. Third-wheeling at least gets me a free drink. Now, I've just got to deal with a crisis of denial."

"You're such a dick."

"And you're being a fucking baby."

Liv pushed herself upright with a sharp intake of breath. She paced along the sidewalk, scraping the back of her neck where Vaughn had touched her. "I'm trying to rationalize the way I'm feeling right now. Telling myself it's just pent-up sexual frustration and not, like, feelings."

"Why can't they be feelings?"

"Because she's—" Liv turned around and searched the blank, smog-bloated sky until she found an answer. "She's great. Genuinely. Such a good person, Lotte, you have no fucking idea. But she's a *Keaton*. That's Vaughn Keaton in there. Tell me I'm crazy."

"I mean... She is incredibly attractive."

Liv put her hands on her hips and glared at Lotte. Her tongue poked around in her mouth. She took several long breaths, which did nothing to slow her racing heart. "That was so helpful, Lotte."

"What do you want me to say? I trust you, Liv. I don't know why I do, because you suck sometimes, but I do; and if you trust her, then she can't be that bad. I hate the Keatons as much as the next person in Corcoran, but you're making a big ask of me to ignore her good faith when you're showing off the prosthetic she made for you. Now, put on your big girl pants and go inside. You ran out of there like a startled cat."

Liv planted herself back on the ledge and returned to her former head-in-hands position of wallowing. Her mind cycled through those pleasant, needful sensations she wanted so badly to ignore. Vaughn's hands in her hair. Around her stomach. Liv's lips against her ear. Pulling her closer, closer, closer.

The door opened, and Vaughn poked her head out curiously. "Hey. Are you feeling okay?"

"The vodka shot isn't agreeing with her," Lotte said. "I should have told you. Liv's a lightweight."

Vaughn stepped fully out of the club's doors. The warm wind sent her hair into disarray, and she tried in vain to tamp it down with her hands. "I started to think the worst."

Lotte's pitch rose almost mockingly. "I wouldn't discount it. I certainly wouldn't send her back in there any time soon."

"Should I take her home?"

"No," Liv said petulantly. "You're having a good time. Go have a good time. Don't listen to her."

"It's not a good time unless you're having a good time, too," Vaughn replied innocently. "Come on. I'll grab your jacket and call Clav for a ride."

"V…"

"Do you need a ride, too, Lotte?"

Mercifully, Lotte declined. "My place is honestly so close, I could just walk. Shame, though. I was having a lot of fun. You should come around the Eight Saints one of these days, V. Our drinks are significantly better than the ones here."

Vaughn smiled graciously and continued fussing with her hair even when it proved useless. She left to collect Liv's jacket from the coat room, and once the doors closed behind her, Liv swatted irritably at Lotte's arm. "You're tormenting me. 'Come around the Eight Saints, V.' Terrible, terrible girl. You awful, sinister—"

Vaughn returned, leather jacket over her arm and cell phone held up to her ear. "I *would* have given you a heads up if I'd expected to be here. I'm sure she's fine. Obviously not sober enough to ride home. Yes, we took the motorcycle. Don't give me that tone; I was perfectly safe. Well, I don't think Liv was expecting this kind of reaction either. Alright. Goodbye, Clav."

Simultaneously, Liv's and Lotte's eyes turned to the ground, and they pretended not to have been listening so voraciously. If Liv was lucky, Vaughn's driver would find badgering her about her motorcycle while she postured insobriety to be pointless and leave her to endure the ride home in silence. She contemplated whether it would be impossible to slip inside and down another shot beforehand. A second might ease the nerves, dull the effects of the first.

"Are you sure you wouldn't like a ride, Lotte?"

Lotte pressed her lips together to hide a smug grin. "That's nice of you, but I'm fine. Thanks. I'll see you around." Then, to Liv, she said, "Text me?"

Liv waved her away. Lotte wasted no time in making herself scarce.

The music pressed through the walls, leaking onto the darkened street. Liv's head swam with unease. As strong as its effects were, the shot didn't last her long, and it left her alone with thoughts that were entirely her own. Dreadful, she thought, to think this much.

Vaughn slowly approached her, perching delicately against the ledge beside her. "Was I too forthcoming?"

"Don't pay attention to her," Liv said.

"She's nice."

For that, Liv was both grateful and annoyed. All concerns related to Vaughn Keaton's identity had been undermined by more trivial concerns, like affected libidos. She had given Vaughn a good time. Lotte had been kind, made Vaughn feel welcome. Liv sabotaged her own celebration. She couldn't think of anything else except how awful wanting someone felt when you could not and (under any circumstances) should not have them.

Vaughn tilted her head back against the wall, shut her eyes, and sighed dreamily. She was still in the haze of the music, in the allure of the nightclub. Liv dared not pull her out of it, not even to commiserate. She gazed at her profile, down the column of her neck, clear of mind. Maybe she was not entirely sober, but she was sober enough to recognize that her fascination had turned to something deeper and irreversible. She'd reached a point in the metamorphosis where she could no longer remain ignorant of it.

The corners of Vaughn's mouth tilted upward. Slowly, she asked, "Do you think changing the world can be accomplished without the world watching you?"

The question evaded Liv. She had no clue what Vaughn was talking about. Mentally, they were in entirely different places. "I don't know. People who try to change the world tend to make a lot of noise. Why?"

Vaughn opened her eyes, tracing a map of her thoughts in the smog above them. "I think *we* could change the world."

"How so?"

"What do you mean, 'how so?' We're already doing it, Liv."

Before Liv could press the subject further, Clav's car turned onto their street, and Vaughn buried the conversation. "God, that was quick. Do you want the passenger seat?"

Liv did not take the passenger seat and felt rather small sitting behind the begrudging driver and Vaughn, whose vodka shot had plied several more big questions out of her. Liv let the driver field those questions, still stuck on what the first could possibly mean. Neither she nor Vaughn addressed each other for the rest of the ride to Morgallis.

She didn't think about what that meant for getting home until the car pulled up to Vaughn's house. Her bike was still at the club. Her home had been less than half an hour away from it, and yet, Clav brought them to Vaughn's place for the night, and he ushered them out of the car, eager to return to whatever nightly routine they'd stolen him from. He'd retrieved them in his pajamas and shooed them away so he could return to his bed.

"Thank you!" Vaughn waved from her doorstep. "You're my hero!"

Clav shook his head mirthfully and rolled his window up.

Still running through possible interpretations of Vaughn's statement, Liv asked, "What did you mean earlier?"

"Hmm?" Vaughn threw her keys onto the kitchen countertop and danced her way toward the refrigerator. "Oh. I was being a little overzealous about that. I should have waited to bring it up until we were sober."

Questions meant for sobriety stressed some extra level of importance. Vaughn's slowness in getting to the point caused Liv to become unfortunately aware of all the places on her body that itched. Vaughn poured a glass of water and slid it across the counter to her. Then, another for herself. She took a large gulp of it. "I got myself into a bit of a jam now. Made you curious. Sit down. Make yourself comfortable."

Vaughn disappeared into the workshop for a minute, leaving Liv seated on the couch at a loss for comfort, her mind jumping to outrageous conclusions. She grabbed the remote from the coffee table. If she was meant to spend the night here, she should find something on the television that made it feel more like home. A new episode of Matchmakers and Heartbreakers premiered in less than ten minutes.

Vaughn returned with several things in tow: her black notebook, an assortment of the physical blueprints for Liv's arm, and some other unfamiliar pages. A pen poked out of her shorts pocket, and when Vaughn sat beside Liv on the couch, it popped out and skittered several feet away. Neither of them moved to retrieve it. "Like I said, I wasn't intending to ask you about this after a drink, but it'd be equally wrong not to explain it if I already brought it up."

Liv had seen most of the work before, but Vaughn—this current iteration of her, slightly buzzed, rosy-faced, and chipper—seemed new. Liv paid more attention to her mannerisms than to the papers she spread out on the coffee table in front of them. "Earlier, when Tewer and Golovsky were over, and we were discussing their thoughts about the drone malfunction, I asked them to take a look at the arm and the blueprints. I hoped Dr. Tewer would have something to add to it. Some words of wisdom or even a criticism. Anything to make it the best it could be. My intentions— No, not my intentions. My late-onset hope was that the technology for this could be used in different kinds of prosthetics."

Atop the arrangement of blueprints, Vaughn laid the stack of unfamiliar pages down. An application. Dense paragraphs filled several of the top pages, interspersed with blank lines meant for names. Liv flipped through them, looking but not truly reading. "But it's not my decision whether this tech has a future in later prosthetics," Vaughn continued. "It's yours. It was always your project, your need."

"You made the thing," Liv said automatically.

"For *you*. I didn't make it for anyone else. Still, now that it's done, I can't help but think of how many other people could benefit from work like this. It's useful, and according to Dr. Tewer, it's foolproof, and I think—"

Flatly, Liv interrupted, "It'll be expensive for people, won't it?"

Quiet and gleeful, as if they were entertaining themselves with gossip, Vaughn said, "Not if we don't want it to be. Yours cost me a bit of money only because of the sheer amount of trial and error that went into building those bones, but now that I know it's possible... How much did your first prosthetic cost?"

Liv couldn't remember. Her original prosthetic, prior to her modifications, had been the least of her concerns, as the hospital stay and the amputation itself took up the bulk of her medical expenses. She remembered being offered something nicer, something refined and less bulky, and choosing the tarnished metal prosthetic because she could not afford more when every second in the hospital's care meant money spent. Money her family did not have.

She eyed the polished silver wrist perched atop her knee. "I don't know. I don't know if I can agree to that—to put something into the world with a price that's unworkable for the people who need it. You lose a lot of money when you lose a limb, V. Not just in medical bills, but time off work and recovery, and the fact that it can become less simple to do things you used to take for granted. I can't make something inaccessible."

"Then, we'll make it accessible," Vaughn said as if nothing could be simpler. Liv wished everyone had that kind of conviction. If relinquishing profit was so easy to do, why could none of the other healthcare executives and pharmaceutical companies do it? Vaughn placed her palm against Liv's left bicep and squeezed, soft and reassuring. "We can do whatever we want with this, Liv. Price it at just enough to recover the costs of production. Keep manufacturing private and out of the insurance companies' hands. But none of it happens until you're ready for it."

"What does this even mean?"

"I want to patent the technology for the prosthetic," Vaughn said sternly. "Not to become another predatory tech guy leeching off the people in need of it, but to make it widely available. I..." Vaughn released her grip on Liv's shoulder and folded her hands in her lap. "I was reading through that forum a couple of weeks ago. Almost *half* the people contributing to it were from Corcoran. The number of people who have become amputees from manufacturing jobs and construction work who get completely discarded after they've become less useful is sickening."

Liv had heard this statistic before in recovery. Bronlow's garage was small and shockingly safe, so she hadn't seen first-hand how common it was for workers in the factories around her to lose hands, arms, or feet until it had happened to her; then, she saw other amputees everywhere. It comforted her, in a weird way, to know that she wasn't alone, but it didn't make it easy. None of them deserved the bullshit the world put them through after their limb loss. They had a solidarity rooted in trauma.

"My offer to help you remake your arm seems rather small-minded in hindsight," Vaughn continued. "What we've done—what we've made together—could help so many people, Liv. And as long as we have our names on it, we can decide to make it as accessible as possible. I asked Dr. Tewer to look over the materials I had. I know what he's worked on. He knows patent requirements, and he says we're ready. We just have to say the word—sign the papers."

Liv reached a page in the application that required a series of signatures. It would be easy for Vaughn to sign it on her own if Liv said no, and Liv felt a strange sort of duty to the people she had grown up with to keep that from happening.

But Vaughn wouldn't do that, would she?

Liv trusted her in spite of herself. Where, at first, trust had been wrenched out of her by circumstance, she gave it willingly, intensely. The expectation that Vaughn Keaton would one day fulfill all the disappointment her family had fed to Liv throughout her life had never been met. Why should Liv keep waiting for that to happen when she didn't want it? When she wanted so badly to be proved wrong?

Liv could trust her just a little longer, too. She tidied the unbound stack of application paperwork. "Let me think about it."

It took a second for the lack of emphatic agreement to register in Vaughn's brain. "Yes, of course. We've been drinking. Shouldn't make these kinds of decisions while impaired."

Contrary to what Lotte had said about Liv's earlier behavior, Liv *could* manage her liquor well. Her mind was crystal clear. Her conflict, intricate as an arterial map. She hadn't asked for time just to sober up; having time at all was valuable and made her feel rich.

Vaughn pressed her hands against the pile of paperwork and pushed it toward the opposite end of the table. A long sigh traveled through her entire body before she deflated against the back of the couch. She pulled a pillow against her stomach and held it tight. "Such a long day." When Liv didn't respond, she added delicately, "A good day, though. I haven't had many of those lately. What the hell is on my screen right now?"

Liv chuckled. "Only the finest reality dating show to sweep the city. Give me one of those pillows."

Vaughn passed a pillow from the opposite end of the couch to Liv, which promptly got stuffed under her head in the corner of the L-shape. Even if she felt sober, fatigue enraptured her. She thanked God for Vaughn's couch and pillows, for her begrudging driver, and the glass of water in front of her. Sleep would catch her sooner than she expected.

She expected Vaughn to move after a while. The couch was plush and obscenely clean, but it wasn't nearly as spacious as a bed. Vaughn left momentarily—Liv assumed to retire from the couch for good—and she returned in her pajamas, with two pillows under her arm and a pile of folded blankets in her hands. She placed one set on the long end of the L for herself and unfurled a second blanket over Liv's body. The extra pillow, she placed on the short end of the L for Liv to grab whenever the urge arose.

"I'm still awake, you know," Liv told her.

Vaughn crawled beneath her own blanket, compacting like a fist under the fabric. "You looked cozy, though," she said, looking anything but cozy herself. Liv glanced at her as she absorbed Matchmakers and Heartbreakers with the utmost studiousness, not brave enough to move closer to Vaughn and show her how to come undone.

Liv closed her eyes. The pillow smelled faintly of floral conditioner. Like Vaughn Keaton.

"Goodnight, Liv," she said. Ever cordial, ever the good host.

When Liv dreamed, it was of having her arms too full of a kind of flower she had never even seen in person.

15

By morning, that dream had morphed to one of a stone-toothed woman made of steel structural beams and stiff, soldered joints looking down at her. Liv woke to an ache in her side. She had forgotten to take her prosthetic off and had spent hours with her ribs shelved against the metal. Among other things she'd forgotten: a call to Maura to tell her she would be gone.

She jolted upright, felt around her shorts' pockets, and found them empty. She abruptly pushed herself off the couch, sucking in a sharp breath to combat the discomfort compacting in her torso.

"Good morning," Vaughn said, standing in the kitchen. Liv wasn't used to sleeping in. She typically rose the earliest among her family, although she had been less strict about it during her time off from work.

Liv rubbed her eyes. The shaders in Vaughn's glass walls were at total light transmission, and the sun beamed white around her. "Hey, have you seen my—"

"Your phone *thingy?*" Vaughn hung the spatula in her hand over the lip of her skillet and fetched Liv's comms device from the countertop. "I answered a text from Maura. I hope that's alright."

"You— huh?"

"You left it in your jacket, and it started buzzing. I sent her a text and told her you were at my house, not to worry, et cetera. It's a neat little device."

Liv flipped through her message history and saw Vaughn's cheery, polite text alongside a response from Maura that read, *thank you honey!!!!* She blinked as if the amount of accompanying exclamation marks had deceived her. Maura was always excited for people to visit, for Liv to have friends worth bringing over. Still, Liv found it odd how little her inner conflict of befriending a Keaton, even one so outwardly considerate and altruistic, seemed to extend beyond herself.

Once the events of the previous night returned to her, Liv's mind was rife with exclamation points tied to no particular coherent thought. She responded atonally, "Thanks."

Vaughn returned to the thin, crisped pancakes on her skillet. "These are almost done. Sorry if I woke you up."

"No, no," Liv said. She couldn't be ungrateful about having breakfast made for her. "Weird dream. Bad ache. I don't usually sleep in my prosthetics."

"Oh. I didn't realize," said Vaughn with an unintended upward lilt that indicated she didn't know whether an apology was warranted. Liv had grown to expect all the weird things well-wishers would say to her about her prosthetics or her amputation; this was hardly unusual.

"Consequences of my actions, I guess."

Liv meant it to be a joke about her ruse of insobriety, but forgot that Vaughn wasn't in on it. She made herself scarce and escaped into the restroom down the hall before Vaughn could ask how she was faring, assuming she was hungover from a single shot, and Liv would be forced to admit, for the sake of preserving her dignity, that she was most definitely *not* so easily conquered by alcohol.

She turned on the faucet, rooted through Vaughn's shallow wall-shelves past an intense selection of pill bottles for a face wash, and slathered it en masse on her cheeks. Hangover aside, she felt awful. She had awakened to the sickening after-effects of last night's comingling shame and desire. It toiled in her stomach like sour milk. She scrubbed her face until it turned red, then flushed her mouth out with water and mouthwash since she lacked a toothbrush. Whether she knew what she wanted from the girl in the kitchen, she could not set a precedent of morning breath.

Pancakes and a mug of coffee waited for her at the counter, as did Vaughn. "I watched several episodes of Matchmakers and Heartbreakers last night."

"Those are, like, forty minutes each."

"And yet, I couldn't bring myself to look away. It was like being back in high school, being surrounded by all the worst people I've ever met, and they were all kissing. Terrible show. I sat through four episodes, at least." Vaughn cut her pancakes with such neat knife incisions that put Liv's side-of-the-fork squishing to shame. "We should do that again, by the way."

Liv gave an indiscriminate, "Mmhm," stuffing her mouth.

Vaughn poked at her pancake pieces but did not eat. Liv's appreciation of the food was encroached upon by the fact that she didn't know how to satisfy Vaughn's suggestions. She could only stay silent until her pancakes were gone. Then, what? "I should go soon," Liv said. "I told Maura I would do something with her today."

Vaughn accepted this as truth, albeit with evident disappointment. "Will I see you soon?"

With her prosthetic rebuilt, Liv no longer knew what the future of their relationship looked like. It had hinged on the completion of her arm, on a work partnership.

And, sitting on the coffee table behind her, was the patent...

"Of course, if you'd rather not—"

"I want to see you again," Liv assured, wincing at how formal it sounded. "I'll have to see what Bronlow's says about me coming back to work, first... Talk to Maura and whatnot."

Vaughn took her first bite and chewed with fervor. She chewed for a long time through such light, soft dough that Liv wondered what else she was trying to break with her teeth, whether she was eating to spite a feeling that was eating through her.

Liv quieted that speculation before it could become something equally as torturous within herself. She pushed it down, swallowed an unchewed lump of her breakfast, and met Vaughn's bedraggled driver outside the glass house.

Her day continued, overcast with a harrowing feeling of disquietude. These penetrating, vague feelings itched at Liv more than the overtly terrible ones did. They hid in sidewalk cracks, nearby sewers, and gaps in doorframes, impossible to evade entirely. She pulled her motorcycle into the parking garage beside her apartment building, and she felt it all around her in the ugly yellow light. She lingered in the garage for a while, tilted atop her bike onto her uninjured leg, kneading an ache in her jaw that had come from an hour straight of gritting her teeth. She could not remember how she responded to Vaughn's touch and thought needlessly hard about whether she hadn't just brushed against the other girl's ear but kissed it, either out of muscle memory or simply because she wanted to.

When she touched down onto the cement, the creaking metal beast shook her from her stupor. Every sound was an invasion. Every bodily sensation, a reminder of where she was. Part of her mind was still tied to the interaction, her body still reeling from being touched, and she didn't want to let that go.

The elevator ding was the worst offender. She was back in Corcoran, in the shitty two-bedroom apartment that couldn't keep the smell of smog out even with its lack of windows. Liv stood outside with her eyes closed and her forehead tilted against the front door. She hadn't been far from home last night, but it felt worlds away, like an impossible timeline.

She stepped inside. Maura sat on the couch, chewing her nails, flipping through the pages of an open book. "Hi, Livy."

"Hey."

"You know what day it is?"

Liv checked her comms device for the date. "Did I forget something?"

"I don't know," Maura said. "Were you not planning on going down to visit Lilia this year?"

Something sharp hit Liv through the dull malaise she'd been wading in. Her birth mother's birthday was only two days away. By this time, she had typically begun writing her annual check-in, a letter she spent collective hours each year poring over to deliver to her mother, Lilia Gonzales. Then, she would ride down the unkept bridge out of the Lower Cities to the Holy Commune and deliver it. It was her only thread of contact, her mother's only reminder that Liv was alive and well, doing her best even if she was not necessarily thriving.

"Oh." She had expected to feel worse about forgetting it, like the guilt of forgetting might flush away the more trivial guilt she'd been feeling over acting stupid at a club, but the tradition had, historically, only ever left her feeling hollow and disenchanted. Each year, she drafted letters for Lilia, divulged her hopes and fears about living in the cities, and took the hours-long journey to deliver them to the station on the edge of the Commune, but her mother didn't respond. Liv couldn't even say for certain that Lilia read or received them.

Still, Liv wrote to her year after year. Stopping now would signal a fundamental change in Liv's life that she wasn't sure she was prepared to face. The thought of letting it go and giving it up frightened her more than the prospect of forgetting to write another unacknowledged letter bothered her.

Liv peeled her jacket off, hung it beside the door, and said simply, "I'll go."

Maura nodded, turning another page in her book. It was a diary; Liv noticed dates in all the upper-left-hand corners, as well as a glazed, distant expression on Maura's face. Liv went to the bathroom to brush her teeth, moved by a sense of urgency that something was wrong. She eyed Maura's motionless figure through the open door. The room was silent, save for the sound of her spit hitting the basin.

Liv went to the couch and sat herself gently beside Maura. "You okay?"

Maura's eyes flashed to the silver arm and lit with a sudden remembrance. She forced a smile on her face. "Much better now," she said and shut the book. "Look at you... Your arm, it's—"

She trailed off and never picked up her discarded thought. She clasped the width of it between her hands and traced the panels with her thumbs. "How do you feel, honey?"

"It's perfect," Liv said, sidestepping the real question. "Vaughn had it waiting for me when I stopped by yesterday."

Maura pulled Liv closer and nestled her cheek against the connection point at Liv's shoulder. Liv was tilted at a discomforting angle, but she didn't move. "What's going on, Maura?"

"Nothing. Just a lot on my mind."

"You want to talk about it?"

"I don't want to make you sad. This is such a big moment, I think?"

Liv lay back against the couch and sighed. "I don't know." She stared at the diary on the table. She had never seen it before. Maybe it was so old, she'd overlooked it.

"I just want you to be happy," Maura said. "That's all I was thinking about."

"That can't be it."

"It is. I was thinking about how much change we've put you through. We've had this breath of stability in our lives, but it feels so temporary, like it could be taken away any second. We didn't have much when we lived in the Commune either, but at least we knew what to expect. The same people. Same routines."

"We have that here," Liv said, trying to assuage Maura during an emotional tailspin that felt all too familiar to her.

"It's different," Maura replied. "Corey told me once that he felt like he was always walking on trapdoors, and the ground could give out beneath him at any moment. We were, at least, adults when we left the commune, but you were so little. I don't even know if you remember what it was like back then."

Liv didn't want to remember. The things she did remember from the commune—vignettes of a past life—were so vague and universal, like scraping one's knees or being late for school, that she often found herself recontextualizing those memories with the city behind her instead. There was no place for her in the Commune now. She didn't have the stomach for yearning, for cultivating beautiful, impossible hopes, not when she worked so hard to write the patterns of her survival in Corcoran.

"I wish we could give you more here," Maura said. "It breaks my heart, knowing how much you do for us. How much you've lost for us. You shouldn't have had to do that. You're our baby. We should have been able to protect you from that, just for a little bit longer, and we couldn't. I feel like I failed you."

"Maura," Liv said. "You did nothing wrong."

"Then why wasn't it enough?" she said. "It was our job to keep you safe and show you how to be an adult in due time, but you grew up so fast. Your childhood lasted all of ten seconds." At this, Maura squeezed hard and began to murmur various terms of consolation. "I want you to be so happy. So so so so so happy, Liv."

For all that Liv lacked, there was no shortage of love in her life. The fact occasionally fell into a recess in her mind because love alone could not keep her alive; the world ran on money, and it was hard to feel rich with anything when life was draining them of any tangible wealth they had.

But without that effusive love and limitless belief Maura gave her, she probably wouldn't have cared so much about anything else. The world she lived in was, otherwise, a smear of dogshit that wouldn't dislodge from the tracks of her shoes. She wanted to make it better for the people she loved, build something they wanted to live in.

Maura wiped her nose with the back of her wrist. "Did you have fun last night?"

Liv couldn't stomach this conversation. She nodded, compliant and easy.

"That's good. Didn't drink too much, I hope?"

"Barely anything," Liv answered, scoffing. "Wish I had."

Without pressing the question, Maura scraped her fingernails in acknowledgment across Liv's arm. "Things are going to be okay one day, Liv. I can feel it. I don't know when, but it'll happen."

To be 'okay' felt like a modest goal, but it was enough for Liv. She just had to maintain it.

She considered the patent. Considered Vaughn again. She had wanted to sit with the thought of the patent on her own before sharing it with Maura, but she supposed she could sit alone with it afterward, too. "Vaughn was thinking... Well, I'm thinking about it too, now. About patenting the technology inside the arm and manufacturing it more widely for other prosthetics. I don't have all the details yet, but—"

"You're going to sell it?"

"I don't know. I haven't decided."

"Is there a catch?" Maura grabbed her near-empty glass of orange juice from the table and stood to refill it. "Otherwise, why wouldn't you? You could make some extra money, maybe even reduce your shifts at Bronlow's. I don't know how profits work with that sort of product... There are a lot of disabled people in Corcoran, though." Then, Maura looked at her squarely. "You *are* doing this for Corcoran, aren't you?"

Liv's expression soured. "Of course I am. Why else would I do it?"

"I don't know if you owed your friend a favor. Favors are dangerous things when you're that rich."

In her throat, Liv's breath grew dry and tight. She had assumed that Maura didn't make the connection between Vaughn and the Keatons. It was possible that she still didn't. Vaughn's Upper City wealth was apparent, even when the knowledge of her family name wasn't.

Liv didn't know if she should tell Maura. If Maura didn't already know, it could ruin all the goodwill she felt for Vaughn. She might regret the comfort she had given over the recent loss of her parent when she found out that the parent was Gaines Keaton.

Liv couldn't blame her for it, but she was struggling to balance a new kind of affection for the Keaton girl, and she could not risk reintroducing animosity.

"I'm not trying to outprice the people who need it," Liv explained. "I'm not even sure if I'm going to agree to this."

Maura handed Liv a second glass of orange juice, which Liv took a large mouthful of before her toothpaste came back with a vengeance.

"I think you *should*. And, if you get a bit of extra money from it, you'll do what's right with it. Pay your bills, stay afloat, clear our debts... Why shouldn't you be allowed to do that?" Maura said this as if it were the simplest matter in the world.

Everything weighing on Liv's mind seemed to weigh so little to everyone else. She wished that thought comforted her. She wished it was all in her head, that none of it truly mattered.

All it did was make her feel like she was facing this grand battalion of inconveniences alone. Shouldn't it have mattered more to them? This thing she had with Vaughn. The potential of becoming the kind of person who had made their lives miserable.

Maybe she was giving herself too much credit. She was a Corcoran mechanic, not a pioneer of industry. She wouldn't disrupt anything. It was enough that she could make anyone's life easier in her small way.

Maura studied the pinched expression on her face. "Hey. Look at me. You've got a good head on your shoulders. *And—*" she prodded Liv's sternum with a bony finger, "a great capacity for compassion. If I trust anyone to take care of us, it's you."

"Thanks, Maura."

"And you have me in your corner for sage wisdom."

Liv deadpanned, "So sage."

Maura lifted her feet onto the coffee table and sifted around her body for the remote. She didn't allude to what had initially been troubling her. Liv was home, which meant she could now catch up on her reality TV show and put her concerns down for a nap.

Liv paid weak attention to the screen. She sat back with her hands folded over her stomach, cycling through a zoetrope of images. The patent paperwork. Her vodka shot. The game-makers, grinning at her.

Vaughn. Vaughn. Vaughn.

Every time the thought settled back onto her, Liv held onto it just a few seconds longer.

16

"Put this on."

The rider handed Vaughn a helmet. The occasion was informal. No tempting seamed stockings. Sufficient riding protection for each of them. This, Liv could handle.

Vaughn turned the helmet over in her hands, mapping the dent from the police drone's dart. "Do you want me to fix this for you?"

Before Liv could slip her own helmet onto her head, she replied, "Do you know how to fix everything?"

"No. If I did, my brother wouldn't be the mayor right now."

Vaughn was zipped up tight in Liv's spare leather garments. She swung her leg over the back of Liv's motorcycle, and she took a few seconds to readjust the bulk collecting around her joints. She was saying something Liv couldn't hear through two sets of padding around her head. Liv twisted around, grabbed the sides of the other girl's dented helmet, and searched for the button on the outside of the right ear.

Vaughn twitched in surprise; the command functions turned on with a sudden middle-pitch beep. Liv pressed the button down in a particular pattern until their helmets were paired. "Is that better?" she asked Vaughn.

"Very much so."

Liv had mentally prepared herself for this moment. She nudged the kickstand back with her heel, and the Keaton girl laced her arms around Liv's midsection, drawing closer. The visor of Vaughn's helmet applied a gentle pressure against the back of Liv's. This was just the way two people rode together. Nothing new. Nothing that should keep Liv up at night.

Folded into her jacket pocket was the envelope marked with Lilia's name. As Vaughn adjusted her grasp, Liv felt the paper bend, the corners becoming sharp within the jacket lining.

It was Lilia Gonzales' birthday. Liv would fulfill two promises today. "Are you ready?"

Vaughn cleared her throat. "I don't know why I'm so nervous. Are you nervous?"

Liv smiled, hidden behind her dark visor. "Don't be nervous. I've got you."

The heat sweltered around them, thick and muggy with the onset of a subtropical summer. They made their way to one of the Lower City bridges, where Liv could finally travel at a more exhilarating speed. The bike pushed itself across as if it were navigating through molasses.

Sweat beaded underneath the collar of her leathers. The thread-thin stripe of skin above it proved to be her only recourse, a treasured inconvenience when she was in such a compromising position. Vaughn squeezed tight, nestled close.

"You're not afraid of the bike, are you?"

Unconvincingly, Vaughn replied, "It's fun."

"Well, we're almost there."

"To the Holy Commune? Already?"

"Sure," Liv lied, only because she thought being close might comfort Vaughn. They hadn't even passed the Lower Cities, and they would need to cross another bridge over floodwaters to touch down on the Holy Commune. Beyond that, several miles of dense treeline hid the civilian crossing.

The ride usually comforted Liv. She treated it like a meditation. It was during this annual journey that she forced herself to reckon with ghosts of has-beens and would-not-bes.

But she usually didn't have another person on her bike. So, Liv distracted herself with other thoughts; chiefly, a bead of sweat rolling from her chest to her belly button. Occasionally, Vaughn would readjust her hold, as if she had suddenly become aware of her hands slipping into her rider's lap, and Liv's focus would shift to that.

The bridge into the Holy Commune was empty as far as Liv could see. No one left, and no one ventured in. Liv glanced in her mirrors and was met with the same emptiness behind her, witnessed through a flurry of Vaughn's windblown ponytail.

The bridge met land, arcing over a shallow, debris-filled reef. The pavement on this end was streaked with hard, packed dirt, and it didn't take long before patches of grass sprouted up beneath their tires, burying the pavement completely. Vaughn surveyed the area around them; the only remaining indicator of the road was the clearing of trees ahead of them. Gnarled, vine-draped trunks twisted upward, dripping with Spanish moss. Though Vaughn could not hear it yet, the cicadas sang at this time of the year, sending their constant, droning responses through the spotty canopy.

The shade was a small blessing.

A low, rusted gate and a line of sentries seated in tied-down lawn chairs marked the civilian crossing into the Holy Commune. Few people came to the Holy Commune, but someone was always required to monitor the crossing. Liv had sunbleached memories of scraping her knees, climbing up nearby trees whenever it was her birth mother's turn to patrol the gate.

Two people flanked the ends of the gate: an older man and a woman in conversation, both wearing fabric bucket hats. As Liv approached them, the woman casually returned to her seat to hoist the strap of a tipped-over rifle onto her shoulder.

These rifles passed through the hands of anyone in the Holy Commune old enough to stand on patrol. This woman was probably a store clerk or a teacher.

The man waved his hands at them to stop. Liv brought the motorcycle to a stop parallel to the gate and floored the kickstand.

"You get turned around on the bridge, or something?" he asked, amused.

Liv unclasped the helmet and pulled it over her head. Vaughn followed suit. "I have something for Lilia."

"Lilia who?"

The Holy Commune had a small, tight-knit population. If he didn't know Lilia, he was a liar. Liv thrust her hand into her pocket, trying to pull the envelope through the catching teeth of its zipper. "Lilia Gonzales. I have mail for her. Can I bring it in?"

The man curled his leathery fingers. Liv dropped the letter into his hands, and he assessed it with mocking slowness. He held it up to the light, squinting over his angular sunglasses. He flipped it over and read the addresses more than once. "This you?"

"Yep."

"What's in it?"

Liv shrugged. Questioning from the sentries always amounted to the same dead ends.

"You got ID?" he asked.

Liv gave Vaughn an exasperated, sidelong glance and gestured for the backpack she had asked Vaughn to hold onto. Vaughn asked, "Does he need mine?"

Louder than Liv could say, "No," the man said, "Let's see it."

Liv's ID was fake, but no one could tell the difference. None of her documentation was official or legal, but the information was correct. Her name read *Olivia Shankly*, not Gonzales, as the only family she had outside the Holy Commune was adoptive.

"You married?" the man asked.

"Do I look married?" Liv said lightly, which garnered no laughter. "Yikes. Tough crowd."

The woman with the rifle assessed her closely, eyes narrowed in judgment. Liv felt contempt from her stare and heard her determination like a dog whistle.

"The names don't match."

"I'm just here to drop off a letter," Liv said. The gate was impassable, despite also being pointless and ineffective as a true boundary. Liv knew she was probing a barrier more akin to a brick wall.

Arcing around her, Vaughn handed the man her ID next, and Liv tried rather heedlessly to push it back into her sole possession.

Sneering, the man pushed his sunglasses higher up his nose. "A Keaton. One of those government suits."

"Yes, but I'm—"

"What makes you think we want you here? I bet this letter isn't even real," he said, brandishing the envelope.

"It *is*," Liv groaned. She threw her wallet and ID back into her bag, ignoring the concern growing on Vaughn's face. "Just drop it at the postal center, alright."

"Don't tell me what to do. Take your government scum back where it came from."

Vaughn's fingers hooked into the sides of Liv's jacket. "I'm not—"

The man flicked Vaughn's ID back toward them carelessly. Liv caught it before it could hit the dirt. She offered it back to Vaughn with the card wedged between her index and middle fingers.

"I can wait out here," Vaughn proposed. "Seriously, I'm—"

"Put the helmet back on, V."

The Keaton girl's distressed expression flitted between Liv, who was already shoving her helmet down over her face, and the sunburnt sentries barring their entrance through a functionally useless gate. The gate could not keep a narrow motorcycle out, only cars and wider vehicles that couldn't easily fit through the gaps in the trees around them.

Liv didn't test her luck or argue further. This journey was an exercise in futility. After the initial year or two of rejection, Liv liked to see what new excuses they could come up with to turn her away. "I hear you loud and clear," she said, before fastening the clip beneath her chin.

She started the ignition. Vaughn pulled herself into position, snuggled needlessly close, which brought Liv a profound satisfaction, if only because it also brought a mild upset to the sentries. "Enjoy mosquito season."

The bike turned, accelerating down the clearing of trees with a roarious urgency. The best thing about the Holy Commune was getting the fuck out of it.

Liv had almost forgotten their helmets were still connected; neither of them had spoken until they reached the bridge to the Lower Cities again, and it was Vaughn who broke the silence. Hesitant, she said, "Liv, I'm so sorry. I didn't think it would be an issue. I shouldn't have come."

A chuckle rose up in Liv's chest, fighting against her best efforts to subdue it. "They never let me in," Liv explained. "It's not you. I've been doing this trip for years and haven't once been allowed through the gates."

"Why?"

"Have you seen me?" Liv asked incredulously. "You couldn't make me look less like a chaste heterosexual. They stick to strict doctrines in there. Only the holy are saved when the rapture comes. Only the holy should have survived the floods."

"What about the rest of us? If we're such *heathens,* how did we outlast the floods?"

Liv angled her head back toward Vaughn, smirking through the dark visor. "I don't know. Deals with the devil. Maybe we got a second chance. We may become holy yet."

A long, comfortable silence stretched between them. Vaughn tipped the lower edge of her helmet onto Liv's shoulder and sighed. The tension in her grip had changed from fearful to wanting.

Trusting.

She left the Commune feeling invincible and unstoppable despite their failure to enter. The barrier had not mattered to her in years, but Vaughn's currently undivided attention mattered to her a great deal. "Hey," she said gently. She had to broach the subject before she succumbed to the fear. The anxiety lodged in her throat was already beginning to calcify. "I asked Maura about the patent the other day."

"Did you?"

Liv's heart gave an irregular thump. "She thinks I should sign it."

"Is that what you want?"

Liv nodded, adjusting her grip on her handlebars. "I know I can't fix a broken medical system. I can't undo anyone's losses. But if you're right, and we can make an accessible, versatile prosthetic, we can make the aftermath of it a little easier." She exhaled sharply, urging herself through another Big Feeling. "I've never had that kind of power before. I want to fix things for people, and medical debt isn't something I've ever been able to manage, let alone fix once the problem showed up. I was going back and forth on whether I trusted myself with the kind of influence this would give me."

"And?" Vaughn asked.

"If I don't do it, who will? Why should I keep this kind of technology to myself? For once, I can make a substantial change in the world. It'd be selfish not to do it. All I've worried about thus far is keeping my family safe, but I could do so much more. I just... I've never had that kind of purpose."

Vaughn giggled. "It's a great feeling, isn't it?"

Liv wanted to tell her how much of the feeling was made up of this moment. Vaughn's laughter right in her ears, the smile evident in her words. It chilled her like a glass of lemonade under the sweltering sun. "I'm taking you to the Eight Saints. It's not a place for dancing, but we can have a drink and raise a toast, if you want. I figured you were owed a do-over for the other night."

"You don't owe me anything," Vaughn said.

"The least I can do is buy you a better drink."

"*I* handled my shot perfectly fine."

Liv pressed her lips together to hold back a retort. Whether it was because she was drunk off a single shot (she wasn't) or the onslaught of Big Feelings had caught up to her, it was true that she hadn't handled any part of that night particularly well.

She sped toward Corcoran with the sun beating against her side.

Despite everything—and almost all of her joy was in spite of something—she felt as if she had the world in her hands, and she had the power to keep it safe. To make it right.

17

They arrived at the Eight Saints early enough to witness Lotte clock in for her shift. The sun dipped beneath the skyline and cast Corcoran in shadow. The streets were clogged with post-work traffic. They parked several blocks away from the bar's entrance. Active police drones buzzed above them, surveying a frequent path of congestion before carrying on.

With their helmets off, in the wake of their agreement on the patent, facing one another took on an intimacy Liv wasn't prepared to deal with. She walked ahead of Vaughn toward the counter, cataloguing the patrons and the napkins just to hide the heat on her face.

The Eight Saints was mostly empty at this hour, and she knew she should sit at a table with her company for the sake of space, but she liked her usual spot. There was something increasingly intimate about showing another person the precise way she liked to enjoy her drinks and the exact barstool she always sat on.

She wasn't pursuing intimacy toward any goal. Along with the patent, Liv had thought gratuitously about this tenacious yearning she had been nursing over Vaughn Keaton and reasoned that it was like any other crush—fun while it lasted, but not insurmountable. She used to be infatuated with the daughter of Bronlow's foreman, too, but as time went on, all thoughts of her had colored over with the presentness of other things, like late car part shipments and her ill-fitting coveralls.

Armed with that knowledge and the knowledge that romance was only as immediate as she allowed it to be, Liv could handle the sight of Vaughn swiping a balm on her middle finger across her full lips on the barstool beside her.

It was not without significant restraint. Liv's mind wandered to the taste of the balm, her eyes to the deftness of Vaughn's fingers, and her hands to the cold, perspirant glass of cherry rum and Coke that Lotte had made her for support.

"Wait!" Vaughn said, twisting her balm shut. "We have to toast first."

"To the patent?" Liv lifted her glass but kept it close to her chest. Vaughn did the same and shot an expectant, pleasant glance at Lotte to grab a drink too. Lotte filled a glass with some sparkling water, unwilling to leave the expectation unsatisfied.

"To new beginnings," Vaughn said. "Whatever that means to us all."

Liv tapped her glass to each of theirs and took her first drink.

"What's your beginning?" Vaughn asked their bartender.

Bewildered, Lotte said, *"Me?* I suppose it's finally getting approved for an apartment of my own. I think I've reached a point where I can safely afford the cost of rent for a studio on my own with the amount of hourly wages I've saved, plus regular tips. As long as the Eight Saints doesn't suddenly tank in business, it's doable."

"Cheers to that," said Liv, staring at the ring stains on the counter. "You should get a fold-out sofa and let me sleep on it."

"And wedge a roommate in my studio?"

"Just every once in a while, when Corey snores too loud."

Lotte dropped her glass into a nearby bus bin. "What about that, Liv? You think you'll ever get out of that apartment?"

Liv's cheeks puffed up with an exasperated breath. "Let's not talk about that."

Although no one verbally pressed the subject, Liv could feel their stares gathering into pressure around her. Vaughn's ankle was swinging gently against the frame of her stool, and it tapped the edge of Liv's like a prompt. "Corey asked me about it a little while ago."

"Is he kicking you out?" Lotte's eyes widened in disbelief.

Liv took a heavier gulp of her drink, willing herself to feel the effects of the rum. "I can tell they want their space. I can't really blame them. They came to Corcoran to make a new beginning for themselves, and they've been stuck raising me ever since. They haven't gotten to experience that yet. And then, on the other end, this is all I've ever known and expect to know for the rest of my life."

A wary glance passed between the others in silence. Liv blinked heavily, shedding her lethargic tone with a small shake of her head and forced smile.

"If it helps," Vaughn offered, "I have much more faith in you than you have in yourself."

With a snort, Liv said, "I have *some* faith in myself."

"Sure, maybe during a Run. But I think you deeply under-estimate yourself when it matters. It's very obvious to me how much faith your parents have in you. And you, Lotte?"

The bartender deadpanned, "No faith whatsoever."

"Ouch," Liv said, covering her heart with her hands.

Vaughn's mouth twitched at the corners, and she suppressed the urge to smile as if she couldn't tell whether it was comfort-ing or condescending. "Well. I'm feeling rather optimistic this evening. And I believe you're overdue for positive change."

Liv gathered from Vaughn's tone that the Keaton girl thought of her as a cynic, that Liv must have lived her life miserable and belligerent, but it was a half-truth, at most. It took a stalwart sense of hope to endure everything the world threw at her. It took total indulgence in the rare silver linings of her life to withstand all the perversity, and she indulged. She studied the passion in the music she listened to every morning. She treasured the days when Maura had enough strength to try a new dinner recipe, even if the food turned out inedible.

She looked for silver linings everywhere. When she found them, she fastened her grip around them unrelentingly.

Except this one. She was looking at the brightest score of silver she had ever seen and choosing to keep it at arm's length.

It seemed impossible that someone so lovely could come from a tree as rotten as the Keaton family. As hopeful as she was, it was safer to trust that some things were inevitable, safer to believe that Vaughn would eventually hurt her.

Somehow, no one else seemed to see it. She'd assumed that everyone would understand her. That they would recognize Vaughn Keaton from where she'd come and see the danger spelled out in unmissable neon.

But she was alone, stuck with another one of her singular feelings, and everyone seemed to want to love the Keaton daughter except her.

An hour and a half passed, making easy conversation, pausing to use the restroom or play a few rounds of Pac-Man on the ancient, flickering machine in the corner of the bar.

She didn't stray too far from her designated barstool. Lotte kept the Keaton girl occupied between drink orders for other patrons, who trickled in and filled the space the longer the night went on. Liv was painfully aware of her own avoidance and the eyes on her back while she wiggled the loose knob on the arcade game.

Damn. She was cornered by digital ghosts.

Returning to her stool, she wedged herself closer to the counter and swirled the settled cherry syrup around in her second glass of rum and Coke for the evening.

"Can I get another drink?" Liv asked.

"Finish that one," said Lotte, though she grabbed what she needed to make a third drink.

Liv obeyed and drained her second glass.

She drank like it was a responsibility, rather than something to occupy her mouth when it had stopped speaking for too long. Alcohol had always had the opposite effect of loosening her lips; it made her quiet and sleepy. Lotte's energy would often dip when Lotte was a couple of drinks in, no longer needing to provide entertaining conversation.

Her heart was pounding, and all she was doing was sitting on a barstool. Losing at Pac-Man.

"Liv?" Vaughn slid her stool closer and gently bumped Liv's knee. "You okay?"

"Yeah. Great."

The reassurance was completely transparent, but Vaughn's smile was earnest and full. She'd barely touched her first Bellini, still clear-headed as when she'd first walked in. Smiling at her anyway. Liv blinked, transfixed by the smoothness of the other girl's brow and the tight angle of her nose bridge.

Around them, the usual crowd of late-night patrons finished their first drinks and grew more raucous by the minute. Vaughn watched them with her chin perched on her hand, delighting in the spirit of a dive bar. She pulled the band from her hair and shook out her ponytail.

"Do you ever think about cutting it?" Liv asked.

"Sometimes. I like having something to touch, though. It keeps me grounded."

Liv, too, thought she might feel more grounded if she could run her hands through it. A strand had hooked around the shoulder seam of Vaughn's loose button-up shirt. She could smooth it down. No big deal.

Vaughn pivoted in her seat toward the countertop shyly. Liv must have been staring. "Sorry," she said preemptively.

"It's not you. I accidentally made eye contact with someone."

This made Liv laugh. Vaughn was *all* large, intense eyes and thick lashes. "Okay."

Vaughn itched the nape of her neck and lowered her voice. "Is he coming over?"

"Who? Should I tell him to fuck off?"

"Is he?"

Liv angled her head over her shoulder only to be met with the man in question, who was approaching them at the counter with an audacity that rendered her speechless.

He seemed to have a few years on them. The stretched collar of his T-shirt revealed a crop of dark chest hair. He cleared his throat and gave Liv a cordial nod, to which Liv's face crumpled in confusion. He leaned between them, putting on airs of nonchalance. "Two of your house beers," he said to Lotte. Then, to Vaughn alone, "What are you drinking?"

She said, politely, "I've just about finished, actually."

"Finished?" He looked at the half-drunk glass beside her and scoffed. "You'd let a perfectly good drink go to waste?"

Vaughn's mouth parted a little, affronted by the challenge. She lifted what was left of her Bellini and downed it. *Why?* Liv bemoaned.

"Now you need another one," the guy said.

Liv cut in. "We're in the middle of something here, man."

"Looks fun. Should we toast?"

"That wasn't an invitation."

Softly, Vaughn whispered her name, which felt less like a warning than a punishment. Liv couldn't understand what she wanted, whether she cared about the man's presence or not. But she knew herself and that she'd felt a defensiveness over

Vaughn Keaton since she first offered to rebuild Liv's arm. Liv didn't want some guy joining them. Vaughn was her trouble. No one else's.

Vaughn perked up like a clicky pen and suggested to Liv in as casual a tone as she could muster, "We were leaving soon, anyway, weren't we?"

Liv hastily tore a few bills out of her wallet, nodding along, and slid them across the counter without asking Lotte for the total.

"Awe," the man crooned, a stale, wheaty breath leaving his mouth. "I didn't realize I was talking to a prude. 'S not the sort of bar for sensible ladies."

Vaughn said nothing and even forced a timid smile onto her face, though her skin was blotchy and red with shame. Liv lifted her belongings from the ground and swung her backpack in a wide arc over her shoulder to mark a bubble of personal space.

He was standing in it, still waiting for the second bottle of beer he had asked for to be uncapped behind the counter. Liv shoved her way past him, which only made him bark a condescending laugh.

He wrapped his fingers around the necks of his uncapped bottles and swivelled toward his original seat, where another man sat shaking his leg impatiently for his drink. "You can change your mind," he jeered, hovering just within Vaughn's orbit. "I recognize a treasure when I see one, you know. You got a shine to you."

He lifted his fingers. Touched Vaughn's hair. The pale girl turned unnaturally paler, as if the invasion had rendered every part of her body dormant.

The act did something else entirely to Liv.

She was already committed to a series of actions that fit the 'flight' half of the fight-or-flight dichotomy when she dropped all her things, grasped one of the man's shoulders, and sank her right fist into his turning jaw.

A shockwave vibrated up the arm to the connection point, a sensation so unfamiliar that it forced Liv's mind back into her body. Someone in the bar yelped. Maybe Vaughn. Liv only saw red.

She hadn't meant to hit him. Well, she *would* have, if Vaughn wasn't there, and now that she'd done it, she couldn't go back. She didn't think, didn't know what her own body was doing. The man lurched forward and levied all his weight, plus two sloshing bottles, against Liv.

Heat blossomed across her right cheek, then pain. She stumbled, just struck by a knobby fist occupied with bottles.

Her vision blacked briefly.

The heavy glass fell somewhere beside them. The leather on her legs was splattered with a long parabola of cold beer now emptying into a puddle across the room.

The man swung his arm downward like a scythe. Liv sidestepped and hurled another punch at the back of his head, but missed.

She was off-kilter. More disoriented than she thought. He slammed his shoulder into her stomach. His size was enough to send her halfway across the room, where she toppled against other bar patrons, who shoved her back toward the unfinished fight like a schoolyard game of Red Rover.

The man smeared blood from the split side of his lip with his hand. A flash of ungodly sleek hair to her left indicated that her companion had developed the initiative to get the fuck out of the bar. Liv probably should have jumped ship, too. She was in the thick of it now.

She raised her fists in front of her face and stayed light on her feet, ready for anything. Vaughn had asked her once why she'd made her metal arm the way she did. Liv didn't totally know, but she'd kept it ready for a fight and other skirmishes like these.

The man looked at the red spooling onto his hand and huffed like a bratty horse. A challenge ignited in his man's eyes. He jerked his chin up at her and said, "Come on, bitch."

Liv swallowed her regret for punching the man and prepared to dodge his next jab. She could only do so much to calm herself down before—

A horn blared throughout the bar. The Eight Saints patrons collapsed in a collective effort to cover their ears and bodies from the sudden auditory assault. It rang through Liv's metal hand into her skull as she clamped hard over her ears. The man's menace crumbled around him. A dozen wrinkles formed in the triangle between his nose and eyebrows as he shut his eyes.

As quickly as the noise had come, it left again. The idle chatter-turned-shocked murmurs reduced to utter silence. The patrons, reeling from their stupor, had lost interest in the impending brawl.

It stunned Liv's body into inaction. Before she could wake it up again, Lotte climbed onto the countertop with a deceptively petite air horn still clutched in her hand.

She pointed it at the fighters like a loaded firearm and ordered, "Knock this shit off! All of you!" Brandishing it at Liv, she said, "You two, get out of the bar. And *you* lot—" She gestured at the other man and his companion, "are going to leave in... In five minutes! Until then, everybody better keep their goddamn hands to themselves or I'm calling enforcements."

Stunned into stillness, the dizzying rush of adrenaline and the effects of being struck were catching up to Liv. Her first step sent her careening into Vaughn's side. The other girl had rushed to catch her and circled her arm around her with a nannying force. "Come on."

"But I can't— my bike—"

"Forget the stupid bike," she hissed. "Let's go."

The Eight Saints patrons parted for them, their faces painted in varying hues of disgust and shock, as if Liv had blasted the horn herself. Her ears rang. She could barely hear what Vaughn was muttering under her breath, and she didn't ask until they were already outside, pivoting on their heels without any direction on where to go next.

"You going to call your driver then?" Liv's words slurred unevenly, in part from downing her second drink but mostly from the pain swelling in her face. Her jaw ached with each word. The wind sliced across the side of her face where the man's knuckles split her skin. Through the tracks of her scars, another tear had formed.

"Can you at least walk a little further before we make any big decisions?"

"What's big about the car, pinstripes?"

Vaughn's lips bowed downward with a reluctant restraint. Her pace was quick, her hands fastened too tightly around Liv to shake.

"He's not coming after us, V."

"You don't know that."

"I'd bet—*ah*." Liv located the epicenter of the punch with her fingertips. "I'd bet you a hundred bucks he doesn't."

Vaughn whirled on her with eyes impossibly wide and angry. "Have you no sense of self-preservation?"

"I'm fine." Liv's saliva tasted like blood. She let it well in her mouth, turned, and spat on the ground behind her. "I know what Eight Saints folks are like, okay? You're making this a bigger deal than it is."

"Oh, wonderful. What a prime opportunity to remind

me I don't fit in in your town! Just when I was beginning to think you brought me here for some extension of camaraderie. Alright then!" The iron grasp around Liv's arms fell away, and Vaughn stomped several paces ahead of her. "You're an idiot, Liv. A hot-headed, mouthy fool who's lucky she hasn't already gotten herself killed several times over!"

Liv's legs couldn't keep up. They slumped beneath her, her side colliding with a nearby lamppost. She grappled for the ridges of the pole, propping herself upright. All the pressure points on her body that the man had struck were becoming nauseatingly, grossly clear.

Vaughn hadn't gone far before Liv's feeble call for help turned her around again. "It's okay," Vaughn begrudgingly said. "I've got you."

Through the pain in her jaw, Liv said, "I didn't plan for that to happen."

"No, I'm sure getting smashed in the face wasn't in your itinerary for the day. Maybe you can tell me where I can find a bit of seating for us before you black out."

"I'm not going to black out."

"Fantastic. We can go a little further. Then, I'm taking you home."

The Keaton girl eased Liv back onto her feet, and when the world bent and swayed, she tucked her arm beneath Liv's shoulders, holding the rider up against her side. Liv's depth perception was useless. Her head weighed a hundred pounds, and it kept tipping over no matter how much she tried to keep it up. She wondered if some integral nerve in her brain had snapped. It was more likely that Liv had just been knocked truly senseless for the first time in her life.

The last time Liv had gotten into a fight was when she was newly twenty, and her opponent had been as spindly as a dandelion stem. She had known then how frivolous the ordeal was, that she could take more, withstand worse; but she couldn't have known what it would feel like until it happened. She had been knocked unconscious and bruised blue all over, but this was different.

She teetered on the precipice of unconsciousness but never fully tipped over. She was entirely present in her own body, forced to fathom the extent of all the damage with gross, agonizing clarity.

Once the bar faded out of sight, Vaughn asked, "Are you going to be sick?"

"I'm not drunk, V."

"So you say."

Liv pressed her fingers to the gash on her cheek again, testing it. Blood smeared thin and tacky down to her jaw.

"Why else would you do something so completely nonsensical?" Vaughn looked up at the sky and huffed. Mostly to herself, or to some unseen entity in the stars, she asked, "What the hell were you thinking, Liv? Look at you. You're...."

Liv was pulled into a shallow alleyway and propped against a brick wall for support, giving Vaughn's hands nowhere to go. One splayed against the bricks beside Liv's shoulder, but the other slid uselessly off her rider's body.

She buried her face into her elbow, unable to follow her own orders—*Look at you.* It was difficult to stay mad at a girl who had just been punched in the face with all the force of a hammer. Maybe Liv's thoughts were too readable for Vaughn to keep enduring.

Vaughn could take one look at the uncomfortable, beating truth hidden beneath Liv's cleaved-open ribs and piece together an answer to her question.

Why did Liv *ever* do such reckless things?

The rider lifted her fingers to her jaw and kneaded until the sharpness turned dull. "Do you honestly expect me to watch someone treat you like a piece of meat and do nothing about it?"

"You don't know how to pick your battles. You were never going to win that fight, Liv. All you were going to do was hurt yourself. That does neither of us any good."

"I stood up for you! So I got hit a bit harder than what was palatable for you. I'm fine. I would have *been* fine. I'm not about to lie down and let someone walk all over you or me before I even try to do something about it. All this I do, and yet you can't even thank me."

Vaughn's words became clipped and haggard. "*I* would have been fine. Obviously, I didn't want to be condescended to. I'm sorry I didn't immediately know how to respond to some man in my personal space, but I'm already plenty aware of what it feels like. I can get over something like that and move forward with my life. I can do it without you making a bloody mess of yourself for me."

They could go for hours cycling through blame like this. Liv had the stamina for it and plenty of fire behind her argument. She wasn't a big enough person to kill the blame game altogether. Not when she held so much conviction. If Liv was wrong, if she'd spent years living angry, fighting so hard for nothing, she wouldn't be able to forgive herself. She had lost too much and risked everything to survive.

She thought of Maura, kissing her hair, able to offer forgiveness to Liv whenever she did something wrong as easily as she could point out to Liv that she'd left her shoelaces untied. Liv's reasons were justified. Her anger, proud and ungovernable.

She shouldn't have expected Vaughn to get it. She was asking too much from a Keaton to look past a defiance of order and rules and see the heart behind it, but she wanted her to. She wanted Vaughn to understand it.

"All my life," she said, struggling to articulate, "I have

fought for Corey and Maura. I did it on the Run course just as much as I do it out here. If you can't see why I would put myself in a situation like that for you, then you don't understand me at all, V."

Vaughn closed her eyes and took a shaky inward breath. The inner corners of her eyebrows tipped up in either concern or pity; Liv didn't know and couldn't stand it.

Grabbing Vaughn by her left shoulder, she slid her hand to the back of her neck and made herself an unavoidable subject. "Look. I don't fight the way you do. I don't have the means of winning that you do. I'm not going to charm anyone with my status or buy anyone's loyalty with my family's money. *This* is how I win. It's the only way I know how. It means I fight dirty. I fight like hell. And I'm not going to stop fighting either, because losing anything in the Lower Cities can mean losing everything. The sooner you get that through your head, the better. But God forbid I let some drunk, handsy bastard at a bar take advantage of someone I care about and do nothing about it."

She laid her reasons out like butchered fowl, explicit and undeniable. Her words were a sharpened cleaver, still slick with red, sticking in the block between them. Vaughn stared at her with such an unabashed puzzlement that Liv wondered whether everything she had just said had been intercepted by an invisible wall.

Vaughn's eyes traversed the hard, trained features of Liv's face, from both of her eyes to the angry jut of her jaw. It shouldn't have been clearer how Liv felt, how rising to the defense awakened her entire body. Vaughn, however, remained unreadable. Like a blueprint, she studied Liv, seeing something in the rider's face that she must not have been capable of screwing into place.

Her gaze landed on the gash on Liv's face, and her

expression betrayed a flash of something that looked like awe. She touched the stain of blood beneath the wound with the pad of her thumb.

"Vaughn?"

She was close enough that Liv could see every flicker of movement beneath her lashes. The path of sight from the empty patch in her right brow to the divot in her lip. She mapped Liv's scar, assessed the shallow tear in her skin, and then, Vaughn was kissing her.

Arms hooked tight around Liv's neck, unwavering and demanding as if Liv wasn't still bloody and lightheaded. As if Vaughn hungered for the taste of blood on her lips.

Liv's brain stalled. Her hands found purchase on the other girl's waist for support, or maybe the craving had brought them there. The girl was a salve, a painkiller. Liv's body didn't comprehend the ache while it was overwhelmed with desire.

Between impatient, uncoordinated kisses, Vaughn asked, "Should we be—"

"Don't care."

Obligingly, Vaughn discarded any follow-up questions and let Liv kiss her without interruption. Her only sounds were muffled sighs planted against Liv's mouth or gentle scrapes from her fingernails in the overgrown hair around Liv's ears.

The pressure from Vaughn's hands bled into the tender parts of Liv's skin. Vaughn kept her close, almost suffocatingly so. The ache of kissing her put all other agonies to shame. Liv felt as though she might shatter if the other girl let her go, like a broken piece of glass being held together by a precarious seam of weak glue.

Liv pinned Vaughn against the bricks. She kissed the Keaton girl again and didn't stop, even as the ache in her jaw sharpened. She wedged her head into the flushed, bare corner between Vaughn's neck and shoulder, and she sucked, leaving different kinds of bruises.

With every part of her body, save for her mouth, Vaughn seemed to say, *more more more*. Liv's hair was petted and gripped until it hurt. Her trapezius muscle, bitten into by the unrelenting hooks of Vaughn's bony fingers.

Liv reached for the other girl's tucked shirt and pulled it out from the waistband of her jeans. She didn't know where she was going with this. How far she could go. She would do anything at that moment, emboldened by need, as long as Vaughn let her. As long as Vaughn wanted her.

She fumbled over the buttons, only to find a flimsy tank top underneath. Liv tugged it upward just as Vaughn pushed her lower. Liv was grateful for the dark, with a face too warm and red to hide her shame. Liv trained it on Vaughn's body—against her exposed stomach, her slim belt buckle, and the center seam of her pants. A soreness radiated around her knuckles where they bent around Vaughn's belt loops.

Liv's teeth scraped the denim. It was a precursor to something more. Nothing on its own yet besides a declaration of need, but no one would have guessed it from the way Vaughn was keening into Liv's touch. Intoxicating, ravenous, and *so fucking hot,* Liv thought.

The thought had drowned out the heavy thump of boots from the mouth of the alley.

A beam of white light hit them.

"Can I help you?" bellowed the first of two police officers hovering in the alley. The light fixated on Liv; another belonging to the second officer fell on Vaughn while she was refastening the buttons of her shirt.

Liv stumbled against the brick in her haste to rise to her feet. Her skin drained of all its warmth, petrified by the looming officers. Her fight and vigor meant nothing against someone with a gun on their hip.

Corcoranites avoided cops at all costs, going ten steps further than folks in the Upper City might. Cops in the Lower Cities spelled more danger and administered more violence. Nothing like a bar fight. Nothing that simple.

Liv doubted they were breaking any laws getting handsy in a dark alley, but she couldn't risk saying the wrong thing. Her body was evidence of some kind of assault, and no cop was going to turn a blind eye to the modifications of her prosthetic. She had been lucky when Vaughn saw them the first time, but it wouldn't happen again, especially not in Corcoran. Not if she was caught with fresh bruises blooming on her cheek. She guarded her face and the bloodstain against the light. Her mind went to the grisliest outcomes. They could wrench the prosthetic apart and leave it unsalvageable.

She couldn't imagine going back to the beginning again. Being without the prosthetic again.

Vaughn straightened up, pushed her hair behind her ears, and stepped toward the uniformed pair. "I'm sorry, officer. We were just—"

"Stop where you are," the first cop commanded. "Lower what's in your hand now!"

"What?" Vaughn's mouth fell open in puzzlement. Neither of them held anything in their hands.

"Lay the weapon on the ground!"

"It's her prosthetic, you moron!"

"Put your hands over your head."

Something clicked, like the safety clip of a gun. Flinching, Liv dropped to her knees and did as she was told. With no weapon to lay down, she flattened her silver palm against the ground.

"I am a *Keaton*, officer," Vaughn stated calmly. "What offense have we committed?"

"Vaughn, shut up," Liv warned and kept her head down,

glancing only toward the second officer's shoes as she approached.

"A Keaton?" asked the first. "In Corcoran?"

"I have my ID," Vaughn said. "I'm sure Caldwell would be pleased to hear about how you terrorized his sister for a perfectly legal nighttime tryst."

"Show me."

Liv felt a ring of cold metal brush the back of my head. "And you?" the second officer said. "You're not a Keaton."

Vaughn slowly placed her wallet in front of the first officer. "If you touch a single hair on her head, I'll have you stripped of your badges immediately."

Liv might have appreciated the defensive tone in her voice if the gun levelled at her didn't imbue her with mortal terror. What would Corey think, knowing she'd been forced onto her knees to cower for what could have only been a simple, exploited indiscretion?

Liv hadn't felt sick earlier, but she was close to retching now.

"With all due respect," the second officer stated, pushing the barrel into Liv's hair, "this one's covered in signs of an assault. Whether you're a Keaton or not, we have grounds to question the bruises." After a considerate pause, she added grimly, "And the blood."

"Jennings." The address came from the first officer. The one holding Vaughn's identification.

A moment passed. The gun shifted against Liv's scalp before being tucked back into its holster, and the female officer stalked back toward the mouth of the alley.

"I'm sorry, Miss Keaton," the first officer said. "It's not often we get visitors here."

"So?" She pulled her wallet and ID from his hand, raked the zipper closed for show, and threw them onto the pile of their deposited belongings. "Do you pull your weapons out for every minor infraction?"

"Folks tend to get a little unruly here. Things escalate more often than not. No hard feelings, alright?"

"Hard feelings?" Vaughn repeated with that shrill, old-money shock that Liv should have been used to by now.

"*Vaughn,*" Liv warned, flush with fear. "Don't push it. Let's just go."

"You should listen to your friend," said the second officer. "It's dark out. You're lucky we were cops and not a couple of vandals. It's not safe here, Miss Keaton. You should take your business elsewhere."

"And you should be more mindful where you point those things," she said. "Otherwise, you might hurt the wrong person one of these days."

18

Liv's lungs swelled with all the breath she'd been holding in the officers' presence. Humiliation burned her everywhere, clouding all her senses, smothering the sound in her ears. Vaughn was saying something, hushed and irritable like a scolded child with a closed door standing between them and their mother.

Like a brand, the barrel of the gun had printed on the back of Liv's neck. A metal unlike her fingertips. Cold in a way she wasn't familiar with. Bracing her arms on her knees, Liv doubled over, wondering if vomiting might alleviate the stress.

Vaughn sensed that her delicate raging was falling on unreceptive ears and trailed off into silence. After a long pause and a wipe of her brow, she said, "That was... thrilling, I suppose. Did they hurt you? Are you—"

"I'm fine."

"I wouldn't have let anything bad happen to you, you know. That was a complete overstep of their protocols, what they did, but—"

"Don't," Liv said. "Don't make caveats for them."

"That's not what I was trying to do." Vaughn placed her hand on Liv's arm.

"*Don't.* Just don't touch me right now."

Everything caught up to Liv at once. She paced to the farthest, darkest end of the alley and back. Her body ached all over. Swollen, broken, angry. She bore the full brunt of it now that nothing could distract her.

That was all this was: a distraction. Worse things waited for her on the other end of the evening, and she'd been pushing them off, letting them accrue power; meanwhile, she was offering herself to the Keaton girl like a silly, obedient dog. Getting on her knees for her, showing her just how desperately she wanted to be touched.

She pressed her palms against her eyes. *Stupid.*

Aloud, with as level a tone as she could muster, she said to Vaughn, "Why did you say that?"

"What did I say, Liv?"

"To that cop."

Vaughn's brows lifted, confusion and impatience written on her face. She tucked her arms around her body sheepishly.

"That thing you said at the end. About hurting the wrong person."

"Well, we haven't done anything wrong," Vaughn explained. "They had no reason to reprimand us or treat us with such aggression."

"You don't get it, V. It's not about doing anything wrong. Being in the wrong place at the wrong time was enough to make us a worthy target of harassment."

"Yes, but—"

"They would have done it anyway. There are no wrong people in Corcoran, V. You can never be good enough or obedient enough to satisfy them. They wait for us to make wrong moves or misstep to fill their fucking quotas. And at the end of the day, the best of us are still products of the place we come from, and some of us need to do more than just misstep to keep ourselves afloat."

Vaughn searched their surroundings. The cars on the street had gone cold, and though the lights were on in apartment building windows, the glass panels were shut. Noises were few and distant. "Liv," she muttered. "Are you angry at me?"

The question made Liv's shoulders tense. She was angry at everything. Most of what angered her outmeasured the small scope of Vaughn Keaton. She was angry at things she couldn't change, troubles Vaughn couldn't take away. "You shouldn't have told them off like that," Liv said.

"But earlier—*you*—"

Being who she was, with that name and status, made her blind to the obvious ways that this could be different from telling off some guy at a bar.

Liv didn't fear the people in Corcoran. Even when they were awful, desperate, and rude. There was strength in sticking together. Their fights were their own. She would not let anyone else tell her how to handle rifts. Not a cop, and not a Keaton.

"I don't know what you want from me, Liv. I'm trying my best here."

"Nothing!" Liv tugged at her hair until her scalp hurt and wished she could scrub the memory of Vaughn's hands away. "I don't want anything from you, but you keep inserting yourself in places you shouldn't be!"

"You brought me here. Unless you forgot."

"Yeah, well." Liv's pitch shifted higher and higher until her words were catching in her throat. "You should call Clav and go home. Forget this ever happened."

"But you—"

"I was trying to keep my nose down and stay out of trouble with that money. You keep bringing yourself into my life."

Vaughn levelled those huge, glassy eyes at her so intensely that Liv had to turn around and scour the bricks for something new to look at. "Liv," she murmured, gravely. "You're being mean."

Mean. Such a small word, yet it stung like a slap in the face.

But 'mean' was nothing. Liv could forgive herself for being

mean if she did the right thing. She had forgotten herself and her principles and let an urge take her too far. Undoing it would be painful, but it was necessary.

Tears gathered in the pinched corners of Liv's eyes. She wiped them as covertly as she could. The graze of her own fingertips against her swollen cheek seared hot. "Go call your driver. It's nicer in Morgallis anyway."

She snatched her belongings up from the ground and exited the alley, pouring into the quiet street like a riot. Vaughn maintained a steady pace behind her. The anticipation of an argument left unfinished made Liv's head foggy.

"I did that for *you*!" True, unbridled resentment laced the Keaton girl's words, made deep and rough by the onset of her tears. Every word felt like a curse. "Everything I've done was to make you happy or make things better! You're so committed to making yourself the biggest martyr in the city, but you don't have to be. Why do you refuse to let anyone help you every once in a while? Why can't you let someone else care about you? Or maybe, you take it for granted, since everyone in your life seems to let you get away with *bullshit*."

"What are you talking about?"

"You treat Lotte like dirt. You lie to your parents. You can't even look me in the eyes right now while you insult me, and yet you have us all in your pockets, forgiving and forgetting and ignoring how much of an asshole you can be."

Liv turned and looked Vaughn squarely in the face.

"I run myself ragged trying to provide. I've given up pieces of myself to make sure my family is taken care of. You think I enjoy having my guard up all the time?" Her voice ricocheted and filled up the silence. "You think I wake up every day and decide to work myself so hard just because I feel like it? Every limit my body has placed on me, I've had to cross, because people were depending on me. I'm exhausted. All I want is a fucking break. I want to go home to a house with a window and fresh air. I want regular time to cook a fresh meal and watch TV with my parents. This is the most time I've ever had to myself, and I'm spending it on edge with a tweaked knee. Every day that I'm not back at work is another day of wages I can't bring in. You will never know what that feels like."

Vaughn's lips parted, as if she had an argument to make, but no sound came out. Liv took a deep breath and trained her voice back to a reasonable volume. "I could take you to every dive bar in the Lower Cities and watch you brush elbows with every after-work patron until your elbows were chafed. Nothing I do will change the way this ends. You're always going to go back to your glass house in the hills, safe from the city and ignorant of the struggles of everyday people, because that's just the world you live in. And this?" Liv gestured flippantly to the place where the officers had stood. "This is the world *I* live in. There's no point in trying to make nice between them. There's no world where you and I make sense."

A scuttle of pedestrians down the street prompted them each to cut their losses and leave. Liv felt cold for the first time since winter. She needed a shower and a night of sleep that lasted at least thirteen hours to get her through the most immediate aftershocks from the night.

Pushing her hair behind her ears with a trembling hand, Vaughn tipped her head down shamefully and muttered, "Fuck you, Liv."

She walked away and called her driver. It was none of Liv's business what happened after that.

PART THREE

19

Vaughn wished she liked her brother. He was the only one who, without fail, showed up for her when she couldn't stand being alone.

She was too embarrassed to ask Clav to keep her company, possibly because she still liked *him*. He had never seen her sent to such a low point by a romantic partner. The whole ordeal felt childish, and for every day that she didn't wake up having slept off the thought of Liv, she wondered what was wrong with her.

It shouldn't have been so difficult to put all thoughts related to Liv Shankly to rest. They had kissed once. For their entire friendship, Liv had been oscillating between gratitude and immense guilt, which was hardly indicative of friendship. But who was Vaughn Keaton to say? She had no other friends except for Clav, and calling him a friend still seemed like a gross misrepresentation she wasn't brave enough to claim.

She was sitting in the workshop when he arrived earlier, doing the same thing that she had been doing for the past weeks, which was staring blankly at the patent documents before her. They had been shuffled in and out of order; their current state was out of order and would probably remain that way. She wasn't planning to do anything with the blueprints now. Not without Liv. She would eventually file them into a cabinet somewhere in the house. She didn't have the heart to do it yet.

Caldwell dressed up for a night out. He took wide strides into the center of the room and did a spin, hoping it would make her laugh. "Why are you not dressed yet? I told you to get ready."

She swivelled her chair toward the workbench with a sigh, letting the pages pile into whatever order they pleased with a swipe of her hand, and stood up to change. "Five minutes," she said.

"Five? You don't want to take ten?"

"You seemed irked that I wasn't ready before. Are we late?"

His gaze slipped to the side avoidantly. He didn't think she looked presentable enough, but knew better than to kick his sibling while she was already down. "Whatever," she mumbled.

"Are you working on something?

"No."

Whether or not they were late, Vaughn wasted little time in her bedroom stripping out of her slept-in clothes and into something fresh. She hadn't gone anywhere or done anything to feel grimy yet, but she probably needed one soon, if only to maintain a sense of general self-care. Water glasses littered the surfaces of her room: three on the little desk in the corner, one on her nightstand, and another two balanced on short stacks of books. Of clean drinkware, her cabinets had nearly emptied.

She held onto the nightstand for support as she slid her feet into a pair of pale, short heels and made a mental note to tidy up later. Enough time had passed that the accumulation of glasses no longer seemed defensible. Caldwell's comment from an earlier visit came to mind. *It's depressing.*

When it became too much to think about, she forced herself out of the room. Caldwell stood directly across the hall, fussing with his hair to achieve the perfect pastiche of disheveled and cool.

No matter what kind of person he was, for better or for

worse, Caldwell would always be her brother. If she could forget the fact, his face would instantly remind her. He looked at it in the reflection of Vaughn's bathroom mirror, splashing water on his face, then towelled it off. Their faces had been near copies of each other throughout their shared childhoods, and though they had begun to diverge in exactness at some point, the similarities were deep and indisputable.

He met her eyes in the mirror and flashed a playful smile at her. "Hey, why don't we stop for a coffee on the way? Have you had any today?"

Vaughn's forehead tilted against the doorframe. Her head throbbed from the combination of intermittent crying and caffeine withdrawal. She had little energy to make her daily pot of coffee. She would lie in bed until midday, force herself to pour another tall glass of water in the afternoon so she didn't shrivel up like a prune (which she would subsequently abandon in her room), scribble self-flagellating musings in her notebook for an hour, and then zone out to Lunokhod's recap of the daily news.

The news only ever made her feel worse. Her mental state was fucked and unchecked. The state of the world around her, even more fucked. Everywhere she turned, she saw her family's influence tarnishing everything. She had such a rotten family tree. Maybe it was only time until she turned bad, too.

Caldwell turned to face her when she did not respond to him. He took her shoulders in his hands and gave them a gentle shake. "What ails thee, dear sister? I will vanquish it."

"You're not allowed to vanquish this."

"I have to do something. It's upsetting me to see you so bereft."

"This is something," she said.

Caldwell scrutinized her with narrowed eyes. She had agreed to accompany him to one of his indulgent gatherings in the city center, which initially brought him such enthusiasm that he reminded her of the brother she used to have, who was full of boyish wonder and passion. "There's my sister," he had said, as if she had been the one to change.

That enthusiasm had since faded, replaced by a concern that something in Vaughn was fundamentally wrong. "You look too nice to be so sad," said Caldwell.

She wore a nice dress of smooth, eggshell-coloured silk, and for Caldwell, a navy sport jacket over finely tailored trousers and accessories that matched the specific shade of light red-brown both twins had growing out of their heads.

"That's stupid."

"It's all stupid." He had not been so close to self-awareness in a long time. "So, coffee? My treat."

There were many years during Vaughn's childhood when she wished she and Caldwell were the only Keatons left. Their mother had died when they were small. Their father had been negligent since the beginning, leaving them with a rotation of nannies and teachers. "Wouldn't it be so cool," Caldwell would tell her, "if we could live in this big house without him? We could have our schoolmates over *all* the time, and we could only do our schoolwork *some* of the time."

Caldwell seemed to think that opportunity was still attainable. No father, social wealth, and ignored responsibility. His parties made this most obvious, and he moved through the crowd atop the Skerville Hotel roof as if ignited by a switch, soaking in the outpouring of love from a selection of family friends, entrepreneurs, and other supposedly famous Morgallis socialites.

Vaughn didn't know any of these people. Caldwell gestured to several of them as though she ought to know them, but every name drew up blank. He returned the greetings lobbed at him by people who had been there for some time already, but he focused on funneling Vaughn toward the bar. "So, no coffee, but maybe you want something to drink?"

Vaughn picked up whatever the bartender was pouring for the servers to pile onto their trays and swirled it around in front of her nose. The wind affected her more up here, tossing strands of her hair around her wine glass. She missed the pony-tail elastic she usually had around her wrist. She had shed that small comfort for the illusion of glamor.

Caldwell picked up a glass of his own and gave the bartender a sharp nod as thanks. "We need to toast to something."

Vaughn cleared her throat to prompt him. She didn't want to allocate the toast.

"To getting out of the house. Making new friends."

"Sure."

"This will be good for you," said Caldwell. "You're in a place where everyone loves you."

"I don't recognize a single person here."

"So what?" He took a long drink. "They know *you*."

Even as an idea, Vaughn didn't think she existed in anyone's mind. She didn't grace tabloids or celebrity news channels the way Caldwell did. In Morgallis, especially now, she felt like an accessory to Caldwell, sewn to him like a pocket. If anyone looked at her, it would be because she was closest to the man with all the power in the city.

It beat being remembered as the failed Warner chip trial subject.

That thought made her down her glass of wine in one fell swoop.

"There you go. Loosen up."

Liv would laugh if she saw her like this. She looked like a different person next to Caldwell. She'd stepped into a more graceful, demure character like a skin, but it was too tight.

But the way Liv had looked at her in the alleyway... Vaughn couldn't scrub that expression from her mind. It haunted her. So much want and triumph in her rider's eyes, like she had been wrestling with her desire for some time, and the desire had finally won.

It'd be easier to get over Liv if she had acted like she hated it. Instead, Liv only hated *Vaughn*. Hated things about her that she couldn't get rid of.

Vaughn placed her empty glass on an empty corner of the drink table where it would not get confused with the others and picked up a second. She cast her gaze past the bar and through the glass barrier surrounding the rooftop. This high in altitude, she could steal glimpses of other rooftops and their humbler happenings. A long pool stretched across an apartment roof in front of her, occupied by a pair of swimmers circling each other. Vaughn meandered toward the glass and watched them navigate a centerpoint like two fish vying for one piece of bait. One of the figures kicked away from the other, prompting a leisurely chase.

Caldwell didn't join her. The purpose of parties was the people, and he understood them much better than she did. Understanding, seducing, and manipulating them. He switched through faces so easily that she could no longer find the seams where one version of Caldwell ceased to be and another was born. He adapted effortlessly.

He shook the arms of strangers en route to a sleek leather couch on the opposite side of the pool. A voice summoned her attention from her left. "I imagine you didn't notice me when you walked in."

Vaughn's teeth clipped together, her fingers shifting along the stem of her wine glass.

"Otherwise," said Greer Margossi, "I'd feel incredibly

slighted by the way you ignored my greeting. Tell me I'm wrong."

The swimmers on the other roof were splashing each other. Vaughn wished she could teleport from her roof to theirs and escape the sight of her ex. "I didn't realize you were here."

While Vaughn had not changed much in physical appearance since they last talked to one another, everything about Greer had become refined. Her dark hair was lobbed into a sharp, even cut just beneath her jaw. The kinks in it had been ironed so flat that her hair resembled a single arc of sheet metal more than thousands of individual hairs. She wore a short dress and long boots in matching shades of eggplant purple, accentuating the sliver of light pink skin on her thighs. Her lips were blushed to a just-kissed shade. Vaughn knew it well. She smothered the recognition as soon as it came.

"You do that," Greer said. "You slip into your head a lot. Is it daydreaming?"

Vaughn shook her head. "Something else."

"I see."

"How are you?" Vaughn didn't mean to start this conversation, but she couldn't bear the silence. Her mind had left the party and joined the pair of swimmers in their pool. Her body was slipping into autopilot.

"Do you really want to know? You haven't said anything to me in over a year."

The forwardness of the question prevented Vaughn from slipping too far away from the event at hand. "You've talked to my brother plenty," she said.

Greer shrugged and swirled the glass in her hand, which was full of some other kind of drink. "It's all work. No play. Nothing to write home about."

"Surely it must be interesting, if you're so keen on it."

"Who says I'm keen? Work is work for a reason."

Vaughn's mouth flattened into a harsh line. She ought to have let the matter of their business die. Liv was gone and likely didn't care about where her money was supposed to go. Caldwell didn't seem to care either. He had moved on to more ambitious endeavors with fewer limits.

The only one who cared was Vaughn.

And she still *did* care.

She met Greer's eyes, which were a striking shade of blue. "You know me. I like work. It sounded interesting to me."

"How much has he told you, then?" asked Greer.

"It's been so long since we talked about it." The wine doled the lie out of her as easily as a lie from Caldwell's mouth. "I've forgotten the details. But I remember being interested."

"That's a generous reaction."

Reaching toward Greer's glass, Vaughn gestured for a sip, brushing her fingers as she lifted it from her. "Remind me?"

The first of Greer's many reservations fell away. She turned her back against the rooftop barrier, folded her arms over her stomach, and made herself comfortable for a long conversation. Vaughn's gaze remained lucidly rapt on the changes in her expression. The first drink hit her sense of comprehension hard, and its resemblance to an attentive version of herself goaded more out of Greer the longer she kept it up.

"I really hate this job," Greer began. "I thought, for a while, that doing something in fashion might still appeal to my parents, but my mother is hell-bent on keeping the family together to spearhead our company. But you know me; I'm not the next great innovator, and I honestly couldn't care less about enhancing the sound quality of modern phones. Margitte's the big thinker. Emmanuel handles most of the business contacts. If I didn't establish some worth in the company as soon as possible, my parents were going to remove me from their succession plan entirely. So, when an offer came in from the

Keatons to buy the rights to our new transmission chip to put in the new security unit patrols, and my family didn't secure it, I took it upon myself to make it happen."

Vaughn tried not to look confused by the idea of security unit patrols. The closest things she could think of were the steel hounds used by the police.

And the drones, of course.

"Why couldn't they secure it?"

Greer made a closed-mouth noise of enthusiasm while she was taking another drink. "Well, I *thought* it was an error on their part, like they had fucked something up and lost the opportunity to provide an essential component to this wide-scale project, but no! For some reason, they declined the offer. I guess Caldwell's offer was for exclusive rights, and Emmanuel thought that was a stupid idea. He nixed the idea before our parents could even catch wind of it, which meant that I still had a chance to secure that deal and gain favor. I just had to do it in a way that Emmanuel couldn't interfere with."

"Hence, the Drone Run," Vaughn supplied. Although she said it casually in an attempt to seem more knowledgeable about the ordeal, Greer looked at her as if she had mentioned something unspeakable.

"I heard you were there that night."

Returning her attention to the swimmers on the other rooftop, Vaughn replied only with a sip from her wine glass. She wanted to ask what else she'd heard, but it wouldn't help anyone to talk about Liv, even if only to gauge whether a target was already on her back.

Greer continued, "I assume he briefed you beforehand, then?"

Vaughn shrugged, posturing what she hoped looked like nonchalance.

"It was all fucked after that. I held up *my* end of the deal, hired a competent rider, laid out the plan... But, as you know, the rider took a spill, and the money went to some other participant. He told me he would get the money to me some other way, and that I just had to hold off Emmanuel's bitching for a little bit longer. But I don't have much say in the company. *This* was supposed to change that."

"So, the deal didn't go through?"

Greer laughed and shook her head, the sleek sheet of her short hair moving as one. "Where have you even been for the past few months? Have you missed everything?"

Vaughn could no longer follow or hide that she was clueless. She acted drunk instead. "I think the wine's getting to me."

"You're hammering those pretty hard. You okay?" Greer lifted her fingers to Vaughn's temple and combed strands back with her nails. Just dizzy enough not to realize what was happening until it was too late, Vaughn let it happen with nothing more than a flurry of bewildered blinks. "Either way, I don't know how you forgot about the deal. It was one of the first things he did after getting into that High Mayor seat. And it all happened on the right side of the table, which did me a solid when it came to bragging rights. I suspected it would be a harder sell if I got the money for it under the table."

"Of course."

"And what are you doing these days?" Greer took a deep breath and leaned her head back against the barrier. Vaughn wasn't ready to move on from the subject. What she needed to know sat out of reach still.

"Those security patrol units—what else did he tell you about them?"

Greer's tongue clicked in disappointment. "God, you're still just as inseparable from your work as I remember."

Vaughn couldn't help her body from shrinking as if it'd been struck by a fist. She remained, in Greer's eyes, as dull as ever. Vaughn hoped that dullness would prove useful, that nothing would seem amiss if she only wanted to talk about business at a rooftop party, but the remembrance of Greer's words made her not want to speak at all.

She shouldn't have come. Why Vaughn thought coming to this party could lift her spirits, she didn't know.

"Goodbye, Greer."

"What? I didn't mean anything by that, Vaughn, I swear."

"I'm sure you didn't." Greer seemed to take this at face value instead of as sarcasm, as Vaughn had intended. *Always a barrier,* she thought, sliding a second empty glass of wine onto the counter. "Excuse me."

Greer looked for another place to go, then built herself up into the picture of confidence like a jilted bride left standing at an altar. She would be fine. She was always fine. Whether she believed it or not, she didn't need proximity to Vaughn to succeed. Trying to keep it when she didn't want it only hurt them both.

Vaughn's heel caught in a crack in the floor. Her ankle twisted sharply, wrenching a yelp out of her. She steadied herself against another person. They turned around, gave her a smile and an arm, which she used only while testing her weight. She felt a little pain, but her eyes started to burn. She didn't want to cry here. Not in front of all these people, these strangers.

Having narrowly evaded a sprain, she made her way through the clusters of people, looking for Caldwell. His suit jacket lay discarded beside him on the couch. Another man with shirt cuffs hiked up haphazardly to his elbows pressed a hand to her brother's shoulders as he bent over a low tabletop. Caldwell's head gave a sudden jerk. A flash of white between his fingers told Vaughn he had snorted a line of what she could only assume was cocaine. Unease knotted up all over her body.

It was too early for this. Then again, it was too early to have finished two glasses of wine.

Vaughn plucked her phone from the thin fold of her little bag and found Clav's number. She half-expected him to ignore her call; three late-night summonses for unplanned rides home would lead to his resignation. She was too tipsy to understand this and would only feel remorse for it once she was home, where she would realize that he was the only person left in her life to care about.

He picked up on the third ring. "Yeah?"

Vaughn's voice was marked by a telling tremor. "I need you. I mean, I need to get home."

"Where are you?"

She slipped into the elevator alone. "The Skerville. I shouldn't have come here. I don't know what I was thinking." An untamed sob burst out of her. She pressed her palm to her mouth and the phone to her stomach, but she couldn't hide it.

"Okay," he said. "Sit tight. I'll be right there. You want me to stay on the phone? Are you having an emergency?"

She could hear fabric shuffling, a belt clicking. "Yes," she said. Then, because he had asked two questions, "No emergency. I just don't know what to do."

"Take some deep breaths," he said. More clicks. Keys jingling. Metal scraping. Vaughn did as she was told, staring up at the blue light on the ceiling. "Everything's going to be okay. I'll be there in ten minutes tops."

She wiped her nose. So much for putting on any makeup. "You're a good friend, Clav."

He said nothing for several seconds. Then, in a rather pitiful attempt at sarcasm, he said, "I could be better."

20

A muggy sheet of grey hung over Corcoran; part smog, part usual monsoon weather. Through intermittent rain, the sound of thunder ebbed in and out of proximity to Bronlow's garage. The region as a whole was waterlogged for half the year, but the end of summer took on the worst of it.

Liv's coworker, Luis, had turned on a radio station, and its signal flickered unreliably. He shut it off with a grunt. Liv could barely hear it over the dull booms of the weather. "I don't think that rain's going to let up any time soon. You gonna ride the bike home?"

"Unless you feel like giving me a ride."

Liv had no other choice unless her coworker felt gracious enough to weather the storm to take her home, and her luck was never certain. He had two small daughters who kept him inundated with after-work activities that needed attending to. Youth soccer and baseball games and school dance recitals took up much of his availability, which was scarce, given that no one except Liv did shifts at the garage as long as he did.

Asking Corey for a ride home was off the table. He was scheduled late again, much to her and Maura's chagrin. While Liv was happy to have one less person for whom she needed to pretend to be cheery, it left Maura with only Liv to talk to. Maura was observant enough about Liv's moods to make up for his absence. Fielding all of Maura's questions, no matter how well-intentioned they were, gave Liv an itch that only grew and could never be quashed. Liv would climb up to her loft bed, having graduated out of her knee brace and back into her bedroom, flustered and unable to keep her hands still. She would ignore everything happening around her to such an impressive degree that she would put herself to bed through sheer determination.

Luis dragged a metal stool up to the side of the lifted car that Liv was doing a routine undercarriage inspection for and slumped onto it. "You think this guy's going to pick up his car tonight, then?"

"Nah. He's coming tomorrow."

"Maybe you should head home now, instead. If the rain doesn't stop, it'll at least be easier to get through when it's light out."

Liv wiped her hands on her dusty blue coveralls, smearing them with dark dirt, and stepped out from underneath the vehicle to check the time. Some of the stains on the garment had lived there for years and were sufficiently grandfathered in. New spots were indistinguishable from old. She expected to work in this garage forever.

"Why are you still here?" she asked. "You should have gone home already."

"I felt bad leaving you alone. Who are you going to talk to if the radio's down?"

She laughed a little. "Go home, Luis. This won't take me much longer."

"Save it for the morning." He gathered his backpack and keys from a break room in the office. When he returned for a final goodbye and found her in the same spot as before, he shook his head and left without looking back.

Liv luxuriated in the silence before getting back to work. She paced in small circles, mostly mulling over the source of the noise this car's driver had reported, but her focus kept slipping into blankness. She had been sleeping a lot lately, which staved off the usual fatigue but introduced a foggy-headedness that she didn't have before. Sleep got her out of the questioning, an easy progression from hiding in her room and trying not to make noise so Maura wouldn't check on her.

At some point within that shift into sleep, Vaughn would come to mind and thwart her best efforts. It was hard to achieve any comfort when the sound of her last words was still so sharp in Liv's mind. They kept her muscles tense and her pulse fast. Everything around her—the things in her life that were present and true and not some exaggerated, recollected haunt—made her jump.

"Hey." A fist knocked against the entryway into the garage and broke her from her stupor. Although Liv had joked about it in the past, she'd never truly been displeased to see Clavernus Lim until now.

Her eyes widened, and she laughed nervously. "No."

"What do you mean, 'no?'" Vaughn's driver unfurled his fist and raised his hands in the air. "I just want to talk to you."

"Okay, well, no. I don't have anything to say."

Liv hadn't once spoken to Vaughn during the month since their fight, and to her driver, Liv had done even less. It wasn't like she had many chances to see him. He was a former Corcoranite with no remaining ties to the city, employed in Morgallis by a girl who, thankfully, wanted nothing else to do with Liv.

Liv thought she had been safe in that assumption.

He eyed the stool left by Luis and lowered himself onto it slowly. "That's too bad... But *I* can talk."

Liv was wearing a scratched-up pair of protective glasses and took them off in a melodramatic flourish. "You caught me at a bad time. I was just about to—"

"You know what else caught *me* at a bad time, Liv? A call. Three nights ago. I was lying in bed, having a go at building a successful beachfront strip in Cities: Skylines IX, when my employer called me. You know. *Vaughn*."

Liv ignored him and fetched a rag from the workbench. She tossed the glasses aside a little too hard and flinched when the lenses scraped against the metal.

"I don't suppose you want to ask how she was doing."

"You know that we don't talk. I don't know why you're trying to act coy about this. It's none of my—"

"Because I don't understand how you could say the things you said to her when she was so good to you unless you were a cold-hearted loser."

"*Wow*," Liv said. "That's rich coming from you, Clav. I expect you, of all people, to understand why I said it."

Clav's brow furrowed low.

"Or maybe you've just gotten comfortable in the Upper City and forgotten what it's like to live in Corcoran under the Keatons," she continued. "How much harm they do. How much they take away. Just because it isn't the case for you anymore doesn't mean thousands of people aren't still struggling with the consequences of their actions."

"Of course, I remember it. How easy do you think I have it now? You think I live lavishly? That I have a place just like Vaughn's and my shit's nice like hers? I live in a one-bedroom the size of a shoebox, but we're not talking about me."

"We're not talking about anything. I'm going home."

Bright white, immediately followed by a deafening crack of thunder, worked to make her look more foolish than she probably was. The rain lashed against the building with an anger that rivalled a scream.

Liv pulled another nearby stool toward the workbench where she stood and folded into it, exhausted. She brought her heels up to the bowing metal rung. Her fingers clasped behind her neck, and her eyes closed as if in meditation. "I don't owe her anything," she said. "Neither do you."

"Sure. I don't owe her anything. At least, not past my job requirements. But I show up anyway, because I care, and because she's good to me."

Liv didn't know what else to say. When she cycled through defenses, she only ever came back to a few. If Clav Lim couldn't understand them, she had nothing else to stand on.

She put her head down on the bench and sighed. What were those defenses for? Not for a girl she had already pushed away, but for herself, and she could poke holes in them as easily as styrofoam. If Liv couldn't convince herself that her reasons were sound, she would have to contend with the loss of one of the loveliest people she had ever met.

It had to be for something. Liv wanted it to be for something bigger than herself, a wider awakening to class disparities and inequity that Vaughn had overlooked, but Vaughn was also just a girl. She couldn't fix everything. She couldn't even fix Liv's original prosthetic.

Some things were simply beyond repair.

Did it make Liv naive to think her world was salvageable? That anyone could fix all the bad things in her life that had lodged into her body like bits of broken glass was an idea so far-fetched; she ought to abandon all hope.

Hope was angry, sometimes. Hope meant that she held onto all that hurt so there would be somewhere to grow from, and she clung to those sharp, broken things that could never be fixed.

Clav approached her warily and squatted down at her side.

"She doesn't know I'm here right now, and I'd prefer that she didn't know. Truth is, I haven't been a good friend to her. I didn't think I owed her anything either. But it's worth something to me that she tries."

"What if that's not enough?" Liv asked, surprised at how

close she was to crying. "No amount of *trying* is going to change this thing that's just too fundamentally different about us."

"No, it won't. Still doesn't mean she isn't worthy of a little grace."

"What do you want me to do, then?"

"Me?" Clav pushed himself to his feet. "I don't care what you do. I just thought Vaughn deserved a friend who would stick up for her. I told you my two cents, and now I'm going home."

Liv laid her cheek in her hand and kneaded her temple with her hard, silver fingertips. With more exasperation than malice, she said, "Nobody ever has any answers."

Clav indignantly threw up the hand holding his keys. "Look, I'm not here to tell you what to want. Just here to tell you that you ought to start thinking about it. Otherwise, you're going to hurt a lot of people who care about you. See you."

He left after that, sparing no further glances or words of pity. Through the tinted panels of the garage doors and the heavy sheets of rain, Liv saw him jog out to his car and throw himself inside. The light flickered on, then faded away, and left Liv alone with her thoughts again. Those evil things.

She reached across the workbench for her discarded safety goggles, not looking. They fell to the ground. Everything holding Liv together seemed to fall, too.

Lowering to her knees, she joined her dropped goggles. She unfurled across the cold floor; the shock against her flushed skin pushed a noise out of her akin to a cough. The car hovered on its lift above her, abandoned. She stared at it for a long time, until another, milder sensation of cold had appeared beside her eyes.

She didn't know how long she had lain there letting the night grow older until her comms device rattled against the metal workbench. Maura must have assumed she was stranded somewhere or had taken a spill in the rain.

Liv rubbed her eyes and nose, putting on a brave face for no one. She was prepared to answer a message from Maura with an excuse as to why she hadn't left work.

Instead, the full and punctuated name of Vaughn Q. Keaton popped up.

Everything is gone. Someone took the blueprints.

Added to the list of singular experiences in Liv's life: speeding through torrential rain not to make amends with a girl whose last words were 'fuck you,' but to show up at her house anyway. Liv didn't have a plan. She was focused on not hydroplaning off the bridge from Corcoran to Morgallis and visualizing twenty feet ahead of her bike in the downpour.

She was sure of few things: that she was soggy, miserable, and unsure of whether she would make it to the house in one piece.

Morgallis had been built to spite the floods, and its walls were made of something absorbent and thirsty. The high-rises drank up much of the rainfall before it could hit Liv.

She left the city having achieved only a brief reprieve before being thrust back into the storm. She resembled a chew toy dropped in a bathtub.

Her bike pushed through the wet dirt of the hillside, valiantly kicking tar-black sludge up her knees. *This must be what hell feels like,* she thought, possibly her only coherent thought. Branches uprooted from nearby sludge and whacked her viciously. She was soaked down to her bones. She would be okay as long as she didn't sink. The house was so close, only a few minutes at her speed.

Her bike was struggling to climb through a particularly

nasty well of debris spanning the width of the road when a car careened down the hill, headlights glowing in the rain.

She swerved. Her bike twisted and stalled in the mud. *"Fuck!"* Barely saved by her bad knee from tipping off, Liv spun around to admonish the car. All she could see were its taillights.

She recollected herself, panting like a dog. In the dark, alone again, she allowed herself to think about what an awful decision she'd made. Mud caked her bottom half. Rain drenched through the rest of her. She could have waited until morning if she had really wanted to come, but she knew that, with a little time to think it through, she wouldn't come at all.

Liv finished the climb toward the glass house grimly.

Alternating patterns of flashing police lights ricocheted off the blackened foliage. In front of the gate sat two cars and one officer; other cars and bodies moved through various tasks behind the clear glass of Vaughn's home.

"Hey!" the officer by the gate shouted. "You have business up here?"

Liv nodded, but her hesitation was clear.

"The estate is closed to visitors for the evening! I'm sorry, you'll have to reschedule!"

"I need to talk to her!"

The officer shook his head. The walkie nestled in a pocket on his uniform jacket beeped, and a message came through. He dipped his head apologetically and returned to his car to exchange words with one of the officers on the inside.

Liv floored the kickstand and pushed aside the strands of hair that stuck to her forehead. She refused to leave until she could see Vaughn. She could only see officers through the glass from where she stood. A dreaded idea seeped into her mind that Vaughn might not even be there. Maybe Clav had come back to pick her up and take her to his shoebox apartment, or her repugnant brother had taken her to the family home that seemed to haunt her. She might have been in the car that nearly hit Liv on the way up.

The girl emerged from her workshop, accompanied by two officers, fidgeting with the band around her braid. A small victory and fear that made Liv's heart stutter.

Liv waved her arms in wide arcs to capture her attention from an impossible distance, watched with impassivity by the officer hiding in his car from the rain.

The officer nearest to the open front door noticed Liv first. The conversation at hand absorbed all of Vaughn's attention; she registered her rider's presence in stages. She looked at her for a while, motionless and blank-faced. She stepped toward the doorway and excused herself automatically as she passed the other officers.

Vaughn flinched at the rain, as if she had forgotten about it until it hit her. She broke into a clumsy jog toward the gate. "Let her in!"

Liv rounded the vehicle, spurred forward by the sureness of Vaughn's steps. The collision of their bodies and the interlocking of their arms happened instinctively. A small noise huffed out of Vaughn's mouth, so close to Liv's ear that she could feel her lips moving again.

Twisting into the fabric of Vaughn's cardigan, Liv's fingers held the other girl with unflinching certainty. The tremors in Vaughn's breath rattled up through her hands.

"Oh, Liv." Vaughn's arms laced around Liv's shoulders. A hand snuck into Liv's sweat-damp hair and held her in place. She glanced warily at the officer behind her and whispered for Liv's ears alone, "You shouldn't have come back."

21

Liv had spent nearly an hour in the rain by the time she arrived at Vaughn's house. Taking shelter was no longer a priority for her; none of her clothes were salvageable from the dirt, and no corner or crevice of her body had been spared by the rain.

She stared incredulously at Vaughn, whose grip around Liv's shoulders had loosened if only so she could observe the filthy state of her former rider.

"Did you hear me?" Vaughn asked. "Your fingerprints are *everywhere.*"

"So? I didn't take anything."

Behind them, the officer that Vaughn had been previously speaking to zipped a hooded raincoat up to his chin and stepped into the downpour to join them.

"I know," Vaughn assured her. "I know exactly who did it, but they refuse to listen to me."

"What? Why?"

"You know why. Caldwell has them in his pocket. They're his drinking buddies, his family friends. Whether or not any of them believes me is irrelevant. My word means nothing against his."

"You think Caldwell did it?"

With a ragged desperation, Vaughn said, "I *know* he did it." Her eyes fell on Liv's face, at first pleading. She became cognizant of how close they remained. She made a futile effort to wipe the accumulating drops of rain from her face and backed away.

Liv, whose gaze had been fixed so stringently on Vaughn, straightened herself out before the officer could get any closer.

"Miss Keaton," he said. The stiff, zipped collar nearly obscured his mouth. "We're happy to spend some more time gathering evidence from the house, but we've got plenty to go on."

"I told you who did it," Vaughn muttered. "You're wasting your time."

"Surely, you must have someone else in mind who could have wanted your plans." As he said this, the officer's attention flickered as fast as a camera flash to the silver poking out of Liv's jacket sleeve. "Look... Trying to assign fault to the High Mayor won't get you anywhere with the folks at the station. I really suggest taking a moment tonight to come up with some names. Otherwise, there's nothing else we can do for you."

Through her visage of professionalism, bitterness leaked through, easy to miss by anyone who hadn't looked at Vaughn's face long enough to learn its subtleties. "That's my brother, Officer Welles, not my High Mayor. And you don't work for him. You work for the people."

"We work for the city he runs, Miss Keaton."

"A city is not one man alone. If I can suggest something, too, it's that you and your station reconsider why you do this at all if not to help."

The visible half of the officer's face tensed. "Very well. I'll have the guys off the property in the next few minutes."

Vaughn said nothing and looked at neither of them. She pulled the cardigan tight around her body and surveyed the landscape around her as it pulsed in unnatural shades of red and blue. She wiped her face again with a barely perceptible sniff. "Excuse me."

Liv had nothing to do but follow her unless she wanted to be stranded in the rain again.

She waited outside, keeping a comfortable distance between herself and the Keaton girl while the rest of the officers who were overturning her house filed out to their cars. One by one, the lights atop their vehicles switched off. Each left with high beams on and minutes between themselves and the next car.

When everyone had left, Liv asked, "Can I come in?"

Vaughn waved her inside, unsatisfactorily miffed. Streaks of mud caked Liv's pants from the ride up the flooding, half-paved road. "Stay here."

Liv was in no position to complain. Vaughn disappeared into her bedroom, and when she returned, she had a pile of clothing and a bath towel in her arms. "You can leave your things outside the bathroom door."

"You don't have to clean them."

"I'm not going to make you sit in them when they're filthy. I certainly don't plan on sending you all the way back to Corcoran in this weather. Why you thought coming here at this hour was a good idea, I have no idea."

Liv bit her tongue and took her unspoken retort to the bathroom with her.

She showered as dexterously as she could in an unfamiliar shower without her prosthetic. With what little time she had to think, she rehearsed all the ways that this could go. She could sit in silence on Vaughn's couch until her clothes had gone through an expedient dryer cycle and be sent home without regard. They could fight again. Vaughn could impress how foolish an idea it was to show up uninvited and unwelcome.

Nothing seemed promising. Still, Liv was here. A fresh change of Vaughn's clothes waited for her on the countertop. The fabric was cold and smooth against her skin. The T-shirt she slipped over her head smelled unmistakably like Vaughn. Liv hadn't realized how much of Vaughn Keaton she had been missing. She brought the edge of the collar up to her nose.

The garments were loose and stretchy, capable of fitting Liv's dissimilar build. Vaughn had left a pair of supple blue socks that rose to the ankle and a matching set of gray sweatpants and a shirt.

Temporary fixes, surely. She couldn't imagine Vaughn wanting her to stay. Liv had a guilty face. She prodded it in the mirror, up close and scrutinous. Why should Vaughn forgive her? She didn't come with a plan or an apology lined up. Vaughn had no reason to let her stay.

Liv thought of the alternative—Vaughn being alone in a house from which her things had just been stolen. Maybe that was enough to want Liv close, even if she hated her. Even if she no longer wanted her around. Vaughn needed *someone,* and the only person at her disposal was Liv.

Vaughn was in the workshop when Liv exited the bathroom. She sat in her swivelly chair, staring at the bare workbench in front of her. She didn't turn when Liv approached her or flinch when Liv put her hands on the bench beside her. "My brother is gone," she said in a tone Liv couldn't decipher. "It's real this time. I've been losing him for years now, but I've held out hope time and time again that something inside him would draw him back. He's gone. He did this, and now he's gone."

"Hey." It was the same meaningless cajolement Corey might have used on her when he didn't know what to say. "Tell me what happened."

Vaughn shook her head. "There's nothing I can prove. Lunokhod was disabled. And the cameras. The only people who know about them are Caldwell and Clav."

"And me."

"You didn't steal the plans, Liv."

No, she didn't, but Vaughn's conviction drew merit from nothing. "You sound so sure of that."

"Because I'm right. I know him, and I know you. Only one of you has the gall to think I would forgive you for something like this." Vaughn leaned back in her chair and swivelled it toward Liv. She rubbed her temple slowly. "But since you're here."

"I didn't take the paperwork."

A smile teased the corners of Vaughn Keaton's lips. "Figures."

"Do you know why he did it?"

After a long pause, Vaughn admitted, "I have... suspicions. I just don't know if I have it in me to care anymore."

Liv pulled up the second chair, which had been moved across the room. She sat close enough that their knees brushed lightly. "That's not true. I know you care."

"At some point, it just becomes too much to handle. How does someone change so much in such a short amount of time and keep nothing of their old self? I don't know how to talk to him anymore. I used to think he was doing this in part to keep me close to him; he would remind me of how we were the only Keatons left, and it was essential that we stick together. But he has changed in a way I can't even fathom, become something awful and cruel. Maybe he just took the paperwork because he wanted to hurt me. That's as good a reason as any these days." Vaughn rubbed the exhaustion from her eyes and glanced at her cellphone for the time. "I need to change the laundry."

She left for the laundry closet, and when she returned, she handed Liv a glass of water. Liv hadn't realized how dry her mouth was until now. The cold glass against her warm hands was enough to make her salivate, and a mere sip was all it took to reinstate her ability to reason.

Liv looked at Vaughn and truly felt the enormity of her

words weighing down on her. Pushing the glass aside, she reached for Vaughn's hand.

"Don't."

"V, you're shaking again."

Vaughn tightened the cardigan around her body as if it could hold her together. "You didn't have to come. I took it seriously, what you said before. There's no point in trying to make this work. We don't... We don't *make sense*." The last words were quiet, as if they hurt to speak.

Liv stood up to reach her level. "So what if we don't make sense? I don't care about that anymore."

"Yes, you do. You've always cared about it."

"And that was stupid." Carefully, Liv grasped her by the shoulders so Vaughn couldn't look away. "I was pissed off and scared. Someone had just put a gun to my head, and I freaked out. That wasn't your fault. I shouldn't have said it."

Prying each finger apart from her shoulders, Vaughn said, "You meant it. You know, deep down, that you still believe it to be true."

She returned to her seat, having to contend with the fact that Liv could not be made to leave when it was storming outside, and her wet clothes were trapped in the dryer for an hour. She hid her face in her hands and propped her elbows on the workbench. "I'm always going to be a Keaton. I'm not allowed to be more than that family name; it overshadows the fact that I'm also just a girl. No matter how much I do for the good of this city, I have my father's legacy weighing me down. And now Caldwell... I'm trying to prove that name wrong and do right by everyone else, but maybe it's pointless. Maybe you're right."

Liv did not take her seat again. She sank to her knees beside Vaughn's legs and spun the chair toward her. "Sure, I meant it," she said. "That doesn't make it right. Doesn't mean I wouldn't take it back if I could."

"But you can't take it back."

"I can say I'm sorry." She looked up at Vaughn and the strand of loose hair at her temple that begged to be sorted out. "You could forgive me."

Vaughn's mouth was a hard, flat line, and the dip between her brows was a few kept seconds away from boring a permanent dip into her skull.

Liv's efforts came up short. She faced a brick wall of a woman who had just been wronged by too many people she trusted. Maybe Liv didn't deserve a second chance. She had been given so many in the past; perhaps, it was inevitable that someone would keep their second chance to themselves.

She laid her cheek on the top of Vaughn's knees, prostrated. "I'm sorry. I don't know what else to do. I fucked up, V. Tell me what to do to fix it."

"Liv," the other girl lamented. Her fingers carded delicately through Liv's hair and around her ear. They hovered over the road scars that trailed down her cheek.

Liv couldn't bear the inaction. She closed her eyes tightly. She craved the touch, the affection. It wasn't forgiveness, but it sufficed in its place.

Vaughn's hand slid lower, easing down the side of her neck to the middle of her shoulders. She gave a gentle command. "Get up."

What she meant was, "Come here."

She cradled Liv's face in her hands and tilted it upward. Eyeing the tension between Liv's brows, she smoothed over it with her thumb. "You look ridiculous down there."

The chair's wheels shifted disruptively. Vaughn pulled her upward and placed a kiss upon Liv's forehead, then her scarred cheek.

Liv's hands found purchase on Vaughn's waist as she

stumbled forward. She felt as if a hand had been pushing down on her chest for weeks, and she had just been allowed to breathe again. Teeth struck teeth in a thoughtless maintenance of closeness. Vaughn's fingers, still quivering, grasped tightly around Liv's borrowed shirt.

An anguished, half-muffled noise wrenched out of Liv's mouth. Vaughn's kiss was demanding and unrelenting, and Liv wanted nothing more than to satisfy her every need.

They followed each other up to their feet. Liv made quick work of crushing all the remaining space that sprouted between them. The desperation in Vaughn's grasp spurred her on, waking her entire body up. She came alive with it, as if it were a heartbeat steadily murmuring the other girl's name. *Vaughn. Vaughn. Vaughn.*

Vaughn pressed her fingers to Liv's chin and gave it a soft push. "Wait— This isn't—"

"No?"

"No, it is. I just—" Vaughn couldn't hold onto her thoughts. Liv had woken her up, too, but in the manner of espresso shots on an empty stomach. "I need you to know this isn't why I invited you."

"You didn't invite me at all." Liv's mouth broke into a smile. Being held so close had an inebriating effect on her. "But this isn't why I came, either."

Vaughn's eyes flickered to Liv's, hopeful and overwhelmed with unspent desire. Her hands fell beneath the hem of Liv's shirt and sealed to her bare waist. "I want this," she said. "Maybe we don't make sense, but everything feels right when you're here. And I'd like it if you stayed."

The implications of a much longer time spent kissing Vaughn Keaton made Liv's face flush. She revelled in the lightness of being next to the other girl, how all her fatigue seemed to slip away.

She would figure it out tomorrow, whether it meant one night or something much longer. When Vaughn drew her out of the workshop, Liv fervently obliged.

Only twice had Vaughn invited Liv into her bedroom before. Both times, Liv waited in the doorway for her to complete a quick task or collect something she had forgotten.

Being dragged into her room now felt like crossing another kind of threshold entirely. She had discovered an elation from which she could never return, and she chased it with chaste kisses. Vaughn closed her door, which gave her little privacy, since the shaders in her glass walls and her requests to Lunokhod went unacknowledged by the disabled AI.

"Goddamn it," Vaughn whispered. She looked at every wall as if she could scare Lunokhod into response. Liv pressed her thumb to the soft hollow beneath Vaughn's jaw and urged it further upward, making space to lavish the length of her neck with her mouth. "I can hang something up on the wall if it's too open for you."

"I don't care." Liv could not imagine anyone would withstand torrential rain for the sake of voyeurism. Nothing mattered to her except for this room, this bed. She could see nothing but Vaughn and regarded little else while she had her melting against her touch.

Vaughn goaded her back onto the bed. Her sheets were white with pale blue stripes—*like pinstripes*, Liv thought. Parting her knees, Liv tugged Vaughn between them and untucked her shirt from the waistband of her trousers. "Take these off."

Vaughn rested her hand on Liv's shoulder and whispered in her ear, "Take what off?"

The unmistakable romance of her mouth along the shell of Liv's felt like a battle won. Liv could see beneath her high collar to the sharp jut of bone and, like a starved animal, she ached to taste it, to devour her totally. "All of it. I want you naked." Naked, trembling, screaming—Liv didn't confess the extent of it.

Vaughn slid her cardigan down her shoulders and unfastened each button of her shirt with methodical slowness. She surveyed Liv's face for a break in her patience. She thought it was a punishment, making Liv wait. As if she didn't enjoy the sight of Vaughn taking herself apart for her. Every piece shed was a reward. A cause for praise.

Liv hooked her index around the little band between her sheer bralette cups and tugged. "How do you want *me*, V?"

She laughed. "Obscenely. Sometimes, when we were working, I would just look at you and forget how to think."

"I didn't know you were capable of not thinking."

Unhooking her bralette, Vaughn replied, "Neither did I. I've learned a lot about myself with you. For instance—" She took Liv's left hand, which rested on her waistband, and brought it to her mouth, kissing her palm. "I never realized how much I missed being touched until you were sitting next to me, with your hands to yourself. It's not something I usually care about, but I would find myself staring at your fingers as you took your notes."

She bit gently into the fleshy part of Liv's palm. "I wanted to do filthy things with your hands, Liv." Then, she wrapped her lips around her thumb and coated it in enough spit that, when she moved Liv's hand to her breast, it left her skin gleaming. "I want them to do filthy things to me."

Marvelling in the rare softness of Vaughn Keaton's body, Liv drew her closer and opened her mouth to the glistening pink bud of her nipple. Vaughn keened against her with a gasp. Liv swirled her tongue around it, as Vaughn carded nails along her scalp. She sucked until it was plump and red. Adored it because it was Vaughn's. She did the same with the other and made unhurried work of unbuttoning Vaughn's trousers so she could turn elsewhere once her breasts were too tender for more.

Liv spun her onto the bed with a suddenness that caused her to yelp. She wanted the Keaton girl under her, gasping for her, relinquishing all sorts of unbidden sounds. She dropped to her knees and pulled Vaughn's trousers off. "Do you want my fingers, then?"

Vaughn let her back stretch across the mattress. "I want to know what could have happened that night, had we not..."

"Fought."

"By that point, I would have let you do anything. I just wanted you to make me come."

Her eyelids fluttered shut as Liv's hands slid up the expanse of her bare chest. Liv's touch was greedy. She followed the path blazed by her hands with her lips and settled both beside her throat with a tantalizing slowness, wherein Liv left bruising love bites up to the bottom of Vaughn's ear, reaching her scar.

"I'll make you come," Liv promised. Evidence of her lips trailed down to Vaughn's collarbone. She looked up at Vaughn, pleased with herself for having left a sufficient signature. "I just want to do it right. That night, everything happened so fast. I wouldn't have been a good lover for you."

She marked her course back between Vaughn's legs with shorter, gentler kisses. "It would've been quick and clumsy. You deserve someone who can fuck you all night. Someone who takes their time to enjoy you. To appreciate you..." Liv splayed her hand across Vaughn's stomach. Her body had warmed. Liv admired the subtle curves of her hips like flashes of a long-forgotten dream. "God, look at you. You're perfect."

Vaughn covered her eyes with her forearm. "I find it completely unfair that I am totally undressed while you still have all your clothes on."

Liv stripped off her shirt to appease her. She resumed her appreciation between Vaughn's legs as if there had been no interruption. With a permissive tug on her underwear, Vaughn's hips rose and fell so Liv could slip the flimsy bit of fabric off her legs.

Liv trailed her thumb along the knobby bone of Vaughn's ankle. She guided it over her shoulder. Pressed her face to Vaughn's thigh and nibbled on it. "I want to give you everything."

Vaughn's nails raked through her hair. "Please," she said hoarsely. "I need you. I want—"

Liv answered first with only gentle pressure against the girl's clit. She touched through a fine layer of damp, chestnut-colored hair. Vaughn's hips jerked upward. A whine tumbled out of her mouth. "Sorry, I should have told you," she rushed. "I-I'm quite sensitive."

Liv soothed her silver fingers along her thigh, bearing it against her cheek while her other hand continued to tease. "You're doing amazing, V."

"I'm not doing anything."

Liv buried her face into that soft flesh of thigh, smiling to herself. She wondered how long she could get away with this minimal touch. How much gentle petting Vaughn would endure before she begged. She couldn't deny herself the satisfaction of watching Vaughn come apart around her. "You don't even know what you do to me. Seeing you in those tights, wearing my jacket. I've never felt less rational in my life." A slow swipe along the pink seam of Vaughn's pussy left her fingers slick. She put them in her mouth, and the taste of arousal nearly made her black out. Thoroughly wet with her saliva, she teased the entrance of Vaughn's cunt before she sank two fingers deep inside her, welcomed by a sudden clench.

She moved slowly, making space where she was warm and

tight, relishing in the way Vaughn's body responded to her. Pressure from Vaughn's heels dug into her back. From her nails, a pleasurable friction on her scalp.

To be wanted with such fervency made Liv feel deranged. To know that the soft utterances of her name and the long, gratifying sounds Vaughn made were just for her shattered any sense of restraint she still had left.

She rewarded her lover with the flat of her tongue and the force of her lips, which doled out other affirmations. "Oh, Liv. You marvelous girl."

Threatening her languid, confident strokes was the niggling insecurity that she wasn't used to using her left hand this way. Only once had she been intimate with another person since she had lost her arm. The sex had been different. She liked wearing a strap, and luckily, the other girl had liked Liv wearing it, too. Liv didn't feel entirely graceful with her hands anymore, but she was committed and eager. She had a mouth that knew how to make girls come and hips that begged to be held tight by Vaughn's long, slender legs. She had stamina that she could put to better use in other ways.

Next time, she thought. Liv had several delicious fantasies that involved Vaughn Keaton on her back or her stomach, stuffed full and deep, and covered in hickeys. But this, having Vaughn's thighs pressed to her ears, was more than pleasurable. Liv wondered if she could come without even touching herself—just watching Vaughn get there with her tongue.

She could feel her pleasure building around her fingers, swelling against her mouth. She looked up at Vaughn, seeing only her arched back and small, raised tits moving in a shallow panting rhythm. Liv suddenly wished she had more hands.

She kissed Vaughn's hip and replaced her tongue with the heavy heel of her palm. "A little more," she murmured. The air kissed her face, where it was hot and sticky. "Come on, V. You can do it."

Vaughn nodded quickly, though she was too breathless to speak.

It overtook her with a sudden jerk and a sharp cry. Her fingers dug into Liv's shoulder blades. Her thighs squeezed tight around Liv's hand, holding it still inside her.

She was indescribably beautiful. How Liv ever thought she stood a chance against her was foolish beyond comparison. She trailed gentle kisses up Vaughn's body, seizing a chance to catch her breath. Her senses returned to her slowly. She removed her hand from between Vaughn's legs and wiped it clean with the shirt she had removed. "Sorry."

Vaughn smiled languidly, gazing at her through heavy-lidded eyes. "Oh, it's so troubling. Seeing you clean me off your fingers. I'd hoped you would keep it there like a souvenir."

Liv pushed Vaughn's knees up to her stomach, kissed them both, and moved them aside to lie down with her. She braced herself on her right arm, silver sinking into the twisted sheets. She could think of so many ways to please Vaughn Keaton, but a thought took root that, maybe, she would only ever do so much. A question drilled into her mind with frustrating persistence. Did Vaughn mind the difference in her palms? Did she care for the feeling of metal against her skin?

Vaughn propped herself on her side and traced the line of muscle down the other girl's stomach to her pelvis with her fingertips. "Hey." Her large, fluttering eyes fixed Liv's gaze in place, as if she knew her mind was wandering into unwelcoming places and she could lure her back to safety. She fitted her face into the bent corner of Liv's neck. Her thumb pressed into Liv's hip, just above the low-slung waistband of her borrowed sweatpants. "Take these off for me? Let me repay the favor."

"I don't mind just making you come," Liv said. "It's a bit of an ordeal getting me there. I'm not— *ah*—" Vaughn's lips parted, and she sucked until light bruises formed above the sleeve of Liv's prosthetic that matched her own. When they were sufficiently noticeable, she gave Liv a self-satisfied hum. "I'm not as sensitive as I'd like to be."

"I'm a fast learner," Vaughn suggested, "and a very enthusiastic student."

Liv touched her rather mindlessly now that they were like this. She was working toward nothing, her only focus on mapping the sequence of ribs and the bend in Vaughn's waist for when she was alone in her room again and needed something to tip her over the edge. She pressed a kiss to Vaughn's shoulder. "You're perfect. It's just..." Liv shook her head with a slight laugh. "Sometimes, I think I've lost some sensitivity from the bike. Or maybe it's just hard for other people to make me come. I can do it on my own, but it takes a lot to get me there, and I... It's probably embarrassing, but I get off on the pressure of, like, *riding*."

"Why would that be embarrassing?"

"I don't know. In my head, there's a conflation to be made between the position and the bike, and I generally try not to be thinking of anything else during sex."

Vaughn surged forward and kissed her with a small huff of effort. Her tongue trailed along the seam of Liv's lips, tasting evidence of herself. Her thigh slid between Liv's. "I should know how to make you come, Liv."

"I'm more than happy being the one to provide."

"I want to." Vaughn nudged the waistband down Liv's hips. "Show me what to do."

"It might take a while. Trust me, I'm horny as hell right now, but my body just likes to take its time."

"I can be patient."

Of all the things she'd said to turn her on, Liv suspected this was not meant to be one of them. She pushed her bottom layers down her legs swiftly. She climbed back on top of Vaughn, aligning their hips in a configuration she knew could work for her. She lifted one of Vaughn's thighs simply to kiss the inside of her knee and have something to hold.

She bore her hips down against Vaughn's, shifting until she found that perfect spot, and until a lightning strike of pleasure darted up her body. Heavenly.

Liv's grip around Vaughn's knee and her ribs tightened possessively. "Is this okay?"

Vaughn was ogling her with her huge, desirous eyes, her hand tracing a path from Liv's hip to her breast. She thumbed at her nipple. "Don't worry about me this time. I just want this to be for you."

"It is," Liv said. "This feels... so good for me. It should feel good for you, too."

Vaughn nodded slowly and watched Liv indulge in her body. The attention overwhelmed her. She touched her forehead to Vaughn's propped-up knee, hiding the deep red flush in her face. In this position, Vaughn could see her more clearly, and it seemed to be the only thing she wanted to do.

"If you keep looking at me like that, I'm going to come in, like, two minutes."

"I'm just looking at you," she said innocently. "Like I always do."

"But you have... such pretty eyes." Liv's lips parted in a moan against Vaughn's knee. She was less vocal than Vaughn, and her sounds were less musical. She knew an orgasm was close whenever her words turned to incoherent babbling. She let them trail off and turn to bites. "They're like... Fuck, I don't know. I'm almost there."

But Vaughn came first, grappling for something to hold onto. Her hips jerked upward. Her body arched into Liv's touch, a ragged sound tearing through her lungs.

Seeing her so unwound pushed Liv over seconds later. She came with a whine muffled against Vaughn's knee, then a rush of insecurity. She hadn't known this kind of intimacy in what felt like years. Beyond sex and bareness, she had not been this undone by any person before.

She closed her eyes and drew another lazy kiss to the side of Vaughn's kneecap. Spent, she mumbled, "I'm going to have to get back in the shower again tonight. It's so late."

Vaughn pushed herself upright, still crushed and panting beneath Liv's hips. She nuzzled the inner curve of Liv's breast, beneath the cutoff of the sleeve for her prosthetic. "I don't think I could forgive you for getting out of this bed right now. I'm feeling rather vulnerable."

Liv gave a hoarse laugh, but she couldn't fathom the thought of being anywhere else but next to Vaughn. The immediacy of the act clouded her thoughts. She would emerge from her sex-drunk stupor tomorrow, but she didn't want to think about it now. How stupid this was. How special she felt.

How she was grossly in love with Vaughn Keaton.

As a rule, she didn't admit those kinds of things just after sex, so she said nothing about it and spoke only of her less precious thoughts while Vaughn followed her begrudgingly to the shower and washed with her.

She wondered if Vaughn lived by a similar rule. She couldn't assume that Vaughn felt as strongly for her or in such similar terms, but she could sense something large and important lingering behind everything she said to her as they dressed in new pajamas and lay on her bed.

She knew it was better this way. Safer for Liv's heart. She could only withstand so many Big Feelings so fast, and she'd have to sit with this one for a while, but part of her wanted Vaughn to give voice to this thing, just to know.

As Vaughn flirted with the edges of sleep, she laid her hand over the tracks of scars on Liv's cheek. "What do you think I should do, Liv?"

"Sleep."

"After that." She combed through the shaggy, loose bits of dark hair hanging down Liv's forehead and added, "I'm never going to get those plans back."

"We'll make new ones then. What are the chances your brother knows what to do with them?" Liv's speech slowed, her eyelids already too heavy to open again.

"He's not an idiot."

"But you are brilliant."

Vaughn sighed. "If he wants to manufacture that technology as-is, he doesn't need to know what to do with the plans. He just needs to have someone else who does. Right now, he has everyone at his disposal."

"Not everyone. Not us." Liv slung her knee around Vaughn's leg and tucked her forehead underneath her chin. She was too warm and cozy under the duvet to think of blueprints. Being wrapped in the scent of Vaughn's body wash was what Heaven felt like. "We'll figure it out tomorrow."

"But what if—"

"Shh." She kissed Vaughn's neck. "Tomorrow."

The Keaton girl deflated, with some relief that she had been permitted to leave her cruel brain and return to the land of the living. Her heartbeat slowed. Her arms slid around Liv's neck and went slack with tension shortly after.

Liv was already asleep, and so, she assumed she had dreamt it when Lunokhod awoke with a two-tone beeping pattern and said, "System override malfunction. Rebooting... Rebooting... Rebooting..."

22

Liv rose at dawn to find the shaders turned to about 50%. They were set on a schedule to lower and rise as the daylight shifted, but Vaughn usually adjusted it manually with a command to Lunokhod. Vaughn was out cold when Liv woke up, embroiled in such a deep sleep that she didn't even squirm when Liv crept out of bed.

Liv reattached her prosthetic, gave her fingers a customary flex, and escaped to the bathroom.

Vaughn's retaliatory marks freckled her throat above where the scuba of her prosthetic sleeve ended, bright red beneath the mirror light. Liv observed the phenomenon, half-satisfied and dread-laden. She tugged the neckline of the sleeve higher, which did nothing to hide it. No garment she owned would cover it up aside from a hooded jacket, and it was the warmest time of the year. Worse yet, she could not even justify a jacket with the rain; the sky was cloudless and empty from the previous day's storm. She would only look guilty, and she had criminally observant coworkers.

But she felt light with elation and mostly absolved from her fuck-up. She picked around Vaughn's cabinets and found an open pack of extra toothbrushes. Another small win to elevate her mood. She brushed her teeth, tamped down her pokey, slept-on hair, and fetched her clothes from the laundry room.

She dressed in the bedroom. Vaughn slept soundly through the shuffling of clothing and *thunk* of her shoes, giving little more indication than a sigh that she was aware of Liv's presence at all. As Liv was pulling her belt tight through the buckle, she noticed something in the room that had not been there when they had gone to bed. A smattering of papers upon which Vaughn had begun to re-draft the parts she could remember from their previous blueprints. She must have woken up at some point and adjusted the shaders to do some work.

Most of the numbers were non-specific, marked with asterisks, the words "Measure again," or "Ask Liv." Apart from what Vaughn had already written, Liv could only remember one or two missing values. She rooted around the disorganized pile for the pencil Vaughn had been using and found it wedged in the pages of her black notebook.

Liv's fingers stalled over the cover. Was this... No, it was a different notebook from the one she was using to conceptualize her prosthetic's design, which Liv rightfully assumed had been taken.

When she flipped it open on the desk, only thin, scratchy diary entries greeted her.

Liv knew she shouldn't pry. Vaughn didn't always tell her everything at first, but she was honest whenever Liv asked her questions. How strong was their trust now? Even if she had thrown herself at Vaughn's feet and asked for forgiveness, wrongdoings didn't typically disappear after a night of good sex.

It was unlikely that she would ever have a chance to see something like this again. To know what someone truly thought of her when they thought she couldn't see it. She pressed the pages flat with her hand and braced for the worst.

Emile from school was on M&H. I don't understand how the most insufferable people find love so easily. That's assuming I believe the credibility of love on reality TV. Even so, I discovered an online following that's willing to pick up the pieces of whatever eventual divorce comes from this show. It must be nice to be wanted like that. He's in that sweet spot of public perception before it tips into parasocial scariness right now.

I thought I was in that spot for a while. I keep to myself and stay out of trouble. I've seen what kind of public trouble Caldwell gets into. How do I end up in the public eye anyway? What do they get out of reporting on Vaughn Keaton when she has nothing to contribute but uneventful trips to the coffee shop to fetch a new bag of beans? I'm getting tired of coffee at home every day. I wish they would ignore me, and I could sit down. I wish I could talk to strangers and not be followed by that suspicion of knowing on their faces that they've seen me before. I can't stand it. I've never spoken for Papa. Caldwell speaks enough for himself. Yet somehow, this name is going to follow me to the grave.

Someone managed to get a photo of me stumbling out of the party Caldwell took me to. I look like a drunk fool, because I was. Even though I was only there for a few minutes before that sordid interaction with Greer. Even so, it's so unfair that I couldn't even be a drunk fool in peace. My nearly-twisted ankle must live on in infamy. Worse yet, I couldn't help wondering if Liv would see it. I wonder if she'd think I was moving on. She's so disconnected from what happens here, I almost envy it. Still, I suspect she would see right through those pictures. I didn't—

A hiss of fabric gave Liv pause and lifted her fingers from the page. Vaughn rolled over with a little sigh, pulling her sheets up to her chin. Her arms wrapped around one of her cast-off pillows, blissfully unaware. Liv thought of abandoning the journal and waking her up before she got ready to leave for work, but Vaughn needed the sleep. It was impossible to miss the dark rings around her eyes when they were so huge. Even in sleep, they looked swollen from a day of crying.

When she was sure that Vaughn hadn't woken up, Liv resumed her reading.

I didn't belong there. I'm starting to think I don't belong anywhere. For a long time, I wanted to believe in what Caldwell was saying, that it was just us against the world, but he's become someone I don't know how to talk to. I don't know which of us is the bad fruit from the tree: Caldwell, who's rotten to the core but everything Papa wanted him to be, or me, who fails to be wicked the way they are but fails at everything else too.

I need to take a walk. I might ask Clav to come with me. I've used up all my excuses for his company. Unfortunately, I might just have to be honest.

Vaughn's driver had mentioned getting a call from her, but nothing about her being with Caldwell. Or Greer. Liv shouldn't have been jealous. Vaughn lay behind her, dressed in evidence of her adoring mouth, in a sleep as deep as death. A pang of jealousy struck her in the chest, but the regret was more affecting. She had extracted herself enough from Vaughn's life and left her to turn to the only other people with some semblance of stock in it.

She sat back on the edge of the bed and applied a gentle pressure to the blanket over Vaughn's calf. "Hey. *V.*"

Vaughn answered by turning her face into the pillow and groaning.

"I have to go to work soon."

She resurfaced, pulling her brows tight. "You're leaving?"

Liv smoothed the fine pieces of Vaughn's hair across her pillow. "I have time for coffee if you get up. I left a car at the garage last night with some unfinished work, and the driver is coming in a few hours."

"You could come back afterwards. If you wanted."

Liv shook her head. "I'm taking Corey to work early the next morning to get the car. Maura has an appointment."

Vaughn's gaze dropped to the fibers of the pillow next to her. She captured Liv's hand and brought it close to her mouth.

"Should I expect you to be occupied for the foreseeable future? Seeing as you've effectively chased me out of Corcoran, I assume you don't want me coming by."

"It's not that I don't want you there," Liv said. "I didn't... I didn't tell Maura what happened because I knew she was looking forward to you coming over again. The place is just small. I have a twin-sized loft bed and no privacy. And the walls are *so* thin, V. It's actually offensive."

Realizing the conversation demanded more attention than she could reasonably afford or undo to resume her sleep, Vaughn pushed herself upright and pulled her knees up to her chest. "I don't mind it. I enjoyed being there. It felt warm."

"That'd be the shitty air conditioning. It shuts out on our floor a lot for some reason."

"It was your family. They were so kind to me. I think about that dinner a lot. It's clear how much you love them, and it makes everything a bit warmer."

Liv wasn't sure how much the power of love could truly redeem that cramped apartment's loft bed with its paper-thin walls for someone who lived in an idyllic terrarium smart home. Eventually, the rose-colored lenses would slip off, or her married neighbors on the other side of her wall would engage in their prolonged, kinky sex, and Vaughn would understand how unromantic the place was. "Why don't we go somewhere?" Liv suggested.

"Like where?"

She suspected that drinks and dancing were temporarily off the table. Lotte had temporarily but unofficially banned her from the Eight Saints. "I could take you to a movie."

Vaughn echoed the words, apparently dissatisfied. "A movie?"

"Or not. We could also do literally anything else."

Vaughn's chest lifted with a heavy breath. She shuffled

close and tilted her forehead against Liv's shoulder. "I need to make some progress on those plans. I doubt I'll be able to draft them so thoroughly without building another prototype from scratch. It's going to take some time, and who knows what Caldwell will do with them in the meantime. There's a high probability I'll be too late to intercept him."

Liv looked at the cluttered desk. She considered asking about that night, saying it was Clav who told her what happened. Whether he did the right thing by ambushing her at work to defend Vaughn's honor came second to the fact that it pissed her off.

Before she could say anything, Vaughn hooked a finger into the neckline of her prosthetic's sleeve and kissed one of the bruises peeking out of it. The warm brush of her breath beneath her jaw sent a shudder down her spine. "It's much less provocative than sitting totally still in a movie theater with fifty-or-so other people making chewing noises, but if you wanted to help me—"

"I'll be there," Liv said. "Just give me a couple of days to take care of things at home. After that, I'm all yours."

A grin teased across Vaughn's mouth. She grazed the side of Liv's nose with the edge of her own as if to lean into a kiss, but didn't follow through. "All mine?" she whispered. Then, turning Liv's face aside with a thumb against her chin, she pressed her mouth to the edge of Liv's ear and said, "All yours."

Maura's regular check-ins happened at Corcoran Regional Hospital. Although Liv drove her, Corey usually aligned his lunch breaks with them so he could say hello and subtly remind the nurses attending that anything about her care would reach his ears eventually. She had these appointments often enough and for so many years that the staff knew her well.

But she had been referred to a clinic in Matrevillea for a trial. A radiologist at Corc Regional had discovered an abnormality in her lungs that had not been seen before. It didn't look like cancer. "Truthfully," he had said, "I can't tell what it is without a biopsy."

He had urged her not to panic. The mass was small, likely removable if not totally benign. A lump was a lump, though. Someone needed to investigate it.

Liv sat in a new waiting room during the appointment. The staff moved in anxious flurries behind the check-in counter, visible stress leaking through the large smiles they were putting on. The urgency—for what, Liv couldn't tell—infected her with unease. As long as she didn't hear anything about Maura, she didn't care. She tried to focus on the television, but two children were loudly punching buttons on the interactive wall in the kids' corner and crying whenever their knuckles would clip the wall around it. This, too, looked new. At least, it looked unblemished for a kids' area. Around the room, a dozen new fixtures caught Liv's eyes.

And decorations. They were celebrating something. Liv couldn't decipher the staff's hushed tones, but none of it seemed celebratory.

A clerk called her over to the front desk. "Are you here with Maura Shankly?"

"Yeah?"

The nurse pursed her lips and looked down at a tablet in her hands. Its screen was notably unscuffed; Liv had encountered many of them during Maura's frequent appointments. "Can you verify the insurance information we have on file?"

She didn't usually answer this question for Maura and found it strange that they wouldn't ask Maura herself. She took the tablet and scrolled through a list of correct policy numbers, insurance details, her home address, and relevant contact information. At the bottom was a signature. Maura had seen it and signed it half an hour ago. "Everything looks fine," she said. "Is something wrong?"

"Your insurance provider is denying the treatment."

"What?"

"They've issued a fraud check on your account. Maybe, you could give them a call and verify if anything's amiss?"

Fraud.

Had all the deposits caught up to them? She didn't know why it would matter to them. They had paid off their debts. If they cared about the money at all, it should have been because they now possessed what they were owed, not because the Shanklys had done something wrong.

"Fraud?" Liv scoffed through a knot growing in her throat. "What kind of fraud?"

"I don't know," said the nurse. "It must have been a recent discovery. We have it on record that her treatment had been approved up until just this morning."

"And they just decided not to cover it, all of a sudden?"

The nurse turned sharply to the sound of a scuffle in the hallway behind her. She forced the smile back onto her face and said cheerily, "It's probably just a mistake! Give them a call and let us know what they say."

Liv's pulse had begun to hammer against her throat. She itched her neck through the sweatshirt hood she had pulled over her head. "How's she doing?"

"Doctor Madison is still with her right now, but she's almost done. You have some time to sort this out, I'm sure. I've even seen providers reimburse patients for errors after they've been paid for."

Liv found it unlikely that their insurance would reimburse them for anything. Their track record of missed payments superseded the fact that they eventually caught up with the winnings from the Drone Run. Liv left the front desk with her thoughts a muddy blur. She took out her comms device. Her hands were unjustifiably unsound. Her fingers shook as they punched the buttons.

A representative from Warner Medical placed her on hold with a wait of two and a half hours.

"Assholes," she muttered, ending the call. The second call she made went to Corey. She had no idea if he would pick up or whether he was sitting in front of a patient. She didn't know what to say when he answered.

"What's up, Chopped Liver?"

"Her treatment isn't covered."

"Of course it is. You know how worried she gets about payments. She didn't want to go through with it unless it was covered."

"Yeah, well, Warner Med just took it back. They issued a fraud check this morning."

Corey said nothing. Liv heard the latch of a door. Wherever he had been when she first called, he refused to stay to continue such a sensitive conversation.

More quietly, Liv asked, "Did you make any deposits recently?"

"Not to Warner. We paid off the remaining debt a couple of months ago. Did you?"

"Of course not. Maura made a deposit at the bank last week, but—"

"They shouldn't be seeing our bank deposits. The debt's paid off. There must have been a mistake."

"I tried to call, but the wait is over two hours long."

Like Liv, all Corey could say was, "Assholes."

A trio of nurses was huddled together tightly about the commotion in the hallways. Liv hadn't asked about it and couldn't help straying to the worst possibilities. What if something had gone wrong in the exam room? She didn't know what else Maura had scheduled for today except the biopsy. It couldn't have gone so terribly wrong. It couldn't be such a large procedure that their provider wouldn't cover it.

The nurses straightened as the source of their discussion neared. A cluster of people—well-dressed, straight-laced suit types—approached the office space and lingered behind the door to the waiting room, engrossed in their layered conversations. One of them laughed, and then the rest of them followed.

The door swung open. The first of them poured through.

With a non-specific gesture, a man in the middle gave a half-hearted thanks to the staff. Liv blinked, assuming she was hallucinating that hair color and that unmissable, deplorable expression of conceit. Caldwell Keaton in the flesh, touring the refurbished facility. He noticed her, total remembrance in his eyes.

Liv dropped the comms device and sent her fist straight into his cheekbone.

23

Liv had been sitting in the uncomfortable, bolted-down chair for almost an hour since she had been transferred to this room, which had no windows but two cameras aimed at the table where she sat. Small red lights blinked at her, prompting memories of the Drone Runs. Her gaze only ever glossed over them, never lingering.

But what else could she do in this room? She'd been made to wait here after being transported, sluggish and unwilling, to the Matrevillea police station only minutes after being placed in the standard cell. High Mayor's orders. She didn't know why Caldwell would want to speak with her directly, but in hindsight, the wait was sufficiently torturous for him to have deliberately planned it.

Her body was riddled with aches as sharp as needles. After she had attacked Caldwell in the clinic, a personal guard standing beside him had shoved her to the ground and crushed her under all his weight. Although her wrists were cuffed and the cuffs were laced through a keyhole in the tabletop, she could still shift and twist in her seat, and she assessed that none of her bones had broken from the impact. At least, none of them had shattered beyond mend. She ached as if she were being held together by fishing wire and office tape and stretched to her limits.

A lack of water only exacerbated it. The minutes ticked by in silence, her tongue parching. Did they expect her to reconsider what she had done? She wished she'd punched him harder and hoped he would be missing several teeth when he eventually arrived.

She flinched at the latch of the heavy door. A thickly wrapped bandage held Caldwell's jaw shut with a sleeve of ice pressed to his cheek. The skin she could see was swollen and red, as if stained by a smear of ineffectively wiped blood. She regretted punching him in such a convenient place for proper aftercare. It should have been her finest work. Her hardest blow.

He took a seat in front of her; Liv saw the force of it reach his injured face. She eyed his puffy cheek, pleased with herself.

When it was clear she didn't intend to break the silence, he shifted his attention to the camera behind her and made a gesture of dismissal to whoever was watching.

The blinking lights of both cameras ceased.

"I thought you were done with my sister," he said.

Liv had nothing to say to him. Not that she believed in the dignity of the police force when Caldwell had them at his beck and call, but she didn't dare give them any more information to use against her. She didn't trust that the cameras were truly off or that no one else could hear her. She had given them enough problems during her booking, made them work for any of her identifying information. Her lack of any proper registration with the city made her, essentially, non-existent to them.

He waved his hand at the level of her neck. "I'm assuming *those* are hers. I saw you up there the other night. Apologies for the... road scare."

She didn't know if she could uphold this principle of silence. He had been in the car that nearly hit her. The one that didn't stop or check to see whether they'd hit her. She expected nothing less from him than the worst. *Despicable little shit,* she thought.

Vaughn hadn't mentioned to her that Caldwell had been at her house moments before she arrived. How Vaughn had not already skewered him with her epee for stealing her plans confounded her.

"I'll make this simple," said Caldwell. "If you're not going to talk, you can listen. Seeing as you have no intention of leaving Vaughn to her own devices, I'm going to propose a truce on the basis of fulfilling a simple favor for me."

"No."

"No?" Since he'd lost the easy motion in his jaw, he could only wrinkle his nose at her in disgust. It unnerved her how much he resembled Vaughn. He possessed all the bad parts that Vaughn was eager to shed, and he wore them proudly. "You'll like this one. Do this favor for me, and I'll correct the issue you're having with your insurance. One call to Stephen Warner, and your mother can carry on with her treatment. How does that sound?"

This couldn't be their only option for relief. She thought of Corey's warning against owing favors to people like the Keatons. She should not have owed her benefactor anything, let alone owed something to her brother.

That was before she had punched him, though, before he had poisoned his father, usurped his position as the High Mayor of the city, and overstayed his temporary welcome. If she believed in a personal debt—and she did, because the effects of every other kind of debt she was acquainted with were too real and unmissable—she owed a much more powerful figure a favor worth his time. Vaughn had been a rarity, not a rule. Liv couldn't expect anyone else not to keep the score.

Certainly not Caldwell Keaton.

"I had a rider in that race. I'm sure you encountered him; he was good, a surefire win. All he had to do was cross, and I would have been able to get my money where it needed to go.

Yet, somehow, you managed to not only cross quickly but keep him from crossing with you."

Liv didn't care for his recap and grew impatient waiting for him to make a point.

"Forgive me if I'm not as accommodating to you as my sister is. The last time I saw you, you cost me a lot of money, so I don't really give a shit what happens to you. But you obviously seem to care about what happens to your mother, and you can be useful to me."

"What—in a race that doesn't exist anymore?"

"*Didn't.*" Caldwell leaned back in his chair and let his head roll back with a sigh. "Its absence has since been rectified."

Liv would have known if the gamemakers had resurrected the Drone Runs. Even if they hadn't told her, even if Lotte wanted her to avoid it for her own good, she was drawn to it. She could sense it. Those who wanted to keep her safe wouldn't also lie to her.

They knew how much it took for her to come back to the Run. Her return always came with a worthy cause.

"My sister seems to have lost something quite valuable to her. Blueprints, she says. I personally have no need for them. It makes no sense that I should have them, which is what she wants to believe. But you might have a reason." He righted his posture slowly, wincing at the rush of blood that colored his face. "Suppose something were to happen to the arm you have now. Suppose something were to happen that left you scrounging for money again. I've done some digging on you. You're a tough person to track, but once I did, it was impossible to get rid of you. Some *deep* debt you have there. It doesn't seem too far-fetched a possibility to return to that, does it?"

Liv's chest squeezed tight, her lungs incapable of holding onto a breath. Her hatred flared up like a fever. She stared at her locked cuffs and the small abrasion they had left on her silver wrist. Suddenly, she wished the punch had killed him. She didn't care what they did to her after that, whether they locked her up or buried her in the floodwaters. It would have been worth it.

It would have been worth it to her.

"Suppose," Caldwell continued, bracing his forearms on the table, "I give you a chance to undo the mess you've made for me. One favor, and we can forget this ever happened. You go home to your sick mother, exempt from Warner Med's badgering, with a criminal record free of theft charges against the Keaton family. I get a spectacle that garners vestments from some of the most influential powers in the Total City, broadcast live on TCFTV for everyone to find thrill in. Then, we can be finished with each other once and for all. Enticing right? All you have to do is ride for me. Well—" A malicious smile pained the High Mayor's punched face. "You'll have to win, too. Different rules, unfortunately. It's not as thrilling when everyone wins. We'll have to cull the weak somehow, make it so only one person reaches the end of the Run course. It may not be on those Lower City streets you're so familiar with, but Morgallis is easy to navigate, especially for a seasoned rider like yourself."

Liv sneered, unwilling to respect him with a proper response. The taste of bile crept up her throat. She let it sit there, gathering in her mouth. This was what unadulterated loathing tasted like. She committed it to her memory.

He sprang forward from his chair, its unbolted legs screeching across the hard ground. "Come on. You need this far more than I do, Olivia. This is a mercy. An *opportunity*. Everything you need taken care of for just one win."

Liv felt the glaring absence in his statement, the black spot staining his idea of everything. It was only everything for her if they ignored the existence of Vaughn Keaton, which Liv couldn't do. His offer didn't include returning the blueprints or Vaughn's close involvement in her life. Perhaps, he thought this was enough, that Vaughn was either a separate issue he would have to deal with later, or that Liv wouldn't consider her a crucial piece of that *everything.*

That Vaughn had spent so long mourning the loss of her brother made Liv arch forward, gather up her saliva, and spit on his hands.

His nostrils flared with barely suppressed rage. He didn't pretend to show her grace or kindness. This was for his personal gain and her blackmail; nothing more.

He kept his hands to himself. The anticipation of violence thrummed through Liv's veins, the disabled cameras offering her no witness. "Five days," he said. "You can decide whether your family's insurance troubles are worth your act of petty rebellion, or you can decide to accept this deal, ride your hunk of metal into the sun, and return to your life as-is. It shouldn't take long. Either you're capable, or you're not. We both know you only have one choice."

Breaking their steadfast eye contact, he reached into his pocket and wallet and extracted a business card. He laid it on the table, gold foil catching the phosphorescent light. Two fingers rested on its corner, and with a slow drag, he pushed it through the bubble of spit she had left on the table.

Proud didn't describe the way Liv left the station. However, she left anyway, her arguments bridled by a tight-laced jaw.

She let Vaughn Keaton do the talking.

The passenger door of Clav's car slammed shut. The girl and her driver descended on the scene like a tidal wave, unstoppable and punishing. Before Caldwell could open his wrapped jaws to speak and his guard could bark a useless warning against

Clavernus Lim, the pair cornered Caldwell. Vaughn stabbed a bony finger hard into his chest. Clav barred anyone from stopping her.

"How could you, Caldwell? You couldn't just steal my work, you had to insult me, too."

"Insult you?" He laughed nervously, splitting panicked glances between his sister and her driver. His guard clamped a hand around Clav's shoulder and drew him back roughly.

He didn't touch Vaughn. A simple, "Wait," out of Caldwell Keaton's lopsided mouth was enough to stop the guard in his tracks.

The officers behind the office windows stood at attention. The Keaton twins, together, could not be stopped from fighting, short of a truly murderous act, unless they wanted to incur wrath from either sibling. They stared at the pair, rapt, and revoked the last of the attention dedicated to making sure Liv Shankly left the premises without causing any further rifts.

"What insult are you getting out of this?" Caldwell took several steps back, but his sister followed, closing the distance until his shoulders met the wall of the station. "You know I've only ever wanted what's best for you. I'm your brother."

"What good are you to me as a brother if you lie to me?" Vaughn seethed. "If you steal from me and break your promises?"

Through gritted teeth, Caldwell swore, "I've kept every promise to you."

"Not this one," Vaughn said, gesturing back to Liv. "You promised me you wouldn't touch her or harm her—"

"And there she stands! Untouched and unharmed by me, as you wished. Oh, do you expect my security personnel to stand by when she assaults me?"

"Don't give me technicalities."

"What do you want then? My dear *sister*... Nothing ever

makes you happy."

"This did," she said more softly, and Liv barely heard it. "So did you, once. I believed in us, Caldwell, but you're just like Papa. Cruel. Greedy. Soon enough, you'll be alone, too."

"I am not—" Caldwell shook his head, sputtering like a dry spigot. "Papa wasn't smart enough to know what he had, but I am. I'm better than that, and you know it—"

Vaughn shoved him hard into the wall and took a large step back. "You're worse. A hundred times worse. I don't know how you sleep at night."

She turned on her heels and made a straight path toward Liv and her driver. She held her head high, but her eyes were trained on the ground, a ruse of strength meant only for her brother.

Liv's mouth had fallen open, stunned. She shut it, looking first to Clav, who had an expression as furious as a rash, then to Vaughn, who cupped her hand around Liv's cheek with shocking sureness.

"I'm taking you home," she whispered. She brought her other hand to Liv's face, and she cradled it gently. "Your home."

Liv nodded. The tenderness of Vaughn's touch cooled the white-hot anger inside her, rendering that flame small and the shadow of doubt around her terrifyingly large. She blinked and found her eyes wet with tears.

Vaughn kissed her once, deeply. "Get in the car, Liv."

Doing as she was told had never been easier.

In the little mirror, over the black frame of his sunglasses, Clav eyed her like she was a reprimanded schoolchild, not for the crime of assaulting Caldwell Keaton (he claimed he would dream of doing it himself, sometimes) but for the way her hand smoothed circles around Vaughn's back as she talked herself down from a panic attack.

Liv would deal with him later. She had enough on her mind without his guilty watchdog behavior.

Vaughn had handled herself just as scathingly as she had intended to. It was the shame of her own satisfaction that she couldn't reckon with. "It's never enough for him," she said, head in her hands. "Now he's gambling with an unlimited pool of city resources. I can't believe it."

"I believe it completely," Clav said, unhelpfully.

Liv had informed her about his plan to host another Drone Run within Morgallis's city limits and his proposal to ride for him. After that, she lacked the energy to say anything else. She needed a nap and a basin of ice-cold water to sink her head into for a few seconds.

These were attainable goals; Clav's car was closing in on her family's apartment. Liv only needed to survive the inevitable impasse between herself and her parents, who had barraged her with concerning phone calls up until news of her release had reached them.

At some point, Vaughn had already warned Corey against going to the station. Liv could only imagine how unhappy he was to hear what Liv had done via a command like that.

"You're not doing his stupid race," Vaughn said, looking at Liv on the propped-up column of her arms.

"I don't have a choice."

"I do. I can cover the treatment Maura needs. None of you will have to worry about that."

"That's not the point, V." Liv removed her hand and tucked her arms around her body. "I owe him something, and he's going to hold it over my head until I pay. I have to clear that debt with him."

Clav sneered, his fists clenching around the steering wheel. "You think the most powerful man in Morgallis cares about your debt?"

"Of course he cares," Vaughn said. "Debt is everything to him. Otherwise, he has nothing. Nothing to hold people down with or leverage power from."

"*Her* debt isn't going to hurt him in any way that matters," Clav contested. "He has all the money he needs at his fingertips. He has recovered his losses from the Run a hundredfold. You're never going to even the score. Nothing is stopping him from doing this again. No obligation of fairness. If he wants something from you, he's going to take it."

"*Stop.*" The command came from Vaughn. It gave Liv a breath of relief, as she was nearing the precipice of a mental breakdown, the longer he forced her to consider the futility of her sense of justice.

A stupid, unenforceable thing. But it was all she had if she couldn't have retribution.

Vaughn pressed her fist to her mouth thoughtfully. "We'll think of something. I'm going to make this right."

Liv wished she could believe her. The hope she had held onto for so many years always seemed to hinge on a race. She'd had nothing so stable that it could not be thwarted by one wrong turn or a shredded tire. For all her efforts, she could barely keep her family afloat. She certainly didn't have the resources to fix the problems.

"I think we should kill him."

"Clav," warned the Keaton girl.

"That's one way to fix it," Liv said passively, though the idea thrilled her.

The driver pushed his sunglasses higher up his nose, as if they masked his growing conviction. "There's an upsetting number of problems we could fix that way."

"I can't kill my brother, Clav."

"Pull in here." Liv pointed out the entrance to the nearby

garage as they approached her apartment building. She rolled her window down and punched a resident code into the call box. No one spoke or even dared to move until the window had gone up and the gate had closed behind her.

"Better yet," Vaughn continued, "an entire station of police officers just witnessed me berating him. It's one thing to poison a politician you're related to when the city thinks you're endeared to each other and another to murder one they know you despise. Everyone will suspect foul play."

"You don't have to kill him," the driver assured. "You just have to stay out of our way when we do it."

"We?" Liv looked at Vaughn. Then, at the door lock button beside her, nestled into the lock position. "I want him dead as much as you do—sorry, Vaughn—but my parents need me. I can't put them through that. I can't make them suffer that loss if I get jailed or, worse, *killed*."

"Come on, Shankly. You don't think Corcoranites would worship you for it? Do anything for a hero?" He turned in his seat to face them, immediately accosted by the grim expression in Vaughn's eyes.

"You're talking about my brother. As if murdering him would be noble."

He took off his sunglasses, regarded Liv briefly as a reminder that his grudge against her was only superficial, and said, "He's a monster, Vaughn. I know you don't want to believe it, but you do. You've seen it. All these years, you've watched it happening—his descent into greed—and you've been too close to understand just how fucked up he's become. But can you honestly tell me it wouldn't be easier for you to have him gone?"

"This isn't about me." Vaughn shut her eyes, knowing she was the only thing that stood between her brother and whatever Clav wanted to do to him. All the things it might fix... All the problems it could undo... If it truly wasn't about her but for the everyday people of the Lower Cities, she would have agreed: Caldwell needed to die. Softly, tamed by understanding, she said, "It shouldn't be about me, Clav."

But this didn't satisfy him. He wanted more from her. More fire, more willingness. "If we want to do this right, I need it to be about you, too."

"What the hell are you talking about?" Liv asked.

"I'm saying I need her to help us. She doesn't have to be the one to do it, but it'll be a hell of a lot easier to do it with her than without her. He's too difficult to reach if we're not in his inner circle of devotees. You are, at most, a pawn for his business ventures, and I am probably the longest-running pain in his ass he has ever known. Vaughn can get us close." He turned to her. "We need this, Vaughn."

The Keaton girl sank in her seat, covering her face. "Of all the favors I would do for you both without question..."

The others exchanged a glance of mutual regret. Liv's lack of continued abnegation sufficed as well as compliance. They were in this together, equally invested in the High Mayor's removal.

And they both felt hideous for asking Vaughn to let them do it.

"It's the only thing I'll ever ask you to do," said Clav. "Please."

Vaughn slipped Liv a silent plea but found only a commitment to the driver's plan in her eyes.

"I need to speak with Liv alone, first."

They would speak after Liv had reunited with Maura and Corey. Corey had taken her by the shoulders, given her a firm shake, and asked, "What were you thinking?" How could she have been so careless? So temperamental? Why didn't she let them try to amend the problem first? Had their sudden fortune truly caught up to them?

She had dribbled loud, embarrassing tears all over his shirt as he crushed her in an embrace and mumbled a slew of other rhetorical questions.

He didn't wait for answers. He was pissed off, pent up with disgrace over being useless when she needed him. Nothing Maura said could comfort him. Nothing Liv could say changed the fact that she had introduced a web of conspiracy into their lives that made the medical debt seem harmless in comparison. Her word was good for fuck all.

They had five days to figure out how to pull off an assassination. That was nothing. She could spend five days working on the same difficult car problem. Five days could pass in silence and leave the problem of Caldwell Keaton open to inflict more misery upon Liv Shankly's life.

"I have to go," she said.

"Go?" Maura's eyelashes fluttered with rapid blinks. "Can't you just stay home tonight? Please?"

"I promise I'll be back tomorrow," she said earnestly. "Everything is okay. I need a little space to think."

"We can give you space," Corey offered.

Looking around the apartment, realizing that she could not recall a single other instance in which it held five people at once, Liv gave an awkward shrug as if to say, *Not much.*

After packing a change of clothes into her backpack, including her equipment for riding, she left her parents in the living room. She had to go somewhere else, do something now, before the enormity of what lay ahead of her rendered her too afraid to act at all. Neither of them could see how much it gutted her. How Liv was stuck between two insurmountable weights.

She handed Vaughn the spare helmet.

"You don't want to ride back in the car?" Clav asked.

"I'll be alright," Vaughn assured him. "Gives us a little time to talk."

"Sure. Talk."

Sensing the sarcasm in his voice, Liv extended her middle finger at him.

He swatted it away and returned the grievance by pressing Liv's forehead like a button. "I need you to keep a clear head, Shankly. I'll meet you at the house. Get her there in one piece."

"Shut up, man."

His face illuminated, amused. He gave his keys a twirl and entered the elevator without them.

His car was gone by the time the elevator came back for them. In the garage, they went through the motions of riding together: leathers zipped up to the throat, connection established through the speakers in their helmets, arms fastened around bodies, and hands around the handlebars. How Liv had gotten herself into such trouble by simply riding bewildered her.

24

They left the garage not long after the driver did, slipping quietly into the night like thieves. The space inside Liv's helmet felt vacuous, barring the extent of the motorcycle's engine noise and making space for words from the Keaton girl that didn't come.

Vaughn saved her pressing thoughts for when they had left Corcoran. All they could see from the bridge were the bright neon lights of the Upper City before them, the water below too deep and black to make sense of where it started.

"Should I do it?" Vaughn didn't have to speak loudly to be heard through the connected call.

Liv hesitated, unsure of how unsympathetic she was allowed to be about Vaughn's brother. "Someone should."

A helmet pressed to the side of hers like a cat nuzzling a hand. "Maybe I owe it to him to do it myself."

"I wouldn't ask you to do it. I hate him, V, more than I thought I was capable of, but he's still your brother. I don't think Clav's asking you to be the one to do it either."

"I know." Vaughn squeezed Liv's midsection. "I don't think I could forgive myself if something happened to either of you because of it. At least, if I did it, I would deserve it."

"I'd visit you all the time in prison," Liv said. "I think you'd look sexy in a jumpsuit."

She heard a sharp breath of laughter in her speaker. "You're so weird, Liv."

"Weird?"

"Everything feels so damning and awful, but I feel like I could weather anything next to you. One would think you're a superhero, the way I regard you so highly. Instead, you're just some perv who wants to see me covered up head to toe in TC penitentiary orange."

Liv's hands shifted around the handlebars. She was fixed in place for the ride, but she yearned to turn around and draw her passenger's face closer for a kiss. She would have few opportunities to enjoy her company if she were jailed. She might miss out on Maura's progress, or worse, any sharp declines in her health that stole what time they had left together.

She couldn't come back from this. Not fully. Even if she miraculously evaded being held responsible for the High Mayor's murder, she would live the rest of her life with his blood on her hands.

It had to be worth it. For thousands of people suffering under policies he upheld, losing games he created. She had always wanted to witness the triumphant aftermath of a revolution. Maybe it would be enough for her to start it.

"I need you to make sure they're taken care of," Liv said, without needing to clarify whom she spoke of. "They've given me everything. Raised me to be strong. I want to come home to them, but if that's not possible—"

"I can do that," Vaughn said. "But that won't happen. I'm going to figure something out, find a way to fix this. I'm going to keep you safe."

A hand lifted up to Liv's chest and splayed flat over her heartbeat. She took a long, steady breath, like an ode to the body she lived in, which persisted in spite of everything and embraced such earnest, full-hearted love from so many people.

Another Big Feeling, to recognize how much she was cared for. It only got bigger among all the bleakness that constantly fatigued her, the way dark shadows in a childhood bedroom were always big enough to swallow up monsters before they could appear in the flesh.

She moved the controls to her left side momentarily to answer Vaughn with light pressure upon her hand. "Good. I was looking forward to seeing a movie with you one of these days."

"Is that truly the only thing you want to do?"

Liv laughed. To envision a future at all, let alone to fill it with good and promising things, required an enormous amount of hope from her that she had been too afraid to spend before. If she was preparing to lose everything, it only seemed appropriate to let herself dream now. "I think I imagined that, if we had gone through with the patent and settled down, and if I was capable of having it all, I would enjoy the simple things more. Like cooking dinner and folding my laundry. All my life, I've had this dreadful urgency attached to everything I do, and I think... I don't think I would need more than what I have now. What did you say the other day about movie theaters? About the, uh... The chewing?"

"That I can't stand the idea of sitting in a dark, crowded room full of people chewing on popcorn?"

"Besides the sensory nightmare, I think movies are the most valuable commodity for people who are rich with time. You sit there, unproductive, and let yourself become absorbed in people who don't exist and stories that don't affect you. And if it's particularly dark, and you've somehow managed to pick a showing that no one else is at, with seats in the back corner, you can spend the entire time just making out with someone you like; and you're incapable of being rushed into something more by the fact that you're in public. You can just languish in a theater. Spend a couple of hours divorced from reality."

"I think your perception of theaters is greatly influenced

by your experience of making out in them."

"You'd get it if you tried it. When we finish this, I'm taking you to a movie, and it'll be something so awful that we'll have no choice but to kill time by making out."

Vaughn sighed and let her hand fall back to its first position around Liv's waist. "By 'finish this,' you mean get rid of my brother?"

It was said without malice or blame, despaired over with the same tone one might use when discovering bugs in their recently bought produce. An unfortunate, inescapable fact of life.

"I know I can't make it easier," Liv said. "I can't fill the space it's going to leave, but I'll be damned if I let you believe that the only person in your corner is Caldwell when there are so many other people who'd kill for you. You don't have to be perfect or useful to be loved. Waiting for everything to be perfect is going to take me nowhere. I would weather a future that's just as bleak as the present, as long as you're in it."

Vaughn held her tight for such a straightforward ride. They made it through the city without delays. The rare lull in the traffic beckoned her to explore and assess the cityscape in anticipation of another Run, but she remained steadfast in her direction. Clav would be waiting for them. If they were lucky, a race within Morgallis's city limits would never happen.

Up the hill, she expected to see those flashing police car lights again and was relieved to see Clav's car parked alone in front of the house. Liv could see him inside the house, doling out commands to Lunokhod, one of which set the shaders to a maximum, making the walls opaque.

Now parked, Liv tore off her helmet and rushed to lift the one on Vaughn's head. She had been made to wait to kiss her for the duration of the ride, and now that she had the chance, she seized it without hesitation. Their noses bumped as they met with mismatched levels of preparedness. A soreness in her neck manifested when Vaughn pushed her nails up into her sweaty hair. Their faces were damp, and their mouths hot from the incubation of their helmets. They kissed until Clav reemerged through the front door.

He placed his hands on his hips and made a patronizing groan of disapproval. "When you're decent, please."

"What?" Liv dismounted from the bike, followed by her passenger. "I have all my clothes on."

"I can practically smell the depravity on you."

"Okay, well, I smell cranky asshole, but I'm not complaining all the damn time."

Liv passed him at the entrance, wrinkling her nose in mock disgust. She set their riding equipment beside the arm of the couch and dropped her backpack into Vaughn's room.

From the living room where the others sat in anticipatory stillness, Clav announced, "I had an idea."

"Already?" Liv returned to find a glass of water poured for her on the coffee table.

"To tell you the truth, I've been knocking vague ideas around in my head since I graduated high school," he said. "Nothing specific or methodical. Just enough to have a reservoir of possibilities for when the time came."

"Have you always been like this?" Vaughn asked, sipping nervously from her own glass. Out of obligation, she had given them all water, but Liv could tell from the discontent in her expression that Vaughn longed for a drink more potent and sedative.

"No," Clav said, letting his head fall back into a cradle of his hands. "But I've never had any loyalty to him, hence an unwillingness to ignore all his red flags. I never told you this, Vaughn, but he accused my mother of stealing from the Keaton estate after she passed."

"What?"

"It's why I didn't answer you for a long time after you first reached out. I didn't think there was a point to it. You were defensive about him. You swore there was some good in him, and that was all you cared to see. He's been an asshole for years. Now, he's an asshole with too much power."

"He'll get what's coming to him," Liv said.

Clav looked pleasantly surprised. "Had a productive chat, then?"

Where they had expected a pitying remark from Vaughn Keaton, they were met with silence. She stared at the water swirling in her cup. She gnawed at the inside of her cheek, considering something hard.

Slowly rising from her seat, she paced toward the kitchen with crossed arms and a lowered head. "Lunokhod?"

"Good evening."

"I want you to shut down."

"Lunokhod is commencing shutdown in five... four... three... two... one..."

She rested her elbows along the countertop and downed the rest of her glass in one large drink. When she finished, she said with the confidence of someone with a lot more sleep in their system, "Tell me about your idea, Clav."

In the days leading up to the inaugural Upper City Drone Run, Liv made herself scarce in every place she was supposed to be. She called out of work, claiming a family emergency had arisen, and to her family, she kept her mouth shut and indulged in all other conversation topics she could sink her teeth into.

It was not entirely on purpose. Clav confided more in his employer than in her, which she understood perfectly well, even if it pissed her off. She played a simple part and didn't need to know the finer details, he'd said. He gave her a list of errands to run, which sent her away and kept her out of the house. After she had fulfilled several of his pointless, low-stakes tasks around the Upper City, she realized that he had given her a map of Morgallis's essential pockets and landmarks to prepare for the night of the Drone Run.

"All you have to do is keep the Run going," Clav said when she returned, miffed. Vaughn had dredged up private floor plans of her family's estate and had them laid out on the coffee table for documentation, but Clav didn't let Liv's gaze stray from his. He stepped into her line of sight. "If the cameras are on you, we have more time to work."

"You want me to stay within the boundaries of the course longer than I have to?"

As she scanned each page of floor plans, Vaughn interjected, "I've arranged for someone to shadow you. You'll have an ally on the ground. Someone to work off. Think of it like a dance."

"Is this ally going to keep me from getting hit by another dart? I thought you neutralized the Upper City drones, V."

"Don't worry about the drones," Vaughn said. She gathered the floor plans into a neat pile. "Shall we burn these?"

"Couldn't hurt," said Clav.

Asking Liv not to dwell on the drones proved unhelpful, and Liv's efforts not to catastrophize failed miserably. She expected ruthlessness from Caldwell. She expected old drones with rusted darts. Darts with teeth that she wouldn't be able to pull out once they had pierced her.

She thought Vaughn might share more with her once Clav left. Instead, wine was poured, inhibitions lowered. The question hung in the air between them, ignored. Vaughn had had enough conspiring for one day.

She finished her glass of wine on the couch beside Liv. Her eyelids were heavy with exhaustion, but her body came alive with need. She drew Liv close, tasting of wine and guilt. In her ear, smooth and seductive, Vaughn whispered, "It's better if you don't know."

Although she tried to fight it, Liv's intent to seduce her for information was made null by Vaughn's intent to fuck her as a distraction. Liv allowed herself to be plied with murmured words of affirmation and needy, lustful kisses. She let Vaughn undress her and drown her questions with promises of safe-keeping and praises.

Liv would have been a fool to take it for granted. She didn't know what the future held for her anymore. If she didn't have an opportunity to put up a fight before she was felled by the powers that be, she could at least go out having been thoroughly manhandled by a pretty girl.

On the night before the Run, Liv lay restless in Vaughn's bed until the black shadows outside the glass lifted to blue. Under the guise of her heavy sleep, Vaughn laid her cheek in the crook of Liv's shoulder and pretended not to notice the way her heart was pounding just inches away. Her arms wormed around Liv's midsection, her legs twining possessively through the rider's. Liv sighed and said a silent prayer to whoever, or whatever, would acknowledge her, uncertain whether an authority like that existed.

Whatever happens, don't let it be for nothing.

25

She had missed out on so much sleep that by the time morning came, all that remained of Vaughn Keaton's presence in the room was a note folded and tucked under the pillow. Liv grabbed it and held it above her eyes to shield them from the sunlight. The script bore no resemblance to Vaughn's but said, clearly, *Be good. I love you.*

Liv stared at it, trying to figure out whether Vaughn had written it for her; the penmanship belonged to someone else. She looked for other signs of life in the glass house. Vaughn had left coffee in the pot for her and a gift box on the counter, wrapped elegantly in a silver bow.

No one answered when she called out their names.

Liv chose to believe the note was for her, anomalous as the script was. She re-folded it and set it aside to fix herself a cup of coffee.

Caldwell had given her clear instructions for the night of the Run, including where to meet him and when. Her late slumber left her with only three hours to prepare, one of which would be spent at the beginning of the course, listening to the High Mayor's introductory speech and partaking in the pre-Run broadcast.

If Vaughn had left these things for her, did she not intend to see her before the race? Liv had expected, perhaps unrealistically, to give her a proper goodbye before she walked into the unknown. None of them knew what lay ahead, and no one less than Liv, who'd been kept in the dark with only the instruction to ride.

Disappointment pressed down on her chest, making it difficult to manage a full breath.

She checked her comms device for new messages. Her conversation history with Vaughn lacked a myriad of messages she knew she had sent. Evidence of their most recent correspondence had disappeared from all of Liv's channels of contact with her. Emails, texts, voice messages, call logs. Everything tender and idealistic she'd shared throughout the past few weeks, leading up to the night when they'd fought—gone.

As if the ground had shifted beneath her, Liv's weight slanted against the countertop. Her thoughts were rife with a conspiratorial sort of insecurity. She selected Vaughn's number and met a dial tone she'd never heard before.

Aloud, Liv murmured, "Did she block me?"

She set her coffee on the counter and groaned. The gift box, with its obnoxious, silver bow, seemed to taunt her in her periphery.

Liv pulled it across the counter, unenthusiastic. Vaughn must have had a reason, but Liv didn't feel like being charitable with that assumption. She could use a hug. Some words of good luck.

In a single night, Vaughn had scrubbed every trace of herself from Liv's life and left her with only a note in handwriting she didn't recognize.

She unlaced the bow and lifted the lid of the box. The matte black dome of a new motorcycle helmet greeted her. No, not a new helmet. Upon further inspection, hoisted out of its box, Liv detected elements of the damaged helmet she hadn't gotten around to replacing yet.

Vaughn had swapped out the shell, though hairline marks extended from the point where the dart had struck the first one, drawn in gloss as decoration. The padding on the inside had been replaced. Her fingers sank into firm, unused sponge.

She examined it from all sides before sliding it over her head and readjusting the buckle beneath her chin. Pulled snug around her face, she tried the buttons in her usual pattern of commands. Everything worked.

Through the tinted visor, Liv noticed another slip of paper hiding on the floor of the box. On it was written a series of dots and lines. Liv recognized the formation enough to know it was made of Morse code dits and dahs, but not enough to know what it meant.

She raised her finger to the button beside her ear and slowly translated the pattern with pressure. A dial tone filled her speakers, ringing once. Twice.

Before the third, the call was answered.

"You woke up late," said Vaughn Keaton. She sounded like she was in a car, and at no point did she inform Liv where she was headed. "I hope you're ready to put on a show."

When Liv raced in the Drone Runs for the first time, the only person she knew was Corey Shankly. She had just turned sixteen and hadn't told Corey the truth about the Run. She needed a benefactor to ride. He cared enough about his kid to know that he hadn't been spending enough time with her in recent months, and he had agreed to join her just to amend it.

Had he known what she'd done—sourced the necessary information about the Runs when it would only endanger her— he would have never agreed to go. The reality of the stakes only dawned on him as the coursemaster was announcing the countdown, and he saw the wrangler send police drones into the air. His voice in Liv's ear became frantic and demanding, telling her to withdraw, to leave the scene.

Liv, only mostly aware of what could happen to her once she entered the boundary of the course, pressed her finger to the button beside her ear and ended the call.

It would take years of racing for her to lose a Run. Years of trust building between them. Trust that Liv would escape the boundary in one piece, that she would return home unscathed, that she would keep her hands to herself during the ride, and focus on finishing, not fighting.

She would give anything to see him now. A crowd of spectators amassed around a barricade. Lights flashed unforgivingly around the swarm of bikes, ricocheting off metal in every direction. She had her helmet on, and she kept it on at Vaughn's earlier command.

The Keaton girl eluded her now. Liv scoured the sea of chaos for familiar faces and saw no one. She'd never felt more alone than she felt now, faced with the snapping jaws of hundreds of hungry vultures.

She considered dialing Corey on her helmet's speakers. She hadn't been courageous enough to tell either of her parents about the awful deed she had committed herself to, but maybe now, as her mind skipped to the worst possible outcomes, she could swallow her pride and tell him she missed him.

Before she could reach for the button, the crowd erupted into riotous cheers over the arrival of the High Mayor's vehicle. Out of that sleek, black car, Caldwell's personal guard appeared, then the little boy overlord himself. The pinstripes of his family's house emblazoned a bomber jacket, not the business jackets or vests he usually made appearances in. A declaration that this would not be business, although he would dip his fingers into it anyway.

Liv had forgotten that pinstripes weren't synonymous with the High Mayorship. They may as well have meant the same thing. She had expected Gaines Keaton to die in that position, and eventually, he did, but not the way anyone had anticipated.

She wished he had died and stayed dead, but his crooked, putrid spirit lived on, and it stared her in the face.

Caldwell threw his arms wide and proud. "If it isn't my sacrifice of the evening. You should relish it, Shankly. How many chances does one get in life to see such a crowd mewling over them?"

He couldn't see her through her visor, blissfully oblivious to the utter antipathy in her face. He wrapped his arm around her shoulder and showed her off to the crowd. Liv anchored herself to the bike with a firm grip, unwilling to be attached solely to Caldwell.

The applause made her stomach turn and her breaths acrid. Cameras observing the other riders converged upon her. Simultaneous flashes and lights disoriented her, sharp even through her tinted visor.

She hadn't raced on a scale so large. Hadn't been scrutinized so widely by so many people she didn't know. How this could please Caldwell, she had no fucking clue. Such an impenetrable ego made him retentive to the praise.

"Try to liven up a bit," he said out of the corner of his mouth. "This is the only time I'm going to be pleased to see you."

Emboldened by the anonymity of her helmet, she said, articulating clearly, "Eat shit, motherfucker."

"Take that spirit to the course and you might do well." He clapped her on the back hard. On the loudspeakers positioned around them, both on the ground and in the skies, a five-note chime summoned a collective silence from the observers. "That's my cue," said Caldwell, before he returned to the safety of his guard and left Liv to her spiraling.

"Welcome," said an obscenely orange broadcaster. She

spoke into a fixed camera, joined by two other broadcasters behind a canopied table on a raised, temporary platform that overlooked the starting line. Though the wind blew steadily, the perfect weld of her hairspray kept every strand of platinum blonde in place. "It's a magical night to be hosting Morgallis's inaugural Drone Run. What a privilege it is to be here with you all."

"Behind a different desk!" the man to her left said.

"Well, it certainly beats the view from the office, doesn't it, Jordan?"

All three of the broadcasters devolved into rehearsed laughter. Liv switched her helmet to noise-cancelling. She couldn't let newsroom banter deliver the killing blow in an all-around dreadful evening.

She ignored the visor faces angled toward her. Some things, like suspicion among contract riders, stayed the same. She braced for trouble on the course, violence on her tail. Caldwell's Drone Run had different rules, not including the disavowal of weapons maintained by the Lower City racers.

She had nothing to show for it. Nothing hidden in her pockets except Vaughn's note.

Be good. I love you.

Liv knew she should listen to the announcers, but couldn't bring herself to focus. On the monumental screens looming off the tops of skyscrapers, scenes of the night played in torturously broken fragments. A needless close-up of a rider's helmet. The woman's orange face twisted in laughter. It disoriented her, made her feel physically ill. The cameras, the crowd, the grating tones of the broadcasters—all of it kept her cognizant of risks, so she chose to ignore them.

Caldwell Keaton had to die tonight. Nothing else mattered to her but making that happen.

"Riders! Take your marks."

She moved her bike to the starting line. She couldn't hide herself anymore or make herself seem non-threatening. The High Mayor had marked her for sabotage. Still, she avoided drawing attention where she could, sat in the middle of the group, and made no sudden moves.

A rider to her right goaded her into acknowledging him. "Hey. Hey, you."

She didn't speak but inclined her visor ever so slightly at him. He pulled up his visor, granting her a moment of recognition.

"Bjorn?"

"Supposedly, I'm your dance partner tonight."

"Dance partner?"

"Vaughn's words, not mine," he said, sliding the visor back into place.

The sight of his weathered face left her discombobulated, but not as much as a bystander lingering beyond the barrier past the sightline of Bjorn's helmet. Liv knew him by stature alone: broad-shouldered, thick around the stomach, gray flecked in his beard. The coursemaster. *Michael.* He lacked the company of his long-term partner. When he brought his hands out of his pockets and began to sign in an unexaggerated manner, she didn't think it was meant for her and turned to see whether Dr. Tewer stood elsewhere, signing in conversation with him.

Liv didn't see him. Right now, having found two familiar faces so suddenly, she didn't think she could fully digest any others before the countdown began.

The coursemaster's signs were meant for her. She turned to him again and watched him repeat the series of signs.

"Ten! Nine! Eight!"

At the level of his stomach, in small, understated motions, he signed *DRONES TAMPERED.*

She didn't know what that meant, whether the drones

whirring to life above her head had been tampered with for the purpose of Caldwell's Run or if he'd done something to them to help her.

"Four! Three!"

She shook her head. She couldn't risk getting hit by one to figure it out. She adjusted her grip on the handlebars, fingers hooked tight around the clutch to keep from shaking.

"Two! One!"

Breath stalled in her lungs.

With a bleating, drawn-out horn, Caldwell Keaton's Drone Run commenced.

The first ten seconds went as usual. Riders fanned out and disappeared through the adjacent streets. The sounds of engines thinning, and then, the sounds of cheers.

Bjorn's bike kept its distance, trailing away and dipping into side streets. It stayed within her sight always, his visor fastened to hers. She checked for drones before giving him a sign through the gaps in the buildings; the sky was empty. They had risen into the air and seemingly vanished.

The smattering of screens above her head, built into the mirrored windows of the high-rises, resulted in complete disorientation and required intense effort to look past. She couldn't keep her head down for a Drone Run, but too much time with her eyes on the skyline would make her sick. Cameras shifted from the broadcasters' engrossed expressions to aerial views of riders dispersing throughout the course boundary.

So, the cameras were up there and, likely, so were the drones. Liv just couldn't see them.

She motioned left to Bjorn when the screens were occupied with another rider. She cut inward, nearly (and deliberately) clipping the front of his bike.

It was her job to dance. Create a spectacle. Where she could not find danger in the drones, she would have to make it on the ground.

Bjorn answered her feint with a sudden acceleration, clinging to her side. A seasoned rider, he was afforded her unmitigated, earnest efforts at unseating. His engine roared in threat. He was equally prepared to spar.

As if from a pocket in the sky, an illusion split from the face of a four-pronged drone. Liv registered its blinking eye only fast enough to see it release a dart at them.

She braked, and it struck the ground at an anticipatory position. Electricity crackled around its tip. The darts had been charged. Perhaps, to stun and, possibly, to kill.

Liv had metal in her body, fused to her by magnets and latches. She sat atop a hulk of machinery—didn't they all? A dart with all that electricity could inflict serious damage, far beyond the effects of the sedative used in the Lower Cities.

The dart split Liv and Bjorn. They diverged down different roads, hiding in the dense urban landscape. When she had escaped the immediate threat, Liv switched the commands on her bike to her left hand and dialed the pattern of Morse code into her helmet.

"Liv? How's it going?"

"Great."

"Really?"

"*No!*" Liv didn't recognize the street she was on from Clav's convoluted route of errands and worried she had driven herself into a dead-end. She reached a familiar intersection with a deep sigh of relief. "They're supercharging the darts in these drones, V."

"I know. I found the plans for them the other day. Focus on riding. Tewer is monitoring them."

"I didn't see him at the Run. Only the coursemaster. I don't think he's—"

"He's with me. At the estate. I'm trying to find where Caldwell hid the blueprints for the prosthetic."

"What? You're not here?"

"We need this first, Liv." Vaughn went silent, leaving Liv alone with the hum of her engine and invasive broadcast updates from above. "Worry about the Run. Dr. Tewer is—"

"Stop telling me to focus on the Run, V. I need to know that Caldwell is getting taken care of tonight."

Sidestepping the point, "Dr. Tewer is monitoring the drones. I've granted him power to override in case of emergency, but he isn't going to interfere with the commands they've already been given until it's *absolutely* necessary. If Caldwell notices something is wrong, he'll jump ship. Keep him entertained. Let me do my job."

Liv caught sight of two other contract riders engaged in a scuffle, speeding down the road. She slowed down, shelved in a dark, narrow space between two buildings, and watched one land a hard kick to the other's knee. Neither rider went down. Like Liv and Bjorn, they split into two.

From her hiding spot, Liv observed the mechanisms of the illusion around the drone fall away. A reflective surface glitched around the seam where two doors opened and the drone peeked through. It lobbed a dart, missing both riders, before retreating behind its illusory mask.

"You better be right about this," Liv muttered.

"I have it all under control. Michael is keeping an eye on the Run for me. Bjorn has an eye on you. I'm going to keep you safe. I just need you to do the same and keep yourself upright. These riders don't operate under the same ruleset you're used to."

"I see that."

"I—" A prompt from the wrangler interrupted her. "I have

to go. Be safe."

Behave. Be safe. Be good.

I love you.

The call ended before Liv could reply. She pushed herself out of her hiding space, into full view of the drone.

She could outmaneuver it easily. She took advantage of the clearing of other riders and gave the cameras access to a lone, audacious rider. Sights of herself manifested on the screens as if on cue. She made for the other edge of the course boundary. She couldn't entirely abandon the goal of the Run without drawing needless attention to her meddling, either.

Her eyes stayed peeled for Bjorn. She'd lost him after the dart and needed someone to derail her steady journey. An unthreatened rider didn't make for a riveting view. The broadcasters appeared again, bubbling with their predictions for the Run's outcomes. Who was this unknown, faceless contract rider racing for the Keaton house?

Liv narrowed into a mention of her silver arm. "I've heard some whispers around the station about new military tech," said the lone male broadcaster. "Something about those roaming Kilgarre bots being weaponized."

"Now, where did you hear that, Jordan?" asked the woman sitting in the rightmost seat.

"An anchor never reveals his sources."

"Don't say that," teased the middle-most woman, Titania, whose name was written on a banner across the bottom. "They'll start to question the credibility of the news."

All three broadcasters laughed. Wicked people, Liv thought.

Was it true, though? Had Caldwell, in the short span of the last week, bastardized the technology in her prosthetic so much that it could be militarized? Weaponized in the bots roaming around Morgallis?

Liv blocked out the sound again, overcome with dread. As she adjusted the setting, she was greeted by the unwelcome sight of an unfamiliar contract rider in her immediate path.

Their bike swerved, narrowly missing Liv's. It inched close enough that she swiped with her right hand to hold the other rider at bay. Their helmet bore a house name she didn't recognize. She couldn't see Bjorn, didn't know how far he was, or how he would know if something had happened to her.

On the screens, multiplied, larger than in her periphery, she saw the rider remove a contraption the size of her comms device. A jammer.

Liv needed her baton, the spikes in her fingers—*something* to take down the other rider before they could wreak havoc on the electronics in her helmet or, potentially, her arm.

This arm didn't work the way her first one did. She didn't know the extent of its digitization, whether the jammer would interfere with a signal or not.

But Liv couldn't summon any of her prosthetic's extensions to fend the rider off without taking her left hand off the bike. "Fuck."

A dart sailed through the air between them, lodging in the exposed slip-up of skin on her assailant's forearm.

Liv screamed as the bike beside her pitched inward, the rider's weight forced down the pavement. Blood smeared across the dark street. The dart snapped at the point where it had pushed through the rider's arm.

The jammer clattered to the ground and shattered from the impact. A louder, singular snap—bone splitting.

Would Dr. Tewer let the drones hit the others? She couldn't tell if he'd done it. Whether he was willing to interfere in such a way that rendered another rider injured.

It was too close to her for it to have been worth the risk of intervening. She wasn't sure how much closer a dart would have to get before Dr. Tewer stepped in. A rider had been downed, regardless. Their spectacle, preserved. Liv had a deathwish to outlast.

Behind her, the spasms of the rider's body ceased. Sedated or dead, Liv didn't know. She had put enough distance between them that he looked no larger than a crooked wood screw.

"Oh!" a broadcaster said. "House DeVoriah has been eliminated!"

"Down she goes!"

The drone hid behind its illusion somewhere above her. She couldn't slow down until she was certain she'd evaded it. To her right, Bjorn's engine swelled in volume. She led him in a chase down another, less visible street.

They couldn't speak to one another like this, the engines too loud and their faces too obscured, but it brought her momentary comfort to ride next to someone she trusted not to knock her down.

They entered another clearing. A prime location for a drone. Liv could sense its presence, even if she couldn't see it. The screen in front of her was fixed in Caldwell Keaton, making passive conversation with someone next to him.

"Did you expect this event to be so brutal, Titania?" asked the voice of the woman to the left: Simone.

"Don't say it's brutal just yet. Unless the selection thins any further within the next few minutes, the Run will authorize a bounty system. Six uniformed participants—bounty hunters, for all intents and purposes—will be given the chance to secure a slice of tonight's winnings if they can take out the remaining riders."

Caldwell's face betrayed his unadulterated excitement. From the open windows of the buildings around them, observers applauded the raising of the stakes.

It didn't matter how awful the High Mayor was or how

visibly he did wrong. Not if the people loved him. Not if they, too, were hungry for violence.

With a camera-ready smile, Jordan faced the lens with all his teeth and shouted, *"Wow!"*

26

Vaughn left the cameras on as she scavenged the estate. She still had access to the house, which had been left to the twins to divide between themselves when Gaines died. She deactivated the alarm system; thirty seconds of unaddressed beeping would turn into a call to the authorities.

"There are no cameras in this room," she said to Dr. Tewer, leading him first to her father's old office. "They'll see you coming in, but you can monitor the Run from here without trouble."

Stanislaus rounded the High Mayor's plush burgundy chair, trailing his fingers along the rare scores in the leather. It looked as if it hadn't been touched since Gaines's death, as if Caldwell had never sat in it.

Vaughn had returned to the house following their father's death when Mirata read the will to them and allocated his assets. Since then, she stayed far away from the Keaton estate, thereby effectively surrendering it to Caldwell's ownership.

Legally, she still had every right to be here. The things in Gaines's desk, hers to sift through.

She removed the copy of Gulliver's Travels from his bookshelf and opened it to the page where she knew his desk key was hidden. "Do you mind if I..."

Stanislaus rolled the elegant desk chair aside for her to unlock the middle-most drawer. Its contents didn't surprise her. Half-used notepads, pens with burst ink cartridges, a consequent sticky spot of congealed ink, and a stapler—no spare staples. She rifled through the pages just in case Caldwell had made copies and hidden them somewhere. Nothing.

She shut the drawer with a sigh, then checked the column of larger drawers on both sides. As she expected, Gaines's belongings had not been touched or contributed to by Caldwell. She knew her brother still had an apartment in the heart of the city, but he didn't use it much anymore, except as a backup for the nights when he felt too drunk or high to be driven home. He had enough sense to know that he couldn't trust strangers in the High Mayor's estate when he was inebriated. Business, however, remained at the family home, the stripe-floored Greco-Roman behemoth of a building. The blueprints had to be here. Vaughn felt it more surely than anything else she felt tonight.

"Wait here," she instructed gently. "I'm going to check the private rooms."

She had a guilty strut, easily noticeable on camera. The feigned confidence of her elongated posture was transparent as glass. She prayed that Caldwell wouldn't be watching from the starting line, absorbed in his phone, observing her like a specimen. At any moment, he could trigger the alarms or, if he wanted to catch her by surprise, alert the authorities without giving her any notice whatsoever.

No warnings. No mercy. She trusted the validity of her claim to the estate, but she didn't trust the authorities to obey their own doctrines. They could deem it irrelevant, gleaning the wrongness of her presence from her guilty strut.

On the other hand, if Caldwell wasn't looking at her, he was, by design, looking at Liv Shankly. Vaughn hated that idea, too.

She opened his bedroom door first. Clothes cluttered the floor. Jackets that were meant for the unoccupied hooks lining the wall beside the door lay discarded around the perimeter, cast aside carelessly after long nights of trouble. Vaughn had assumed his political ventures would shape him into something more refined, more adult. His room still looked the same as when he was sixteen, ten years ago now. He'd brought his mess with him into office, and he'd let it seep into his dealings.

Lifting the layer of clothing off his floor garment by garment, Vaughn searched for evidence of concealment. Of paperwork, she found only a few unrelated notes: phone numbers, quick math, and reminders to himself. He had a desk next on the other side of his nightstand from his bed, the way her room in the glass house did, although its surface was covered in coffee stains and pockmarks. The notes that were on it had been stuck to it for, presumably, months; Vaughn had to peel them off to look at them. He'd written nothing of value, but also a note to himself that said, "Call V before end of week. Tea at the rose garden?"

For as old as the note was, she had never been asked to join him for tea. With a sharp pang in her chest, she wished they could still go. If she went through with this, there could be no forgiveness. No chance to redeem him. No rose garden.

She opened his desk drawer and saw nothing of interest. She immediately regretted opening up his nightstand and wiped her hands rigorously down the front of her trousers upon closing it. There was no room on his shelves to hide her blueprints or her notebook; she checked under and behind his childhood collection of sailing trophies and snowglobes and went as far as to lift the backs of his picture frames.

Finally, she crouched down next to his unmade bed and pulled out the flat tub she knew held a variety of novelty boxes and flat keepsakes. Here, he kept the participation certificates that didn't result in trophies, birthday cards, and reminders of their mother. His private stash always held the same sorts of things, and Vaughn didn't expect to find her blueprints there, but she checked anyway.

After she confirmed that nothing of note had been added to the tub, she lowered her cheek to the ground and peered into the dark space beneath the bed where the tub had been. For a spot that went unacknowledged most of the time, Vaughn noticed a startling lack of cobwebs and, dragging her finger across the hardwood, *dust*.

Her finger caught on a splinter and jerked upward reactively. Her knuckles hit the underside of the bedframe and burned up with a rush of blood. The sound it made was muffled by something gentle, like a plastic bag.

Their childhood beds had the same build. The frames were made of wood and wrought iron. Caldwell had shoved something into the slats. She pressed her body flat to the floor and wormed her arm as far in as she could manage, feeling for the end of the plastic. She hit the plastic corner of what felt like a sleeve or flat pouch.

Vaughn pulled without much success. She lacked leverage from this angle, so she pushed herself upright and lifted the mattress.

The blue-tinted sleeve didn't contain her blueprints or her journal. She guessed drug paraphernalia from the presence of white powder. The other contents puzzled her. She removed a small, unlabelled vial.

The burner phone in her pocket buzzed. "What's happening?"

Clav was parked half a mile outside the estate with his lights off and the engine on. While Dr. Tewer had a direct line to the coursemaster at the Drone Run, Clav was one of only two people who had a direct line to her.

"Have you found anything yet?" he asked.

"Still looking. Is it all clear where you are?"

"Dead silent. Trying not to let it get to me."

Vaughn held the vial up to the window, turning it in front of the full, yellow moon. It had a pearlescent finish to it and a viscosity that left the glass streaked in colors. She didn't know why, but it made her mouth water. "Have you, um…"

"Seen anything from the Run?" Clav huffed, which made Vaughn brace for bad news. "Three riders downed. Liv and the other Corcoran rider are still active in the Run. Several others, too."

Though her voice held no hint of relief, Vaughn was relieved nonetheless. "Good. That's perfect. Can I ask you something? About *drugs.*"

"I'm not on any, if that's what you're asking."

"No, that's— I mean, are you familiar with what they look like, generally?"

"What are you looking at right now?"

"A small vial. About as tall as my pinkie finger. It's about a third of the way full of a clear liquid with an iridescent sheen. It's unlabelled."

The line went quiet for several seconds. When she began to wonder if the call had disconnected, she asked, "Clav?"

"I looked it up. Could be GHP—gamma hydroxybutyrate."

"Which is?"

"If that's what it is, it's a date rape drug."

Vaughn closed her fist around the vial and let it fall to her side. Her stomach turned with unease. "Do you think it could be anything else?" Maybe she sounded foolish for wanting to prove that suspicion wrong. It wouldn't have made a difference to her whether or not he was capable of something so vile; he would be dead soon, and she couldn't turn back now.

But Clav didn't argue. He'd be the first to point out Caldwell's hideousness. "I think it might be what he used to kill your father."

The door to Gaines's office slammed hard, shaking the structure of the house. Hurried footsteps bounded up the staircase. Vaughn kept her driver on the line and said, "Tewer's coming up."

Stanislaus raised his phone's volume and handed it to Vaughn. "I'm here," she said, holding both phones in her hands.

"There hasn't been enough action on the course." Michael's words were nearly indecipherable above the raucous cheers around him.

"What do you mean? That's good, isn't it? To have people active in the race?"

"They're sending a second wave of threats onto the course to thin the selection. New riders with an incentive to take out the first. There are too many people still standing."

"I need time," Vaughn anguished. "What about the drones?"

"I don't know... They haven't been pulled from the Run. I suppose they're sending them out together. I don't know how easy it'll be to hold them both off, but we can't control the new riders if they're released."

Vaughn handed the wrangler's phone back to him, forgetting the call with her driver was still active. "Vaughn. Vaughn, are you there?"

"I'm thinking."

Though Stanislaus was the only person in the room with her, she felt crushed beneath a disproportionate weight. She twisted her fingers into her hair and pulled as if the tension would siphon out a useful thought.

"When they send those riders out..." She shook her head, wondering if she could be as intentionally wicked as Caldwell. "When they send those riders out, can you tell me if the drones register them as targets, too?"

The wrangler looked at her sternly but without disbelief. He didn't dissuade her. No one else spoke up to ask whether this was what she truly wanted.

"If they don't, override that command. If they're going to hunt my rider, they ought to know what it feels like, too."

27

Although Liv couldn't hear Bjorn from where he sat, she felt the collective collapse in their ease as the bounty riders crossed into the boundary of the Run course. "Shit," she whispered. Could she afford to let the guise slip and give Bjorn a clearer command? The screen wasn't on her, but the cameras likely were.

They looked like every other contract rider already on the course, but they lacked house affiliation, judging by the blankness on their helmets and lack of uniformity in their gear. Where the organizers had sourced these riders, Liv didn't know. She wondered, treacherously, if any of them were from the Lower Cities. Enough need would drive anyone to these measures.

It had happened to Bjorn. She had forgiven him easily enough.

His visor tipped toward hers. Liv accelerated forward. She didn't know if she needed to entertain their dance any longer. What use was perpetuating their chase when an honest threat descended on them?

Fuck the High Mayor, she thought. Then, unwilling to afford him any respectable title, she amended to herself, *Fuck Caldwell Keaton.*

A ringtone filled the inside of her helmet. She answered it swiftly. "What's happening?"

"Don't worry about the drones," instructed Vaughn.

"They're not repealing the drones, V. The riders are an added threat, not a replacement."

"We're handling it. Focus on outlasting the other riders."

The distant sounds of engines seemed to multiply. The screen drew her attention with echoes of the route she and other riders had just taken, as if the bounty crew were following their tracks. Maybe they were. They would reach her quickly if they had tracks to guide them. It was only her first time on the course. She rode with limited confidence and less familiarity with the city.

"I'm getting nervous," she said, finally giving voice to her panic. It was a bad move. She could no longer deny or suppress it, but she couldn't give it power either.

"You're doing beautifully," Vaughn replied.

"Did you find the plans?"

"Not yet, but we will. I just need a little more time."

Bjorn split away, careening down another street. Liv refrained from following him now that the dance was futile, but he'd left her alone. Truly alone.

"We've found something else, though," Vaughn assured her. "I think it's what Caldwell used to poison Papa."

"He still has it?"

"If this is what I think it is, I'm just as surprised as you are. He has it in a stash with other paraphernalia, so I could be wrong, but—"

Bang!

The closeness of what Liv could only assume was a firearm caused her grip to jerk.

"Liv? What was—"

"They're armed. The bounty riders."

All around her, magnified across the screens, were broken pieces of machinery, the splattered guts of a bike. A contract rider had been downed already. Thrown off their bike, they struggled to reestablish a steady footing. Close behind, a bounty rider dismounted their bike. They shoved an odd-looking firearm into a holster on their chest. Their motions were clumsy and unpracticed, as if they weren't accustomed to this configuration. With more certain movements, they took out a taser and aimed it at the stumbling contract rider.

"Point one!" Simone said amidst thunderous, supportive shouts. "How do you think these riders would fare on the course as normal participants, Titania?"

The center broadcaster drawled, "*Great* question, Simone. In fact, these riders are not only vying for a cut of this race's grand prize winnings. They're riding to secure a position in the next Drone Run."

"Liv!" Vaughn's voice pierced her focus. "Can you hear me? What's going on?"

"They've already downed one rider. I don't know where they are on the course."

"Where's Bjorn?"

She couldn't see him. She wondered if Caldwell had placed something on her bike or if something tracked them from the skies. The bounty riders had been able to find the first rider quickly.

"Liv, are you still there?" Vaughn's voice, commingling with the rising volume of encroaching engines and quips of all three broadcasters, produced a cacophony of distractions. A shooting pain travelled up Liv's jaw from clenching her teeth.

"I... I can't focus right now." Liv ended the call, unable to think clearly or think better of cutting off her last connection to someone who could help. They'd given her this prerogative and told her to ride.

But the longer she stayed on the bike, the less she could hold onto her focus.

The downed contract rider lay twitching in the aftermath

of the electric shock. The bounty rider approached them and let a yellow handkerchief fall onto their body, a mark of conquest that only stoked the frenzy of violence in the crowd.

They returned to their bike at a leisurely pace, as if securing other riders didn't concern them. Liv wondered what it would take to win a spot at the next one.

The next one. No, there couldn't be another Drone Run in Morgallis, nor could she allow herself to think of participation as a prize.

She turned her eyes to the sky. Her ears remained vigilant to the nearing engine noise.

Too much, too much. She couldn't think, didn't know what to do. If she could reach the end of the course the way the Run asked her to, there'd be enough happening on the course to keep Caldwell occupied.

Liv made a sharp turn, righting herself directly toward the end of the course. She was going to finish the Drone Run. It was foolish to think that choosing that goal made the task at hand any simpler. If she trusted Vaughn to carry out the plan, it wouldn't matter whether they found the plans for the prosthetic. Caldwell needed to die, and Liv needed to absolve herself of any blame. Even if she could do only one of those things, nothing was more important to her than seeing her family again.

She wanted to go home, to kiss her girlfriend, to throw herself remorsefully at her parents' doorstep. She'd let them scold her as much as they wanted. She'd let them put locks on her bedroom door and keep her confined to that apartment forever. It was a dreadful place to go old, but at least they could do it together.

Another rider went down. Aerial view. They'd been hit by a drone, then marked by a bounty rider afterward.

"Is that legal?" Jordan asked the other broadcasters. They

shared a mutual confusion. The camera panned to Caldwell, whose attention had strayed toward something his personal guard was whispering in his ear.

There was no rule in place for marking a rider after they'd fallen. Liv watched him make it up on the spot and announce with condemnable pride, "No point for riders you don't hit."

The camera returned to the bounty rider, focusing in from afar. They had returned to their bike, assuming their mark was valid for a point. Caldwell's declaration instilled them with visible discontent.

They abandoned their bike. Pulling a firearm from their chest holster, they turned back toward the downed rider. It was Bjorn, already wounded by the sharp dart from the overhead drones. His body lay mostly intact, having been struck through the fleshy part of his calf, but his movements were sluggish and affected by the shock.

He dragged himself across the asphalt. With one hand pressed against his punctured leg and the other straining against tire-marked cement to pull himself behind the bike, he cried out in anger. Liv saw it shake through his body, but couldn't hear.

"No." She said it to no one, alone in her helmet and on the course.

Propelled by their grievance toward the High Mayor's ruling, the bounty rider lifted the firearm and aimed it at Bjorn.

The panel in the sky re-opened like jaws and spat out a second dart. The bloody tip protruded from the bounty rider's shoulder.

They slumped to the pavement alongside Liv's ally. The gun went off, bullet askew.

The crowd's gasp was not one that indicated the wrongness

of the moment. It was a testament to their unfettered engross-ment in the sport. The loud noise and sudden jerk from the dart penetrating an unexpected body was a welcome disrup-tion that only furthered their interest.

No simple observer had gleaned the collapse of the ruse being put on by Vaughn.

But Caldwell did.

The cameras first panned to the broadcasters, whose mouths hung open in disbelief but closed out of professional-ism. If they suspected something was amiss, they didn't say it on camera. They had a job to do and masses to entertain. So, those slack jaws gave way to riveted, white-toothed grins.

Then, briefly, the cameras panned to Caldwell's seat. It continued panning as the High Mayor was fleeing from his chair down a crowded aisle. People parted at the command of his personal guard. Their eyes were wide and wistful as he passed, starry with adoration.

Liv wished she still had Vaughn on the phone. She couldn't afford to remove her grip from the handlebars to punch the code into her helmet anymore. The bounty riders approached; the sounds of engines increased every second. She gauged at least one to her left. She took a sharp right.

She remembered, after she had already crossed several intersections, that Bjorn had come this way before he was hit by the drone. She noted movement on the road. Both his body and the bounty rider's sat propped up against their bikes. She wondered how long they would have to sit there before someone came to administer aid.

On the screens, another rider narrowly escaped the shot of a drone. With Caldwell gone, Liv had, at least, a few seconds to talk to Bjorn without prying eyes on her.

She slowed to turn and sidled up to him. "I can take you with me."

He took his helmet off and discarded it in frustration. "What? Are you crazy?"

"You're bleeding, Bjorn. No one's coming to help."

He surveyed the emptiness at Liv's back and considered the offer. "Come back for me when you're done. If no one else comes to help me, at least you'll have finished the Run."

Liv nodded. The urge to fight his decision rose up into her throat like the taste of bad meat. She left before the drone could reappear and punish her for the moment of respite.

Her only focus was finishing.

She had raced this way for years, keeping her hands to herself and her eyes on the road. That road had never felt so unfamiliar or so bright. And it was true that no Drone Run had ever been watched by so many eyes and with such hunger. The wager had always been high. Lives were staked on Liv's ability to reach the end of a course since she was young. It would be untrue and unfair to her family to say that this Run was worth more than the ones that kept them above water.

Caldwell might have been worth more financially, but in his hands, one ego trip away from being crushed and obliterated, were the lives of thousands in the Total City. It was unfair that they should all be held in such a precarious grasp, balancing on the short temper of an unqualified, spoiled brat. She cared about each one of them more than she had ever cared about him.

Anticipation could age a person quickly. Paranoia could scourge deep wrinkles in young faces and tire the heart with too-fast beating. A slow death could be just as violent, and that was what her family had been driven to.

The road ahead looked clear and quiet. Liv didn't trust it, although she didn't totally trust anything.

She usually trusted her intuition doing the Drone Run—so many years of riding and racing had made her good at picking up mostly imperceptible and inexplicable shifts in the atmosphere—but she thought she might be overreacting this time. She knew the course less intimately and the people not at all.

Continuing down that eerily blank street, she tried to calm her heart rate and recalibrate all the impacted functions of her body.

Shots were fired for several minutes. Engine noise vanished nearly completely.

Her job had been to ride, and she'd done it.

The boundary of the course grew closer and closer, while everything else seemed to stay exactly where it was.

She should have known it couldn't be that easy.

The bounty rider lurked in a narrow alley. Shadows masked the smooth, black metal on the front of their bike. Liv's thoughts were turbulent enough that she didn't notice the start of its engine until she had passed it.

She was on a narrow street. Any turns would slow her, and the straightaway would grant the bounty rider a perfect target.

The screens showcased a different contract rider, drawing a chase out on a wider road somewhere Liv didn't recognize. She heard shots and couldn't tell if they were coming from behind her or above her on the screens. She dipped her head instinctively, but no ammunition crossed her.

The bounty rider behind her hadn't tried to take her down yet. They accelerated their motorcycle but could only gain on her so much unless something changed about the course. Liv was committed to riding straight and fast until she came across a wider intersection for which she could afford the slowdown of a turn.

Minutes passed with no viable turn in sight. The streets were small, her drift unsteady. The bounty rider's bullet seemed inevitable, and she braced to be hit with it at any moment. Why it hadn't come already, she didn't know. Their lack of action seemed almost leisurely.

The road began to pinch. It had been four lanes across when she first turned onto it, and it reduced to two. Up ahead, she could see her lane break away and turn the opposite lane into a one-way.

The bounty rider's inaction unfolded before her. The turn would drive her away from the course's boundaries. If she barrelled down the one-way, toward the end, something would be waiting for her.

Liv couldn't be corralled into the easy sightlines of multiple riders; she wouldn't withstand it. She had no frame of reference for what happened to those injured in the Run, and she doubted Caldwell would care enough about her to attend to her injuries. Had anyone come for Bjorn yet? The other felled riders?

The contract racer on the screen went down. A pink handkerchief, the color of a washed bloodstain, claimed success for another bounty rider.

"Do you know what this means, Simone? There's only one original racer on the course right now."

"Tell me, Jordan, there has to be some kind of prize for being the last one standing."

Last one.

The bounty rider returned to their bike, hiked their leg over the seat, and set off into motion.

"I'm afraid not. While only the first of the original racers to cross the boundary is allowed to take home the grand prize money, they'll need to cross it. This win is contingent on more than outlasting your fellow participants."

"What does this mean for the High Mayor's rider?"

The pressure alone made her feel like her bones were erupting into tiny fractures everywhere.

"It means she has a hell of a last few miles ahead of her."

That was all she had. A few miles. If the rider behind her was waiting to shoot, they were cutting it short to start aiming.

With one member of the bounty crew trapped next to Bjorn, five could be waiting for her at the boundary. She could only assume the one with the pink handkerchief was en route to her, too. She had no clue how close they were.

All six had been vying for a point toward the next Run. If the rider behind her wanted a point, it made no sense to drive her into the clutches of the others.

She eyed them in the reflection of her left-hand mirror. The stillness unnerved her. They possessed a readable confidence in knowing that they were pushing her into more dangerous territory.

She took the upcoming turn away from the course's end, prolonging the chase.

She would probably hate herself for it later.

With no one else to follow, the cameras engaged on her bike.

"She's still going," said Titania.

"I'm not sure how much fuel those things hold, Titania, but I'd be worried about it running out."

"Of all things to worry about—"

"I've never gotten on one!"

They laughed again, their masks of good humor slipping from their faces as they were forced to be on camera a little longer than necessary.

Liv didn't pity them for it. They had no drones following them. No venators on their tails. Safe on their raised platform and shielded by the drones' commands, they had no threats levied against them.

Liv, on the other hand, could see the bounty rider behind

her remove the gun from their holster and aim it clumsily at her. She veered into a side street so abruptly that her tires lost their grip on the pavement. "Fuck!" The bullet careened over her helmet.

The rider couldn't follow. However, her moment of isolation lasted all of ten seconds.

Returning to a main road, she faced two riders, each encroaching on her position from a different shadowy alcove. Above her head hovered a drone.

Pink and yellow handkerchiefs hung on the riders' hips. With one point to each of their names, they found enough promise in each other as they did in the capture of Liv Shankly. They reached for their holsters. Yellow fumbled their grip, which gave Pink enough time to aim it at the front wheel of their rival's motorcycle.

Yellow veered out of control. They braked to total stillness. Liv could see their distant figure dismounting and pushing their bike to the ground in a blind rage.

But Liv's eyes were on Pink. She had gotten lucky too many times tonight. She could only stave off their attention for so long before something—whether it was Pink or the drone—finally hit her.

The drone lobbed useless darts at her. Their aim was indicative of the wrangler's tampering. She prayed one of them might arc conveniently toward the pink rider; but what would that change? She had turned back from the boundary crossing and given the remainders space to plan their attacks.

She thought of surrendering. What that would mean for her if they couldn't get rid of Caldwell: her end of the bargain rendered a failure, his promise to leave her family alone rendered null and void.

Caldwell wasn't even watching.

A dart struck her leather jacket, tearing through her left

sleeve. Pain seared up through her arm. Air slipped through the gash.

Her handlebars jerked from the force. She kept herself upright, but another dart followed closely after.

The wrangler didn't disable it or move its aim; it was reasonably close for a perfectly functioning drone. Red bloomed from the hole in her jacket. The wind pelted her like shards of broken ice. She couldn't tell how badly she'd been hit. She hadn't fallen, and that was something.

She struggled through a turn and—

A bullet lodged in her tire.

Her body was thrown upward. Her limbs flailed to find purchase on something steady. She hit the ground: ribs first, right shoulder, helmet, then legs. The air punched out of her chest.

She couldn't move. Her cry for help was limited to a soundless breath. She could still move her arm, albeit slowly. It shook and fell to her stomach weakly. She'd broken something. She forgot what ribs were supposed to feel like, but this was wrong. Her left arm, too.

She couldn't lift her head to gauge the damage, but she could turn it toward the bounty rider, who braked only a few feet from her. The gun had been re-holstered, and he approached with determination in his strut. She mouthed, meekly, "H-help. I broke—"

They pulled the handkerchief out of their hip pocket. Had they hit her, too? Had she missed a bullet entering her body somewhere? She knew she was bleeding. Felt the blood all around.

She hadn't forgotten what a bad crash felt like, but even this was different.

Pink raised their arms above their head, culminating in applause from a city's worth of observers. They waved their handkerchief triumphantly and paid her no mind.

"Stop!" shouted Titania. "Stop the race!"

Liv wanted to laugh. What race? The race had ended when Caldwell left. This was a bloodbath.

Through failing vision and a tinted visor, she saw the camera focus on the blurry faces of the broadcasters. "The High Mayor has just been shot."

28

Vaughn was covered in blood. It pooled across her stomach and fell in thick rivulets down her sides as she pushed herself upward. Some of it belonged to her, but most of it belonged to her brother.

"V. Did you..." Caldwell's last words trailed off into silence. His body slumped sideways. The rug beneath them muffled his dead weight.

"No," she whispered. "No, please, wake up,"

She held no weapons. Her father's ceremonial saber had been knocked out of her grasp by the force of Caldwell's knee. The cause of all that blood was held in the wrangler's fragile grasp—the gun from Caldwell's personal guard.

It wasn't supposed to happen this way. The alarms in the house had been reactivated by the guard upon their entry. The police would arrive any minute and see everything. The guard subdued at the entryway of the house. The wrangler's finger-prints all over the gun. The private rooms, ransacked. It was all on camera, too.

Vaughn rolled her brother onto his back and placed her hands over the deep hole in his chest. His eyelids remained open, but all the light had left them. "What do I do?"

Broken from his stupor, the wrangler's feet began to move again. He left the room and brought back with him the harried driver.

"Fuck," Clav whispered.

"He's not moving," she said.

"Vaughn, he's—"

"This wasn't supposed to happen!" she screamed. Pain sliced through her body as she moved. Caldwell had her pinned to the ground when Stanislaus pulled the trigger. They had been fighting for minutes that felt like hours, throwing mostly harmless jabs at one another as they argued. He pulled her hair. She had pulled his. She'd shoved his face against a desk, which would have exacerbated the color of his existing bruise if his blood still moved. The skirmish had resulted in several sore points and abrasions across her body. She would find bruises on herself eventually, once the dust settled.

She clasped his face and searched for signs of life. Signs that they had not completely ruined everything, and her brother could still be saved. Sure, she had meant to kill him, but not yet. Not now. She was supposed to have a little more time.

Her ears grew desensitized to the consistent alarms. Her mind looped through a pattern of her brother's name. A lifetime flashed before her eyes. Opening presents on their birthday. The first time he convinced her to sneak out of the house. She thought this sort of thing would only happen when she died, but perhaps, being twins, Caldwell's life was so inextricably tied to hers that she felt something vital inside her dying, too.

The officers found her cradling his body, kissing his forehead. They pried away the hands of her driver and the wrangler, who tried in vain to pull Vaughn apart from her brother.

None of them walked out of the house on their own feet. The wrangler was in full-body restraints, unable to speak. Clav shouted at the officers to release the hard cuffs around the wrangler's forearms to let him sign, and he was subsequently sedated via a needle in the crook of his neck.

Vaughn had no energy to fight, but she didn't have to. She

had the privilege of her name on her side and their perception of her as a devastated, terrified woman lamenting her brother's death. "Miss Keaton," said an officer. "Look at me. Can you tell us what's going on?"

In her shock, she felt incapable of lying. She'd lost the ability to see reason. "H-he attacked me."

"Who did? Can you point to him?"

The officers standing around her didn't know what to make of her saying Caldwell's name instead of pointing to either of the restrained men. "They didn't hurt me," she said.

"What about the gun? Do you recognize it?"

"It's not his," she said, nodding to Stanislaus. "He didn't bring it."

She had enough wits about her to withhold the full truth of what had happened, though it was damning enough against her brother that she could have.

They didn't put her in police custody. Clav was booked, but he didn't stay long.

However, no one could anticipate how long Stanislaus Tewer would remain there.

Vaughn sat beside her lover's hospital bed. Internal bleeding, the doctors had said, among a litany of broken bones. It came as a shock to them that the rider hadn't paralyzed herself. Still, she hadn't woken up for more than a few minutes at a time.

Clav stood beside her chair. Tape sealed a small gash on his cheek. He had nowhere else to be after his release except beside his friend. The camera in the room was off, and the room itself was clear of hospital staff. Liv Shankly was stable and being monitored. Vaughn just needed a few minutes to herself to think.

"Have you heard how Stanis is doing?" Clav whispered.

Vaughn's arms were folded atop the bars of Liv's hospital bed, her cheek flat against them. "Michael should be here with news soon. He's at the station with my lawyer now."

"Anything about Caldwell?"

"Like what? He's dead. There's nothing more to it."

"Yes, but—"

"They have access to the video footage. If they have doubts, they can visit his body in the morgue and feel how cold he is."

Clav paced to the other side of the room. Vaughn didn't know how to talk to him, but she needed him there. Liv couldn't comfort her. All Vaughn could ask her to do was keep breathing, and even that felt like too much. She had asked her for so much. Her life was not an equivalent exchange for the work Vaughn had done for her. She wouldn't be able to rest until Liv woke up again and told her, in her own words, that things were okay.

"How's Liv?" he asked, finally.

Vaughn shrugged. "Alive. I have to be content with that for now. I don't know if I could handle losing her, too. Her doctor says she's stable, but I don't know how long it'll take for her to wake up."

"Not for a while, I imagine. Her body's been through a lot of stress and trauma in the past forty-eight hours. Yours too."

"I just want to talk to her." Vaughn's shoulders lifted and fell slowly. She took Liv's hand, which was adorned with clips and identifying wristbands. The warmth of her palm gave Vaughn more comfort than anything up until this point.

But it had only been a day. The longest day of her life, sure, but a single day, nonetheless. Liv hadn't had the time to rest sufficiently. Vaughn hadn't even started to grieve the way she knew she could be capable of. She clung to the fact that she hadn't yet lost Liv to temper the overwhelming ache of losing her brother.

His awfulness didn't make it any easier. His death had left her the last person to bear the Keaton name. Such a heavy thing, that name. She didn't want it. She had shared it with her brother, though, and he had once been a boy who made her feel proud to have it. She didn't know if she was strong enough to rid herself of him entirely.

Michael entered the private room with a quick knock and weary eyes. Vaughn regarded him apologetically. About her lawyer, Vaughn asked, "What did Camilla say?"

"Well, he's... He's facing murder charges, obviously, and for the assassination of a High Mayor, terrorism charges aren't off the table. If she gets her hands on that footage from the house, she has the potential to get the charges reduced significantly, but it'll be a hard fight. Caldwell was—"

"A murderer," Vaughn said. "The court will get a murderer, and it won't be Stanislaus. I'll get Camilla that footage. We cleared ourselves a path forward before we even started, but we have that evidence on our side now."

Michael sank to his heels beside Vaughn's chair with an aged, groaning slowness. "Do you really think we could get those charges reduced?"

Both sets of eyes landed on her, but she kept her gaze fixed on Liv Shankly and watched for signs of waking. Vaughn needed this. So much so that all other concerns paled in comparison to knowing that she would wake up and go home to her family.

"I think we can get them dropped," she said. "Camilla is a marvel. She'll know what to do."

Michael laid a large, gentle hand on his shoulder. "I hope you're right, kid. Do you know if Shanks's parents were called? In less dire circumstances, I wouldn't intervene, but..."

"They know. They left about an hour ago to get some food. I've never seen parents dote so lovingly over their child."

The others looked at her with a mix of disbelief and pity, as if a parent couldn't be anything but doting and loving to their child.

Vaughn knew better. She'd been loved much less. "I told them I couldn't see her for a long time. No details; they know nothing about what happened to Caldwell, except that he's dead now. But I need someone to be able to tell her why I'm gone when she wakes up."

"Gone?" Clav folded his arms and furrowed his brows at her.

No one hated the sound of that more than Vaughn did. It made her flinch, and it felt too loud. She wondered if that word could wake Liv's body out of its stasis. The rider was so stubborn. So unwilling to let go or give up on the promise of something good.

Vaughn clasped Liv's warm hand between hers. She brought it to her mouth and kissed her knuckles before rising from her chair. "We've made a disaster for ourselves. It's not her responsibility to clean it up."

The trial was televised, and Vaughn wore her least expensive chambray blouse and baggiest cardigan at the request of her attorney. No one could be allowed to think she was handling the grief well. Vaughn assumed that would be easy enough to deduce from her face alone, but she wore her cheap blouse and oversized sweater anyway. She tied her hair in a loose ponytail at the nape of her neck and left the top button of her blouse undone for an unobstructed view of her throat, as if to compare it to the photographs of her from that fateful night and say to the occupants of the courtroom, "This is what it looks like without the bruises from my brother's hands."

With several weeks gone, her body had healed, but her

mind was still fractured. She hadn't spoken to Liv or returned to the hospital. Clav had urged her that Liv would understand. Stanis's case came first, and they'd built the illusion of happenstance off a disconnect between her and the theft of their prosthetic technology. With no deep ties to Liv Shankly, they could argue that they had no motive to premeditate murder. No reason to lash out against Caldwell Keaton.

Liv's absence stole a much-needed leg of support from Vaughn Keaton. She couldn't think. She was absorbed in worry, closer to losing everything than she had ever been before.

She felt the shadow of Liv everywhere she looked. She needed her there, needed the courage of knowing Liv had made it out alive, so she could, too.

Officers from the Morgallis Police Department who had been at the Keaton estate that night gave their recount of the scene. The unmistakable fingerprints on the gun, Caldwell's pacified personal guard, and the other minor injuries on the High Mayor's body pointed clearly to wrongdoing. Vaughn could feel Michael Golovsky's eyes boring holes into the top of her spine, pleading for her to correct the course somehow. He could sense it going too far in favor of his partner's conviction.

In front of her, Stanislaus's body was rigid in his chair.

"Miss Keaton," said the judge. "You're to provide a testimony today, yes?"

The forcedness of her smile worked in her favor. She looked willing to share, but not too much. Grief-stricken, but never unreliable. She was a pretty kind of sad, Camilla had told her. A tragic beauty. The audience would love seeing her wide eyes glassy with tears.

She smoothed the stray hairs away from her forehead as she approached the witness platform. It was a round dais on which only a built-in stool sat, offering a clear view of her body and all its anxious mannerisms. Her knees pressed together.

She made a visible effort to straighten her back and gather her strength.

"Miss Keaton," the judge began. "Dr. Tewer accompanied you to the Keaton family estate, is that correct?"

"Yes."

"Did you witness Dr. Tewer pick up the firearm and shoot it at Caldwell Keaton?"

She nodded. "Yes."

"You claim this was not premeditated murder but rather a defensive action. Is that correct?"

Watchful eyes filled the room. She faced a number of camera lenses and lost track of the question, counting them in her mind.

"Miss Keaton."

"Yes," she answered. "It was Dr. Tewer who saved me. Had he not intervened, I suspect Caldwell would have killed me."

The city prosecutor interjected, "This is speculation!" He was promptly silenced by the judge's raised hand.

"I'm inclined to agree with him, Miss Keaton," said the judge, "unless you have anything to support that claim."

In a series of silent exchanges, Camilla provided the evidence of Caldwell's drug paraphernalia, returned to her seat, and waited for the judge to read over the former High Mayor's toxicology report.

"He's capable of it," Vaughn said.

"Capability to act on an urge means nothing. If you were aware of his actions to poison Gaines Keaton, why didn't you—"

"I didn't know enough at the time to convince anyone to believe me. It's a deep flaw," she said, momentarily meeting the eyes of a familiar police captain, "that no one should believe in a valid concern because it contradicts someone in power. Nevertheless, I found what Caldwell had been hiding."

The barricade of reporters pressed against the back wall murmured updates into their cameras as the judge quietly examined the finer details of the report. What he found would be enough to justify Vaughn's fears of retaliation. It justified Caldwell's violent outburst enough to consequently justify Stanislaus's actions.

But Vaughn wanted more than justification. She wanted the wrangler's freedom. She wanted the city to understand what could have unfolded under Caldwell's reign, because he was more than capable of terrible things; he sought them out like a bloodhound.

Before the judge could proceed with his initial questions, Vaughn said, "I love my brother. But I didn't trust him by that point. I was almost certain he'd done away with our father, but of course, he would never say. There was no telling what he could be capable of. But I know why we were there that night. I'll tell you all of it in my own words. I'd like for you to gauge what kind of man you think Caldwell Keaton is and tell me how someone like that rises to power, if not with an abundance of cruelty. We can't let that happen again."

29

The past few years of Liv's life consisted of recovery. Her body was tired, and her morale deflated. She cried a lot in the months following her hospitalization. The only way she saw Vaughn was through a screen.

She watched the Keaton daughter confess almost everything to the Total City. From the first Drone Run she attended at her brother's request to the stolen prosthetic blueprints, Liv found traces of herself in the story, which was mostly true. Vaughn Keaton was an exceptional liar in that she didn't lie at all, until the end. She maintained a reasonable assumption of the truth, and then—nothing.

What happened after the theft of the blueprints bore little resemblance to the truth.

By then, Liv was hanging onto every televised word with the anticipation of Vaughn eventually letting the wrong thing slip. She might have believed her version of events, too. Vaughn didn't trip over words or confess with any less conviction than the rest of her story.

She'd barely been there for the assassination plan, hadn't she? She'd been kept in the dark about the details of their plan; it was possible that she had overestimated how much she had actually planned to do.

All mentions of Liv Shankly had ceased by then. This was a good thing, but Liv sorely missed the reminders that Vaughn was thinking about her. Vaughn didn't mention the fight outside the Eight Saints or the nature of their relationship, but they'd parted ways in both stories around the same time, that version of Liv leaving because she had gotten her arm and needed nothing else from her. They were friends at most. Vaughn's phone, like Liv's, showed no history of contact between them after Liv's arm was complete.

Liv had time to obsess over Vaughn's television appearances. Bedridden (or couch-ridden, in her case), she and Maura found new things to watch until she knew that something related to the trial would be starting, at which point Liv's mindless chatter would give way to silent engrossment. She wondered if this was what a celebrity crush felt like.

She wished Vaughn could see her. She probably would laugh at her for it, and Liv missed her laugh. The trial had no room for expressions of joy, and it went on for months. Whether Vaughn was speaking that day, Liv could always count on seeing her sitting behind Stanislaus Tewer. Even Michael took days off. When Liv watched live and noticed him missing, Liv often thought of calling him, but didn't have his contact information.

Two months passed. Broadcasts of the trial fell out of priority at the news stations, replaced by regular traffic and weather updates and feel-good stories about the tax-driven generosity of big corporations.

Liv found herself losing interest in television after that. She could only handle so much reality TV before her faith in humanity started to crumble.

When it ended, she'd heard nothing about it. The joy of one man's release wasn't as interesting to broadcast as a story that unlaced the mask of corruption from the High Mayor's head, even if they were entwined issues. Vaughn had given them what they wanted to see: a spectacle and a villain.

They didn't need a hero.

It took another month to find out the wrangler had been released. Liv's days looked less like reality TV binges and more like long walks when it was dry outside to regain her strength. The bulk of her strength wore thin around her body. The hard muscle had become soft, and her surgical scars became less harsh and visible. Still, everything hurt to do. She didn't know if she would ever get back to normal, or if she would have to endure a normalcy that changed forever. Maybe waiting was pointless.

She was at Bronlow's when she got the news. She couldn't return to work in the garage yet, but she came every few days to bother the office clerk and watch Luis work on his cars when she got bored. She had arrived when it was still dry outside and, to her coworkers' chagrin, she lost the opportunity to leave when a storm rolled through.

Luis mentioned the wrangler's release casually when they were talking about some drama with the staff. About another mechanic, he'd joked, "I want to strangle him sometimes. You think they'd let me get away with murder, too?"

"What do you mean, 'too?'"

"You know, like that guy who killed the High Mayor. It's a free-for-all out here. I think I could get away with it."

Liv nodded. "They let him off?"

Luis laughed and stretched his arms above his head. "I didn't think they'd do it. I mean, it really shows you how much they actually care about each other up there, if they don't protect each other. Never thought I'd see the day the High Mayor got publicly denounced by his confidants."

Liv got up from her stool and woke up one of the unused office computers. She typed Stanislaus's name into a search bar. "Holy shit."

The office clerk, Janna, looked at her screen. "Where've

you been?"

Liv opened her mouth, but nothing came out. She'd been right here, stuck in the same place by the circumstances of her recovery, waiting.

She closed the site. "Under a rock, I guess. Sorry."

All day, the rain shifted back and forth between two dissatisfactory modes. She watched her other coworkers leave at the end of their shifts. Luis left. Finally, Janna. The glowing sign above Bronlow's Garage turned off automatically.

The weather couldn't persist like this. Liv occupied her wait with trivial web searches on one of the company computers. She looked up Dr. Tewer. All updates of his case ended with the completion of the trial. They gave him privacy, or they no longer cared. She hoped it meant that he was safe from the press's ruthless attention. She looked up Vaughn's name next. Like the wrangler, she seemed to vanish once the trial was over.

When nine p.m. approached, she considered calling a bot-driven cab. She couldn't wait much longer for the rain to die down. Maura asked for frequent updates. It was late enough that she could ask Corey to pick her up. Too late, even. She hated doing that after he had already gotten home. He liked to change into his pajamas quickly.

Safe underneath the lip of the roof, Liv stood outside and stretched her arm into the rain. Abysmal. She should have checked the weather before she decided to come.

She leaned back against the doorframe and pulled out her comms device. Looking anything up on it proved inconvenient. Liv was about to turn back toward the office to look up a cab service with bot units nearby when someone shouted at her.

The silhouette was unrecognizable; arms braced the fabric of a raincoat over their head, creating a shape that resembled a thin-legged walking triangle. The swift gait, however, jogged an instant remembrance.

"Vaughn? What are you—"

The Keaton girl's features manifested under the outdoor wall light. "I wasn't sure if you—"

Liv shook her head, throwing her gaze pointedly toward the sheet of rain careening off the garage's roof. "Not for a while."

She had expected different first words with which to begin this conversation, and the slight divergence threw her off-kilter. After deciding that she was safe from the rain, Vaughn slowly lowered the tail of her coat from her head.

"Maybe I should have waited until we had better weather," she said. "This is dreadful. Terrible weather for riding."

Liv's face pinched in confusion. "Did you seriously come all this way to talk about the weather with me?"

Vaughn snuffed out the traces of amusement that gathered on her face. "So banal, isn't it, to talk about the weather? It's almost as nauseatingly pedestrian as sitting in a movie theater."

Knowing she'd kept that conversation alive in her memory allayed Liv's worst suspicions. Vaughn wasn't the kind of person to laugh her way through a difficult task; she agonized and assigned things needless gravity even when they were perfectly simple. Her laughter was a heady thing that smoothed the tension out of Liv's hardened expression.

"He's home now," Vaughn said, and Liv knew she meant Dr. Tewer. Her large, pillowed eyes were hopeful. "I mean, he's been home for a little while, but he just had his final meeting with the court staff today. He's facing a lot of restrictions, obviously. There's a limited amount of space he can occupy. No travel. Weekly check-ins. I'm not sure how long it'll be before house arrest is lifted for him, but he's home."

"So that's it then."

"I... For now. There's some paperwork I need to finish before I can wash my hands of it fully, but nothing to do with

Tewer. Just the house."

Liv answered with a satisfied hum. She wrapped her arms around herself and let her weight fall against the spackle-bumped wall of the garage. It was comforting, in a way, to be proven wrong in her expectations of this moment in a way that was so quintessentially Vaughn. So much had changed in the past months, but she was just as industrious. Business came first.

Vaughn mirrored her posture sheepishly. "I'm selling the Keaton estate."

"Oh. I'm sorry."

She shook her head. "I hated that place. It's a relief to have it out of my hands. I feel like I can finally breathe again."

A wave of rolling thunder joined the conversation. Liv let it speak in her place, since she didn't know what to say.

"I'm selling the glass house, too."

"What?"

"There's nothing left for me. I used to think I needed the isolation to keep me safe, but all it did was make me feel worse. I can't keep relying on Clav for company. If it's friendship I need, it can't be contingent on paid service."

"You fired him?"

Vaughn smiled a little. "Not without a substantial payout. He's okay. I gave him the world's most glowing letter of recommendation to a new employer, and he just started driving for them this week. Better yet, he still comes around when I'm no longer paying him. It does wonders for the psyche, having a friend show up just because they can."

She knew she should be happy for Vaughn. Deep down, she admired the way the girl had freed herself from her family ties, but Liv had needed her in those past few months. More than she had ever needed one person. Vaughn's silence had kept her in a miserable purgatory of waiting. Her sympathies were lacking.

"After the trial…" Vaughn inched toward her and surveyed the premises for bystanders, of which none appeared. "Mayor Hokada reached out to me. She asked about you."

"About me? I've never met her."

"About the rider I'd mentioned. My lawyer didn't want me to meet with her privately, but no one else had asked me about you. For the most part, you were the only thing we discussed. She wanted to know why I made the arm for you. What I got out of it. She didn't want to believe that I was just like Caldwell or Gaines and that I had ulterior motives for making something like that, and I think… I think hearing about you, in the limited capacity that I was allowed to admit to, cleared up my intentions perfectly well. How's it working, by the way?"

"Oh. It's fine."

"I was afraid the Run had damaged it."

Liv scoffed. "No. Just me."

After another ripple of thunder passed. "I never found the blueprints, Liv. Presumably, we could have closed the trial even sooner if we had proven that he took the blueprints, too. If he sold them to someone, no one was willing to admit to buying them."

"Tewer got out, though," Liv said. "It doesn't seem possible."

A smile grew across Vaughn's face. "I know. And I'm ready to wash my hands of it now. Get away from Morgallis."

Liv's throat constricted. Getting out of the Total City was a feat Liv could only dream of. Morgallis had the only airplane landing strip in the cities, and few things passed in and out of its small planes except heavyweight cargo that the shipping drones couldn't carry.

Months of waiting. Months of healing from a bodily trauma she didn't know if she could ever truly reverse, just to be left. She didn't know what she'd been expecting. Vaughn could do anything, go anywhere. They'd spent enough time apart that Vaughn could ignore all the investment Liv had sunk into her.

"You're saying goodbye, then."

The creases beside Vaughn's smile smoothed. "I've been offered a political sanctuary. Officially, I have the trial to blame. The only people I would potentially have to fear retaliation from are loyal friends of Caldwell, and you and I both know he doesn't have them. But unofficially, I've been asked to redraft the prosthetic and submit a prototype for Mayor Hokada's consideration."

"Surely, you're not moving to Corcoran."

Vaughn cautiously raised her fingertips up to Liv's temple and pushed them through her hair. "I don't have to. Not if you say so. But I'd like it if you said yes."

"This place... There are so many places you could go, V."

"This is the place where you live," she said. "I have no family to stick around for. No allegiances, except maybe Clav. Apart from my contributions toward new prosthetic technology, no one else cares about what happens to Vaughn Keaton."

Her unspoken sentiment stretched between them: *But you care.* Even if Liv had spent months denying it. Even if Vaughn's later months of silence had caused her to lose faith in the reciprocity of that care.

Liv reached into her shorts' pocket for the fraying note she kept in it. "I've been wondering whether you wrote this for me. I know your handwriting, and this—" Liv dropped the note in her hand. "I know this isn't it."

Vaughn's gaze toward the faded script softened. "I thought it would have spoiled the ruse to put my handwriting on something that could disprove the way I talked about you in court if it ever came to that. I figured—"

Liv clipped the end of Vaughn's sentence, pulling her into a calamitous, urgent kiss. With the note wedged between her fingers, Vaughn cradled Liv's face in her hands. Once her mind caught up to the pressure around her body, she met the kiss with equal desperation and indiscernible mumbled attestations of want against Liv's mouth.

The rider ripped away and said, "I'm sorry. That was—"

"No, no. It wasn't."

Liv caught her breath, held close by Vaughn's unyielding grip. She wouldn't think of letting her go. Vaughn's nose followed the path of hers with a delicate pressure. She touched her with admirable patience.

"Corcoran's a grim place, you know."

"Maybe, you need a different place." Vaughn smiled, full of uninhibited adoration. "Somewhere without loud neighbors adjacent to your bedroom wall."

"I need to make sure my parents are taken care of."

Held firm in Liv's arms, Vaughn kissed her again as if she had no other choice and could think of nothing else. She made no protest to the tight pressure or the metal against her ribs. She relished in Liv's scarcity of her and all the longing that came with it. "All my life," she said, "I've dreamed of having a family like yours. I wanted my family to give me that, and that was never going to happen. But I can still have it. I can't presume that they'll love me the same or forgive me for what I did to you, but I'll treat them well. I'll take care of them with you. Find a place that fits us all. There's no place I wouldn't go for you. Nothing I wouldn't endure for you, Liv. You're the best part of every room I walk into. I want that room, and that life, to be something we make together."

Liv unwound her arms from Vaughn's waist and wiped an echo of rainwater from her cheek. Vaughn tilted her head into her palm. She stared at Liv with her large, dark eyes with a plea, *Say yes.*

Liv studied the pattern of rain as the thunder grew distant.

She estimated a gap in the downpour. Not a complete lapse, but a break from the heavy rate of it. "Do you want to come over tonight?"

Vaughn nodded, as if nothing could please her more. "I might have to borrow a change of clothes if the rain continues like this."

"Anything you want. Wear my clothes. Use my things."

They kissed under the narrow lip of the roof until the torrent subsided. Vaughn could feel the ridges of scars around Liv's body through her shirt. She would have to take it off for her later. Show her how much had changed. How much she had missed.

Maura embraced Vaughn in her drenched state. She stood on her toes to kiss Vaughn's cheeks and scrubbed the water droplets from her brows with her thumbs. Corey emerged from the bathroom to an impassioned reunion and followed Maura's lead. Liv fetched clothes for her guest. She wrung Vaughn's hair out in the bathroom sink as her parents huddled in the kitchen over their respective dinner tasks. She wasn't sure why she had worried so much about this place. It made Vaughn happy, which she cared about more than all the things the apartment lacked.

They had time to broach the subject of Vaughn's relocation. For once, they had time in abundance. Their apartment was full of things that needed to be sorted out and packed for moving, but that could come later.

Liv languished in the nearness of Vaughn. The mending rift between her two worlds. She couldn't keep her eyes or her hands to herself, afraid that she might miss Vaughn slipping away like an illusion.

When her parents retired for the evening, Liv led Vaughn up the ladder to her creaky loft bed. "God, it's taller than I expected."

"It's a space saver," Liv said, in defense of the bed she'd had since childhood. She angled her torso upright, and Vaughn wedged herself along Liv's side, tucking her face into the pocket of Liv's shoulder.

"What will you do when we find a house that's full of space?"

Liv applied an honest effort toward picturing it, but Vaughn's breath against the sensitive expanse of her neck distracted her, regardless of whether Vaughn intended it to. "Are you sure you want to stay in Corcoran?"

Vaughn thought about it for a long time. It was during these quiet moments that Liv wished she could explore Vaughn's mind like a library archive. "It seems wrong to leave. Even if I didn't break this city myself, I have to make it right."

With a sigh and another gratuitous kiss to Vaughn's forehead, Liv said, "You can't fix everything. Total City is just too broken, V."

She raked her fingers through Vaughn's stringy, damp hair. A hand splayed across her ribs, a thumb stroking gingerly along her side. She could forget the smallness of her bed when something as lovely as Vaughn Keaton took up its extra space. It didn't seem like too much to want her in it forever. To fall asleep next to her every night.

And she could have more now. The possibility alone was what she had always dreamed of.

"We'll make something new," Vaughn promised. Her eyelids became heavy with sleep. Big confessions weighed her down and loosened her frame against Liv's. She sighed against Liv's collarbone. The sound had never held so much hope. "We're rather good at that."

ACKNOWLEDGEMENTS

I have a lot of folks to thank. My first book, *Modern Divination*, was written partially in front of an internet audience. My second and third books were written almost entirely alone and talked about after the fact. With *Heavy Metal Lover*, my fourth book, I was never without a community of other writers and friends. Through one of the toughest times in my life, I was lucky enough to be supported by so many people.

I have no cohesive way of listing you all, so you're getting bullet points.

- Sheyla Knigge, my agent and professional hype woman.
- Kelsea Yu, for all the tea and for sitting in my car a lot.
- Courtney Gould, Rosiee Thor, and Megan Lally, for the cheap steak bites.
- Sophia Slade, my confidant and jeans model.
- Sarah Underwood, for your steadfastness.
- Andrea Cayasso, for our godforsaken Instagram DMs.
- Grace Alberti, for your wisdom.
- Seth Haddon, for your invaluable help and friendship.
- Emma Holland, for your resilience and constant support.
- Bri Boehm, for being a connoisseur of fictional lesbians.
- Yves Donlon and Harvey Baxter, my Arcane enablers.
- Teagan Olivia King, for so much.

- K. M. Fajardo, for the blurb and the drool-worthy cyberpunk baddies.
- Ren Rice, for helping me, even though Ingram made it a pain.
- My Patreon supporters, especially Selah and Lainey, for stoking my fire to create.
- Noreamea, my incredible cover illustrator. The moment I saw your work, I knew I could have no one else on this cover.
- For my last job, for sucking so much that I finished my books out of spite.
- Relevant Coffee and Honey Latte Cafe, who see me most days of the week.
- Gabrielle Marchicelli, the only person I watch movies with.
- Briar, my science girl, butterfly queen, little drink afficionado.
- Trevor, for the fried tofu and free use of your espresso machine.
- Mosse, my grey earl, royal advisor, drum occupant.
- The queer community in Florida, namely St. Petersburg.
- Rose Glass, for directing Love Lies Bleeding, starring Katy O'Brien and Kristen Stewart.
- Tamsyn Muir, C. L. Clark, Allison Saft, August Clarke, and Tamara Jeree, for writing some of my favorite lesbians.
- The music of: Bat For Lashes, Yves Tumor, MUNA, Lady Gaga, Magdalena Bay, Pixel Grip, The Japanese House, King Princess, Wolf Alice, and Desire.
- The readers who followed me back to self-publishing from *Modern Divination*. What a journey it's been. May the road ahead be long and prosperous and full of good stories.

ABOUT THE AUTHOR

Isa Agajanian (they/them) is a queer author and illustrator currently living in the Pacific Northwest. A lifelong lover of SFF fiction, Isa, along with their beloved cat, Mossie, can be found haunting late-night coffee shops, offering unsolicited tea recommendations, and looking for magic in the mundane.

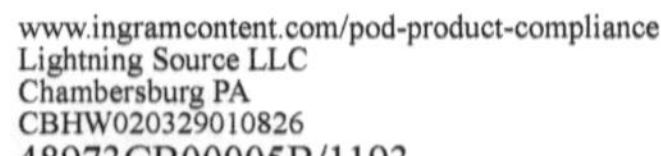